For Candi —
The truth is not to
Welcome to the City!

THE
PROMETHEUS
EFFECT

Truly,
David Fleming
10-6-18

DAVID FLEMING

Copyright © 2017 by David Fleming

All rights reserved. This book or any portion thereof may not be reproduced or used in any manner whatsoever without the express written permission of the copyright owner except for the use of brief quotations in a book. Requests for permission should be addressed to the publisher.

The Prometheus Effect is a work of fiction. Names, organizations, places and incidents portrayed in this novel are either products of the author's imagination or are used fictitiously. Any resemblance to actual, events, locales, or persons is purely coincidental. No underground secret organization made the author state this either.

Published by:
David Fleming

Edited by:
David Gatewood (www.lonetrout.com)
Crystal Watanabe (www.pikkoshouse.com)

Cover Design by:
Susan L. Harlow (www.slharlow.com)

Ebook and Print Formatting by:
Crystal Watanabe

First edition, 2017

*For Stephen
an honest man*

and

*Tom & Rebecca
the greatest of friends*

CHAPTER 1

Fall 1945

"Who are you, Jack?"

A simple question.

But Jack knew better than to tell the whole truth to a politician. Blurting out, "I'm the man on the verge of creating fusion!" would likely land him in a government bunker while they destroyed the world. He valued life too much to allow that to happen. And if they were armed with his creation, power-worshipping men behind imposing desks would be virtually guaranteed to wipe humanity's slate clean in the worst way.

I gave him the answers he asked for, Jack thought. *Let his deeds be recorded in history; mine will direct the course of it. We don't have time for these questions. Now, thank me and let me get back to work.*

"Just a man," Jack answered.

"You're only nineteen years old. More a boy than a man."

Jack calmly rested his hands on the polished leather arms of his chair. This man wasn't the first person to try to intimidate him, nor would he be the last. Still, the situation called for a modicum of respect.

"What can I do for you, sir?"

The politician drummed his fingers on the file sitting atop his desk, his intense hazel eyes never leaving Jack's calmer brown. Great men had sat in Jack's chair, and no doubt some of them had fidgeted and babbled before this politician. But Jack sat comfortably and waited for an answer.

"I have read your proposal," the man said at last, opening the file. "How did you come up with it?"

"It seemed reasonable." Jack noted the unique strokes of his own handwriting in blue ink on the exposed page.

"Reasonable?" The politician goggled at him, then lowered his eyes to the file. "We presented our problems to the best minds available to us. Some managed to address the most serious issues, but not one of them even approached anything I would call 'comprehensive.' Yet you covered every issue—including a few we hadn't thought of. Atomic weapons, dictators, pandemics, population, natural resources, and crazy things I've never even heard of before." He looked up from the file. "Do you really think fossil fuels are going to cause so much trouble?"

"Undeniably. The problems are all interconnected." Jack leaned back in his chair, his expression unchanged.

"Why does the implementation of this have to be so damned secret? I would feel a lot more reassured if it had an oversight committee. They could also be sworn to silence."

"Those who peddle power for a living tend to have trouble keeping secrets. They use them as barter to advance their positions. If any of the organization's solutions become common knowledge before they're needed, then they become problems themselves." Jack steepled his index fingers before him and asked, "What do you think your enemies would have done if they had known about your atomic weapons project?"

"They would have attacked us sooner."

"That's best case scenario. Worst case, they would have waited until they developed enough atomics of their own and then annihilated us. Imagine Pearl Harbor over every city, with atomic weapons."

"Point taken, but why does the existence of the organization need to be invisible?" He tapped the file. "This is the only copy, by the way."

"Two reasons. First, any knowledge of this organization, no matter how insignificant, would invite scrutiny. And scrutiny is like an open wound. It would attract all sorts of infectious processes that could kill its effectiveness. Second, in intervals of peace, some might consider dissolving the project. Yet peace does not obviate the need for this organization. The future is bound to be paved with trouble."

"Very well; I'm no stranger to secret societies," the politician said. "Incidentally, your physics professor committed a serious breach of national security by sharing our problem with you."

"He knew he could trust me," Jack replied.

"Can I trust you, Jack?" The politician locked eyes with the teen. "More importantly, can the country trust you?"

"What do you mean, sir?"

"As you read in the classified documents your professor provided, we came close to losing the war. The Germans managed to skip decades ahead of us in theoretical technology. Japan failed to follow through and step on our neck after they knocked us over. It was only through brute force, sheer luck, and a bit of trickery that we managed to end the war. We emptied our bag of tricks with Fat Man and Little Boy. And still, millions died. How many do you think will die in the next world war?"

"All of them," Jack replied without pause.

The politician raised an eyebrow. "You're being a little melodramatic, aren't you, son?"

Jack held the man's gaze silently.

"Well." He leaned back in his seat. "That's why we appealed to the geniuses. That's why you're here. I'm authorizing the inception of your proposal, and you are the person I want to lead the program."

A self-preservation instinct impelled Jack to his feet before the politician finished his last sentence. *I did them a favor by outlining a path to a peaceful world. Now they want me to pave it for them?* Perhaps Jack was the best choice to lead this project—no, not perhaps; he knew he was the best choice—but he also knew that anyone involved with the organization would never have a normal life. To the rest of the world, the organization's members would cease to exist.

I should have seen this coming. And if I hadn't been so focused on my discovery, I would have. You don't bring a problem to someone unless you have a solution, and you don't provide a solution unless you're willing to do it yourself.

He decided the situation called for a bit of obsequiousness. With his hands on his hips and his head bowed, he asked, "Why me?"

"It's your idea; I can't think of anyone better qualified. And it would make you a very powerful young man."

That it would. This was a ticket to absolute power. Yet power and fame held no value in Jack's moral code. Truth—that was the only standard by which he lived. He had never considered immersing himself in a field where lies and deception were the norm.

"And if I won't?" Jack asked.

"You're the genius. What do you think?"

I think I should have known better than to trust a politician.

After a brief pause, Jack replied, "The way I see it, you have two choices. One, lock me in isolation for the rest of my life. Or two, kill me."

"I really hadn't thought of the first one," the politician said. Jack discerned no humor in the man's tone.

And there it was. Jack had no real options. From the moment he'd submitted the proposal, his fate had been sealed. And if he was honest with himself, perhaps he'd known that all along. He would never have trusted anyone else with the execution of this plan.

So be it.

"You understand that in order for this to work," Jack said, "it has to be implemented exactly as written. There are no line-item vetoes here."

"Does this mean you're accepting the position?"

"Yes." Jack stepped forward and took the file from the politician's desk.

"Good luck then, Jack."

"With the level of secrecy involved, and the type of people I need to acquire, you're likely never to see me again," Jack said.

"Like Jack the Ripper?"

"I'll do a better job of it."

Jack turned to leave, his heart racing and his mind several steps ahead. But before he reached the door, the man asked from behind him, "What are you going to call this organization of yours?"

Jack stopped to ponder the question. In comparison to the function of the organization, the name seemed meaningless. "It won't have a name," he said. "That would only draw unwanted attention."

"It has to have a name," the politician urged. "Otherwise you and your people are forever going to be saying, 'Let's get back to the you-know-what, wink wink.'"

A valid point. Jack thought for a moment—and then it came to him. Something simple and unlikely to raise suspicions if overheard. "I'll call it the City," he said.

"Very well then. I will arrange your security clearances… and your death," said the politician.

"Thank you, Mr. President," Jack said, and he left the Oval Office.

***

One week later, Jack's cremated remains fertilized an unmarked apple tree seedling in his hometown. The official story was that his truck had blown a tire and skidded into a ravine. The fuel tank ruptured and his vehicle was engulfed in a fireball. By the time the volunteer fire department arrived, there was nothing left that could burn. The charred skeleton inside was identifiable only by cross-matching the serial number on the engine block to the registered owner. According to the coroner, the driver was dead on impact. He never felt a thing.

***

The City currently had a population of one.

Near a dry lake bed in Nevada, recently used for bombing and artillery practice, a nineteen-year-old man sat at a surplus military desk in an aluminum-clad house trailer. Stacks of personnel files from all branches of the military cluttered every flat surface, and a humming space heater took the edge off the chill. In the trash, a crumpled obituary lay among several Black Jack chewing gum wrappers.

And as the man rotated the dial on his Western Electric 302

telephone to set up another interview, he couldn't help but think:
Damn, I loved that truck!

CHAPTER 2

Late Summer 2039

Mykl held the world in his hands. Continents and oceans spun in a blur before his eyes. As they slowed, he gave Greenland another swipe with his tiny fingers and sat mesmerized by the illusion of power rotating in his lap.

"Put the globe away Mykl. We have to go," a gentle voice said from behind.

A slender woman with raven black hair cascading over her shoulders stood patiently in the doorway of the one-bedroom apartment. Rays of warm light from the setting sun accentuated her petite figure. She wore preposterously high heels in an attempt to create a fantasy of height, while fishnet stockings hugged her legs, sparkling magically from ankles to hips with calculated purpose. A leather corset peeked through the opening of her jacket. One pale hand hung relaxed at her side, while the other tapped polished red nails on the doorframe. A lock of hair masked one side of her angular face.

Her fierce blue eyes stared purposefully at the small boy across the room. "Now, Mykl."

He placed the globe atop his cluttered desk. Giving it one last spin, he danced his fingers across the keyboard of his disposable computer, closed his calculus book, and dashed to take his mother's outstretched hand.

"We won't have to live like this much longer, you know," she said as they walked to the car. "In fact, I may even be done by tonight. Then we can finally be with your dad."

Mykl tilted his head to gaze up at her. She rarely spoke of this man he had never met. It was as if he were some great secret. His mother had many secrets, and she kept them well.

She kissed his cheek as she checked his seatbelt. "I named you after him, Mykl. He's going to be so happy to see you."

He probably has a weird name too, Mykl thought. No one ever spelled *his* right, and everyone who saw it written down pronounced it wrong. It would be a lot easier if he spelled it like every other Michael.

They drove in silence to a child care center that catered to night shift workers. Mykl leaned forward in his seat so the air conditioning would blow harder across his face. His body felt tingly as his mother reached over with her free hand to scratch his back. These brief moments spent with her were wonderful.

Today marked the first night at her new evening job. Once she finished her shift at the club, she'd pick him up, drop him off at a second child care center, one nearer their apartment, and move on to her day job. She never talked about work or why she needed so many jobs. Another secret she reserved for herself. She never explained why she wouldn't let him stay at home and play—though that was an oft-debated point between them. She had treated him like a child for as long as he could remember. He was quite capable of taking care of himself. After all, in another three minutes and seventeen seconds, he would be four years old.

Waning rays of sunlight teased the solar arrays on the eastern mountains. They were unable to produce electricity as well as advertised, but residents had learned to adjust to the arrays' limitations, similar to the way they had with water several decades before: limited resources went to the highest bidders. And in Vegas, those bidders were the owners of the garish neon signs and dazzling strobes that beckoned patrons to an adult playground of sensory overload and sinful fantasy. Even with war tensions running high and the world in crisis, high rollers and power brokers still migrated to Vegas to indulge in wanton spending, every one of them with an irrational hope of a lucky streak—a hope that would eventually crash into the concrete wall of probability. All of the glamour and glitz boiled down to the simple exchange of ten dollars for nine.

Their car came to a stop in front of the care center. Mykl let out a deep sigh and leaned the full mass of his meager weight into the door as he pulled the handle.

"Hey, short stuff. Aren't you forgetting something?"

Yes, I'm forgetting to remind you it's my birthday. Stretching across the seat, he gave his mother a kiss goodbye before scooting out. As he leaned into the door to close it, his mom called out, "I love you, Mykl."

Her warm smile melted any misgivings he had about her forgetting his birthday. "I love you too, Mom." He trudged away to his humdrum shift inside with the other unfortunate kids.

"Happy birthday, Stinker!" his mom yelled to his back.

Love for his mom and guilt for doubting her assailed him simultaneously. The lump in his throat left him speechless.

"We'll go get your present after I pick you up," she said. With a wink and a wave, she was gone.

***

The insistent chiming of a phone in the next room stirred Mykl from a deep sleep. Heavy grogginess made him feel like a bag of sand on his tiny cot. Breathing mounds of slumbering children encircled him in the multipurpose room. Why was he so tired?

A quick squint at the glowing wall clock answered his question. 2:37 a.m. Much too early to be awake. Mykl rolled over in relief when someone finally answered the phone. But his eyes popped open again when he overheard his mom's name spoken. Quickly, he ran to listen.

"Yes, she has a child here... No, she's listed as a single parent... No, she's the only person we have a contact number for. Why, what's wrong? ... Oh my God."

Mykl didn't want to believe the likely meaning of that "Oh my God." *It can't be true. No. It can't.* She was going to be picking him up in a few hours. She was. She had to. They were talking about someone else, something else… anyone else besides his mom.

The lady set her phone down as if it had become too heavy to hold. Mykl stepped into the room to face her. Tears already rolled down his cheeks, as well as hers.

"I'm so sorry, Mykl," she said to him in a hoarse whisper.

Grief and uncertainty threatened to crush him under their immense weight. His legs would no longer let him stand. He lowered himself into a fetal position on the cold tile. Merciless serpents of anguish and despair coiled about his chest and throat, robbing him of breath. His mom was all he had. Her loving smile touched his mind. He tried in vain to hold her image close, only to lose it in a cold fog. Angrily, he flicked a mental lash at the beasts already beginning to feed on her memory. *You can't have her,* he thought. *She's mine!*

Maybe they'd made a mistake and it wasn't her? She changed her name and hair color like the days of the week. Maybe it was a lady who wasn't a mom? That way there wouldn't be a kid left all alone. The most beautiful person in the world would then show up with a warm hug and make the pain in his chest go away. He could tell her how much he loved her and always would. Then they could celebrate his birthday, get his present… and meet his dad.

All of that was gone now. His heart no longer served a purpose. Life without her wasn't worth living.

The care worker knelt beside him, placing a hand on his back. "The police are sending someone to get you, Mykl."

Her voice sounded so far away. He scrunched hands into his teary eyes. Another voice echoed in his mind. *"Happy birthday, Stinker!"*

"Where will I go?" he managed to ask.

"I don't know, Mykl. I don't know."

CHAPTER 3

Late Winter 2040

Sebastian Falstano felt as uncomfortable passing through the hatch into the submarine as the crew who had called it home for the last six months did at his entry. While his discomfort originated from suppressing claustrophobic thoughts, the crew's came from having to share their space with a stranger working for the CIA. Sebastian wasn't concerned with them, however; their orders forbade them to speak to the spook for any reason other than an emergency. Sebastian cared only about his mission: determine the validity of newly discovered evidence of supposed extraterrestrial technology, and the impact it could have on the world if made public.

Bookended by the submarine commander and his XO, Sebastian made his way through narrow passageways. He had been assured by his superiors that he would receive special treatment and enjoy private quarters, and he was looking forward to it. His arduous route to the sub had required clandestine connections and blindfolded transportation switches that had left no chance for relaxation, and with more than forty-eight hours clocked and thousands of miles traveled, he could smell his own funk. A cigarette, shower, and a decent meal were in order.

They passed the galley and its enticing aromas. As Sebastian was deciding what would come first—the shower or the meal—two men with no-nonsense expressions stepped out from behind a bulkhead.

With grips like iron shackles, they took hold of his upper arms. One pressed a pneumatic syringe against his left jugular vein and pulled the trigger.

Darkness engulfed him.

***

Back in his quarters, the commander sat down heavily at his small desk. His executive officer had followed him at his unspoken order, which had consisted of a concerned look and a jerk of his head.

"Close the door, Kyle," the commander said. When it shut completely, he continued, "I don't like this, not one bit. Why would they pull us off a critical recovery mission?"

"The rocket debris will surely still be there when we return. Brass must think it can wait," said the XO.

"Dammit! This is a prototype stealth submarine, not a taxi! *And*, that smug son of a bitch didn't even have the courtesy to ask permission to come aboard. Now we're sailing with a dark navigation plot, without bearing, speed, or depth, while some satellite feed takes over our course headings. You know the consequences if we're discovered. Did they take the self-destruct commands from me as well? No, I don't like this at all. The sooner he's dead or off my boat, the better. These orders put my boat and my crew in unnecessary danger. There's something very odd about this mission."

The XO, standing at ease, said, "The orders came with Juliet Romeo priority."

"I've never even *heard* of a Juliet Romeo priority before!" the commander railed. "The damned thing required more authentication codes than it takes to launch a two-megaton Novabird. I've been serving on tin cans for twenty-seven years. They should trust me enough to tell me where we're going."

"Perhaps that's why you were selected, sir. You have a reputation for making correct decisions, even in the poor light of dimly explained orders. Maybe it's better that we don't know where we're going. They've obviously invested a great deal of resources to accommodate this man, yet they still regard him as expendable. What's to keep them from thinking the same of us?"

"You've got a really sick mind. You know that?" The commander withdrew his sidearm from its holster and slid the magazine out. After racking out the loaded round, he inspected the breach with a critical eye. The XO froze, his eyes widening slightly in concern. "You did a great job cleaning this," the commander said. "It'd be a real shame if I had to dirty it up on that spook."

"Yes, sir. It would."

CHAPTER 4

Flat on his back, naked and cold, in a tiny deserted infirmary, Sebastian pounded the back of his head progressively harder against a sliver of pillow. The numbing buzz from his rattled brain seeped into his body and through to the thin, unforgiving mattress. Stiff leather straps bit into the flesh of his limbs and torso. Porous IV tape compressed folded gauze pads over standard injection sites and tugged painfully at the fine hair of his inner arms. A pea-sized dot of fresh venous blood seeped through one of the pads. That single bit of evidence, and an ache in his groin, told him the IVs and a catheter had recently been removed.

He had no means of calculating time. The thought of countless days strapped down and sedated rapidly fouled his mood. To make things worse, his body smelled like a dirty diaper soaked in vinegar. Days of intravenous feeding had left him craving anything he could chew more than twice before swallowing.

A spinning spoked wheel at the heavy, sealed hatch announced visitors. Sebastian's thoughts coalesced into a dangerously reckless attitude.

The commander of the sub tossed a set of clothes into his face as the hatch swung open. "Get dressed. It's time you got off my boat." The ship's med tech followed the commander inside, swiftly unfastened Sebastian's bindings, and promptly withdrew.

"Where are we?" Sebastian asked as he put on the same clothes he had started his journey in.

"Our location is classified," the commander said.

Sebastian's expression transformed into one of arrogance. He considered informing the commander of the importance of his mission. But before he could utter another word, the commander's icy tone stopped him.

"I don't care what clearance level you have, Mr. Falstano, or how highly regarded you come. Your orders state that you are to keep your mouth shut from now until you are safely sealed outside my boat. If you speak to any member of my crew, I have explicit orders to shoot you. In the head. Without question or repercussion. Understood?"

Sebastian noted the commander's empty holster and the deadly black semi-auto pistol gripped in his right hand, safety off and finger indexed above the trigger. Even with frangible bullets, it was a breach of standard safety protocol to draw a weapon inside a submarine, unless one intended to use it. "Understood," Sebastian replied.

A quick sniff of his wrinkled shirt revealed they hadn't bothered to launder his clothes during his forced hibernation. The commander's crooked smile confirmed the insult was intentional. Muscles along Sebastian's jaw bulged as his clenched teeth fought to contain the seething comments swimming in the back of his throat.

"Ready when you are, *Commander*," Sebastian said with enough insolence to erase the last trace of smile from the commander's face. The commander made a terse gesture with his pistol to direct Sebastian out of the infirmary.

An eerie quiet greeted him as he stepped into the deserted passageway. Apparently the commander had taken steps to remove any opportunity for him to commit suicide by inadvertently talking to a crew member. Sebastian chuckled at the thought as his long strides took him to the forward hatch.

The submarine's Executive Officer stood at attention in a shaft of greenish light below the hatch as they entered the airlock chamber. His eyes darted to the pistol in his commander's hand before he saluted and stepped aside. "The cavern is secure, sir," he said, dropping the salute.

Sebastian had considered the commander's threat during his short walk—and had deemed it to be a bluff. His mission was much too important for him to be executed for the trivial act of speaking to someone. It wasn't as if he would be divulging mission specifics, and he desperately desired information on his whereabouts. Besides, their treatment of him prompted an irrational urge to test the commander. With one hand on a rung of the ladder leading up to the light, he flashed an impudent grin and drawled to the XO, "Where the hell are we, Ensign?"

The crisp click of a gun hammer strike sounded behind Sebastian's head, shattering his grin. He turned to see the red-faced commander holding a pistol centered on his forehead. A flicker of confusion haunted the eyes of the two men on opposite sides of the weapon. Before Sebastian could regain his wits and laugh at the commander's misfortune, a crushing pain in his abdomen lifted him off his feet. The XO, his fist firmly planted in Sebastian's gut, whispered harshly, "Get out!"

Unable to retort for lack of breath, Sebastian scaled the ladder and crawled through the hatch to collapse on the outer deck. The hatch slammed closed inches from his head, leaving him alone in an artificially lit concrete cavern.

***

The XO climbed down from securing the hatch to find the commander's pistol directed at him. Without a word, the XO calmly extended his hand, palm up, for the weapon.

"I loaded this weapon myself!" the commander exclaimed, ripping the slide back. The unfired round tumbled in the air above the ejection port, and the commander deftly snatched it into his hand. An unscathed primer stared back at him from the 9mm cartridge.

He released his grip on the pistol as the XO took possession of it. Still staring at the primer, he asked, "Why did you remove my firing

pin, XO Smith?"
 "I had orders to, sir."

CHAPTER 5

Sebastian fish-gulped painful breaths as he acquainted himself with his new surroundings. That crazy bastard had looked as if he actually meant to kill him! What had he hoped to accomplish by pulling the trigger of an unloaded gun? Then again, he had to consider the sobering thought that it may have been loaded and his life was spared by an all-too-rare misfire. *If they were willing to kill in order to protect whatever's stored here, then it must be something extraordinary.*

Normal breathing came back gradually, but a residual ache still filled his abdomen. That XO was going to find himself unclogging shitters on a carrier when Sebastian got done with this assignment. His prior intelligence-gathering operations—not to mention a few surreptitious finds in forbidden files—had provided him enough embarrassing details on Navy brass to make revenge a certainty.

The submarine let out a sigh of air and began slipping beneath the waters. Sebastian scrambled to his feet and leapt to a rusted ladder bolted to a natural stone wall. Hanging from a rung, he watched the last of the electronic sensor masts vanish into an inky black swirl.

A moment of inspiration struck him, and he climbed down to dip his hand in the water. It felt on the warm side and—he brought a moistened finger to his lips—tasted salty. At least he could rule out the larger freshwater lakes accessible to sub traffic.

"We have drinkable water up top if you're that thirsty," said a sultry female voice.

Tilting his head back, Sebastian saw a gorgeous blonde wearing a plain white lab coat standing at the top of the ladder. A brief glimpse of pink panties under her skirt brightened his mood. "And what else do you have waiting for me up there?" he asked suggestively.

"Don't tempt me, Mr. Falstano," she said, turning sideways to brandish her pistol and block his leering view.

"Why does everyone want to shoot me?"

"You were selected because you're the most qualified to execute this assignment. My orders carry specific instructions on what you may be shown and what you are to evaluate. Any deviation *shall* be met with lethal force. The sensitivity of this mission makes even you expendable if you show signs of instability."

"Oh, really?" Sebastian feigned indifference, though his gut was full of aching doubt. As he climbed the ladder, he surreptitiously plucked a piece of crumbling stone by a ladder bolt and tucked it into his left shoe. She appeared not to have noticed.

When he reached the top of the ladder and stood, it irked him to discover that he was significantly shorter than his host. A freakishly tall Amazon holding a gun didn't bode well for his chances to get to know her better.

"Where the hell are we, darling?" he asked as he surveyed the crudely made cavern.

"I don't know. They didn't tell me, and I knew better than to ask."

"Who are 'they'?"

"The people who gave me the gun."

Sebastian smirked. "What day is it then?"

"No idea."

"Time?"

"Sorry."

"Well, what *can* you tell me?"

"You were brought here under strict security to determine the validity of the artifact stored in this facility. Your credentials in science and energy, along with your clearance level, made you the best candidate. Beyond that..." She gave a shrug and an elegant flick of her wrist.

Sebastian carefully composed his face. But as he ran a hand through his hair, he couldn't help but frown at the pungent body odor wafting from his armpit. Unwashed and unarmed—she had the better of him. "Fine then. Take me to the artifact, so I can get on with the assignment and be done with this place."

"As you wish," she said, her eyes flicking up to a security camera, then indicating he should lead the way to the massive vault door serving as the cavern's only dry exit. Pretending not to notice the discreetly mounted lens, Sebastian passed over the vault threshold, the woman at his heels. With mechanical assistance the door thundered shut behind them, leaving them in complete darkness.

As a child, Sebastian's mother had taken him on a cave tour beyond city limits. When they were deep inside, their guide had turned off the lights to show them how dark the cave appeared in its natural state. It was a darkness so complete that one's eyes could never adapt to it. The guide pressed on with his droning monologue in the dark, not realizing that Sebastian had panicked and wet his pants.

This new darkness tugged at those memories. Sebastian sensed his inner panic rising; it threatened to take over his mind and, once again, his bladder. But as he opened his mouth to scream, the hallway lit ahead of them, allowing him to regain his leash on sanity.

"Everything okay, Mr. Falstano?"

"Fine," he managed to croak after a convulsive swallow.

As they walked down the hallway, Sebastian ran his hand along the rough exposed aggregate in the concrete wall; this place had been constructed hastily. The hallway had no turns, and ended at a ten-foot-square metal door that was even more imposing than the one they had just passed through.

The Amazon rapidly scribbled a pattern code into a circular touchpad next to the door. A high-pitched whine began resonating through the heavy air, causing Sebastian's nose hairs to tingle. Reflexively, he raised an index finger to his nose and rubbed it in an attempt to alleviate the discomfort. The inescapable harmonics in his skull were like having a dentist drilling all his teeth at once.

"Annoying, isn't it?" she said as she regarded him calmly, absentmindedly tapping the pistol on her left thigh.

"It's torture!" Sebastian's eyes watered. "What's the reason for it?" he barely grated out.

"One of many security measures. The noise is just an insignificant side effect." She showed no signs of discomfort.

Insignificant side effect?

An eternity of two minutes passed before silence once again fell upon them. Another few seconds and Sebastian would have divulged national secrets for a moment of peace. For a moment, he had even thought of going for her gun; by the way she handled it, he could tell she wasn't trained in its use. But the cameras told him there had to be someone else in the cavern, and it wasn't worth the risk to find out if *they* knew how to use a weapon. Besides, even if he did manage to wrest it from her, they could quietly turn out the lights and leave him to rot. If he was expendable, she certainly was too.

"Go ahead, Mr. Falstano," she said, gesturing toward the door's tiny handle.

With a skeptical glance at his minder, Sebastian gave the handle a tug. The three-foot-thick door swung toward him with surprisingly minimal effort. As he stepped around it, his eyes widened in surprise. A large section of the other side of the door he'd just pulled open looked like it would protrude several feet into the wide hallway of the next room in its closed position.

A small forest of wide silver columns ran the entire length of the new hallway, obscuring his view of the far end. Pointing down from the ceiling was an inverted pyramid—a perfect match to fit into the door protrusion below. He suddenly understood. The entire ceiling was designed to move up and down to prevent entry. The columns must be massive hydraulic pistons, and their pumps were no doubt the cause of that god-awful noise. The number of pistons employed meant that the moveable ceiling had to weigh hundreds, if not thousands, of tons.

Anyone unfortunate enough to be inside when it returned to its locked position would be squashed into goo. It was the most massive security feature he had ever seen. It would take days, if not weeks, of drilling and high explosives to defeat.

"This is… wow."

"Proceed." The Amazon waved him into the hallway with her pistol.

Sebastian hastened his step, devoutly hoping the hydraulic system possessed safeguards to prevent his worst claustrophobic nightmare from coming true. After winding his way through the pistons to the end of the hall, he faced a circular hatch similar to those on the submarine.

"Turn the wheel and pull. It's unlocked," the woman said.

"With all the rigmarole I've just been through, you leave this one unlocked?"

"We have other security measures that render locking this door unnecessary."

"Measures like…?"

She cocked the pistol with her thumb.

"Fair enough." Sebastian turned to the door and opened it.

Beyond the hatch was a dark chamber of unknown size or depth.

"Okay, where's the light switch?"

"There's a flashlight on the floor to the left of the door, just inside," the woman said.

Sebastian arched a carefully groomed eyebrow at her.

With a feminine shrug of her shoulders, she volunteered, "We ran out of funding, and security weighed more heavily than convenience."

"Uh-huh." Against his better judgment, Sebastian stepped into the darkness and felt around on the floor. His fingers found the flashlight. "Got it. Hope you could afford batteries." He fumbled for the ON switch.

"Rotate the end counter-clockwise," the woman said from the door.

"Yeah, yeah." The flashlight came on. Its beam revealed a low, dome-shaped ceiling spanning a circular room. A pedestal stood in the center, on top of which a pristine white cloth covered a rounded object.

Sebastian had to crouch as he approached the pedestal. Only when he was next to the artifact was the ceiling high enough for him to stand at his full height. Holding his breath, he carefully lifted the cloth.

A blue-hued sphere, heavily scarred and pitted, sat atop the pedestal. It measured approximately sixteen inches in diameter and its center glowed faintly. Sebastian slowly went to his knees as if in reverence. He absentmindedly dropped the cloth and hovered a hand over the sphere. It radiated heat.

"Is it radioactive?" he asked, drawing away in concern.

"No. It stays at a constant fifty degrees centigrade. The means by which it generates heat or light is unknown."

"But you had to have run tests?" He leaned toward it until he could feel warmth on his face.

"X-rays, spectrographs, MRIs, chemical makeup—you name it, we tested it. Without all of the surface damage, it would be a perfect sphere of diamond, with a few trace minerals. We didn't wish to cut it open—yet—for fear of damaging it… or us."

"Is it carbonado?" Sebastian asked.

"Similar, but not like any carbonado we've ever seen. The most disturbing test result came from the analysis of the light it emits. While it's too fast to be detected by the human eye, there is a pattern to it, not unlike a timer."

"Timer? Like a countdown?" Sebastian felt a seed of fear take root in the pit of his stomach.

"Possibly. It's more like a simple count based on fractions of the speed of light. If the scientists and mathematicians are correct, their extrapolations from the count suggest the artifact is well over one billion years old."

Sebastian had trouble wrapping his brain around a timespan of one *billion* years. The implications… This artifact had the potential to shatter the foundations of religions, cultures… of the very foundations of the human race. Here was an artificial energy source that predated most life on earth—and it certainly wasn't created by a bacterium and protozoa in some lichen's garage.

"Where was this found?" he asked, never taking his eyes from the wonder before him.

"The moon."

"*What?*" he half shouted as he snapped his gaze from the sphere to the woman. "This was discovered during the moon landings? That long ago?"

"No. It was found last month."

Sebastian blinked, dumbfounded. "Since when…"

"As you know, you aren't privy to all the covert operations going on." The woman lifted an elegant leg to rest a sandaled foot on the bottom of the raised hatch opening. Silhouetted as she was, Sebastian couldn't help but conclude that she could rule the fashion world as a model—if she traded her attitude for a pair of high heels. "There's one more thing you should see. Shine your light into the sphere from the side."

Tearing his gaze from her leg, Sebastian did as he was told. Hazy shadows appeared inside the sphere. With the tip of his nose almost touching the artifact, he identified the shadows as three-dimensional symbols. Glyphs?

He twisted back to the woman. "This could be a lang—"

The woman's gun fired. For the second time that day, someone had pointed a gun at him and pulled the trigger. He staggered back, ears ringing, blinded and stunned. A sticky wet warmth flowed from the center of his chest. As his knees buckled, he was stung by a cold anger. Before consciousness abandoned him, he attempted to vent that anger in one last word of defiance.

"Bissh!"

Fear slipped in to dine in darkness as he collapsed to the ground.

***

A man in a well-tailored suit stepped through the hatch. "Well done," he said.

"Can I shoot him again?" she asked, removing her earplugs.

He chuckled. "I'm afraid not."

"Please?"

"Not, now. The situation is far too advanced to be fixing problems one at a time. Besides, I get the next shot here."

"I hope he doesn't disappoint you," she replied. She bent to rescue the cloth from the trickle of blood inching away from Sebastian.

"Individuals with his qualifications never do."

CHAPTER 6

Summer 2040

Jessica labored at her desk in disciplined concentration, analyzing data from the military's latest experiment on subatomic particles. A prototype circular particle accelerator lay hidden in what the public believed to be a nuclear test crater deep in a Nevada desert. To all satellites, foreign and domestic, its details were no different than any other poisonous radiation pit scarring Nevada's barren soil. But while nearby craters had originated from underground nuclear detonations, scientists had conjured the accelerator crater with conventional explosives. And to Jessica, this crater offered a means of pursuing a lifelong dream she had mortgaged her body and soul to achieve.

Jessica believed that life's rewards were directly related to the effort invested in their pursuit. As simple and naïve as that might have been, she also fiercely believed in her own abilities.

Jessica had suffered through the necessary evil of high school, enduring indifferent teachers and watered-down classes. But before she made it to college, the economy tanked—and college scholarships evaporated. Young people were needed in the work force, not in school. And it wasn't just colleges that were downsizing; public school districts changed minimum proficiency policies in order to accelerate graduation. Once a student demonstrated minimum competency, they were summarily graduated. There just wasn't money available to keep everyone in school.

Most teens were ecstatic to graduate early, but not Jessica. She kept her grades less than stellar in order to stay in school, thereby retaining access to library facilities, computers, and textbooks. She knew that dedicated self-study provided her the best chance of college admittance. She was determined to get a college education.

Unfortunately, the cost of attendance had risen beyond the means of all but the very rich—or those desperate enough to gamble with their financial future. To encourage applications—and thereby revenue—colleges removed the government middleman from the equation and began offering high-interest loans themselves, to anyone who could pass their entry level placement tests. Fees for these placement tests soon surpassed tuition as their main moneymaker.

Jessica earned the money for her tests by working odd jobs after school. Her parents offered no support, feeling it was a waste of money. They said her life would be better served by getting a *real* job. Her mother managed the trailer park they lived in, and her father walked two miles, each way, every week, to collect his disability check and a case of beer.

Jessica passed her tests with ease and opted for the fifty-year payment plan. Requirements also mandated that she submit to temporary chemical sterilization—the college's way of providing additional motivation for its students to pay them back. If she kept current with her remittance, she could have her sterilization reversed after ten years. Jessica fully intended to pay back every penny much sooner. The alternative was a lifetime of lonely poverty and garnished wages.

But during her first three years of college, she discovered a horrible fact. Acidic practices were corroding higher learning from within. Instructors doled out material like the carnival game in which one shoots streams of water into a clown's mouth until the balloon above its head pops. In the new education game, everyone won when their brain was full, no matter the amount it took to fill it, or the quality of the filling. Knowledge took a back seat to blind attendance—and the occasional nod of compliance.

Yet the moment Jessica penned her signature to that student loan, she had committed herself. She had no other choice but to make the most of it. So once again, she immersed herself in the rigors of self-study. A handful of professors gained her attention and admiration. She took every class they taught regardless of whether she needed them for her physics degree.

When the time came to enroll for fall classes in her fourth year, the college mandated that all students take committee-selected classes dealing with the social and cultural appreciation of third world countries. The powers that be wanted to force their students to be sympathetic to the growing problems of dying cultures, thus sending forth a new generation of minds to alleviate the tensions threatening to destroy civilization. Jessica had other goals. Lining the pockets of professors teaching moral fluff was not among them.

So she proposed a different course of study, one revolving around her thesis that an infinitely large universe presupposes an infinitely small one—and that there were yet to be discovered subatomic particles that could be key to solving the world's energy problems. It was a groundbreaking concept; her research had revealed that only one other person had ever made mention of the idea. That mention was made in a journal dated before the Second World War ended, credited to a man by the utterly generic name of J. Smith. She found no other mention of the man in post-war academic writings or the science community at large. As impossible as it seemed, this man ahead of his time had existed only long enough to publish a few lines of text.

But Jessica encountered an unrelenting force preventing her from moving forward with her research: a corrosive indifference to new knowledge.

"Cold fusion?" said the dean of physics. "Don't waste your mind. You're a bright girl, Jessica. Why don't you develop a new insulation for multifamily dwellings? That's what will be needed when we run out of fossil fuels in two hundred years."

Jessica stormed out of his office, too disgusted to argue. She met with her two trusted professors. One taught advanced physics, the other philosophy. Both sympathized with her situation but were powerless to do anything. They did point out, however, that she had learned all she could in the educational system, despite the best efforts of the educational system itself—and that there was a different institution that might even *pay* her to continue learning: the United States government.

Two months and six civil service tests later, Jessica sat at a desk in a brightly lit windowless room, the pancakes she'd eaten for breakfast skipping around like flat stones over the acid pond in her stomach. A closed question booklet with a blank answer sheet tucked neatly inside loomed on the scarred laminate surface of her desk. She had applied for a civilian physicist position within the military, and a noisy clock now ticked away the seconds as she prepared herself to delve into her seventh entry-level exam.

She wasn't superstitious, but she devoutly hoped number seven would be her last.

Her six prior attempts had taken place in convention centers and auditoriums alongside hundreds to thousands of other applicants. She had enjoyed a degree of cozy anonymity in the company of so many strangers. But now she was the solitary person in a space not much larger than a closet, the walls reflecting and amplifying her anxiety. As did the sound of that stupid clock! At least there wasn't an anti-cheat spy camera watching her, just a spindly black spider, high up in a corner, starving in its empty web.

With a deep cleansing breath, she opened her booklet and began.

The early questions challenged her undergraduate limits. If not for her self-imposed study regimen, she would have been at a loss for how to unravel the trickier problems. It took over an hour to complete the first page alone.

Upon turning to the second page, she found that someone had circled all the answers from that page forward, making only a halfhearted effort to erase their marks. She didn't think much of it: the instructions allowed for writing in the test materials, and she couldn't be held accountable for these markings. Besides, she wasn't going to trust the answers of the preceding test-taker. But as it turned out, the next two pages proved ridiculously easy, and she discovered that her answers matched up perfectly with the poorly erased circles.

She scanned the rest of the booklet. Ten pages remained, and much to her chagrin, they were filled with technically advanced questions that would require tedious calculations. The ticking clock gave her less than two hours to complete the exam—not remotely enough time.

She leaned back to contemplate a moral dilemma. She could complete the test using someone else's answers; or she could turn in the compromised test booklet for a clean one, muddle through as much of the test as she could, and almost certainly lose another job opportunity.

It was an easy decision. She wanted her achievements to be on her own merits. A clean conscience would allow her to sleep well at night, regardless of the bleak future awaiting her if she failed.

She stood quickly and knocked at the closed door.

"Finished already?" the proctor asked, peering in.

"No, ma'am. Someone marked the answers to all of the questions after the first page. I thought it would be best if I turned this in for a new test booklet."

The proctor took the booklet and flipped through the pages. "Well, aren't you the honest one?" She left to retrieve a replacement booklet, discarded the first page, and handed the rest to Jessica. "Finish the test with this. The questions are different, but the knowledge required for them is the same. I'll take the answers you have so far. Unfortunately, I can't give you any extra time to complete the test."

Jessica nodded and returned to her desk. She managed to finish another four pages before time expired. She left the building with low expectations for the job.

So it was to her great surprise when, two days later, she received a phone call requesting she come in for an interview the next day. Two men and a woman—who looked more accustomed to wearing military uniforms than the crisp civilian suits they had on—interrogated her on background details for less than ten minutes before dismissing her. When she asked what she had scored on the test, they merely replied that she had passed and should wait in the lobby while they deliberated.

Jessica fidgeted on the edge of a couch cushion, pondering how palms could sweat so much. She made a mental note to never eat such a large breakfast before testing or interviews.

An hour later, a secretary ushered her into a completely different room to complete the interview. An Army colonel in full dress uniform stood alone behind a cheap folding table.

"Sit," the colonel commanded. After Jessica settled herself into an uncomfortable chair, the colonel seated himself and asked, "Why do you want to work for the United States military?"

The fact that she heard the same question at the beginning of every other civil service interview did nothing to alleviate her anxiety at having to respond to it again. With hands folded calmly in her lap, she took a breath, straightened her back, and answered, "I've reached a point in my education where I believe practical application of what I have learned will be more beneficial than remaining in my degree program. I know the military has abundant facilities and resources to engage in scientific research. It's public knowledge that the military has been attempting to develop alternative energy solutions. Given the opportunity, I would like to continue my thesis work and help you achieve that goal."

The colonel took no notes, nor communicated anything through his facial expression or body language. She may as well have been trying to convince a frowning statue to smile. As if someone flipped a switch, he recited his next question. "The current global climate hints that we may be on the brink of another world war. While we can't give you any specifics, your performance on our entrance exam showed that you may be proficient in areas that will allow you to participate in other projects. How would you feel about that?"

Damn. I was afraid they were going to ask me something like this. Developing new weapon technology was the last thing Jessica wanted to be involved with. She hoped they wouldn't hold a candid answer against her. "To be honest, I would prefer not to work in the development of new weapons. If I can aid in areas other than that, I would be happy to do so."

She detected an upward twitch at the corner of his mouth. *Is that a hint of a smile? Am I really going to get this job?*

"Our current operations are extremely sensitive and require the utmost discretion and secrecy. Are you willing to disappear from society for the next ten years to assist in classified experiments so you may pursue your thesis?"

Ten years? She would be in her thirties by then, an old woman. Still, her parents wouldn't miss her. If she left, they could spend more on nickel slots. Her so-called friends would only miss her up until the next big party—then they'd make new best friends and forget about her. Ten years engaging in her passion for science in exchange for alienating herself from the outside world? *I tend to be a recluse anyway. At least I can get paid for it and potentially make the world a better place.*

The colonel was waiting patiently for her answer.

"I am willing, sir," she replied.

"You have until tomorrow morning to change your mind. *If* you choose to accept the position, be at the executive terminal of McCarran Airport at eight a.m." The colonel made a notation on one of the forms neatly stacked in front of him. He then added, "At the end of your service, the government will pay your outstanding student loan, and after five years, your sterilization will be reversed. You will not be permitted to bring any belongings other than hard copy notes pertaining to your thesis. Before boarding the plane, you will be required to take an oath of non-disclosure."

The colonel stood, extending his hand to end the hiring interview. Jessica rose and returned the colonel's firm grip. "Thank you, sir," she said. She smiled, knowing her path in life now had a direction.

***

Late the next morning, Jessica found herself on a sun-bleached airstrip at what the public believed was an abandoned military base. Her history classes had taught her that the base had been mothballed because of radiation fallout from early aboveground nuclear testing as well as toxic contamination from the first stealth aircraft programs. Conspiracy theorists, however, claimed the government used the base to test alien technology, including working spacecraft. Of course, all of this was categorically denied.

Prototype stealth aircraft and spy planes had once graced the massive hangars; now they served as a haven for dust and scorpions. Jessica patiently endured an orientation and tour of the base. Ominous pictographic signs forbade her from venturing near pits in which toxic materials had been dumped, burned, or stored. The only interesting relic of the tour wasn't something her tour guide showed her, just a curiosity that caught her attention—a name and date scrawled in the gritty concrete of the oldest hangar:

Jack the Ripper 2/14/55.

CHAPTER 7

Shadowed by two armed guards and her supervisor, Jessica presented security credentials to an elevator control pad. Only two buttons were available inside the elevator: up and down. She pushed the down button.

Today marked her fiftieth day of employment, but it was her first time taking this descent. As the elevator dropped, her anxiety level rose. With no way to count floors, her imagination took over. Her ears popped, and still they dropped.

The guards swallowed and glanced at her supervisor, an ancient man in his ninth decade of life. He rarely spoke, opting instead to hand her almost illegible written instructions or—to her frustration—to simply point in the direction he wished her to go and wait until she figured out his intention.

When at last the elevator stopped and the doors opened, he pointed "out"—one of his easier commands to decipher.

Five finger points later, as they strolled through a maze of corridors and unfamiliar faces, they came to a dead end. A vault door with no recognizable handle, hinges, or keypad of any kind stood closed before her. The eccentric old man merely pointed to it.

Jessica stepped closer, raising up on her tiptoes to examine the top, then bent to a knee to check the bottom, looking for some hidden locking mechanism. Finding none, she glanced back to see the old man smiling at her, as if his secret door held great humor.

Words of wisdom from Jessica's philosophy professor entered her thoughts: *Try before you pry.* She stood, and without looking away from the old man's eyes, pushed on the cold steel surface with her palm. She was rewarded by the old man's beaming smile and a door that swung open with little effort.

"Well done, young woman. Please step inside," the old man said without pointing. The genuine praise in his voice shocked her more than hearing him actually speak.

A short walkway led to a narrow door, its top slanting toward her. Without waiting for him to point, she touched it; it slid up to disappear in the low ceiling.

A dim polyhedral-shaped room opened before her like an immense, hollow diamond. All along the interior surface, sparkling points of light moved in perpetually random patterns. She traced the source of the lights to a softball-sized sphere hovering over a stout reclining chair on a pedestal in the center of the room.

Jessica moved to examine the sphere closer. A strong odor of cheap men's cologne tickled her nose. Before she could say anything, the old man said, "You have thirty minutes. Good luck," and touched the door. It closed softly, leaving her alone with a head full of questions.

Great. Another test to add to her workload.

With her hands in the pockets of her lab coat, she walked a cramped circle around the perimeter of the room. She could find nothing to explain what was levitating the sphere, and she could identify no reason for the room's unusual shape. She turned her attention to the chair. Indentations in the thick padding hinted that it was designed for extended periods of use. It possessed a standard data entry touchpad mounted on a swing arm for use while seated, along with a miniature view monitor, its screen dark and unresponsive. There was no ON switch.

Sitting in the well-worn chair seemed the reasonable thing to do, so she sat. And as she pulled the touchpad to a working position, the walls vanished into a seamless darkness and the sphere projected a three-dimensional holographic star field all around her.

Overwhelmed by a surge of acute vertigo, Jessica squeezed the arms of the chair with a white-knuckled grip. She hovered in space with no visual reference for up-down orientation. It was just space, her chair, and the sphere.

A small octagonal cursor trailed along the star field wherever she looked. The chair smoothly rotated and tilted, centering on her field of view when she moved her head to mark a star. She soon realized that face direction turned the chair while eye movements altered the cursor. This virtual reality technology was so far beyond civilian consumer level that Jessica's mind spun with possible applications for it.

She selected a twinkling star and tapped the question mark symbol on her pad. A holographic information screen flashed to life in front of her. *Spica, brightest star in the constellation Virgo, a blue giant 260 light years from Earth.* Jessica stared at the flashing cursor circling the star. They wouldn't go to the trouble of developing cutting-edge secret technology just to bury a planetarium in the desert. There had to be more to this thing.

A few glowing pictograms were arranged well below the text on Spica. Jessica selected one labeled "Current Projects." With a touch of her finger through the hologram, a constellation of information clusters replaced the star data: *Atomic Particles*, *Lunar Sensors*, *Precision Weapons*, *Satellites*, *Fusion Research*, *Space Exploration*, *Stealth Limitations*, and *Personal*.

It's no wonder the chair had seen so much use. I could spend weeks in here and never satisfy my curiosity.

She dug deeper into the Fusion Research cluster. It revealed that they had not only discovered its secret but also how to regulate and maintain the reaction. Applied uses were still forthcoming. Bubbling with excitement, Jessica opened up Space Exploration next. It had been recently accessed, according to the security timestamp. Inside were clusters on *Pioneer*, *Voyager*, *Cassini*, *Viking*, *Pathfinder*, and others.

Jessica recognized them as early NASA-launched space exploration vehicles that had been reported as either nonfunctioning, lost, or destroyed.

Jessica touched *Voyager I*, which had the same access timestamp as the root cluster. Her chair immediately shifted to face a blinking blue disc in the star field—no doubt the current position of the spacecraft. According to the display, the craft still actively transmitted data: the right half of her holographic screen showed a star field from Voyager's camera feed, and a digital date and time readout ticked away with blurring microseconds. The thing was ancient by current technological standards, and the fact that *any* part of it still functioned amazed her. And she couldn't help but wonder why they had bothered to deceive the public all these years in claiming that *Voyager* was lost.

It was all very fascinating, but Jessica still struggled to understand the point of all this. It must have taken billions of dollars to build this facility and who knew how much to maintain it. She shook her head at the sheer scope of wasteful government spending as she tapped one of the scroll arrows below the camera feed.

The image shifted immediately.

Jessica blinked in surprise; it took her a moment to digest what had just happened. As she scrolled the camera around its range of motion, it came to her. *Voyager I* was over fifteen billion miles away from Earth. It would take almost twenty-four hours for any signal to reach it, let alone for an image to be transmitted. Yet the commands she was giving to the spacecraft were executed *immediately*. Whatever technology was at work here was achieving faster-than-light communication, and to Jessica's cynical mind, that made it ridiculously beyond the impossible. Then again, if it was legitimate, it certainly justified the secrecy and the oath she had taken to be here.

She checked the other spacecraft data feeds and found them all to have the same instantaneous responses. Her brief scan of the other folders proved enlightening but had nowhere near the impact of FTL communication and fusion.

That left only the personal folder. It was unlocked, and it begged to be opened; its timestamp showed it to be the last file accessed prior to her entering. Jessica reached out to touch it, but paused to work through her conflicting emotions. She had clearance for top secret level work and was now inside what was perhaps the most secret place on the base. Yet, it didn't feel right for her to peek inside someone's personal folder.

An empty red hourglass icon flashed before her. *I guess my thirty minutes are up.* She withdrew her hand, and as she pushed the keyboard back to its original position, the star field and holographic screen disappeared, leaving Jessica once more anchored in the solid confines of the polyhedral chamber.

She rose and walked to the door, which once again slid upward as she palmed it. Even the locking mechanism held a secret. She took one last look at the sparkling sphere, then left with new hope for the limitless possibilities it represented.

CHAPTER 8

The day after Jessica's "test," two uniformed military police officers entered the accelerator control analysis lab. Their eyes rapidly scanned faces until finally locking on target.

"Jessica Stafford?" one asked.

"Yes?" Jessica replied without looking up from her screen, completely absorbed in a rhythm of data input.

"Come with us. Leave the lab coat."

Jessica blinked until the officer's words sank in, still not fully registering their meaning. She stood and draped her lab coat on the chair. "What's this about?"

"Our orders are to escort you to the colonel," the officer said, lifting a hand to his sidearm.

The hairs on the back of Jessica's neck prickled in alarm. Coldly emotionless faces and postures like coiled snakes warned her not to provoke these men. With arms limp at her sides, Jessica slowly walked with them out of the facility, to a waiting helicopter.

Jessica pinched the bridge of her nose with eyes closed in concentration as the helicopter lifted off the ground. She had done something wrong. That had to be the reason for this. But nothing came to mind, and the MPs never said a word. Fear prevented her from even making eye contact with them, but she was certain they never so much as blinked under the tension of the stuffy flight back to the base. They extended hands to assist her to the ground upon landing, then shadowed her to the colonel's office as if she might try to flee.

"Sit, Miss Stafford," the colonel commanded in a tone that would make a mountain tremble. "It has been brought to my attention that you have been falsifying data on a critical research project."

Jessica opened her mouth to speak. The colonel immediately cut her off with a terse hand gesture. "This isn't a forum for discussion. I have documented proof of your actions. Due to the sensitive nature of our business here, we cannot tolerate employees who lack integrity. Your contract is terminated, effective immediately."

Jessica closed her eyes and shakily expelled air through her nose. This couldn't be happening. Her eyes stung. This wasn't the place for tears. She bit the inside of her lip to fend them off.

"Do you understand why you are being terminated?" asked the colonel.

"No! This *has* to be a mistake. Falsifying data? What would I have to gain by such a thing?"

The colonel's face hardened into an unforgiving wall. His words flowed without mercy. "It's not so much what you have to gain as it is about what we have to lose. We can't afford to take the chance. You are fired. Do you understand?"

They made up their minds before they even brought me here. Jessica knew her every argument would be dismissed, and her pride would not allow begging. "Yes, sir," she replied, lowering her head.

"Do you have any questions?" the colonel asked. But his tone issued a command: *Don't ask any questions.*

"No, sir," she answered.

"Read this aloud and sign it. *Again.*" The colonel slid a document to Jessica. As his fingers withdrew, she saw it was the same non-disclosure agreement she had signed less than two months ago.

Jessica read aloud. "I understand, under penalty of lifetime, solitary imprisonment, that I may not divulge, discuss, or record in any manner the nature of the work that I participated in or may have witnessed while in the employment of the United States. Only a person presenting military credentials with the code name 'Jack the Ripper' may authorize me to break this oath." She signed on the line marked with a red X, still silently hoping the colonel would change his mind and tell her it was all a joke.

"You will be provided a change of clothes and escorted off the premises. From there, you will be driven back to Las Vegas. The rest is up to you. Dismissed."

The colonel retrieved the document and added his own signature, then acted as if Jessica ceased to exist. The angular lines of his signature on her discharge papers cut a permanent scar on her future.

The guards who had been standing at attention behind her stepped forward to escort her out. Jessica followed the lead guard while the other trailed. *This must be what it's like marching to face a firing squad*, she thought. And in a sense, that was exactly what she was doing. They were tossing her back into civilization, and that was almost as deadly for someone with a black mark of dishonor on their record. The fact that almost everyone else on the planet shunned any opportunity to be honorable mattered not. She had committed the unforgiveable sin of being caught—and that made her an inferior breed. Regardless of her abilities, few would be inclined to give her another chance. Fewer still would ever believe the tragic truth—that she was innocent.

***

As soon as the trailing escort left the office, a man with graying hair and a well-tailored suit entered from the colonel's private sitting area.

"You should start evacuating as soon as they're gone," he said.

The colonel's countenance was that of a man who had just taken a beating. "You're a real bastard, Jack."

"Signatures don't give value to an oath, only actions," Jack said. "You of all people should know that by now."

"The fact that I know *exactly* what is going through her head at this moment doesn't make it any easier," the colonel declared.

"Only those of the finest moral character ever make it through the Lazar Test, my friend. As much as we need the likes of Jessica, we have to be certain."

"She's a good kid. Nothing like that piece of work we processed yesterday. Insolent prick. I wanted to shoot him."

"I'll add your name to the list," Jack said.

CHAPTER 9

Sebastian had no earthly idea how they had returned him to the States after losing consciousness from that drugged bullet. A puncture scar in the center of his chest and the rock in his shoe were the only tangible items he'd managed to return with. The rock might be valuable if he ever wanted to discover the location of the secret cavern—although it was a long shot. Still, he had hollowed out a pocket under the insole of his shoe to keep it safe.

After his return, he had spent the better part of seven months debriefing higher pay grades on his mission findings and their sociopolitical ramifications. When the agency at last gave him the authority to continue analyzing the potential consequences of the discovery, he insisted that they first reveal their other covert operations—in order for him to better formulate a contingency plan if the information became public. Somewhat to his surprise, they did. And when he encountered the room housing faster-than-light and fusion technology, he could barely contain his excitement. The classified folder he peeked into contained his own assessment of the artifact, along with several scientists' strong recommendations that it not be moved from its present location until all dangers could be ruled out. But it offered nothing regarding the artifact's location.

Sebastian knew the power of information as well as anyone. A career in the secret services meant he knew things that no one else could. And that knowledge gave him job security. They couldn't possibly fire him with the knowledge he now possessed.

***

Several days later, Sebastian found himself handcuffed to a seat in the back of a sweltering bus. They had fired him on grounds of sexual harassment—and all he'd done was promise career advancement to a young secretary for a few special favors. *Of all the stupid things*, he thought. If he was guilty of such a time-honored method of asking a girl out, then what they had done to him was nothing short of rape. The indignity of a strip search had rankled him; the rough cavity search had left him feeling violated. Armed guards had treated him like a prisoner when they marched him into the colonel's office.

Sebastian's threats to go over the colonel's head had shattered against the man's stoic face. His insults about the colonel's ability to command seemed to have an effect, but the steely look the colonel leveled at Sebastian got him to mind his attitude. He'd seen that look before: right before someone pulled a trigger.

"I have to take a piss!" he yelled to the bus driver.

The driver reached behind his seat to retrieve something, and with a backhanded throw, he hurled it at Sebastian. With his right hand secured by the cuffs, Sebastian made an awkward attempt to fend off the spinning projectile with his left. It ricocheted off his wrist to his forehead and settled into his lap.

Sebastian scowled down at a dinky bottle of water. "Thanks!" he yelled sarcastically. As much as the heat made him thirsty, he really did have to urinate, and water would make things worse. And even if he emptied the bottle, there was no way it could hold the contents of his bladder. It seemed that everyone he encountered lately had been trained in subtle forms of torture.

***

MPs walked Jessica across a scorching hot parking lot to a plain black and white bus with dark tinted windows. Without air conditioning, the old bus was like a dry sauna, and the interior smelled of dusty creosote. The driver benefitted from a stubby fan mounted on the dash, vibrating in its struggle to produce a cool breeze in the harsh desert heat. With a nod to the MP, he started the engine.

Only one other person occupied the bus, and he sat in the very back. Jessica had no desire to speak to anyone, so she bent to sit in the first available seat. But the guard behind her caught her arm. "Sit in the back next to the other one," he said. He kept a firm grip as he all but pushed her along the aisle.

A quick glance at the other passenger confirmed that he was watching her closely. When she took a seat across the aisle from him, she saw that his wrist was secured to a sturdy rail below the window. A metallic clinking and silver flash from the MP's utility belt told her she was in for the same treatment. Giving in to the inevitable, she presented her left wrist. The disappointment in the MP's expression said everything. With fluid movements, he secured her wrist to the rail and left without a word.

In Jessica's peripheral vision, she discerned that the man across from her was still staring. She inclined her head to the window, pretending to be interested in something beyond the sand-pitted glass as the bus began to move. Maybe he would get the hint if she ignored him.

"What did they get *you* for?" he asked.

She clenched her jaw at the familiarity in his tone. Why did they have to lock her up next to a twit like this? Being handcuffed to the drive train under the bus would be preferable.

Her attitude changed when a familiar odor reached her nostrils. It was the same cologne she had detected in the polyhedral room. *He was there too.*

The man had his free hand extended toward her in greeting. "I'm Sebastian," he said. "How do you do?"

She regarded his proffered hand as if it were holding a dead mouse. Like a crab retreating into its shell, she shifted closer to the window.

"Hey, I recognize you," he continued. "You were in the facility where they work on fusion..." He cast her an appraising gaze. "Did you study the artifact?"

Jessica couldn't believe what she was hearing. Was this some sort of sick, twisted test? He had to have taken the same oath she had, and he certainly wasn't Jack the Ripper. And what did he mean about an 'artifact'? Could that be the information contained in that classified folder? He shouldn't be talking about *any* of this anyway. It was life-alteringly dangerous to do so. She wouldn't be surprised if they'd hid a microphone in the back of the bus to listen in on their conversation.

"What's the matter?" he persisted. "Listen—" He leaned over as close as his restraint allowed. "With all the classified information in your brain, they can't possibly get away with firing you. They're counting on us honoring that oath. But all we have to do is go to the media and we'll be treated like celebrities. They'll even pay us! If we go together, we'll have more credibility. What do you say?"

Holy shit.

Jessica closed her eyes. He kept babbling on and would not shut up. She wished someone would shoot him. He had a point: if they went public, any subsequent 'mysterious disappearance' would only make their stories more believable. But it wasn't worth it. It wasn't worth losing her self-respect to side with someone who had none. She would stay true to her oath, no matter the difficulties it caused. It was the right thing to do—and that made the decision simple. With sweat beading on her forehead, she pinned a cold glare on Sebastian.

"Would you like some water?" he asked, brandishing his bottle.

"No thank you. We have a long ride, and I doubt they'll stop to let us use the bathroom."

CHAPTER 10

Fall 2040

Mykl stood proudly among the towering snow-covered pines. Gripping a twisted metal sword, he pondered a pale glow in the distance. Leaden gray clouds weighed heavily in the sky, absorbing any hint that the sun had ever existed. He had snuck to this spot and battled this enemy many times before. But today, it was time for a different outcome.

A brilliant flash, followed by a thundering crash, announced the arrival of a demon. Time was the third enemy demanding his life now; he must hurry. With great strides, he set off toward the glow.

At the edge of a clearing, he stopped. On a patch of glistening white snow, in the center of a glowing circle, another demon awaited him. An electric rope of fear spiraled down his spine as he saw his image reflected in the demon's eyes. Raucous gusts of steamy breath blew through venom-stained fangs, and its fetid odor carried past him on the icy breeze.

Mykl's fear had nothing to do with the demon standing before him; it was reserved for the person he knew was approaching him from behind. With scant seconds remaining, he dashed into the circle—and threw down his sword.

He grinned as the demon sank its fangs into his shoulder and began rending his flesh. It consumed his limbs in ragged, sloppy gulps. Bright red spatters of blood dotted the snow around steaming entrails. Mykl watched impassively as his life drained away. He no longer cared... Just a few more moments...

***

"MYKL! GET OFF THAT COMPUTER! *NOW!*"

Mykl stared into the flaring nostrils of the demon-woman fuming behind him. She stood more than three times his size and raked his body with her dark, lifeless eyes. He sighed. He wasn't even allowed to enjoy his own boredom. His gaze transformed into a forced scowl.

"Don't look at me like that! You're lucky to even be here. There are more deserving children who should be, that's for sure." Lori's voice oozed contempt as she advanced on him. "You're nothing special. The world is filthy with unwanted five-year-olds. Do you think because your mom was murdered that you deserve to be here more than anyone else? You're no better than the drug-addicted newborn that died on our doorstep yesterday."

Mykl turned his head to the security video monitors next to the computer and closed his eyes in disgust.

Lori caught his unspoken accusation and declared, "It wasn't my fault. I was on my break!"

In his fourteen months of life in the "Box," Mykl had cataloged all of the excuses in Lori's repertoire. *I was on a bathroom break. I was on my lunch break. She wasn't my responsibility.* The excuses held as much weight as the smoke from her special "cigarettes." She hated children and said so daily. Why she had chosen to manage a house of unwanted kids, Mykl would never know.

Linda, the night shift assistant manager, strolled past to pick up her coat. Lori lashed out at her. "Why do you let him use the computer?"

"It keeps him out of trouble."

"And *how* did he get the password?" Lori's eyes slitted in anger, and her greasy black hair threatened to slither out of its scalp-stretching bun.

Linda reached for the grimy keyboard and flipped it upside down, revealing a well-worn strip of masking tape stuck to the bottom. Ten tiny letters written in red ink seemed to shrink guiltily in the light. Mykl feigned a look of innocence as Lori shifted her dark gaze from the tape to his face.

Linda pointed from Lori to the tape. "Of all people," she said, "*you* should be able to memorize *that* without having to write it down and sticking it where any simple-minded child can find it. I'm sure you can think up another one."

"I put it there because *you* couldn't memorize it," Lori replied caustically. "It's a wonder you can even remember to come to work."

"Whatever, I'm going home now," Linda said, marching for the exit.

While Lori reigned as queen demon of the Box, Linda played the indifferent serf, who couldn't care less what the children did as long as they didn't inconvenience her. It was that indifference that made it possible for Mykl to sneak out of the dorm at night to use the office computer without reprisal from the mean kids, or from Lori.

The "office" was really just a large semicircular desk that arced out into the dayroom. It served as a post for direct observation of the children coming and going from the dorms. Black and white security monitors recorded events from strategically located cameras.

Lori set the morning paper among the clutter on the desk. Her pale skin took on a greenish tinge under the hum of fluorescent lights as she stared down at Mykl. "Go watch cartoons like everyone else."

Mykl had no desire to watch meaningless cartoons. They barely deserved his apathy. He turned back to the computer screen. Even living vicariously in a fantasy world as a magic sword-wielding hero had lost its appeal. He needed something more tangible. It was time to find a new form of entertainment on the computer—but it would have to wait. He would resume his adventures in the evening, when Linda was once again on duty, and after the rest of the Box had succumbed to sleep.

Pushing away the filthy computer mouse, he hopped off the chair and started to leave.

"By the way," Lori spat, "someone called yesterday to schedule an adoption interview with you for tomorrow evening." Her voice dripped with toxic glee. "There's no escaping this time—his background and income all check out. Your stay here is about to end. Good riddance!"

Threats from Lori were like cockroaches: they came in varying sizes, and you were bound to be confronted by at least a dozen throughout the day. Adoption threats were far from original for her. He ignored her as he joined the other children in the dayroom.

Mykl tried his best to be invisible to the other denizens of the Box. Barely over five years old, he was a small wisp of a boy, and his delicate features, copper-colored eyes, and chocolate brown hair would be considered cute if not for the serious expression he wore as a shield to hide his inner terror and grief. Still, he was a target for kids in need of punching fodder to justify their existence. The unwritten rule of the Box allowed bullies to pick on anyone smaller than themselves, and Mykl dwelled at the bottom of the food chain.

The flickering television in the dayroom already held kids captive as they waited for the breakfast bell to trigger the morning stampede. Sniffles and coughs leaked from children varying in age from five to seventeen. Mykl felt lucky for never falling victim to the illnesses that so commonly plagued others.

A tattered old couch looked like a living creature as eleven squirming figures jockeyed for position. The rest of the bodies in the room appeared to have tumbled off the couch earlier in an orphan landslide that had left them sprawled haphazardly on a gaudy rug. The kids lay on their stomachs, their heads propped up high. Putting one's face too close to the rug only intensified its revolting odor.

A public service announcement interrupted their viewing with a piercing sound and flashing red text ticker. The face of a beautiful woman brandishing a fake smile delivered the bad news of the day and an update on the latest end-of-the-world predictions. Civil unrest in the European Union had degraded into border skirmishes involving tanks and mortars. Militarily superior neighbors were taking sides and adding fighter jets to the mix. Body counts were rising accordingly. The strong language of peacekeeping efforts offered little protection from RPGs, airstrikes, and landmines. Oh, and apparently there were increasing nuclear tensions in the Middle East—*again*. Ever since the dirty bomb detonation at a crowded concert in New York's Central Park, terrorist attacks around the world had become as common as pigeon shit on a park bench. And the media reveled in it. They stoked public fear and fed on increased ratings like starving parasites.

Mykl wanted no part of it. He wondered if things would be better off if they just launched all the missiles and called it a day. He began to walk away, only to be halted in his steps by the announcement of an upcoming exclusive weekend interview with a former clandestine government worker-turned-whistleblower. The woman pumped the story, promising proof that the government was withholding fusion and faster-than-light technology in a secret military base. Mykl shook his head at the thought. *Faster than light?* What a crackpot. Faster-than-light approached the speed of Santa's sleigh. And fusion filled the holy grail of science. Together, they formed the cheap bubblegum that held together most science fiction. *Fusion, really?* If that technology existed, why wouldn't they have implemented it already and gotten the world out of this energy mess?

The announcement ended, and Mykl shifted into invisible mode. No one ever noticed him when he put his mind to seeking solitude. Soundlessly, he glided across the dayroom in his ratty socks, taking care to avoid any movements noticeable by those watching television. He doubted the kids absorbed in their cartoons could be aware of anything but the mindless drivel pouring out of the ancient box anyway...

"Myyyyyklll?"

... except James. Mykl had never been able to hide from James. It baffled him to no end.

The hulking lump of man-boy called James shuffled toward him. A frightening mass of sleep-matted hair gave him the look of a madman. He came off as seventeen going on seven and made his way around the Box in a slack-faced slouch most of the time. If he ever stretched to his full height of six foot three, he would have been an imposing presence.

James's gray eyes twinkled with child-like mischief. "Myyykll," he drawled in a nasal twang as he flashed an impish smile. "Fixes shoes agains?"

As usual, the voices in James's head had told him to tie his shoelaces into elaborate knots. His knotting skills approached Gordian art. At least he hadn't tied his shoes together again.

"Sure, James, I'll fix your shoes." Mykl knelt to size up the latest knot puzzle. He soon realized it was going to take a focused effort to remedy.

"Where's Dawn?" he asked.

"Dawn outside with kitteh," James said.

"How about we go out there and keep her company while I work on your laces?" Dawn had lived on the planet two years less than James but exhibited much better conversation skills.

James nodded several times in agreement and trundled across the dayroom to the door leading out to the quad.

As Mykl followed him past the office desk, he ignored the chilly look Lori leveled at him as she industriously tapped away at the computer. She appeared to be installing new software. *I didn't know she was smart enough to do that*, he thought with a shrug.

As stark as a penitentiary, the quad was a square patch of disintegrating blacktop, thirty feet on a side, enclosed by a weathered, twelve-foot, chain link fence. Tattered shreds of sun-rotted trash fluttered on long-barbed razor wire topping the fence, and rusty bolts penetrated deep into the exterior stucco to secure the fence to the Box. Reddish brown stains flowed from the bolts like battered children's tears frozen in time. In the center of the quad, a lone pole of galvanized metal with a short length of rusted chain attached at the top—the remnant of some neglected entertainment device for children—listed at a slight angle, its use long forgotten. Some charity group had installed a rosebush planter against the building in an attempt to beautify the area, but its singular purpose now was to serve as a symbol of what happened to life in the Box: it was mistreated, flowerless, and struggling to blossom.

An old metal folding chair was the only other object in the quad. Dawn was sitting in the chair with a scrawny white purring kitten curled up in her lap and a soft smile on her lips.

The light morning breeze carried a noticeable chill as Mykl stepped outside. It was mid-October, and fall had finally decided to announce its arrival. Everyone had greeted the recent change in temperature as a much-welcomed gift after the sweltering summer that had ruthlessly taxed their tired air conditioner.

James lowered himself to the blacktop near the chair as Mykl peered over Dawn's shoulder. "How is Teeka this morning?" Mykl asked.

The kitten made a stiff-legged stretch and yawned mightily. "Warm and happy," Dawn said. "She wolfed down my scraps as fast as I pulled them out of the bag. Has James been amusing himself with his laces again?"

"How could you tell?"

Dawn stroked the kitten's soft fur. "He giggled when he passed. I figured he must be up to his usual mischief."

Mykl sat cross-legged at James's feet and began tugging the laces with practiced finesse. "You figured right. He did a doozy today!"

While Mykl's deft little fingers worked their magic with the dingy size thirteen shoes, James's gray eyes gazed up at Dawn with infatuation. The low morning sun was sneaking into their dismal world to illuminate the greatest beauty within the Box: Dawn. It was difficult to tell which was brighter, the sun or Dawn's translucent radiance.

Feeling the sun on her face, Dawn took a slow, deep breath as if trying to capture its warmth into her body. Her head was held high and her slim shoulders were back, without fear of the world or the evil it could throw at her. Pale blue eyes the color of a cloudless desert sky gazed beyond their confinement. She owned the Box with her quiet elegance.

But while those she encountered marveled at her beauty and strength of spirit, her view of the world didn't extend beyond her arm's reach. She knew light only as warmth. Colors were useless names for old memories. Shapes manifested themselves exclusively through touch and imagination. Such was the life of the blind.

At age seven, a doctor visiting the Box had told Dawn she would never see again. He blamed her condition on a combination of malnutrition and some childhood disease she hadn't been immunized against. At fifteen, she still suffered from headaches as a result of that illness.

Teeka hopped off Dawn's lap and pounced on James's laces.

"Kitteh!"

"Hold her for me, James," Mykl said.

James gently picked up the squirming kitten and held her protectively under his chin.

Loose bits of trash filtered through the fence and danced across the asphalt. Mykl looked up to survey the quad and shook his head. "That razor wire is depressing. It makes this place look like a prison."

"I don't mind it," Dawn said.

"Ha ha. You're the only one who wouldn't," Mykl replied flatly.

"Keeps out Ass Angel." James said it as a simple statement of fact. Mykl and Dawn said nothing.

The Asylum Angel—as he had called himself in his haunting letter—was referred to as the "Ass Angel" by those in the Box. A security camera had captured him taping an envelope to the asylum's main entry door. When Lori read the letter, she called the police in a panic. She later explained to her charges that the psychopathic Angel had threatened to send all the children to heaven unless they were immediately adopted. Mykl secretly wondered if it was all a ploy to make them more agreeable to adoption.

Also included in the letter was some type of crude cipher. Lori made a copy for herself before the police arrived, and she readily flashed that copy, with good effect, whenever certain individuals misbehaved. And when a local paper published the cipher and a pixelated image of the Angel, Lori allowed it to circulate, uncensored, among the kids. Even those who couldn't read knew the crazy symbols meant they were marked for death. Lori seemed to enjoy hearing them talk in fearful whispers.

"Don't worry, James," Mykl said. "He can't get inside here. After all, we have this beautiful twelve-foot fence topped with razor wire."

And it was true: for all its dreariness and uncaring staff, the Box offered safety. Unfortunately, the kids were treated like unwanted pets in a pound. They were fed and watered, and the television stayed on all day long to keep them occupied, but they had little hope of ever being adopted. At least they weren't put to sleep when they got too old; instead, they were summarily kicked out. But even a dog about to be put to sleep got a pat on the head every once in a while.

When at last Mykl unraveled James's knots, he carefully retied them with his own special James-proof version. "There. Now leave them alone for the rest of the day!"

"Yes, Myyyklll." James placed Teeka back on Dawn's lap. "Have kitteh back, pretty Dawn."

Just as Dawn reached out to receive her, Lori burst into the quad. "What are you doing with that mangy cat?" she growled.

Teeka responded by puffing up in a fury of fur and claws. She wriggled out of James's grasp, flew across the quad, and disappeared under a gap in the fence. Even an innocent kitten had the sense to run from the demon-woman.

Mykl saw Dawn mouth the word "bitch" in mute protest. Lori never seemed to notice Dawn's insults.

"You know the rules," Lori said. "No pets. Don't let me catch any of you with one of those vermin again. Now get back inside!"

Yelling and screaming from the Box drowned out all but the first peal of the breakfast bell. James assisted Dawn to her feet and escorted her inside. Mykl glanced back at the fence and saw a young white furry face with a black smirk of a mustache peering around a crumpled garbage can. Mykl kept his smile to himself and walked past Lori with firm control over the sharpened words prickling the tip of his tongue.

James and Dawn were disappearing into the cafeteria, and Mykl had to double his shorter strides to catch up. He was pleased to see that they were serving his favorite breakfast today: oatmeal and orange-flavored water. It must be a special day; they hardly ever served orange-flavored water.

James guided Dawn to an empty space at the end of a long table. "Stay with Dawn, James. I'll go get our food," Mykl said. He grabbed a tray to get in line behind the others waiting for their daily gruel.

Boredom radiated from the pimple-faced drudge behind the counter. "Three please?" Mykl said. He held up three tiny fingers and wiggled them. He knew math wasn't a strong point for the volunteer kitchen workers.

With three steaming bowls on his tray, he made for the drink counter. He was handicapped by his size and five-year-old muscle strength, and adding three overfull drinks to the tray made transport even more of a challenge. Slowly… Slowly…

"Mykl? Are you letting my oatmeal get cold?" Dawn asked with a smile.

"Hold your kittens! I'm coming, I'm coming!"

James applauded when Mykl finally delivered the tray to the table with only minor spillage. "Tank you, Myyykll."

"Yes, thank you, Mykl. Did you happen to bring spoons too?" Dawn asked innocently.

Grumbling, Mykl fetched spoons as well.

They ate and bantered among themselves, with James and Mykl taking the brunt of Dawn's sharp wit. "When are you going to grow, Mykl? Are you sure you're not some sort of government experiment gone horribly wrong?" she teased.

Mykl flicked a pebble of hardened oatmeal at her chest. She flinched, and James blew a snot bubble through a snort of laughter. "No fair!" she exclaimed. "You should be ashamed of yourself for picking on a poor little blind girl."

"Not me. It was James!"

"James no flick booger!" he cried in defense.

"Booger? It was a booger?" Dawn snorted as well, which only caused the boys to tease her, and soon they were all lost in a massive giggle fit.

After breakfast, while Mykl scraped their bowls into the trash, James escorted Dawn to the dayroom. The two were inseparable. James gladly served as her eyes and valiantly took on the duty of guardian angel, and in turn, Dawn shared her kindness and friendship.

Mykl ran to catch back up to them. He found Dawn stretched

out on a threadbare tan couch, her eyes staring into infinity, her pose reminiscent of a hieroglyph of an Egyptian princess Mykl had once seen on an Internet travel site. James sat at her feet in peaceful admiration.

With a running start, Mykl jumped high into the air and plopped into the middle of an old beanbag chair nearby. "I saw Teeka hanging out by the fence after Lori scared her off. She should be there waiting for you in the morning."

"I do love that little rat," Dawn said.

"Teeka no ratteh. She kitteh!"

"James, what are you going to do in six months when they make you leave for being too old?" Mykl asked. but it was Dawn he looked to for a reaction.

"Mehbe James stay and serve boogers?" he replied.

"Lori would never let you. She *hates* us," Dawn said. "God, she pisses me off." She closed her eyes and hugged her body tight as if fending off a chill. Abruptly, she sat up and rose in a swift graceful motion. "I have a headache. I'm going to my room… No, don't get up, James, I can find my way. It's not like anything ever changes around here."

James looked sad as his perfectly postured princess disappeared up the stairs.

"C'mon, James," said Mykl, "we may as well go too. It's better than hanging around here and waiting for Lori to yell at us for existing."

James struggled to his feet. "Yeeaah, why she so mean?"

"I don't know. The whole world is that way. We just happen to be stuck in our own little slice of it. It could be worse—we could be adopted by the Ass Angel."

James scowled. "Not funnily, Mykl."

Tina, a shy, blue-green-eyed girl Mykl's age, walked past them on her way to the quad. She was a relatively new addition to the Box. "Hi, James. Hi, Mykl," she said in a small voice.

"Hi, Tina," they said in unison. Mykl was watching her walk away when James poked him in the shoulder. "You likes her," he teased.

"No I don't!" Mykl turned his back on James and lengthened his stride toward their dorm. "She's a girl!" But all the way down the hall,

James chanted, "Myyykll likes Teeenaa, Myyykll likes Teeenaa," while Mykl countered, "Shut up! Shut up! Shut up!"

A lingering stink of urine and vomit saturated the dorms. One acclimated to it, eventually. Girls lived upstairs to separate them from the boys. Mykl and James shared a space downstairs. The odd pairing went against normal practice—the customary system paired individuals of similar age—but Mykl had little to complain about. James slept in the upper bunk, didn't snore too loudly, and his size kept the mean kids at bay.

As soon as they stepped inside their dorm, James promptly set to work on one of his peculiar pastimes: dots. All six foot three, two hundred twenty pounds of him plopped down at the child-sized desk they shared, and a lock of roughly cut ash blond hair hung below his brows, bouncing rhythmically, as he hunched over a pencil and made pages and pages of dots on blank sheets of printer paper that Mykl had liberated from office supplies. The activity appeared to be therapeutic and kept him from making knots in his shoelaces, so Mykl never troubled him over this particular quirk.

It certainly isn't his only quirk, Mykl thought as he spied an old newspaper opened to the crossword puzzle lying on the floor. James never paid attention to the questions that went with the puzzle; he just filled in the blank squares with words of his own choosing, using his unique style of spelling. To Mykl's amazement, James always filled in every box, and every word made sense—down *and* across.

James also had a pre-bedtime habit of pounding out dozens and dozens of pushups and sit-ups. It kept him extraordinarily fit. When Mykl asked him about it, James replied that he'd once heard someone on television say that you had to do those exercises if you wanted to be healthy. Mykl simply arched an eyebrow at James's rare display of common sense.

Mykl once overheard a member of the staff commenting that James was autistic. Mykl did some research on autism on the Internet and decided to challenge James to a game of solving square roots. James always calculated them faster. He was smart in his own eccentric way.

Perhaps that was why Mykl sometimes likened James's situation to his own. When Mykl had first encountered children his own age, he'd thought there must be something wrong with them—before quickly coming to the realization that *he* was the odd one. At the age of three, it was already obvious there was something unusual going on. Others his age didn't act or think like he did. Adults mistakenly attributed his quiet demeanor to some type of mental abnormality. His incredible ability to absorb and compile an adult vocabulary had only served to justify their diagnosis. Though he was usually very careful about revealing his abilities, sometimes his filter would give way, such as when a snappy retort was too good to keep to himself. That often happened with Lori.

Did James realize that he was odd, too?

I don't care what other people think of him, Mykl thought. *James is my friend.*

If only he could be taught to leave his blasted laces alone.

CHAPTER 11

Late into the night, a wailing ambulance siren pulled Mykl from the serene depths of sleep. He opened his eyes and stared at the sagging, exposed wire mesh that somehow managed to keep James and his tattered mattress from crashing down and killing him in a bone-crushing instant.

Mykl rolled over and hugged his pillow. Before being awakened, he had been dreaming of his mother. Thoughts of her still haunted him. He loved her. Why did she have to die? And why did she keep so many secrets—use so many names?

And where was his father? The only thing he knew about his father was that they supposedly had the same name. Yet even armed with a full name, his Internet research had yielded nothing.

And that had left Mykl stuck here, at the Las Vegas Foundling Asylum.

The orphanage.

Mykl knew that foundling asylums had virtually disappeared from advanced societies for a number of decades, in favor of foster care. But the foster care system had broken down, as legitimate foster parents had become vastly outnumbered by abusers who simply took in as many children as legally allowed to get the maximum government stipend. Too often that money bought alcohol and cigarettes, instead of food and clothes, and local politicians decided that the money was better off kept in their own expert hands. And so it was that the foundling asylums, operated by the governments themselves, replaced foster care as the most popular means for dealing with unwanted children.

This didn't result in an increase in the quality of care. Underfunding was the norm, and the politicians were always looking for ways to spend even less. Revised sterility laws proved to be the most popular solution to the problem of unwanted children.

Sterility laws had long been in place for pets. In hindsight, it had only been a matter of time before their success led to similar ordinances for people. Habitual criminals, welfare recipients, and those who wished to live in subsidized housing were soon all required to submit to chemical sterilization. Infertility could be reversed with a drug, but it was available only by court order. Careful screening measures claimed to sterilize only those who weren't worthy of being parents in the first place. But the policy had little effect on the growing number of homeless children.

Mykl got out of bed and crept to stargaze at the window. It was a clear night, and if he pressed his cheek to the cold glass, he could almost see Orion's Belt between the security bars. He loved looking at the stars and often snuck into the quad late at night to stare awestruck at the grandeur of an open sky.

James rolled over, and the protesting squeal of wire mesh echoed through the still air. Mykl looked around. At this hour, Lori should be long gone, and Linda would be in charge of the Box. Mykl chuckled. All Linda ever did was show up and go to sleep.

He shuffled to his dresser to retrieve a pair of socks. They all had holes in them, but he had only himself to blame for that. He'd long ago decided that shoes were too noisy; socks were ever so much stealthier. Choosing a pair with the fewest holes, he gave them a sniff and sat on the scuffed linoleum to pull them on, taking care to avoid enlarging the tears. Then he slipped out the door and padded softly down the hallway. A quick reconnaissance of the dayroom confirmed that Linda was earning her keep for the night by warming the full length of the couch.

The office computer was his ultimate goal, but first Mykl wanted to visit the quad. A security camera kept watch on the door, but he doubted anyone ever bothered to check the security recordings. In any case, no one had ever confronted him about his nighttime forays—or his petty pilfering of office supplies.

The door to the quad was locked at night. It was unlocked by a button at the desk, but would remain unlocked only so long as the button remained pressed—and while it was pressed, an annoying buzzer alarm sounded, so taping the button down or leaving a heavy object on top of it was not an option. But in his early days at the Box, Mykl had developed a method for unlocking the door without raising suspicion. It involved a ruler, a paper clip, a wad of paper, and three strips of tape, all of which could be found among the office supplies.

After bending the paper clip into the shape of a flat square with an "X" in the middle, Mykl inserted it in the crack between the door and the jamb, resting on top of the bolt. He then shoved the end of the ruler just below the bolt, taping it into place to catch the paperclip. The second strip of tape covered the crack where the bolt lay; its purpose was to keep the reconfigured paperclip from tumbling out after it slid past the moving bolt and landed on the ruler.

Mykl then returned to the desk and tapped the button, causing only the slightest bit of buzz from the alarm. Linda never stirred. When the bolt slid aside, the paperclip fell, landing on the ruler. And when the bolt attempted to slide back again, locking the door, it was blocked by the paperclip. The locking mechanism was defeated.

Mykl pulled the door open slowly—it often produced a high-pitched screech if opened too fast—and heard a soft plaintive meow from outside. Teeka lay curled up under the chair, patiently waiting for Dawn to come feed her in a few hours. Mykl shoved his wad of paper into the strike box and used the last piece of tape to secure it as insurance against the door relocking. Closing the door softly behind him, he slipped outside and knelt to pet the hungry kitten.

Mykl's fingers combed through fur that was soft and cold—too cold, in Mykl's mind. He knew what it felt like to suffer through a chilly night. All he had to offer the kitten were his socks, so he sat and removed them, then gently laid the holey offerings over the purring, curled-up beast. She gave him a slow blink of loving trust.

Stargazing would have to be brief tonight. The cold was already seeping into his toes; he wouldn't last more than a few minutes before they began hurting.

Mykl looked up. Light pollution limited his viewing to only the brightest celestial bodies, and Jupiter dominated the sky this evening. He had often seen pictures of it in tattered books and on the Internet, but nothing compared to seeing it with his own eyes. He had been cooped up in care centers and the Box for too long, and it had kindled in him a desire for adventure. Gazing at stars and planets granted him a momentary escape from his dreary prison.

Someday I will be free, he thought. He only hoped there would be a world worth exploring when the time came. The way things on Earth were heading, they all might be living in caves soon.

An aching cold sent a shiver from his toes to the base of his skull. Time to go back inside. The stars held enough patience to wait another night. He stopped to give Teeka a pat on the head, then returned to the stale but warm air of the Box.

After gathering up the evidence of his escape and returning the ruler to its drawer, Mykl turned his attention to the computer. The cheap refurbished monitor gave off an eerie glow as the screen saver cycled through random colored patterns. Nicotine stained the keyboard and mouse; Mykl's fingers always smelled like an ashtray when he finished his computer adventures. He feathered the handle to raise the pneumatic chair to its full height, then sat down and tapped the spacebar. The computer prompted him for a password. He typed it in:

[nomorekids]

The computer responded: *Invalid password.*

Damn. She changed it. Mykl looked under the keyboard. A fresh piece of tape with the words "Good Riddance!" had been placed over the old password. Ha! She had a sense of humor after all—she'd obviously written that for him.

Still, he had to try it to be sure.

[goodriddance!]
Invalid password.

Yeah, he didn't think she was that stupid. Now, what would she have changed it to?

[bitchqueen]
Invalid password.
[devildemon]
Invalid password.
[skinnyslut]
Invalid password.

This was getting him nowhere. *C'mon, Mykl, think. How are you going to gain access to this computer?*

An idea popped into his head, brilliant in its simplicity. Two people knew the password. One made a living as a cold-hearted bitch—but the other went through life like a free-roaming vapor, conforming to the path of least resistance, malleable as monkey poo and as predictable as gravity.

"Hey, Linda?" he called to the sleeping figure on the couch.

"What?" she asked, obviously annoyed at having been woken up.

"What's the new password to the computer?"

"Linda's sleeping."

The vengeful demon spares no one.

[lindassleeping]
Invalid password.
Sarcasm strikes again. "That didn't work."

"No more cats. Now quit bugging me and lemme sleep."

"Thank you, Linda."

She waved dismissively and rolled over.

[nomorecats] granted Mykl the mind-escape of online access again.

"Sick bitch," he muttered under his breath. Why couldn't there be more Lindas in the world? No. There were already too many Lindas. The Loris just made them seem more desirable than they actually were.

"Where do I go today?" he mused. He'd already mined all the information on the computer's hard drive. It stored a database of vital statistics on every child in the Box. Once a year, the state required that a proficiency test be given to every child in a foundling asylum; the results were used to assist prospective parents in choosing a child. Specifically, they were included in what was essentially a sales catalogue of unwanted children, a document that detailed everything from physical characteristics and handicaps to intelligence and proficiencies.

Mykl found it strange that the kids who were adopted most often were not the smartest or the ones who showed the greatest potential. People didn't want a child smarter than them. They also didn't want an especially dumb kid or problem child. No, they wanted an average kid—someone they could bully, dominate, bend to their will. The meanest of the kids who teased Mykl, Donzer, had been adopted—and returned—three times already. His wicked streak increased with every newly earned scar.

Box-lore said the truly intelligent kids, the ones who excelled on the tests, were taken away by the government. Rumor had it that these children were put to work in dark places as menial laborers, never to see the light of day or a starry sky again. Of course, these rumors came from the same kids who believed in the Tooth Fairy. But the truth mattered not to Mykl; he just knew that he had to keep his intelligence a secret, his proficiency scores on the lower end. According to the Box's records, he had no more intelligence than a potty trained turtle.

Of course, that wasn't a guarantee against adoption, which he definitely did not want. The realities of life beyond the Box frightened him. He had seen too many fresh bruises on kids who were brought back like defective merchandise. But so far he had been fortunate.

He turned his attention back to the computer. A firewall prevented him from accessing sites deemed inappropriate or nonproductive—but fortunately for Mykl, it failed to block sites providing information on how to defeat firewalls, and he'd gotten around it long ago.

He considered once more what to do with his stolen computer time. Perhaps that puzzle website? It had been a few months since he'd visited it, and his mind longed for some decent exercise. Even at the hardest level, the puzzles on the site had barely challenged him, yet they were still entertaining. He'd have finished them all already, but the server providing web access had crashed before he could finish.

He activated an anonymity program of his own design and logged on. The site had a completely redesigned welcome page. This was promising. Perhaps they had improved the puzzles as well?

He soon found that they had. In fact, to his delight, each puzzle interlaced with previous ones. He had to keep track of everything he'd done in order to keep up. Every detail held meaning to be used in some future puzzle. Altogether, it was like a complex symphony of logic the likes of which Mykl had never been exposed to before. His mind reveled in heavenly rapture. It seemed as if an intelligence behind the screen was creating puzzles specifically for him.

As soon as he entered a solution, another problem would appear on the screen. The speed at which they came increased subtly, undetected by Mykl, due to his unwavering focus. Strategy problems, number regressions, pattern recognitions, and word associations flashed before him. Mykl's eyes narrowed in concentration, his fingers pitter-pattering across the keyboard. His mind had never been pressed this hard. The world inside the Box ceased to exist; time compressed, he had to pee, didn't care, he knew the answer, his fingers blurred over the keys, <enter>, another question, got it, fingers starting to tire, <enter>, next, answer keyed—

The puzzle disappeared before he could hit enter. Mykl raised his fists, ready to bring them down in anger.

The screen blinked, and a new image appeared. A cipher. Something familiar about it. Clever, but not clever enough. James wrote in a similar way. The author had omitted all the vowels and purposely misspelled words phonetically before encrypting them... and peculiar words at that... Done! What does it say...?

The reality of the Box came crushing in on him. A rising sense of panic grew in his belly and moved up to threaten his pounding heart. He realized now that he had been duped. He wasn't entertaining himself with puzzles—he was taking a test! The last cipher had seemed familiar, and it didn't seem to fit in with the pattern of the previous puzzles—and now Mykl understood why.

He had been tricked into solving an unpublished cipher of the Asylum Angel.

Driven by fear, he erased his solution and shut off the computer. His mind still racing, he ran back to his dorm, trying to comprehend what had happened and who was behind it. How could he have been so stupid? Someone out there now knew the secret he had kept for so long. Would his anonymity program protect him? Doubtful.

He buried his face in his pillow and wished he could disappear from the planet. Cipher symbols burned white hot in his mind. He knew where the first victim of the Asylum Angel would be found—and the grisly details of how they would be killed.

CHAPTER 12

"Hello?"

"We've found him, sir."

"Found who?"

"The user who almost aced the Level II puzzle page a few months ago."

"Yes. I remember. The trace failed to pin down a location due to a server problem and a rather ingenious anti-tracking program."

"We reset his logon to take him to the Level I trials if he ever came back. He did. He didn't submit the solution to the last puzzle, though."

"The Level I trials were designed so they couldn't be finished. They're only a measurement tool."

"I don't think you understand, sir. He *did* answer the last question, but it appears a computer issue prevented him from entering it."

"That more than justifies acquiring him."

"We believe something he saw on the computer frightened him. We have the recording from the user's office security camera."

"Age?"

"Five. Las Vegas Foundling Asylum."

"Bring him in. He'll be the last. We don't have time for more."

"There's more, sir."

"What?"

"An incident at the asylum."

THE PROMETHEUS EFFECT

***

Awakened by an anguished scream rising from the quad, James bolted from his bunk and was gone before Mykl could sit up. Mykl had been in bed for about an hour and had never quite fallen asleep.

The scream died, then was resurrected in hysterical wails. It sounded like Dawn, but he couldn't be sure. With foreboding thoughts, he peeled himself from under his covers to follow James.

James had Dawn secured in an embrace. Her thin body shuddered with wracking sobs. James kept whispering, "No cry, no cry," but she was inconsolable. A crowd of children had gathered around them. Most looked horrified, a few wore malicious smirks.

Behind Dawn, a pool of dark blood glistened beside a small pair of holey socks. A limp white tail drooped off the back of Dawn's chair.

Mykl's heart sank.

"Ha ha! The Ass Angel killed your cat!" yelled Donzer. His flippant tone and lack of surprise made it obvious he was the one who had killed Teeka. The vicious bastards—Donzer's grinning minions no doubt participated—even placed the body on Dawn's chair to be sure she would be the one to find it.

Guilt threatened to turn Mykl inside out. He didn't like to cry, but leaning against the wall with his cheek pressed to the coarse stucco, he found himself incapable of holding back tears. His stupid socks had encouraged Teeka to stay put, making it easier for them to find her.

The crowd parted a bit, and Mykl saw more than he would have liked. Apparently they had pulled up a piece of the broken blacktop and used it to crush Teeka's skull.

His face became hot with anger. He had never experienced such hate before. He wanted to drag those who committed this heinous crime to the center of the quad and bash their skulls in with the same piece of bloody rock. Knowing that his size prevented any such fury-driven revenge only tormented him further.

He recognized his own rage reflected in James's face as he held Dawn. James's eyes were fixed on the same chunk of blacktop. James could very well kill with his bare hands, and he looked determined enough to do it.

The thought sobered Mykl, and he composed himself to join in the embrace. He reached up and grabbed James's arm to get his attention. "No," he whispered, shaking his head slowly. James merely nodded once, closed his eyes, and allowed his tears to fall into Dawn's obsidian black hair.

In a whirling blur, Dawn let out a guttural growl and ripped herself from James's grasp. Donzer, caught flat-footed, barely drew a breath to scream before Dawn had a fistful of his hair and was winding up for a roundhouse punch to his face. At the cost of a few dozen follicles, he managed to dodge the telegraphed blow. But his attempt to laugh stalled against gritted teeth as Dawn stepped in close for leverage and flung him to the ground in a breath-stealing slam. She straddled him and proceeded to rain down a hellacious fury of righteous white knuckles. Donzer cowered pitifully behind crossed arms, which only managed to block about half the raging storm of fist-sized hail.

Lori's shrill voice scattered the crowd. "Everyone back inside!"

James, who had been standing in awe through the whole melee, his arms extended as if trying to determine the best way to pick up a ferocious animal, found an opening and plucked the still-swinging Dawn off Donzer. Her knuckles dribbled blood from wild misses hitting asphalt. She buried her flushed face into James's chest.

Donzer yelled, "The Ass Angel did it!"

"Donzer!" Lori pointed at him. "If you think the Angel is bad, don't you dare cross *me*! Use that word again and you'll be cleaning urinals with a Q-tip!"

Donzer wiped his bloody nose, and he and his cronies skulked away. Any punishment involving bathroom duty was no laughing matter.

Lori pulled Mykl toward her by the fine hairs on the back of his neck and roughly spun him as she bent to snarl, "See what happens when you feed the damned things? This is *your* mess. You clean it up!"

She ushered everyone back inside. James cradled Dawn in his arms and carried her. Lori went in last and slammed the door shut behind her, leaving Mykl shivering barefoot in the cold in his pajamas

Mykl's fists and jaw clenched white with anger. Deliberately not looking at the chair, he scanned the quad. He saw nowhere to bury Teeka, and he couldn't bring himself to just toss the body over the fence or throw it in the trash. The neglected planter was the best he could do.

Ignoring the cold, with his bare hands, he dug a deep hole in the dry dirt next to the plant's shriveled roots. Fresh tears sprang up when he lifted the lifeless kitten and carried her to the tiny grave. With great reverence, he placed his socks on top of her and refilled the hole.

Unknown to Mykl, Tina watched him through the grimy window above the planter. Tears streamed from her blue-green eyes and fell to her hands, which held the few scraps of food she had saved from last night.

***

James had been allowed to carry Dawn to her room but was forbidden from going inside or staying to give comfort. No boys were allowed in the girl's dorm; that was the rule. So now he sat at his desk, his face flushed with anger, furiously stabbing dots on a sheet of paper.

Mykl grabbed a towel from the hook on the back of their door. Blood stained his hands, his pajamas were filthy, and he hoped a shower would wash away any memory of last night and this morning.

The boys' sanitary room was anything but, which was why cleaning it was one of the most feared punishments in the Box. Mykl crossed the threshold and retched as an ammoniated reek of sour urine struck his nostrils. He tried to take shallow breaths through his mouth until he could acclimate; but it only provoked the need to take a much deeper breath when he reached the point of no return. Speed and economy of motion would be his best defense.

Eight shower nozzles leaked cold drops at random intervals in a four-by-ten-foot space with no partitions. The leaks left an orange-colored, hard water stain streaking to the green-tinged drain. Mykl hung his towel and stripped off his pajamas. Bloodstains on the front gave him a moment's pause before he threw them in the shower violently, hoping the waste water would rinse them away. Using both hands, he muscled the hot water handle and leaned to the side to wait for the weak spray to heat up, with complete disregard for Lori's rule about wasting water.

The warm stream felt good running over his scalp and neck as he lathered up. But though his body began to feel cleaner, his soul remained stained with a guilt that would never wash off. He should have known better than to encourage Teeka's trust of children when the likes of Donzer existed in the Box. He could have shooed her off back to the alley to wait until Dawn called for her. Anything would have been better than what he had done.

Would've, could've, should've; it wasn't within his ability to change things that had already happened. He hoped Dawn could forgive him.

He rinsed, wrung the water out of his pajamas, and dried himself off. With the towel around his waist dragging the ground, he took a deep breath and dashed through the stench back to his dorm.

James was gone when he returned, so he draped his wet pajamas on the back of the chair. Fresh pages of dots littered the desk. That wasn't like James; he was usually very meticulous about putting them away. But considering the morning's emotional roller coaster, Mykl could understand how he might be put off his normal routine.

Mykl gathered the pages and put them away in James's "dot drawer." The dots never made any sense to him. They rambled along haphazardly with no rhyme or reason. At first Mykl had thought they might be some kind of writing, but James didn't put them on the paper the way one would normally write. He would work on as many as five pages at once, front and back, right to left, down to up, and round in circular loops. There was no way anyone could make anything of it but what it was— pages of random dots contrived and valued by a brilliant simpleton.

But looking at the dots reminded him of the Angel cipher. He couldn't tell James or Dawn about what it said. They were already upset, and it wasn't as if they could do anything about it anyway. Telling Lori was out of the question. For one thing, he didn't think she would care, and for another, she would punish him for having used the computer. No, his best bet was to wait until after his interview, then he would access the computer again, make a throwaway email address, and use it to anonymously notify the police about the Angel's intent. Then, as much as he hated the idea, he would have to stay away from the computer until the ramifications of his latest adventure played out. It wasn't the greatest plan, but it was the best he could come up with after having been awake all night.

With a yawn, Mykl crawled into his bunk, hoping this time to get a few hours of sleep.

CHAPTER 13

"Myyykll?" James prodded him. "Myyykll?"

Mykl groaned. "What time is it?"

"Lunches times. Dawn no comes down yet."

Mykl stretched. "Well, if she won't come to food, then we will have to get the food to her."

"James helps!"

"The fake and shake routine."

James's eyes went wide.

"Are you up to it?" Mykl asked.

James nodded vigorously.

"Do you remember how to make it believable?"

"James do good. No worry. Mykl takes care of Dawn."

Mykl dressed while James rocked and fidgeted impatiently. "Let's go. I'll get the food, then when I give the signal, you do your thing."

Mykl had taught James how to fake a seizure; it was an easy way to distract the staff and even the other kids. It came in handy for things like stealing office supplies, avoiding punishments… and sneaking food into the dorms.

***

Mykl pushed his pre-nap worries to the back of his mind as they walked through the hall to the dayroom. He and James had grabbed a couple of sandwiches and desserts they knew Dawn liked; now they just had to get them to her.

James swung his muscular arms, his lips pursed together in firm determination. He would do anything to see Dawn happy again. She was his obsession, and he showed his love for her not through words, but through his devotion to her needs. Mykl loved her too, as a big sister who never ceased to inspire him. He hoped that seeing Dawn might grant him a chance to begin atonement. At the very least, he could apologize for his role in Teeka's death.

James positioned himself in front of the television among a group of younger kids watching cartoons. Almost immediately, he rolled his eyes into the back of his head and fell over with his body rigid. Then he began to convulse.

The kids around him fled, screaming, while others came running in to see the cause of the ruckus. Lori let out a stream of curses and left her desk to investigate the latest interruption of her day. And Mykl skipped up the stairs unnoticed. Behind him, he heard Lori yelling for someone to bring her a towel, because James had wet his pants—the *coup de grace* of successfully faking a seizure.

If James could perfect a fake seizure so well, Mykl wondered, why couldn't he learn not to mess with his damn shoelaces?

He found Dawn sitting alone in a plastic chair, her head bowed toward the window, the sun beaming down on her. Slow-running tears crusted her cheeks. Mykl knew the warm sunlight on her lap reminded her of Teeka.

He hesitantly stepped into her room.

"Hello, Mykl. I'm not hungry," she said without turning, her voice barely above a whisper.

Even in her grief she was sharp enough to realize that the sound of crinkling paper from a sandwich bag could only mean that he had come with food.

"I... I'll just leave it on your desk then." He set down the food, then rushed to Dawn's side and hugged her. "I'm sorry, Dawn. It was my fault. I saw Teeka there last night and gave her my socks to keep her warm. She wouldn't have been there for them to hurt her if I hadn't…"

With a hand on his arm, Dawn leaned into his hug and moved her head from side to side. "No, Mykl. Never apologize for an act of kindness. I certainly don't blame you. I blame those who indiscriminately kill the innocent just for being innocent. If it wasn't Donzer, then it surely would have been someone else, eventually. And you know, as much as life in here seems horrible, it's getting much worse out in the real world. Teeka may have been the lucky one."

She sniffed. "James told me you have an interview this evening. You're a smart boy, Mykl, smarter than anyone I've ever known. You're also a good judge of character, so I know you won't end up with bad parents. If you do find someone you like, go. Don't stay here and let your life go to waste. Don't let that brilliant mind go to waste."

Talking seemed to be doing her some good. At least she'd stopped crying.

Mykl thought a bit of privileged information might make her feel even better. "I have a feeling that the Angel will be caught soon," he said. "And don't worry about my interview; I'm more than happy to stay here with you and James."

Dawn turned back to the window. Mykl took that as a sign he should leave.

"Well. I should get back downstairs," he said.

"Wait. Please? Read to me?"

Mykl smiled. "Sure. Same book?"

Dawn nodded.

A box of fantasy novels had been donated to the asylum some months ago, and Dawn had taken one as her own after the first day Mykl read it to her. Its pages told an inspiring tale about handsome heroes, beautiful heroines, ferocious dragons, and good conquering evil. She kept it in her bottom drawer, next to a box of pictures of her family. Pictures she couldn't even look at.

That was one of the things Mykl found inspiring about Dawn: she never gave up. She kept those pictures because she believed that one day, she would see again. And when she did, she would want to look once more on the family she'd lost.

Dawn didn't talk about her family often, but she had told Mykl the story of their death. Her parents and her older sister were all killed in a terrorist car bombing at a hospital. Her mom and dad had both been doctors, and her sister was at the hospital for Take Your Child to Work Day. Dawn would have been there too, but she was too young. No organization ever even bothered to claim responsibility for the attack. It was as if terrorists no longer even had a message to send, demands to make. They just killed.

Mykl retrieved the book and sat on Dawn's bunk. He liked this book too. Opening the cover, he began to read: "Michael stood proudly at the top of a gleaming white palace…"

CHAPTER 14

Mykl read to Dawn until it was time for him to get ready for his interview. Along the way, he finally coaxed Dawn into eating by telling her of James's extra efforts to make the delivery possible.

Just as Mykl rose to leave, she grabbed his arm. "Lori's coming up the stairs. You better hide."

Mykl set the book on her lap and crawled under the bed. Two roaches of the extra-large variety were waiting to keep him company, antennae waving ominously at this intruder in their realm.

The telltale sound of Lori's heel-pounding stride stopped at the doorway. "What are you doing?" she asked in an accusatory tone.

"Reading," Dawn replied, stretching out the word as if the fact should have been obvious.

"Very funny, missy." Lori snatched up the remnants of food and brandished them without eliciting a reaction. "Listen up, you prissy bitch. How many times do I have to tell you? No food in the dorms! If you think I won't punish your pathetic ass because you're blind, then you're in for a real treat."

Mykl watched Dawn's feet as she stood to face Lori. "Do you think because I'm blind, I can be cowed by your threats? I would rather live in darkness than watch a pitiful woman with so little self-worth lash out at innocent children. You make me sick. Touch me or any of my friends, and I will *own* you!"

Dawn lunged at Lori, and Mykl was certain she'd taken a swing at the evil woman. He wanted to cheer as Lori's feet turned to leave without a word.

***

When they were alone again, Dawn led Mykl to the stairs, her keen ears listening to make sure Lori wouldn't catch him sneaking from the girls' dorm.

"Did you take a swing at Lori?" Mykl asked.

"Bitch deserved it."

James ran to meet them, stumbled, and fell at their feet, saying that Lori was in the cafeteria. Dawn endured his bear hug before declaring that her head was pounding and she needed to return to her room. "Thanks for the company, Mykl. Good luck on your interview."

"James waits here. You go gets readies," James said, gently shoving Mykl down the hall.

As Mykl headed toward his room, he heard a huge pop from the direction of the dayroom, followed by Lori launching into a tirade at James. James had adopted Mykl's habit of jumping onto the beanbag, and it sounded as if the old stitching had finally succumbed to the rigors of life in the Box. Mykl was sorely tempted to go back and survey the Styrofoam carnage, but that surely meant tasting more of Lori's vitriol. So reluctantly, he continued to his room.

Dawn's forgiving words had helped lift the burden of guilt from his chest concerning Teeka, but he still had a lot on his mind. The message in that cipher, for one. And the motivations of whoever was behind that test he'd been tricked into taking.

And now, this interview.

Mykl inspected the interview clothes that Lori had left on his bunk. They were nothing special, just a sampling of the better clothes donated every year. He could keep them if someone adopted him, otherwise he had to return them for someone else to use.

He dressed quickly, ran his fingers through his hair, and stretched on his tiptoes to give himself a cursory glance in the dusty mirror. Dark hair and a pair of inquisitive copper eyes stared back at him. He wondered if he was going to have to sleep in a strange home with new parents tonight.

A cockroach skittered across the scuffed linoleum in attempt to escape through the open door. Mykl stomped it on his way out.

***

James ambushed him with a hug as soon as he entered the dayroom. "Maybe this times you be lucky! James still be your friend if you blows it again."

Mykl slugged him in the stomach as hard as he could, but didn't elicit so much as a flinch from his large friend. He then returned the hug with a huge grin on his face. He would miss James terribly if he had to leave, and he still worried about Dawn.

James reached down to fix Mykl's collar with a flip of his fingers. "You better goes before…"

"*Mykl!*"

Carried on a banshee's wail, his name careened throughout the Box. Lori was calling for him, and it was best not to make her wait, lest she be antagonized into even greater feats of bitchiness. Then again, why should Mykl care? She never offered an ounce of affection to her charges—ever. There wasn't a child inside she hadn't threatened, and the only time she ever betrayed any semblance of a good mood was when kids talked about the Angel. She would have to work for it if she wanted his obedience.

He looked up at James, touched a finger to his lips, and scampered behind the couch.

"Mykl! Where is that worthless child?" she demanded of James, who shrugged and began picking his nose with his middle finger like Mykl had taught him. She shook a threatening claw-like finger at him. "Your days are numbered too, retard! Six more months, and you'll be eighteen and out of my hair for good."

She turned to leave the room, and James stuck his tongue out behind her.

"Mykl!"

"Yes?" Mykl answered. He stepped in front of the couch and stood there in wide-eyed innocence as if he'd been there all along.

Lori grabbed him roughly by the arm and began drag-walking him back to the office. "You little shit." She shoved him ahead of her. "Get your ass into that interview lounge. Your new dad is waiting. He seems to be the perfect person to put you in your place."

Mykl's arm stung, and a red welt rose where she grabbed him. He couldn't help but chuckle. Perhaps she was venomous after all.

CHAPTER 15

The interview lounge had doors on opposite sides: one granted access to the dangerous external world, the other back to the Box, via the office. Its décor consisted of a worn brown couch, a fake plant, and an uncomfortable wooden chair for the hopeful adoptee. In the corner, a ceiling-mounted security camera adorned with spider webs watched passively through a dusty lens.

Electronic locks, controlled from the office, secured both doors. This not only prevented anyone from kidnapping a child, but also thwarted the children from running away—either to the outside or, more commonly, back into the Box. Each door had its own "request" button. When someone pressed the request button for the door opening to the outside, it meant a successful adoption. An asylum representative would step in to collect a signature and make sure the child was not being coerced, and then the adoptee would be free to leave with their new parents. A request signal from the door opening into the office usually meant an unsuccessful match, and the child would be returned to the Box.

Lori pressed a button on her desk to buzz Mykl in. "Good luck," she said, her voice thick with insincerity. The door thumped closed behind him with the finality of a coffin slamming shut.

A pale, fat slubberdegullion with a receding hairline slouched on the couch. His face melted into stubbly chins that jiggled gelatinously above a shabby shirt, unbuttoned down to the first greasy stain above his navel. The remaining buttons strained to contain his belly, and looked prepared to fail catastrophically at any second. His dark slacks and slip-on shoes were equally stained. He burped, and noxious vapors spewed through wet fleshy lips. Even from across the lounge, Mykl breathed in the odor of beer and cigarettes. The man's eyes were unfocused, but still Mykl felt his appraising gaze.

Mykl slowly took a seat. His feet dangled several inches above the ground, and he gripped the armrests in a conscious effort to anchor himself. He had made up his mind about this man the moment he'd entered the room, but he thought it might be entertaining to give him an opportunity to speak before breaking the bad news.

The man didn't bother to sit up straight before slurring, "You're kinda…"

"Are you going to hit me?" Mykl interrupted.

"Now wha' kinda question is that? You need to learn ya some manners, little boy. I'm jus' the person to teach ya, too. Gonna put ya to work, tha's wha' I'm gonna do. You jus' mind yer tongue an' we be gettin' along fine. Learn ya to not in'errupt…"

"Are you going to hit me?" Mykl asked again, louder.

The man wheezed and impatiently rotated himself more upright. *All I have to do is twist a bit more, and this loose screw will bolt*, Mykl thought.

"The nice lady in that there office told me I's gonna be able to leave here wi' ya, so ya may's well git used to the idea of me bein' your pa. Saves ya from the Angel. So how's 'bout it? Ya ready ta go?"

"Are you going to hit me?" Mykl spoke slowly and enunciated clearly, as if speaking to someone who didn't understand English.

"If ya don' listen ta me when we git home, yer gonna get the belt!" His face glistened red from the effort of speaking.

"Will I be able to go to school?" Mykl arched an eyebrow. *I may as well have some fun with this before I go back inside.*

The man leaned back at the change of subject. "No." He waved a hand dismissively. "School is too 'spensive. I got me a bar and need someone to see to dishes and cleanin'. Ya won' be allowed to serve no drinks 'til ya turn twenty-one, o' course." He winked at Mykl.

"I don't want to."

"Ya really got no choice. The lady done said so."

"The stove in your home, is it gas or electric?" Mykl asked with a spark in his voice.

The man blinked at the unexpected question. "Gas—Why's ya ask?"

Mykl released the arms of his chair to calmly lean forward and stare into the man's eyes. "I know how gas stoves work. Do you know what happens when someone disables the igniter, blows out the pilot light, and then turns on the gas? I do not want to be your *boy*." His heated stare grew in intensity.

Puzzled bewilderment blossomed on the man's face, then gave way to an explosion of clarity. Mykl understood. The fragile, dark-haired boy politely sitting in front of him had transformed into a flesh-searing demon before his eyes.

"Ya sick bastard!"

A button rocketed off the man's shirt like a bullet as he tumbled off the couch. He fled through the outside door, leaving Mykl alone with the man's lingering odor.

Mykl stared in surprise at the natural light streaming through the door as it closed on its own. The man hadn't even pushed the request button; the door had been unlocked. That could mean only one thing: Lori wanted him out of her life even if it meant breaking adoption rules. That harpy wasn't even going to bother with stepping in to make sure everything was okay. *She would be rid of me and could write whatever she wanted in the adoption documentation.*

Mykl shook his head and grinned. *She's going to have to try harder if she wants to outsmart* me.

He hopped off the chair, reached up to the office request button, and stopped. He glanced back at the other door. Freedom was only a few steps away. *Where would I go?* The world beyond that door filled him with fear. With his size, he was no match for bullies and creepers on the streets. And smarts would only carry him so far. As much as he dreaded it, he had to return to the Box.

He reluctantly pushed the office request button and waited.

Lori would not be happy at his return. He decided that playing meek and dejected was his best ploy. He gazed at his feet and counted the seconds before a slight change of light told him that someone was looking through the narrow window in the door. An expletive filtered through the door, followed by a brief pause, then it opened.

Lori struck a belligerent pose and blocked his path. "What happened? Why did he leave without you?"

"He said I didn't look healthy enough. Probably had something to do with bad genes on my father's side of the family." Mykl shrugged and moved to get past her before she could interrogate him further.

With a gleeful look in her eyes, Lori thrust her knee viciously into his sternum, knocking the air from his lungs and sending him flailing backward onto the floor. Stunned and struggling to breathe, Mykl curled into a ball and willed himself not to cry in front of her. A fiery pain radiated from his chest to his limbs.

"I'm going to save your life if it kills you," Lori said before turning away and slamming the door.

Mykl's lungs wouldn't work; when he tried to inhale, he only managed to make short high-pitched squeaks. *It's just the wind knocked out of me*, he told himself to quell the rising panic.

He pressed his face to the cold tile and concentrated. Breath gradually returned to him in short, shallow gasps. *Well, this is new*, he thought. *She's handled me roughly in the past, but she's never physically struck me before. I must have finally found the line not to cross.*

Minutes passed as Mykl lay there trying to normalize his breathing. He used the time to evaluate his situation. Pushing the office request button again was certainly out of the question: if Lori even bothered to open the door at all—which he considered unlikely—the outcome would be the same. No, his only option now was to leave through the other exit and try to find an adult who would help him.

With one hand clutching his chest, he pushed himself up and

CHAPTER 16

Jack sensed the dark desert rushing underneath the helicopter and mentally urged it to go faster. He berated himself for not checking in earlier. This boy had been hiding in their shadows for over a year. Now he was off the grid with information about the Asylum Angel. For all he knew, the boy might be the next target.

He had seen the recorded images of the boy's adoption interview. The audio cut out early, but something the boy said had obviously had an effect on the man trying to adopt him. An ugly fear chased him outside, and exterior video showed him running all the way back to his vehicle. The boy eyed the closing door, looking torn for a moment before pressing the request buzzer to go back inside.

And then the video went to static.

The external feed also went to static, as did the feed from the asylum office—right after showing the asylum manager reaching for the camera's cord. Clearly she had disconnected all three cameras. But why?

When the video feeds returned, all seemed normal again. That was two hours ago. He'd already initiated tracking on the manager's phone, but she'd made no new calls since.

"Your agent is on tactical channel bravo-nine, sir."

Switching his headset over to B9, Jack spoke calmly. "Have you traced the license plate?" He paused to listen. "Good. Get to that address. And keep me updated."

***

Dawn was sitting huddled on her bunk, her knees hugged tightly to her chest, when she heard footsteps at her door.

She tilted her head. "Mykl?"

"Myyykll gones."

"James, what are you doing up here? Even Linda might punish you if you get caught in the girls' dorm."

"Lori gots rid of Myyykll."

"What are you talking about? You mean he was adopted?"

"No. Lori gots rid."

So, it finally happened. Mykl was gone. "Well," Dawn said, trying to sound strong, "she would certainly like to get rid of *all* of us if she could—and Mykl most of all for the way he pushed her buttons. Though… I was fully expecting he'd come sneaking back to tell me how he ran off another deadbeat. Oh, James, I know you're sad—I am, too—but we have to let him go. He's free of this place." She leaned back to the wall and spoke to the ceiling. "And if he allowed himself to be adopted, he must have found someone worthy. Don't worry, James. Mykl can take care of himself."

"Lori turns off sneaky cameras when Mykl insides."

Dawn sat up and stretched a hand toward James. He stepped closer and took it. "What do you mean she turned off the cameras?"

"She turns thems off, thens backs ons when he gones. Leaves door unlocks too. She no even checks to makes sure he okay. Just looks scary and smiles."

"What?" That meant Lori had broken at least four rules that could get her fired. For all she knew, the Angel himself could have adopted Mykl. "That bitch has gone too far. Even she has rules to follow."

More footsteps approached, and then Linda's voice spoke from the doorway. "James. You know the rules. Out."

brought his shaky legs underneath him. He checked the window in the office door once more before he left; it was empty. *She's not even looking in on me.*

He moved toward the outer door. For a moment, like it or not, freedom was within his grasp.

And then the outer door flew open, and the man who had tried to adopt him came rushing back in. He grabbed Mykl painfully by the arm and wrenched him out the door.

Mykl's adoption had turned into an abduction.

***

While scrounging for a late snack in the cafeteria, James heard the inner request buzzer sound. So—Mykl had rejected another one. Continuing his rummaging, James found a half-eaten bag of chips to share with his friend in celebration. He stuffed the bag in a hiding place for later, smiled, and shuffled back to the dayroom. The children were watching television, leaving Lori alone at her desk—precisely the way she liked it.

James ambled up to her. "Where Myyykll?"

Lori's face wore an expression that puzzled James. She looked… content. No, stranger—she looked *happy*. "Mykl hasn't finished his interview yet." She glanced at the clock, then back at James.

Sensing something amiss, James started walking toward the interview lobby.

She immediately rose to block him. "Go to your room, retard."

He held his ground, searching her dark eyes.

"Don't make me tell you again." The phone in her hand chimed, and she answered without looking away from James. "Back? Good, you're all set."

From the interview lobby came the sound of the outer door opening. Almost immediately, it slammed shut.

Lori reached over to her desk and pushed the button to lock it. "Well! Another successful adoption! You should be happy for him."

With a swipe of his arm, James pushed her aside like a curtain and ran to the lobby window.

The room was empty.

James's heart sank.

He turned away, and a flicker in the corner of his eye caught his attention. The security monitor on Lori's desk—it showed only static. He looked closer, and saw that its cable had been disconnected.

His blood turned to ice, and he shifted his haunted eyes to Lori.

She cackled. "Why, whatever is the matter, James? You look like you've just seen the Angel."

Dawn brushed around James. "Linda, someone needs to be told about Lori. James told me that she all but shoved Mykl out the door."

"Lori already told me the details. You know how James exaggerates. He misses his friend, but he'll deal with it."

"But Mykl might be in danger!" Dawn pleaded.

"He's gone. End of story. Now James, go to your room, or I'll tell Lori when she gets back."

James released Dawn's hand with an exaggerated sigh and trundled away, and Linda followed, closing the door behind her.

Dawn flopped onto her bed and clenched her fists. The frustration of unseeing eyes, plus hands that were tied by Linda's incompetence, left her feeling powerless.

Then again, if anyone could think his way out of a bad situation, it was Mykl. She just wished she could send a guardian angel to him.

To the emptiness confining her, she whispered, "Be strong, Mykl. Never give up."

***

Back in his room, with his hands in his lap, James sat staring at the newspaper on his desk. It wasn't a crossword that held his attention; it was the headline on the front page written in huge block letters: ASYLUM ANGEL. Below the block letters, the paper had published his newest cipher in its entirety, with a reward announcement for the person who could break it.

James turned toward the dark sheet of glass filling the window. The reflection of a handsome seventeen-year-old boy stared back at him, and beyond that, a cascading torrent of lightning leapt from cloud to cloud across the sky. Its intensity illuminated a secret no one still living had ever witnessed: a fiery intelligence in a pair of titanium gray eyes.

CHAPTER 17

Mykl cradled his arm. It didn't feel broken, but it hurt to move. The man had grabbed him above the elbow and lifted him bodily off the ground. With the tips of his shoes scuffing the sidewalk, he was dangle-dragged to a microvan and unceremoniously pushed into the back seat.

"Behave yaself now!"

Child locks effectively prevented Mykl from escaping. Typical of most vehicles in Las Vegas, its windows were tinted limousine dark to tame the oppressive summer heat. No one would see his attempts to get their attention.

As they drove away, he sat back in his seat with his head against the window, feeling the cold glass on his forehead. He wished he could enjoy this feeling of a vehicle in motion, but his mind wouldn't stop spinning wild and horrific thoughts about their destination.

"Just ya wait 'til we get home. Ya mom's gonna teach ya some manners."

Mykl angrily kicked the back of the man's seat. The man drove to a neighborhood near the Box. Over the tops of the house, just a few miles away, the flashing signs of multibillion dollar hotels lit the sky. Their vivid colors sharply contrasted against the porch lights, whose dim bulbs seemed to apologize for revealing dilapidated houses and weedy lava rock lawns. This part of town had existed during the age of aboveground nuclear testing. The houses were indistinguishable from one another, block upon block of square, cookie-cutter homes resembling shingled cinderblock bunkers; the only distinguishing features were the differing patterns of dead trees and rusted cars parked in front. Poor insulation made the houses feel like ovens in the summertime and meat lockers in the winter. Wind from the coming storm whipped garbage cans over the road like urban tumbleweeds.

Mykl watched without emotion as the man pulled into a driveway and activated a remote on his ripped sun visor. In front of the microvan a rising panel of peeling paint unveiled a cave of clutter, with piles reaching like stalagmites to exposed rafters. Darkness enveloped him as the garage door closed behind them, then Mykl squinted as a dome light flicked on with the opening of the man's door.

The man floundered out of the van. "All right, out wit ya."

Mykl glared. *Does this crapulous minion really think I will cooperate and submit? Does he think I'm bluffing about filling his house with an explosive gas?* Mykl wasn't afraid to go on the offensive if passive resistance failed.

Defiantly, he crossed his arms and pushed himself back into his seat. "Do you expect me to call you Dad?" he said, dropping the last word as an insult.

The man laughed. "I ain't gonna be yer pa! That was jus' a sham so's yer new mom could git ya. They won't let her adopt no ones, so's she paid me to do it for her. Ha! Gave me a hun'ed dollars and said she's bring'n me 'sumpin special' when she comes to picks ya up." He winked at Mykl. "Now git out."

Mykl's mind worked feverishly over this new bit of information. Being adopted by an easily manipulated drunkard would have been simple to deal with. Being adopted by proxy for someone who was already deemed unfit for a child was a different matter entirely.

Mykl slid himself across the seat and hopped out. If he could escape even for a moment and tell his story to a neighbor…

He maneuvered his way between piles of junk and stopped at a panel of plywood separating the house from the garage. The man reached over Mykl's shoulder and pushed it open. The stench of stale cigarette smoke, rotting garbage, and rancid sweat poured over him. It may as well have been an asylum-scented air freshener. The man firmly assisted him over the threshold and down the short section of an L-shaped hallway. Mykl barely had time to glance down the longer hallway to the main part of the house before the man shoved him into a room with no windows. Its furnishings, if you could call them that, consisted of an unmade bed, frayed carpet, and an empty closet.

"Ya mom'll be here shortly. Don't gets too used to tha place. Ya ain't stay'n." The man padlocked the door and left Mykl alone in the dark with his thoughts.

***

"Nellis is requesting we alter our flight plan, sir. They have live-fire military exercises in progress over the bombing ranges."

"Skirt to the east and cut through the Groom Range. We need the shortest route to Vegas." Deadlines were nothing new to Jack, but he devoutly hoped they could find the boy before his deadline became literal.

The pilot frowned over his navigation plot. "Sir, that's going to take us over—"

Jack cut off the pilot with an icy stare. "I understand very well where that will take us. I'm the one who built it in the first place. They have *nothing* that I don't already know about."

"They still aren't going to like us in their airspace, sir," the pilot replied, altering course.

"If they give you any flack, tell them the Ripper authorized it."

***

A search of Mykl's new Box revealed two useless light switches. Whether the bulbs were burned out or missing didn't change the fact that he sat in the dark. The only light came creeping in from a gap under the door, and it stopped after a few inches, as if too afraid to enter. Mykl put his cheek to the scratchy carpet by the gap. He could just make out the longer hallway beyond, but it revealed nothing more than weak shadows and flickers of light. He heard muffled television sounds coming from another part of the house.

Mykl sat up and rubbed his eyes with the heels of his hands until random patterns and colors shifted behind his eyelids; it was a habit that helped him clear his mind when he wanted to concentrate. He considered his situation. He guessed that Lori was getting paid to run some sort of adoption-for-cash scheme. It suited her personality to sell children as chattel without regard for their happiness or safety. But the most pressing danger was not to him; it was to the person in the Box who had been targeted by the Angel. For all Mykl knew, the Angel could be on his way to the Box right now. Mykl had the cipher solution, but how could he get it to the police?

I have to figure out a way to conquer a smelly dark room. Dawn lives in a world of eternal darkness, and she would never give up; so neither will I. Even in your absence, you inspire me, Dawn.

He found nothing to write with... unless.

The empty closet loomed in the darkness. Merely thinking of the idea that popped into his head gave him the willies. Dropping to his hands and knees, he carefully began feeling around the bottom of the closet. Holding his palms flat with fingers splayed out, he made long searching sweeps, trembling with anxiety as he did so. He ran a finger in between the carpet and the wall molding— "Ow!"

Mykl pulled the pin out of his finger and stuck the bleeding digit in his mouth. He had confirmed a trivial fact he remembered reading on the internet: all closets have pins on the floor.

He pulled the finger out of his mouth lest he waste precious blood. *I need to work quickly or I'm going to have to stab myself again.*

He milked his finger to keep the blood flowing, then used his own blood to write on the back of the door. He knew no one would see it unless they came in all the way and closed the door, but if they did, well—a message written in blood was sure to attract attention.

Blood stopped flowing after only one letter. As Mykl stabbed his finger again, he decided he'd have to make some compromises when it came to spelling. He hoped whoever found this message had some intelligence.

The doorbell rang, and it was followed by the sound of a muffled voice—a female voice. Mykl quickly put his cheek back to the carpet by the door. Incoherent babble from the television masked the conversation, but Mykl could hear a certain gaiety in the woman's laughter. That lifted Mykl's spirits some. If she was capable of laughter, she couldn't be all that bad.

Mykl hurriedly went back to work on his message in blood. Anticipation played a deadly game with his breathing. His fingers began to tingle from hyperventilating.

He finally finished his message at the expense of four sore fingertips. *At least now if the Angel claims someone, they'll be able to find the body—maybe.*

He had to admit, that was one massive "maybe." This was one message, written on the back of a door, in a dark room that no one ever entered or bothered to clean. The truth was, the only way anyone would find his message was if the Angel came and killed the man who kidnapped Mykl. That was a happy thought. *If I'm lucky, the Angel is a nice psychopath who simply wanted notoriety. If that's the case, then everyone should be safe… I hope.*

Footsteps pounded down the hall and stopped outside Mykl's door. He rose from his listening spot and backed away. Someone shoved a key in the padlock, and the door opened.

"Hello, Mykl. Ready to take a ride?"

CHAPTER 18

"People can be so stupid," the ambulance driver said as he spotted a man dodging cars in the middle of a poorly lit street.

His wizened partner said, "Think of it as job security. If people didn't do stupid things, we wouldn't have anything to do, right?"

Harsh alarm tones blared through their radio, followed by a synthesized dispatcher's voice. "Unit 23, proceed to the intersection of Las Vegas Boulevard and Sahara for a vehicle accident. Auto versus pedestrian."

"Twenty-three copies." The driver pushed the button for the emergency lights and reached for the siren switch.

"Hold off on the sirens for a minute," his partner said. "We're next to the asylum. Those kids have it bad enough with the Angel stalking them. They don't need us waking them up in the middle of the night."

***

Dawn lay in bed with her fingertips touching her face. As her substitute eyes, they gently followed the contour of her profile. She tried to imagine what she looked like. Turning them away from her, she urged them to remember Mykl's face. *I miss you already*, she said in her mind. *How long will it take before my hands forget?*

James was the sole friend she had left in the Box—and she knew he would be forced out soon. She took a deep breath and rolled to her side. "Don't give up. Never give up."

She closed her eyes to the comforting sound of a siren wailing in the distance. As long as there were sirens, it meant people were willing to risk their lives to make the world a better place.

CHAPTER 19

Mykl staggered back and fell against the bed.

"Did you miss me?" Lori asked in a chilling voice as she grabbed his hair and yanked him off his feet. Mykl fought and clawed at her hands as she dragged him through the hall by fistfuls of hair.

"Let go!" he screamed, though he knew the uselessness of his words before they left his mouth. His kicks at her legs missed wildly. What the hell was she up to? If she was in league with the Angel, then Mykl was in serious trouble. If she wasn't, then his life was about to reach new levels of misery. He twisted violently, attempting to break free, only to be rewarded with searing pain and a ripping sensation under his scalp.

When they reached the living room, Lori retrieved a dark device from the coffee table and pushed it into the back of Mykl's neck. Sharpened points of cold metal penetrated his soft flesh.

"Good night, shithead."

Mykl's tiny body spasmed in waves as she switched on the stun gun. Muscles from his jaw to his diaphragm contracted involuntarily, silencing his screams. His vision narrowed and dimmed to darkness, and he fell unconscious.

***

Mykl blinked himself awake uncounted minutes later to the awful sound of tape being stripped off a roll. Face down and unable to move his limbs, he tried to make sense of his situation. Lori couldn't be the Angel, but the gag in his mouth and the tape binding his arms and legs were done up almost true to the cipher—except that the Angel was supposed to allow his victim to move their hands and feet for a specific effect, whereas Mykl had been taped so securely he couldn't move at all.

Lori noticed that he had regained consciousness. "We've got a long drive ahead of us. Can't have you wiggling free and hurting yourself. That would be terrible." Her wicked laugh pierced him like a twisted blade.

As Lori gathered some things into a heavy duffel bag and carried it down the hall, Mykl turned his head to the side and saw the man—his kidnapper—lying prone on a couch, unconscious. His breathing was slow and shallow and his skin was tinged with gray. His future was as bleak as Mykl's; they would both be dead soon.

Mykl closed his eyes. *At least they'll find my body in a few weeks after the smell causes someone to search the house.* If *they find my message.*

Lori returned and took the man's keys from his pocket. "He won't need these anymore." Dragging Mykl by his feet, she pulled him through the house and onto the filthy floor of the garage. The tape bridging his shoulders and feet provided a perfect purchase for her to toss him into the back of the microvan like a suitcase. She then retrieved a heavy vest from her duffel, draped it over him, and secured it with more tape. It weighed more than he did and severely hampered his ability to breathe.

Finally, to Mykl's horror, she placed a new Asylum Angel cipher under his chin. "Here's some reading material while you wait."

Mykl battled to contain his fear. She knew he commanded at least enough intelligence to recognize it for what it represented. But she didn't know about his deciphering abilities—so she wasn't aware that the actual content of the message was what caused Mykl to scream through his gag and begin to cry.

"You really are dumb. It took you until just now to realize I'm taking you to the Angel?" She double-checked his gag and retrieved a fresh pair of rubber gloves. "Got some work left to do. Wait here." She winked.

Mykl's falling tears caused the cipher's ink to run. It would surely cause a media frenzy when they got their hands on it. Even more so if she added a bloodstain. He berated himself for such odd thoughts. *It's not normal for me to think that way.*

The words, "You're not a normal boy, Mykl," played in his mind. Dawn had told him that. She was right. She was also the Angel's next intended victim. The cipher spoke of a beautiful blind girl and the horrible things he would do to her.

Lori returned and took the paper from under his face. She examined the tear-smeared cipher with a critical eye. "Nice touch. I'll have to remember to do that again." She laughed. "Oh, I guess it won't have the same effect next time." She shrugged. "Though I'm sure I can get her to cry *somehow*… Don't you think?"

She sliced him with a dissecting gaze for a moment and reached into her bag for the stun gun. Mykl's jaw clenched on his gag as thousands of volts assaulted his body once again. "This is so much fun!" Lori gave his hair a vicious yank before slamming the van shut.

CHAPTER 20

"We're approaching Vegas airspace, sir. There are thunderstorms moving in from the south. It's going to be a rough ride."

"Fine." Jack tightened the straps on his seat harness and resumed monitoring his data pad. They had lost the phone trace in the vehicle they were tracking—the low signal strength from a bad battery on a retro phone had rendered their technology useless—and the vehicle had too many probable routes to make an effective decision regarding its destination. To make matters worse, clouds and lightning from a wicked thunderstorm nullified the capabilities of Jack's available satellites. Their next-gen satellites would take hours to relocate, and his drones were being reconfigured for other duties. All he could do was send orders to his agents to cover the most likely destinations.

To his pilot, he said, "Refuel at the air base. We'll wait there for further word. Keep the blades hot; I want to be able to leave on a moment's notice."

***

Cab drivers and independent transport operators jockeyed in a zippered line of competition to seize another fare. One leaned forward in his seat, mesmerized by a luminous pane of lightning veiling the horizon.

A polite tapping on the passenger window drew him back to his dreary reality.

"Hop in. Where you headed?"

The passenger stated a destination.

"Where? You do know that's going to be expensive."

The fare ducked into his back seat and reached forward with a closed fist. The driver opened his hand and gasped as several high-denomination casino tokens fell into it.

"I'm not supposed to take these—and I don't have any change," the cabbie said.

His fare backhanded an accepting wave and leaned back.

"Wow, thank you!" the cabbie said, and pulled his cab into the stream of traffic.

The prospect of earning a huge tip sat well with the cabbie, but a man eager to spend so much for a ride to the middle of nowhere troubled him. The cost of this trip might have been reasonable decades ago, when a bustling oasis of a resort graced the shoreline—but how times had changed.

The cabbie surreptitiously checked his rearview mirror. The eyes staring back at him possessed the disquieting quality of a lion stalking its prey. This wasn't the first time he had been hired to drive someone out of the city, but he felt a growing sense of trepidation as he drove toward the developing storm.

CHAPTER 21

Thunder rumbled displeasure at the lightning invading its clouds. Mykl loved watching electrical storms in the desert, but sadness stifled his ability to enjoy this one. Reliving five years of life in a one-hour drive killed his morale.

A day spent in the Box always dragged for an eternity, but now, they echoed like blinks in time. *I want to live!* he screamed in his mind. Even if that meant existing in the Box.

He rubbed his face on the van's filthy carpet to scratch a nose itch. His arms and legs had gone past the pain of immobility and had settled into a burning numbness. *Maybe I can use that to my advantage. If the Angel keeps true to the cipher, I might have an opening to talk my way out of this.*

"We're here!" Lori said cheerfully as the engine sputtered to silence. Cold, damp wind buffeted Mykl as she opened the van. In stark contrast to his deadly predicament, the air smelled fresh and alive. He winced as she savagely ripped the tape from his mouth. He had expected its removal, though—the details of the cipher stated the victim's gag would be removed. The Angel wanted hungry coyotes to hear his victim's screams echo off the desolate mountains.

The upper campground of an abandoned lake resort made a perfect location for the Angel's grisly work. Years ago, the lake had dropped so far in elevation that it had left the resort miles from any water. Its once busy harbor now resembled an empty bowl of rock and sand. But the government continued to supply power to the light poles in the campground—typical government waste.

Lori pulled out Mykl's gag. "Get out," she demanded.

Mykl worked his parched tongue around a mouth too dry to articulate words.

"Oh, that's right. You can't move. How silly of me. Here, let me help you." She removed the weighted vest and stuffed it back in her duffel. The removal of the extra weight left Mykl with a floating sensation.

"What? Nothing to say?" Lori slung the duffel over her shoulder. "I tell you what. I'll go smoke while we wait for the Angel to show up. Give you some time to think about what you'd like to tell him."

Mykl peered out the side of the van. Sharp fragments of gravel littered the cracked asphalt.

"Don't fall out," Lori said. "It's not a long drop, but it looks like it would hurt!" She cackled as she hastened to the front of the van and disappeared.

CHAPTER 22

"Written in *blood*? Damn..."

Jack disconnected the call and yelled up to the pilot. "Time to go! Lake Mead, Echo Bay, upper campground!"

One of his agents had just made entry into the house of the man who had abducted the boy. He reported that the man was dead on the couch with his throat slit, and the only sign of the boy having been there was a message written in blood on the back of a bedroom door:

Eko bay
upr cmpgrnd

***

Lawrence Hansen, retired from the Green Berets after twenty years of service to his country, had now been a National Park Service Ranger for almost twenty-five years. His seniority had kept him from losing his job when the government initiated cutbacks in the region, but even so, his salary had taken a hit. Whereas he previously lived in a modest home by the lake, he now resided in a tiny trailer on the outskirts of Vegas near the park entrance.

The nature of his job had changed as well. Back when a lake existed here, his area of responsibility consisted of one resort. Now he was responsible for no less than five, all dry rotted and deserted. Incidents requiring his attention—usually suicides—normally occurred less often than rainy days, which were few. Unfortunately, crazy weather patterns worldwide were increasing those rainy days significantly. Not that the weather had anything to do with the suicides.

Making his rounds for the day had become a boring routine to be completed automatically, in silence, with no more thought than one gives to breathing. But it was his duty, and he still respected the need for it. He had never done anything in his career that could tarnish his honor, and he slept very well at night because of that.

He added another set of initials to his checklist and flipped the page. Two resorts left to go.

In front of him, a flash of lightning revealed the obvious markings of a taxi turning onto the road. Other rangers might ignore the rare spectacle, but a taxi leaving the entrance road to Echo Bay Resort definitely qualified as an unusual incident worth investigating.

Lawrence sparked up his emergency lights and followed the taxi to a stop on the gravel shoulder. He noted the cabbie fidgeting nervously behind the wheel as he approached from the passenger side. The cabbie rolled down his windows just as a few large drops of rain began thumping and plunking in the tranquil desert.

"License and registration, please," Lawrence said.

The cabbie presented him with the requested documents.

"What brings you out to an abandoned resort in the middle of a thunderstorm?"

"My fare requested it, officer."

"And where is your fare?"

"He asked to be let off at the cattle guard, right before the first campground." The driver shrugged. "He already paid me, so I stopped, and he got out. The customer gets what the customer wants, you know? Great tipper, too."

"What did he look like?"

"Big guy, about two hundred pounds—crazy hair. And a real

determined look in his eyes."

Something about the description tickled the back of Lawrence's mind, but he couldn't bring it into focus. "He didn't ask for you to stay? Or to pick him up later? Or say that he was meeting anyone?"

"No. He said he'd be fine and not to worry about him."

Lawrence recorded the cabbie's name and contact information. "Okay," he handed back the license and registration, "you can be on your way. Thank you."

"Thank you, officer," the cabbie said with relief in his voice. He drove off.

Lawrence trotted quickly back to his truck and hopped in to escape the rain. The interior light shone on a newspaper on the passenger seat. He shuddered as though the Angel himself had stuck a knife in his spine. A headline in large block letters solidified in his mind the significance of the cabbie's passenger description.

***

On a rocky hill overlooking the dark campground stood a lone figure. Rain darkened his light hair and ran in rivulets down his angular face. His body, tall and lean, glistened like a marble sculpture. Once a runaway with an uncertain future, he now had a crystal clear goal to achieve. An abusive family, and a world that shunned his talents, had forced him to be an outcast. He had but one love and one friend; both would be served by his actions tonight.

His lips curled back in a demonic snarl as he sized up his prey below. He ducked as a truck turned the final corner before the campground entrance some half mile away. Lightning, followed by a sharp crack, briefly converted night into day. With the stalking movements of an apex predator, he made his way stealthily down the hill.

CHAPTER 23

"The Angel's here!" Lori sang out as she stepped back into Mykl's field of view.

He twisted to see who else was there and found no one. Confused, he glanced back to see Lori, with hands on her hips and a rain-soaked lock of hair sticking to her face, watching him with a frosty smile. She now wore the heavy vest, along with large kneepads and preposterously oversized boots.

Mykl's head fell back in surrender. The pieces of the puzzle slammed into place with fatal inevitability. This was the psychology of the Angel: to create terror. By delaying her reveal as the Angel, she had prolonged the anticipation and anxiety of her victim. She had wanted his fear to build exponentially to the climax of her announcement. And she had succeeded. As much as he tried to hide his fear, Mykl knew his trembling gave him away.

Lori reveled in it. "You disappoint me, Mykl. No screaming? No begging? No smartass comments? Are you just going to give up and let me have my fun?"

Mykl swallowed a retort that would surely earn him a slap.

"I have a present to show you." She reached to pull something out of her back pocket.

Mykl's mind flashed. This was his chance. "An antique T-handled corkscrew," he said, before she could reveal it.

Her sharp intake of breath gave him hope. He had surprised her. Now he had to take advantage of it.

"I figured out your cipher last night and sent an email to the police," he said.

Lori's face wore a mask of concern. She was buying it. Now to finish the sell.

"No more cats."

Mykl set his jaw in determination and watched Lori calculate the ramifications—though he knew he still had a long way to go to talk her out of killing him.

Lori stepped back from the van and clasped her hands on top of her head, her eyes closed deep in thought. For a minute, an agonized look warped her features—and then she smiled, lurched toward him, and delivered a spiteful backhanded slap.

"*I'm* the one who flashed that cipher on your screen, and I remotely disabled the computer right after. You couldn't have sent an email. I would have seen it on my end! So there's no way you could have notified anyone outside the Asylum." She laughed. "But cheer up: it was published in the paper this morning, and that retard friend of yours took the paper this afternoon. Maybe he'll figure it out and come to your rescue!"

Mykl's shoulders slumped in defeat.

"You didn't even figure out the Angel was involved until I put my new cipher under your nose," Lori continued. "You—" She paused. "Ahhh, now I see why it affected you so deeply. You know that Dawn is going to be praying with me next. Perhaps you're not so stupid after all. It looks like I'm not the only one who had something to hide." She gave him an appraising look. "Very clever of you to keep your proficiency scores low so no one would want to adopt you. My ciphers aren't easy. The police have had weeks to work on the first one and you had, what? A minute at most? Not bad. A mind like yours might have done something special for this world. Instead, it's going to leak out into the sand!"

She brought the corkscrew into the light and examined it. "Maybe

I should change things up and crush you the way I did that mangy cat this morning?"

Mykl couldn't withhold a gasp.

Lori smiled. "Kinda funny, isn't it? Donzer was right when he said the Angel killed your cat. Don't worry, I'll get to him. He was supposed to be the first, but your smart mouth moved you up the list. I have all the time in the world. Although, I'll have to rethink my ciphers. If a five-year-old can figure it out, then who knows who else might be able to?"

Mykl stiffened as she reached for him. She slowly rolled him to the point where he precariously balanced at the edge of the seat. Then, with a swipe of her fingers, she flicked him beyond the balance point and let him fall out of the van.

With his hands and feet bound, there was nothing he could do to break his fall. He hit the asphalt knees first, then grunted as his left shoulder impacted, followed by his face.

"Oops," she said. She dragged him by his hair to a nearby light pole. Mykl had to grit his teeth to keep from crying out.

The old bulb in the fixture above flickered like a candle in a graveyard. Mykl stared past it and up into the dark sky; there were no stars to wish upon. Rain streaked through the light to pelt his face. He asked in his mind, *Is anyone out there?* Only a weak flash of lightning answered him. The thunder never came.

He blinked. *Wait. That's not lightning; it's the beam of a headlight.* But it was quite a ways off.

Lori's face loomed over his; she hadn't noticed the headlights. Her steaming fetid breath wafted past nicotine-stained teeth to his nostrils. Mykl didn't understand why, but there was something terribly familiar about all this.

"What do you think of my toy?" Lori asked. She brandished the corkscrew in front of his eyes. "I wonder how this will feel. Should be interesting…"

"Why do you do it, Lori?" Mykl asked. *If I can keep her talking…*

She pressed the corkscrew to the base of his throat. "There are already too many kids in the world. You're like a virus that keeps on multiplying. The media thinks I'm a monster, but to everyone else, the Angel is a savior. Every child I kill will be one less mouth for their taxes to feed, one less consumer to drain resources, and one less mind to compete for jobs. Plus, no one cares about you, and no one is going to miss you."

As twisted as it sounded, Mykl saw some logic in her thought process. He had wondered every so often what his impact on society was, and now he had a madwoman's perspective on it.

"Are things really so bad that the extermination of a few kids will make a difference?" he asked.

"Of course not. You'd have to kill millions to change anything. But that's not going to keep me from doing my part. And you know, what I do is nothing compared to what is being done *legally* in other countries. Every *day* they kill a hundred times the number of children I'm going to do by letting them die of starvation and disease! It's a terrible way to die; it takes months or years. I'll take care of business in a few hours or less. So let me ask you, Mykl: who's the greater monster?"

Mykl closed his eyes and willed his mind to think. His life now hung on his ability to answer her question. But the solution that came to him seemed as dark as the soul hovering over him.

"Well?" she asked.

He opened his eyes. "You would have to kill every child born on the planet for the next one hundred years to make a difference, and you couldn't possibly do that—so why even try?" He hoped she would give the idea some thought before draining him with the corkscrew.

"You're right about that. I can't possibly kill them all, much as I'd like to. But there's another reason why I do this, and to be honest, it's the most important one." Lori paused to drag the tool down his body. Her eyes turned black. "I like to watch you little bastards squirm!"

She thrust the corkscrew into his right leg, inches above the knee, and twisted. It made a slight pop through his pants, punctured the first layer of skin, then tore deep into muscle. Mykl screamed as pain shot from his leg to his abdomen. He clawed futilely at the harsh desert soil under his back. His legs kicked involuntarily in an effort to escape the siege on his senses. And he knew the end result of his struggling would produce the sinister signature of the Asylum Angel. Evidence of his terror would show like a snow angel in the bloodstained soil.

Lori stared into his tear-filled eyes and began slowly twisting the corkscrew deeper, every excruciating turn taking him to new levels of agony. Then, in one swift movement, she ripped it free.

Pain robbed Mykl's mind of the ability to think.

Gasping for breath, he gazed along the length of his body. For a moment in time, the world around him seemed to slow, as if the air had grown too thick. He didn't see bits of tissue and blood spiraling down to form a fat drop at the end of a vicious instrument of torture, nor did he see the hand that held it. Through the rain, and a fate he was beginning to accept, he saw a tall figure materialize, loping lithely toward him.

With deliberate intention, Lori brought the corkscrew to Mykl's left eye. A drop of blood fell from its tip. But before it touched his eye, two things happened at once: a bolt of lightning ripped a jagged line through the sky, and the running figure leapt into flight, a muscular missile cleaving a path through the rain directly at Lori.

A shower of sparks and a blinding flash froze the raindrops in place. The last thing Mykl saw, before painful light created blissful darkness, was the most intense pair of titanium gray eyes he had ever seen.

CHAPTER 24

"Bring up the infrared. It looks like that last bolt knocked out power."
"We might be next if one of those hits us."
"That boy is worth the risk. There! Heat signatures. Land as close as you can."

***

Windshield wipers swept back and forth aggressively, flinging rain off Lawrence's windshield. His ringing ears and momentarily blurred vision had robbed him of two much-needed senses. Burned into his retinas was an image of a massive lightning bolt and a figure flying horizontally through the air.

He blinked until the image faded. And as he drove toward the smoking light pole, his headlights illuminated a lifeless lump. He grabbed a flashlight with his left hand, stepped out of his truck, and drew his sidearm. As he advanced, the lump transformed into a small boy bound in duct tape. A thin stream of blood stained the puddle of water surrounding him.

"Let go! I can't breathe!" cried a woman's voice.

Lawrence brought up his flashlight and his weapon. He had been so focused on the boy that he hadn't even see the woman a few yards away.

A man stood behind her, holding her in a crushing embrace. He was young and muscular; she was petite and thin.

"Help me!" she shouted at Lawrence. "He's the Angel!"

"Let her go, son," Lawrence commanded. He leveled his gun at the man's forehead. He heard the thump of helicopter blades approaching from the west, but he had no attention to spare.

"She Angel," the young man said simply. "No let her hurt Mykl."

"Let her go and we'll figure this out." Lawrence's finger rested lightly on the trigger.

The young man reluctantly released his hold on the woman. She tore herself out of his grasp. The subtle movement of her arm, as if to hide something, was not lost on Lawrence; neither were her gloved hands, vest, and oversized boots.

A low moan escaped the boy on the ground.

The woman took a step toward the boy. "He's hurt. Let me help him."

The helicopter circled high above. An intense spotlight shined down upon them.

"Stop!" Lawrence shouted.

She ignored the warning and lunged at the boy. Lawrence dropped his flashlight. Before it had even hit the ground, he had drawn a precision stun gun from his left holster and fired twice. Two barbed darts slammed into the woman, one in her neck and the other in her left buttock. She fell short of the boy, incapacitated and screaming obscenities.

Lawrence proudly wore two identical service medals on his uniform. Grandmaster marksman, right *and* left-handed.

The young man who had been holding the woman extended his arms in front of him and clapped stiff-handedly. "Nice shots!"

There was something strange about that boy. "Thanks. Now who are you?" Lawrence knelt to handcuff the screaming woman, never once releasing the flow of voltage from the stunner.

"James. I helps Mykl now, please?"

"Put some pressure on that leg wound of his, James."

"Yessirs." James stumbled over to the boy—Mykl—and firmly

placed his hand on the injured leg. "Myyykll?"

Rain bombarded them in thick sheets as thunder echoed all around. The black helicopter had landed, and now sat atop a hill about fifty yards away, its glistening blades gradually slowing.

Lawrence had secured the woman in handcuffs, but he continued to pin her to the ground with his knee as he watched three men deboard the helicopter and approach. Two were in military uniform—one of whom carried a medical bag—and the third man wore a black suit. The man in the suit walked with confidence, seemingly oblivious to the rain soaking him and his expensive shoes. When he stopped a pace away, he knelt in the mud to pick up a shiny object—Lawrence's nametag, which had fallen off. Lawrence felt an immediate affinity to this stranger who didn't care a lick about ruining nice clothes.

"Yours, I believe?" the man said, offering him the nametag.

"Yep, thanks. Damned thing's always popping off this new jacket. Drop it in my breast pocket if you would."

The man did so. "I'd offer to shake your hand, Mr. Hansen, but you seem to have them full at the moment." The suited man directed the medical technician to check on Mykl.

Lawrence gave a wary smile and yanked the woman to her feet. She sulked, sullen and defeated. "Who are you and why are you here?" he asked the suited man.

"Jack Grey, Federal Bureau of Investigation." Jack presented his credentials. "We recently solved the latest cipher of the Asylum Angel. This is the place where he—she," Jack pointed to the handcuffed woman, "intended to commit her atrocity. But it looks like you beat us here—fortunately. Nice shooting, by the way. I've never seen anything like it." Jack beamed with genuine admiration.

"All it takes is dedication and practice." Lawrence returned the smile. "Well, what happens now? Are you taking custody of this demon?"

"No. I've notified the Las Vegas Metropolitan Police Department to rendezvous with us. They should be here in about twenty minutes to take her off your hands. We will, however, be taking the boy to get some medical attention."

"What about the other one?"

They looked over to where James anxiously observed the medic attending to Mykl. He sat on his bottom, hugging his knees to his chest and rocking back and forth rhythmically. Concern clouded his face, and he softly called out the boy's name over and over.

"I'll be taking him too," Jack said.

"All right, I'm going to secure this beast to my truck until Metro gets here."

Lawrence's prisoner made a frantic attempt to tear herself from his grasp, but succeeded in achieving only a half a second of freedom before Lawrence reapplied power to the silver darts still embedded in her flesh.

"Listen here, missy, there's another twenty minutes worth of charge in this, and I have two extra batteries. I'd be more than happy to drain them all on you, but I'll leave that up to you. Choose carefully, because it's likely the last choice you will ever get in this life."

The woman launched a curse at Lawrence's manhood.

"That's the spirit," he replied.

Lawrence handcuffed her to the heavy-duty bumper of his truck. Unable to dodge the rain, or her fate, she slumped to the ground.

***

Mykl's head buzzed like it was full of honeybees, and his body tingled all over. Where did all these people come from?

A man in a park service uniform held a jacket over him as a makeshift umbrella, although the rain seemed to be letting up. Mykl's tape bindings were being cut by a man in military attire wearing pilot's wings. The medic tending him ripped his pants to expose his leg. "Ow!" he cried out.

The medic looked up apologetically. "Sorry about that. I need to get this wound cleaned so it doesn't get infected. It looks to be a simple soft tissue injury. You're going to need a tetanus shot though."

"A shot?"

"What's the matter?" The medic furrowed his brow at Mykl.

"I hate shots."

A man in a soaking wet suit knelt next to Mykl and chuckled before saying matter-of-factly, "Oh, come on. You were abducted by the Asylum Angel, stabbed in the leg with a corkscrew, knocked unconscious by step voltage from a lightning strike, and who knows what else? Can a simple injection with a short sterile needle be all that bad?"

"Okay, you made your point. I still don't have to like it." Mykl pouted in pure five-year-old fashion.

"How are you feeling?"

"I'm thirsty, my leg hurts, and I have to pee. Who are you?"

"My name is Jack." He extended a hand.

Mykl's mind was now regaining some of its normal clarity and suspiciousness. However, it lacked the ability to filter his dry wit. He put his hand in Jack's and asked, "Like Jack the Ripper?"

Mykl saw the pilot's eyes dart to Jack. Jack paused, then said, "Yes. As a matter of fact, my friends call me Rip. Pleased to meet you...?"

"Mykl. That's James, my dorm mate from the asylum." He pointed to James, who was tying knots in his shoelaces. "He saved me. Though I have absolutely no idea how he got here. James? How *did* you get here?"

"Taxis," he said without looking up from his laces.

"Taxis?" But before he could interrogate his friend further, three black SUVs with dark tinted windows pulled in behind the park service truck. Mykl didn't need to look at the official plates to identify them as government vehicles, for they so perfectly fit the stereotype seen in so many bad movies. The men exiting them were so unremarkable that they would be invisible the moment they stepped into a crowd. Only the raptor-like way they scanned their surroundings set them apart.

The park service man, Lawrence, lifted his chin to the SUVs and asked Jack, "They with you?"

"Yes. They'll be providing transportation for me, the boy, and his friend."

"You're not flying out on the bird?" Lawrence stared wistfully at the sleek helicopter on the hill.

"No. Company policy prohibits children on the aircraft, and I would freeze in these wet clothes." Jack grinned. "Here, please take my card. If there's anything I can ever do for you, don't hesitate to contact me. And I may be interested in offering you a job sometime in the future." Jack offered the card, along with a handshake.

"A job, huh?" Lawrence accepted the card and returned the handshake. "I'm getting a bit too close to retirement to be switching careers, but one never knows. Thanks."

Jack turned back to Mykl. "Well, Mykl. Are you ready to get out of here?"

"No, I still have to pee. James, pull me up." James helped him up and accompanied him as he hobbled behind a dead oleander bush. "No peeking!" he said to James.

"Ha ha. James no peeker." James turned his back on Mykl to give him privacy. "Man in green shirt saves you too. He shoots Lori with zaps gun."

"Really? I'm sorry I missed that. I was too busy playing lightning rod. I'll definitely have to thank him for showing her what it's like." Having finished, he shuffled back to James. "So, how *did* you find me here?" he asked.

"Long stories. Tells other times," James replied cryptically.

"Indeed you will." Mykl stared up at his friend with narrowed eyes. "Right now, let's find out who this guy is and where they want to take us. This might be our ticket out of the Box, so…" Mykl backhanded James in the stomach. "Leave your freakin' laces alone! We don't want to blow this."

"Yes, Myyykll." James adopted a remorseful expression and assisted Mykl back to the adults.

"James go see pretty hecalopter," he said.

"Okay, just don't break it or they might make us walk home."

Mykl shook his head in wonder as he watched James amble clumsily over the rocky ground to the helicopter. The lightning bolt had wiped Mykl's memory of James's agility and his heroic dive, but he retained a vague recollection that James had somehow done something to save him.

Mykl started to shiver. Lawrence knelt and wrapped him in his jacket. "Are you going to be okay?"

"I am now, thanks to you and James." Mykl extended his small hand to Lawrence from inside the opening of the jacket. Lawrence's huge paw of a hand swallowed Mykl's like a warm wet mitten.

"I was just doing my job. I'm sorry I couldn't have gotten here a few minutes sooner to prevent that witch from hurting you."

"Please, don't let her get away!" Mykl shuddered.

"Of that you can be assured." He ruffled Mykl's hair and told him to keep the jacket before going to have a word with the helicopter pilot.

Mykl eyed Jack warily. "You look like you have something on your mind," Jack said.

"Who are you?" Mykl demanded. "My mom told me never to accept rides from strangers."

"Your mom was a stripper who barely spent any time with you."

Jack may as well have slapped Mykl.

But before he could reply, Jack added, "I didn't say it to be mean; it's a recorded fact. I know everything in your record, and I now suspect that some of it isn't quite true." Mykl schooled his face to kitten-eyed innocence. "I'm also the one who designed the test you aced last night. At least, before Lori interrupted it."

Mykl stared at his feet and muttered, "Oops."

"You could have saved all of us a lot of trouble if you had submitted the solution to that cipher."

"Sorry, I was scared. And Lori shut down my computer." Mykl side-eyed Jack with a crooked smile and asked sarcastically, "Well, I guess you're not a stranger then. So, where are you going to take us?"

"Back to the asylum," Jack replied.

Disappointment washed over Mykl. He looked over his shoulder at the Las Vegas glow reflecting off low-hanging clouds to the west. When he was minutes away from death, he had wished he could go back to living in the Box. Now he dreaded it. *Be careful what you wish for*, he thought.

"Metro is ten minutes out, sir," one of the SUV drivers reported.

"Can you walk, Mykl?" Jack asked.

"No, but I can limp pretty well." Mykl yelled for James to come back. Then to Jack he said, "Before we go, can I talk to Lori for a second?"

"Sure. Just keep your distance."

"Do I look stupid?"

Jack opened his mouth to respond, but Mykl raised a hand to cut him off. "Don't answer that. I'll keep back."

Mykl hobbled over to Lori and stopped beyond her reach. Her hair had slipped out of its bun, creating a wet curtain across her face. Kneeling in a puddle, she reminded him of a nightmare creature from a video game. He expected her to lash out at him, to berate him, to do anything other than what she did.

She smiled. "Hello, Mykl," she said softly.

Her surprising demeanor momentarily robbed him of words.

"Angel got your tongue?"

"No. James kept you from getting that far down the list."

"It doesn't matter. I'm not done yet."

"How do you figure?"

"I'm insane. Doesn't it show?"

Mykl understood why she smiled, and it caused a thread of fear to weave into his subconscious.

"Come now, Mykl. They don't execute the insane these days. They lock them up in institutions where they can be cared for—and rehabilitated. Think about it: what sane person would go around killing helpless children? No, they won't kill me. They'll make me *better*. You'll see. They'll all see."

Mykl had heard enough. "Goodbye, Lori," he said, and he turned to leave.

"Goodbye, sweetie. See you later," she said in a serrated voice.

It took every ounce of concentration Mykl could muster to not shiver from the demon's icy-clawed words raking down his spine.

The SUV had two rows of bench seats behind the driver. James had already belted himself into the rearmost seat, leaving a place for Mykl to sit next to him. But Mykl stood by the door, feeling small; the bottom of the frame came up to his chest. It would require extra effort to get in with two good legs, let alone one gimped up with a corkscrew puncture.

Two strong hands slid under his armpits and lifted him inside.

"Sorry about that, son," said the driver. *Son.* He had called him son. No man had ever called him that before. It made him feel warm inside. Mykl turned to smile and salute the man. He returned the salute with a wink and a reminder to buckle up as he closed the door.

As Mykl buckled in, the helicopter on the hill lifted off and disappeared quickly into the night. It had no navigation lights and made so little noise that it virtually disappeared the second it lifted off.

Jack climbed into the passenger seat. "Let's move," he said to the driver.

"We're not waiting for the police to show up?" Mykl looked through the back window at Lawrence, who stood talking to Lori.

"No, the ranger can handle things from here," Jack replied.

"What will happen to Lori?"

"I wouldn't worry about her. Society still has enough redeeming qualities to take care of the likes of her."

The three SUVs left the campground without even turning on their headlights. The driver wore some kind of goggles; they must have allowed him to see in the dark. They drove on for a few minutes, then all three SUVs pulled off to the side of the road. And for a moment, Mykl felt a strange sensation: like being lightheaded and disoriented. James tilted his head and closed his eyes.

A minute later, a small caravan of police cruisers, laser strobes flashing and sirens wailing, came flying along the crumbling asphalt road. Air pressure waves from the speeding cars rocked the SUV as they passed. None bothered to stop and check on them.

Mykl leaned back in his seat. Thoughts of returning to life in the Box dampened his spirit almost as much as the prospect of getting a tetanus shot.

***

The police took Lori into custody and secured her in the uncomfortably molded seat of a transport cruiser.

"Good job, Ranger," said the Metro sergeant. "The children of the asylums should sleep better once news of the Angel's capture gets out."

"Just doing my job, Officer."

"Where are the FBI agents?"

"They left a few minutes ago in three black SUVs. Didn't you pass by them on your way in?"

"No. We were the only vehicles on the road between here and Vegas."

"Well you must have missed them. Perhaps they took the long way back to town?"

"I suppose so."

Lawrence shrugged and walked back to his truck, looking back in the direction the helicopter had disappeared. Under his breath, he muttered: "FBI, my ass."

CHAPTER 25

They rode in silence all the way back to the Box. It was after midnight, and the wet streets gleamed with distorted colors from stoplights and neon signs. James patiently fiddled with his fingers and never once looked up to peer at the city.

When they arrived, Jack helped Mykl step down to the curb by the entrance to the interview lounge.

"Is this where we say goodbye?" Mykl asked, feeling disappointed.

"Goodbye?" Jack looked amused. "Hardly. This is where you go gather your personal belongings before we leave for your new home."

"But I thought…"

Mykl trailed off when he looked at the three SUVs parked at the curb. They were no longer black, nor did they have government plates. The one Mykl had gotten out of was now gray. The other two were white and red, respectively. Mykl pointed to the gray SUV and looked back at Jack, his mouth attempting to compose a question.

Jack touched a finger to his lips and said, "There are a few things we need to talk about, but this is not the place."

Mykl furrowed his brow in confusion. *A color-changing vehicle?* He had never heard of such a thing before. It seemed like the kind of technology that would be used by some sort of unknown secret government agency…

The fairytales about smart kids being appropriated by secret agencies suddenly crystallized into reality. *I'm being saved from one embodiment of hell, and now I'm on the verge of being sent to another.*

James stumbled out of the SUV. "Dawn comes with us?" he asked. Apparently he'd heard everything.

"Hang on, James," Mykl said. "I need to talk with Jack. You can go tell Dawn that I'm okay, if that's okay with Jack?"

"That's fine," Jack said. "We need to get someone to let us inside first."

"Linda should be in there sleeping on the couch at this time of night. Push the button on the wall. She'll get up—eventually."

They waited five minutes before Linda finally responded to the buzzer. An irritated, sleepy voice spoke through the intercom. "Do you have any idea what goddamned time it is?"

"I sincerely hope I didn't wake you. My name is Jack Green, from Child Protective Services. I have two of your charges here with me, one of whom seems to have escaped within the last four hours, and I would very much like to discuss the matter with you." Jack's voice burned with sarcasm, and his last comment came out as a threat.

"Shit, shit, shit," Linda muttered. "Come right in." A click announced the unlocking of the door.

Mykl followed Jack into the interview room, where Mykl's abduction remained vivid in his mind. Linda met them and paled noticeably when Jack showed her his credentials. The identities he had portrayed in the last hour had Mykl on edge: Jack Grey, Jack Green, FBI, Child Protective Services... Who was this person, and how many other aliases did he go by?

"Linda? Is that your name?" Jack asked.

She flushed and stammered, "Y-Yes." She spared a glance at Mykl, and the expression on her face made him suddenly conscious of how he must look, wearing an oversized green park service jacket with ripped and bloody pants showing through the jacket opening. "Mykl? What in the world happened to you?" But it was Jack she looked to for an answer.

"Mykl here has been through a bit of an ordeal and will be taken into our protective custody. You need not concern yourself about his well-being any longer. You will probably find that you are going to be shorthanded in the morning, so you should plan accordingly. As for right now, you may wish to make sure all the *rest* of your children are present and accounted for."

"Hi, Lindas," James sang, as if on cue.

"Um, yes, okay." She turned as if in a daze and drifted back inside.

"Kyle, go with her, check to make sure they aren't missing any more kids."

"Yes, sir," said the SUV's driver, who had joined them in the interview room.

"James go say hi to Dawn?"

"Go ahead, James," said Jack. "And you might want to get some dry clothes on while you're at it."

Jack and Mykl stood alone, Mykl leaning against a chair to take weight off his injured leg. The man and the boy appraised each other, trying to read the other's secrets by their facial expressions.

Mykl spoke first. "You're from the government, aren't you? I've heard stories about smart kids being taken and made to work in sensitive areas doing the drudge work that no one else wants to. That we're regarded as *expendable*."

Jack smiled down at Mykl. "I *am* from the government. That much I can tell you. The specifics will have to wait. As far as kidnapping children to take out the trash and then disposing of them, well, think about it: do you really think we would go to all this effort just to find a janitor?"

Mykl scratched his ear as he realized how silly and farfetched that sounded. "Then why?"

"Mykl, I designed that test to find the best minds in the world. You're the first person who ever came remotely close to finishing the test in its entirety. Do you know how special that makes you? Not to mention how effectively you've managed to hide your true intelligence for so long. It takes an exceptional mind to pull that off. To put you to work as a drudge would be almost as great a crime as Lori attempted to commit. Although," Jack paused dramatically, "you will be expected to clean your own room."

Mykl paid attention not only to this man's words, but also his tone and body language. In Mykl's opinion, Jack resonated sincerity—and Dawn had always claimed he was a good judge of character.

"So this is like an adoption interview? I don't have to go with you if I don't want to?"

"I would rather have you come with me of your own free will. So, if you wish, yes, we can treat this as an interview."

Mykl's features became hard and cold. "Are you going to—"

Jack interrupted before Mykl could finish his standard opening question. "No one will ever hit you."

Mykl narrowed his eyes and paused to reflect on how Jack could have anticipated his question. He glanced at the spider-webbed camera in the corner. Having reasoned it out, he followed up with, "Do you swear to God?"

"Do you believe in God, Mykl?"

"No."

"Then why would you want me to swear to someone you don't believe in?"

"You're not the only one who can test people."

Jack knelt to place a hand on Mykl's shoulder and spoke in a fatherly tone. "I swear on my life, and my love of it, that you will be treated with kindness."

Mykl felt his throat tighten. He chastised himself for being so childish. "Will… will I be able to go to school?"

"Absolutely. You will learn everything you desire, and more."

"Are…" Mykl wiped his eye. "Are you going to be my dad?"

It was Jack's turn to swallow a lump in his throat. "Not exactly. But I promise, I will treat you as if you *were* my son."

That was good enough for Mykl. He released the chair so that he could, for the first time he could recall, hug an adult other than his mom. He felt that he had now been delivered from evil.

Jack returned the hug and willed the boy to be strong, for he had yet to show him all the evil that existed in the world.

CHAPTER 26

Calculating the implications of what Jack had told him, Mykl stepped back with a mischievous gleam in his eye. *If he thinks I'm so valuable that he's willing go to such extreme efforts to get me, then perhaps he's prepared to go a bit further to keep me.*

"I'll go on one condition."

Jack folded his arms across his chest. "And what might that be?"

"James and Dawn have to come with me." Mykl folded his arms in imitation of Jack. "They are my friends, and they both played roles in saving my life. They deserve the same opportunities I do."

Jack looked to the ceiling as if he were deliberating. What he was really doing was trying to keep from bursting out laughing at the precocious five-year-old posturing in front of him. The kid had spunk. And Jack would take every child in the asylum if that's what it took to have this boy agree to go.

But Jack couldn't afford to show weakness and simply give in. "Very well then, we will trade value for value. Promise to keep your room clean and we have a deal." He tried to keep a serious expression, but failed. Mykl, too, cracked a smile.

"Done!" Mykl just hoped he had it in him to actually follow through on his promise.

"Of course, your friends have to be willing to go with us," Jack added.

"Leave that to me. Here," Mykl entrusted Lawrence's jacket to Jack, "I'll go change and let them know."

Mykl limp-skipped to his room in barely contained exuberance. Not only was he about to be free of this soul-sucking hellhole, he had finagled his friends' rescue in the bargain.

He changed clothes as quickly as he could, being careful of his injury. The frayed and faded old clothes felt downright luxurious against his skin compared to the wet garments he peeled off. Unfortunately, he only had the one pair of shoes, and they still squished when he walked, so he carried them, and grabbed an extra pair of socks. In the event he had to put on the shoes, he would have a dry pair for later.

There was no use in trying to pack anything. He didn't have a suitcase or even a trash bag to toss personal belongings into, which was fine, because he *had* no personal belongings—unless he counted the jacket Lawrence had given him. He really should get that back to the ranger somehow.

He sensed a draft coming from the window and went to close it. The hinged security bars were slightly ajar. That explained how James had gotten into the quad, anyway; how he got over the razor wire was still a mystery.

Carrying his drippy shoes, an extra pair of dry socks, and nothing else, he made his way to the dayroom. A cockroach raced him down the hall and disappeared around the corner.

Linda labored at the office computer with Kyle hovering over her shoulder. *Poor Linda; she's going to actually have to do some work to earn her pay now.* Mykl crept past them both and went to the stairs to the girls' dorm. He wanted to leap up the stairs, but thanks to his wounded leg, he had to climb the stairs slowly, gingerly.

When he reached the top, he could hear James excitedly recounting the story of Lori's capture and Mykl's rescue by the park ranger. James was completely downplaying his own part in the tale.

Mykl tapped at the open door. "Did I miss anything while I was gone?"

"Sees! Myyykll backs!"

"Mykl, what is James babbling about?" Dawn said in muzzy-headed exasperation. "He claims Lori is the Ass Angel, she almost killed you, you both got struck by lightning, and then there's something about cars that change color!"

"Well, Dawn, it's all true. Every bit. Except James is leaving out the part where he escaped and took a taxi to come to my rescue."

Dawn buried her face in her hands. "I am *soooo* confused."

Mykl took that as an opening to drop his bomb on her. "You can be confused later. Right now there's a man downstairs who wants to adopt us. *All three* of us."

Dawn dropped her hands a few inches.

"He's from the government," Mykl continued, "but you said I was a good judge of character, and I think he's okay. And he's gobs nicer than any other adult I've ever met. We can even go to school!"

Dawn sat back on her bunk. Whether it was because she needed to concentrate or was simply unable to remain standing, Mykl couldn't tell.

"Before I agree to anything, I have to talk to him myself," she said. "Take James with you. I'll dress and come down."

James and Mykl walked down the hall together to the stairs. James had to mince his steps to maintain pace with his injured friend.

"James carries?"

"Oh, no, James, that would cause my leg to bend too much. Thanks, but no."

Still, when they reached the stairs, James lost his patience. He wrapped his arms around Mykl from behind, grasping him high on his rib cage, and lifted him up so that Mykl's legs dangled. Then he carefully walked down the stairs.

"Well, that works."

"Weeelcomes, Myyykll."

They found Jack wandering about the dayroom, his eyes taking a visual inventory of the place.

"James," Mykl asked, "do you have anything you would want to take with you if we go with Jack?"

"Dots."

Mykl peered up at him. He should have guessed it. His pages of dots were the only thing James ever bothered to save. "Well, you might want to go get them. And change into some dry clothes while you're at it. Yours are starting to smell a bit gamey."

"Okays." But instead of heading for the boy's dorms, James shuffled over to Jack. "Jacks wants dry clothes too? James has more clean ones."

Jack examined his suit as if he just now realized it was soaked through. He smiled up at James. "Thank you, James, I would appreciate that very much. It looks like your clothes are going to be a little too big for me, but I can live with that for a while."

James flashed a bright smile and grabbed Jack by the hand to lead him to the dorms.

Well, that's two out of three votes for Jack, Mykl thought. He hoped Dawn found him acceptable too.

When Dawn entered the dayroom, she called to Mykl with her right arm in front of her and her palm slightly upturned. Her way of asking for a guiding pair of eyes. She cradled a bundle of extra clothes and a book on top of a shoebox in her left arm. He took that as a positive sign.

"Mykl?"

His leg was really beginning to stiffen up now. Awkwardly, he hopped over to her on his good leg while letting the other slide behind.

"Mykl, what's the matter? You sound like you're hopping around like a bunny rabbit."

"Lori screwed up my leg. It'll heal, but it's very sore and stiff right now. Jack just went with James to get some dry clothes. They should be back in a moment. You want to wait for him on the couch?"

"No, I want to speak to him in private. Take me to the cafeteria and then tell him I'm waiting there, if you would?"

Mykl guided her into the dark cafeteria, then returned to the dayroom to wait for Jack.

He had to cough to cover a giggle when Jack returned. The man looked ridiculous in the too-large, mismatched garments that James had donated to him. The outsized clothes drooped on Jack's lean body like the clocks of some famous artist Mykl recalled from his Internet browsing.

"It's okay to laugh, Mykl," Jack said. "I chuckled myself when I looked in the mirror."

"It's a good thing Dawn is blind!" Mykl exclaimed. "She's in the cafeteria waiting for you. She wants to talk to you alone."

"I shan't keep her waiting then."

***

Jack wondered if Mykl had forewarned him about Dawn's blindness on purpose. Either way, it was good information to prevent him from accidentally offending her.

The cafeteria was dark, and he chose not to turn on the lights. A weak red glow emanating from an emergency exit sign reflected off the slick floor in a blurry red slash, outlining the sharp silhouette of a beautiful young woman sitting silently at a table, her eyes closed and head slightly bowed as if she were battling an inner sadness. Yet strength radiated from her confident posture. Anyone with the ability to maintain such spirit in the malnourished atmosphere Lori maintained was well worth salvaging.

"Hello, you must be Jack," Dawn said to the darkness.

"Hello, Dawn. Indeed I am. May I sit?"

"Please do."

"Thank you." Jack took a seat opposite her. "Mykl said you wished to speak to me before making a decision to come with us."

"Of course. My mother told me never to accept rides from strangers."

Even in the darkness, Jack could detect her radiant smile. "Funny, I had the same conversation with Mykl less than two hours ago," he said with a smile in his own voice.

"I trust Mykl's judgment, but I would be remiss if I didn't make my own life-altering decisions. Someone else made the decision that put me into this abyss of neglect. If I am to be thrown into another, I want only myself to blame." She clasped her hands in front of her on the table. Jack recognized her pose as that of one ready to enter into negotiations. "You didn't complain about the lack of light when you entered. Why?"

She had left the lights off on purpose; he was being tested.

"Mykl told me you were blind. This is *your* interview, therefore, you get to dictate the atmosphere. You've had to live in a world of darkness; if you wish for me to experience a brief fraction of the obstacle you have to endure every day in order for me to better understand you, then I am happy to oblige. I can't promise to make you see again. Nor can I promise that you will be happy where I take you. What I *will* promise is that you will have a chance to *pursue* happiness through a great many more opportunities than you will ever have here."

"What kind of opportunities?"

"An education, for one."

"I haven't seen my own face in eight years," Dawn vented. "I can't read anymore, let alone write. Who's going to have the patience to teach a blind girl anything?"

"You need only have the patience to learn. Our teachers will take care of the rest."

"And if I become a burden to you?"

"Our resources, both human and material, are more than enough to prevent any one person from taxing them."

"I want to be productive and earn my keep. This charity shit makes me sick. Endless days of sitting on my ass, regardless of your ability to provide for me, would be nothing short of torture. What have you got for an uneducated blind girl to do so that she can feel like she's making a difference in the world?"

Jack felt like standing up and cheering. What Mykl possessed in raw intelligence, Dawn possessed in exceptional spirit. She had spent eight years in this asylum, yet not only had she survived, she had maintained a fierce desire to be more than a barely existing charity case.

And he had the means to grant her an unbelievable dream.

"While I can't tell you any specifics about the nature of my job, I can tell you that we as a species are headed for dark times. You've lived more than half of your life in darkness and still managed to retain a vibrant spirit. Strength of will like that is extremely rare. You can help us find our way through the coming storm by maintaining that never-surrender attitude. You can earn your keep—of that I have no doubt."

Dawn knew he was holding back significant details, and his creepy talk of a coming darkness piqued her survival instincts. But his voice sounded kind and honest. Mykl was indeed a good judge of character. And she felt as if she were about to be delivered into a new world where she would be limited solely by her desire to succeed. There was only one more question to ask.

"And James. What will become of him?"

"James appears to be a savant of sorts. What he lacks in certain areas, he more than makes up for in others. I think he will find plenty of chances to use his skills. In fact, I expect he and Mykl will make a pretty good team." He leaned across the table to lay a hand gently over Dawn's. "Dawn, I will not force anything. I am not in the business of kidnapping children to turn them into slaves. Ultimately the choice is yours. But I would like nothing better than to bring all three of you with me."

Dawn hoped Jack could not see the tears trickling down her cheeks. She squeezed his hand in acceptance of his offer and softly said, "Okay. Walk me to the door, please?"

***

Mykl and James watched as Jack emerged from the cafeteria with Dawn holding his arm. She looked like she had been crying, but she wore the serene smile of someone who had recently been emancipated.

"Kyle, we'll be escorting three to our home," Jack said with satisfaction.

"Yes, sir," Kyle replied. He was still hovering over Linda.

"How are things looking with the records?"

"She's clear. There doesn't appear to be anything that would show collusion or incriminate her. The rest of the children are all accounted for."

"Very well." Jack turned to Linda. "As I told you when I got here, you have a tough road ahead of you. I suggest you mind your duties to the children here and treat them better than stray animals. As for these three, they're coming with me."

Linda swallowed once and nodded. Mykl felt bad for her. She was still expecting Lori to show up to relieve her in the morning. She had no idea.

"Shall we go?" Jack asked of his traveling companions. He draped the ranger's jacket back over Mykl's shoulders.

Mykl was overcome by a sudden impulse. He looked up at Jack with what he hoped was his most innocent smile. "Can we stop for an ice cream cone?"

Jack stared down at Mykl intently.

"Hey, you might think I'm some kind of genius, but I'm still only five!"

"Are you sure you're only five years old?"

"Might be six, I don't know. I do know that I like ice cream."

Jack laughed. "Sure. We can stop for ice cream."

***

"How long will it take to get there?" Mykl asked as he licked at his ice cream cone.

"About five hours," said Jack.

"And where are we going?"

"North," Jack replied cryptically.

"Then how come we're headed south?"

"We need to switch into a different vehicle. Our storage area is to the south."

"What's wrong with this one?"

"It's going to feel a bit cramped after a few hours of driving."

"What are we going to switch into?"

"You'll see when we get there."

"I don't see why we couldn't go in this one."

"Have you ever traveled long distance with a five-year-old before?"

Mykl puzzled over the question. "No. Why should that matter?"

"Trust me."

"Okay." After a pause to lick his ice cream cone, he added: "Are we there yet?"

CHAPTER 27

Motor homes, boats, and travel trailers filled the storage yard. Rows upon rows of recreational vehicles sat gathering layers of dust and spider webs. Given the price of fuel, it could cost an average person almost a month's wages to fill a tank, so they rarely saw use.

In front of an average-looking motor home, another SUV waited for them, this one green. The man waiting beside it exhibited an air of wizened distinction. His silver hair glowed like a halo in the ghostly light. Jack got out and greeted him like an old friend.

Mykl's leg had stiffened up, and he had difficulty getting out of the vehicle. Kyle quickly came over to help.

"Think you can tolerate me carrying you into the motor home so Dr. Johnson can have a look at it?"

Mykl wasn't looking forward to being carried, but he wasn't sure he could even walk at this point, so he had no choice. "Please don't jostle me too much?"

"You got it, kiddo." Kyle carefully lifted Mykl into his arms. James followed, guiding Dawn.

At odds with its dusty exterior, the inside of the motor home smelled fresh and clean. Kyle set Mykl on a bench seat near the entrance. A man stood waiting—a doctor, judging by his medical bag.

"Hello, Mykl. I'm Dr. Johnson, but call me Stan," said the doctor.

"I need to have a look at that leg of yours to see if it's going to need any stitches."

Mykl shuddered involuntarily. Stitches meant needles.

"You're going to have to drop your pants though. I don't want to have to cut these up," he explained as he tugged slightly at Mykl's pants.

Mykl glanced over at Dawn.

Dawn must have sensed his reluctance, as she said, "Oh, come on, Mykl. Do you think I've been faking this blind bullshit all these years? I promise I won't peek."

"James no peeks either," James said. He turned his head to gaze at the back of the motor home.

Mykl grumbled and bared his legs for Stan.

Stan removed the bandage that had been applied to Mykl's wound. "I doubt she bothered to sterilize that corkscrew before she stuck it in you, so I'd better give you a dose of antibiotics as well as a tetanus shot. The good news is, you don't need any stitches."

"*Two* shots?" Mykl whined.

"I'll kiss it and make it better if you like," Dawn teased.

"James gives hugs too," James said, turning around.

"You're not supposed to be peeking!" Mykl said.

James quickly covered his eyes and sucked his lips between his teeth to suppress a smile.

"Two shots, that's all," Stan said. He removed two syringes from a zippered pocket in his bag. Pulling out a padded red pouch, he selected two vials and began drawing their contents into the syringes. Mykl's eyes widened with growing trepidation.

"Tetanus shot first," Stan said. He wiped Mykl's shoulder with an alcohol prep. The harsh antiseptic odor of the alcohol caused Mykl to tense up and grit his teeth in preparation for the coming sting.

"There. That wasn't so bad, now was it?" Stan said as he stuck a small bandage over the injection site.

"Um, no. I guess not." Mykl rubbed his shoulder.

"See. Don't be a baby, Mykl," Dawn taunted.

"You're not the one getting the shots!" he shot back at her.

"All right, one more and we're done."

Mykl twisted to offer his other shoulder, but Stan raised his bushy eyebrows. "Sorry, Mykl. The antibiotic needs to go in your butt cheek. You can choose which one though."

Dawn tossed her hands in the air. "I take it back. I'm not kissing it to make it better!"

"Very funny." Mykl leaned to the side to let the doctor finish his task. "Ow!"

***

Less than two hours into their trip, Dawn discovered that she suffered from severe motion sickness, and claimed sole possession of the only bathroom in the motor home. The doctor hadn't come with them, so it was just James, Mykl, and Jack in the passenger area. James slept. Kyle drove.

Mykl had an uncomfortable feeling. "I have to pee," he declared.

"There's a rest stop about thirty miles ahead. Can you hold it until then?" Jack said.

"Nope."

"Kyle, find a place to pull over for a pit stop."

With assistance getting down the steps, Mykl and James—and Jack and Kyle—took care of business at the side of the road. Kyle's shoes crunched on the sharp rocks; the others, in their socks, took mincing tender-footed steps. It was three thirty in the morning, and breath-foggingly cold.

Mykl gazed into a dark, moonless sky and gasped. Stars. Brilliant stars. Too many millions to count, the likes of which he had never witnessed in the quad, dazzled his eyes. He turned a slow circle to take in the majestic spectacle.

"Beautiful, aren't they?" Jack asked.

"I never knew they could look like that."

"The dark skies out here are the next best thing to actually seeing them in space."

Mykl was much too distracted to catch the implication of Jack's words. He just stood there, staring up with his mouth agape, shivering.

"Let's get back inside, Mykl. It's too cold to remain out here very long without a coat or shoes."

"Stars pretty, Myyykll," James said as he stumbled into the motor home.

"Yeah, they are," Mykl replied absentmindedly. He took one last gander before following James. "How much farther, Jack?"

"Another two hours or so, you may as well try to get some sleep." Jack leaned over to whisper to Kyle, "Stop at the next town, see if you can find some motion sickness medication for the girl."

Everyone slept while Kyle drove toward the sparse lights in the distance. Everyone except Dawn—feeling no immediate relief from the anti-nausea medication, she continued to endure her woes in the bathroom.

***

The glow of an imminent sunrise greeted them as Kyle pulled the motor home into an old ranch and parked inside a faded barn. Mykl stretched, and discovered, much to his surprise, that his leg already felt better. He rotated his arm and found that his shoulder no longer hurt either—weird. Not that he was complaining. He'd had enough of being punctured for one day. "Where are we, Jack?"

"We are almost there."

"But Kyle said…"

"This is as far as we go in the motor home. The rest of the trip will be taken by tram."

Having emerged from her private accommodation, Dawn let out a miserable groan at the prospect of having to suffer through another moment of rolling motion.

"I'm sorry, Dawn. Rest assured, we have less than thirty minutes of traveling left before you can stand on solid ground and sleep on crisp clean sheets."

Dawn let out a long sigh that ended with, "Clean sheets, mmmmmm."

Crepuscular rays of sunlight shot warmth at Jack and his charges as he led them to the farmhouse. Inside, Jack directed them to the basement. No one appeared to live here, but it was clean, well kept, and obviously had electricity as evidenced by the lights that switched on automatically. The basement had no casement windows, only one entrance, and shelves of unmarked boxes everywhere.

Jack opened one of the boxes and withdrew several coats. "Here, put these on. The temperature is a constant chilly fifty degrees inside."

James took two and helped Dawn button hers up before donning his own. Mykl still wore Lawrence's coat.

Jack withdrew his phone and began drawing patterns on the back with his fingernail. He didn't appear to be making a call; and why the back instead of the touchscreen? Mykl opened his mouth to ask, but was interrupted by a muffled clunk that he felt through his feet. Half of the opposing wall began to swing away from them, shelves and all. The swinging end glided along a shiny metal track that arced into a hidden space. A faint scratching noise filled the suddenly hushed atmosphere.

"Anyone want to tell the blind girl what's going on?" Dawn asked of her speechless companions.

"Wall now door," James replied.

"Wall now door? Thanks, James. Mykl, what's going on?"

"Well, the wall," Mykl scratched his head, "has opened up like a door." He peered inside. "And it appears that there's an even larger metal door on the other side."

Jack stepped through the opening and drew another pattern onto the back of his phone. A massive clunk sounded behind a massive steel-clad door, about eight feet high and twelve feet long. When Jack pulled it open, Mykl saw that it was around four feet thick, like a vault door.

"There are stairs on the other side leading down," Mykl said.

"That's creepy," Dawn declared.

"They're the stairs that lead to our ride," Jack explained. "The only creepy part is the feeling you get from knowing that you will be traveling for eighteen miles at more than a half mile underground."

"I have to walk down a *half mile* of stairs?" Dawn asked.

"Not to worry. The stairs only go two levels to the elevator."

"Silly me. Mykl, remind me to thank you for this adventure someday."

"At least you have two good legs to walk on."

"Kyle can help you," Jack offered.

"That's okay. My leg is actually feeling better. I'll follow behind so James doesn't squish me if he falls."

"Okay then, Kyle, drive safely. I'll see you soon." Jack gave his driver a brief hug and then gestured for James to lead Dawn to the stairs.

"You're not coming with us?" Mykl asked Kyle disappointedly.

"Afraid not," replied Kyle. "Don't worry, we'll meet again." He extended his hand to Mykl, who shook it.

Mykl's ears popped twice during the long descent in the elevator. When they finally stopped, the doors opened to reveal a sleek, black, bullet-shaped tram car awaiting them atop narrow-gauge tracks. A cool draft whispered from an eight-foot-wide half-moon-shaped opening before the lead car.

Jack slid open the tram doors. "All aboard."

Mykl stepped inside. "Wow!" Indirect lighting showed four rows of plush seats, three deep, filling its interior. Soft gray carpeting lined the rest of the inner surfaces. "This is nice. What was this all made for, Jack?"

"It's a secret government installation."

"Well, duh," Mykl intoned, "that much is obvious. As I think we're all beyond the point of no return now, can you tell us exactly *what* secret organization you're with? I know it's not the FBI, and it's *certainly* not Child Protective Services."

"Would you believe the NSA?"

Mykl gave Jack a blank stare.

"How about the Center for Implementation of Alien Technologies?"

"CIAT? Now you're teasing me."

"Patience, Mykl." Jack guided him to a seat. "I promise I will tell you who I work for when we get to the other side."

The other side of *what*, Mykl couldn't begin to guess.

Dawn and James sat in the back. Dawn held her book to her chest as if it were a shield to ward off danger. James kept one hand resting on the dot pages sitting on his lap as he looked out the window. The walls glistened like glass and conjured the illusion of flying underwater. A gentle pushback feeling into the plush seat offered the only evidence of motion.

"It doesn't even feel like we're touching the rails," Mykl said.

"We're not. The rails are for backup now. Our current system uses magnetic strips encircling the tram for levitation and propulsion. It's extremely smooth and efficient."

"You've got no complaints from me," Dawn said.

"I'm glad to hear it. We'll be at our destination in about ten minutes." Jack yawned. "Then you can settle in and get some decent sleep."

Ten minutes later, the invisible force pushing Mykl relaxed, then slightly pulled him forward, as the tram slowed to a stop. Jack pushed a button above him, and the doors slid open to reveal a vestibule almost identical to the one they had just left, along with another blast door.

Mykl tapped Jack on the shoulder. "I understand the possible need for blast protection up top, but down here, a half mile below ground?"

"That's precisely *why* it's needed—and there are actually two doors at this location, another behind this one. Faults crisscross the area, and a large enough earthquake could crack the tunnel wall, allowing groundwater to flood in. The two-door system enables us to send in a rescue crew without endangering those on the other side."

Mykl walked over to examine the shiny wall—his limp was much less pronounced now. The wall was smooth, dry, crystal clear, and looked to be about five inches thick with an underlying metal lattice of some sort.

"We developed a technology that can draw the carbon out of the rock and crystallize it. Once crystallized, it's deposited back on the surface to seal and enhance structural support."

Mykl rapped the surface with his knuckles. "Crystallized carbon? Isn't that…"

"Yes. Diamond," Jack said. He assisted Dawn out of the tram.

Eighteen miles of five-inch-thick diamond. Mykl ran fingers along its surface. Enough diamond gleamed under his tiny hands to ensure a comfortable living for the rest of his life. The value of an entire tunnel was unfathomable.

Jack must have read his thoughts. "If you think that's valuable, it's nothing compared to the value of what's being protected on the other side."

Jack opened the first door and ushered his adoptees into a sort of airlock. "Safety protocols prevent me from opening both doors at once," he said. He closed the first door behind them, then opened the second. "I welcome you to the City."

Mykl walked through the door to a precipice overlooking a cavern that was almost inconceivably immense. He felt like a single plankton being swallowed by a whale. An entire city spread out before them, its buildings sprouting from the bedrock like glistening windowed stalagmites. The streets were bustling as open-topped vehicles noiselessly made their way around. From far above, artificial light from long strips filled the space with a pleasant warm glow.

Mykl felt his mouth getting dry and realized he had been standing there with it hanging open. He closed it and shot a glance at Jack, who had been observing his reaction.

"All right, we're inside now. You promised to tell me who you work for," Mykl said.

"I work for myself," Jack said. "I am the director of this facility and am in charge of the mission for which it was conceived. After World War II, our government commissioned a panel to determine the best way to avoid and counter any potential threats that might arise in the future, so as not to be caught by the unexpected ever again. The solution is what you see here: a clandestine collection of the best minds in the world, all working on problems that threaten our world today—or may threaten it in the future."

Mykl was fascinated, but his body was exhausted; he couldn't hold back a yawn.

"There is much more to tell," Jack said, "but we all need to get some sleep first."

"One more thing," Mykl demanded.

"What's that?"

"What is your *real* name?"

Jack chuckled. "I don't think you would believe me if I told you."

"Try me."

"Jack Smith."

Mykl rolled his eyes. Dawn chortled, and James fidgeted with his dots. "You're right," Mykl said. "I don't believe it. But we're here, and this place looks a lot more interesting than the asylum, so you can be whoever you want to be: Jack Grey, Jack Green, Jack Smith. It's all the same to me."

"You forgot one," Jack said with a kind smile.

A multi-seated cart hummed to a stop in front of them, and a man in a white lab coat got out and walked up to Jack. "Hello, Rip. Welcome back. Love the new look."

"Thanks, Tony. I'd like to introduce you to our new arrivals, Dawn, James, and Mykl." He gestured to each in turn with an open hand.

Tony looked them over. "You guys look like you haven't slept in days. Hop in the cart and I'll take us down into the City. We'll get you a quick breakfast and then settle you into your rooms."

The City grew in size as they rode toward it in tired silence. Mykl struggled to keep his eyes open, and his head kept falling forward against his will. He felt James's arm reach across him to hold him up. It was like having a warm secure seatbelt. His thoughts drifted like clouds through an evening sky, and images appeared in his mind like stars peeking through the haze. Faces of children in the Box, a pouncing kitten, a white page with strange symbols, a twisted length of metal, a blinding flash, and—his body twitched—a pair of eyes he didn't recognize. His last clear thought before succumbing to sleep was: *I'm going home with Jack the Ripper.*

CHAPTER 28

Dawn arrived at her room after a brief visit to the infirmary. She hoped the analgesic they had given her would tame her wild headache. James and Mykl had already gone to their own private rooms in the short time she was away; she suspected both were already fast asleep.

An infirmary assistant walked her through the room's layout and amenities. The walls contained sensors for simple touch commands. Should she find herself disoriented in her new domain, she need only tap any wall twice with a finger, and a chime would sound over the exit. Three taps for the bathroom. She benefited from a memory quite sufficient to recall the location of two openings without the need for cues, but it felt discourteous to dismiss her guide when he was trying to be supportive. A constant tapping, she was told, was for emergencies, and would summon help immediately.

With her guide now gone and Dawn enjoying true privacy for the first time in her life, she had only one thing on her mind. Without need of chimes, she left a trail of asylum clothes in a beeline to the bathroom. Standing naked in the dark, she faultlessly located the control panel for the deep tub and tapped in the commands for a hot bath. Jasmine-scented. With bubbles!

After many years of being tub-deprived, she luxuriated in steamy silence until her fingers had pruned to her satisfaction. Reluctantly, she opened the drain and toweled off. Using the damp towel as a barrier to protect her new freshness from the foul discards of asylum life, she plucked her old clothes from the carpet and deposited them into the trash. Among drawers filled with necessities, she found a nightgown softer than anything her fingertips had ever experienced. The silky feel of it slipping along her body made her quiver with feminine sensuality.

She ran fingers through damp hair and pulled a tress across her face. The delicate floral scent still lingered. Going to bed with damp hair was going to make for a mean case of bedhead when she woke, but—she smiled—nothing another bath couldn't cure.

The bedsheets welcomed her as softly as her gown. Plunging her head into the fluffy pillows, she gave a heavenly sigh.

As Dawn finally succumbed to fatigue, the bed drew her deeper into the depths of its sumptuous spell. Her breathing slowed and her heartbeat swam to a slow pulse in her neck. The pulse slowly traversed to a throb in the back of her head. The throb began drumming on her consciousness. She awoke to a pounding monster in her skull that would not stop as long as her heart still beat.

Disoriented by a bed suddenly grown too large and walls in the wrong places, Dawn grabbed handfuls of hair and rolled to escape the pain. She fell to the carpet and crawled, flailing an arm in front of her until it hit something solid and flat. Survival instinct kicked in, and she began slapping it over and over. Through the viscous haze of her hellish headache she sensed the object of her attention was not a wall but a drawer. In anguish, she twisted her body and reached out with her other hand. It met with something more solid. She tapped it twice. A chime added its din to the roaring beast in her skull. The walls, a moment ago so far away, now threatened to crush her skull like a vise. Lying flat on her back, she fought to focus purely on her fist and its beat against the wall.

Pounding.

Pounding.

Pounding.

CHAPTER 29

Mykl rolled over in search of a clock, but didn't find one. *How long did I sleep?* He experimentally flexed his leg. Much better range of motion now. It was healing quickly.

Eating French toast and drinking *real* orange juice was the last thing he remembered before falling asleep. He must have conked out right at the table and been carried to bed. He was certain he would have remembered this bed if he had been awake for it: it was *huge*. From his warm spot in the middle, he couldn't stretch a hand or foot to any of the edges. And he was dressed in incredibly comfortable dark blue pajamas. *They must have filled these with my limp body before pouring me into bed.*

The walls of his room glowed with enough light to see by, but by what means, he couldn't tell. There were no lamps, light fixtures, or switches; the surfaces themselves emitted the glow. Mykl pulled the covers over him and crawled to the wall—still not leaving his bed—to investigate. Touching the wall caused a perfect square to illuminate under his fingertip, which disappeared the instant he removed it. He placed his palm where the square had been, and a larger version of the square materialized. He slid his hand to the side, and the lit square followed, cool under his palm. He rapidly slid his hand up—and the entire room was illuminated with a blinding white light.

Mykl quickly dove back under the covers, blinking furiously. *Wow, that was amazing!* Venturing a guess as to how the lights operated, he snaked an arm out from under the covers and dragged his hand down the wall. The light dimmed appreciably, but it took a few moments for the afterimage of his silhouetted hand to fade from his retinas.

With the light finally at a comfortable level, he rose from the bed and walked around, examining his living space. It had a simple design, yet it was downright palatial compared to the Box. Along with his bed, he had a dresser, closet, bathroom, and a desk with the largest computer screen he had ever seen. One dresser drawer even held dozens of *new* socks. Mykl slipped on a pair, then wiggled his toes through cottony rapture, reveling in their luxurious springiness.

His first day of freedom in his new home fueled his desire to *live*. And not at the computer. He was too wound up for that. Something active, something fun, something…

The bed loomed in front of him. A crooked smile erupted into a broad grin on his face. His mother had never let him do it. It's too dangerous, she'd always said. But Mykl had endured a year living under the oppression of the Asylum Angel—he was confident he could survive a few moments jumping on a comfy bed.

With a running leap, he dove into the air and landed in the center. Rotating his knees underneath him, he tentatively began bouncing around the bed's perimeter. The ceiling called to him, so he tumbled back to the center and used the bed like a trampoline. Each jump took him higher and higher, but there wasn't enough spring effect to allow him to touch the ceiling. It didn't matter. This was still the greatest thing ever. *Every kid should have this much fun*, he thought. He bounced on his butt, back to his feet, then grabbed his knees to his chest and cannonballed from corner to corner…

The sheets had him entangled when a sharp knocking came from the other side of his door. *Oh, crap.* The last thing he needed was to get in trouble on his first day here.

"One second!" he yelled, flinging off the sheets and fleeing to the bathroom. He turned on the tap and splashed cool water on his face to mask the sweat built up in his exuberant acrobatics. Only then did he crack open the bedroom door.

A friendly-looking woman in a light blue smock peered down at him and smiled.

"Hello, Mykl. My name is Heather. The doctor would like to take a look at your leg again—if you're up to it." She must have noticed the moisture on his face and his heavy breathing, because she kneeled to feel his forehead. "Are you okay? You seem a little feverish."

"Yeah, I was... testing my new socks by running around the room," he said. He knew it sounded stupid the moment it left his mouth.

"Running?" she asked, her face awash in surprise. "I'm sure the doctor will be very interested in such a rapid recovery."

Great. Just great. I've earned myself another shot. Frowning, he asked, "Is it Stan that wants to see me?"

"No. Dr. Johnson is on assignment outside the City. Dr. Lee is in charge until he gets back." She stepped back and motioned for him to come with her. "You're fine in your pajamas and socks if you like; we won't be going far."

"Okay." Mykl slipped through the door, only opening it enough to allow him to pass, lest Heather see the mess he had made of the bed and figure out what he had *really* been doing. He didn't need any more trouble in his life. "Can James come too?" he asked.

"That's our next stop," Heather replied. "He's right down the hall."

The gray-green carpet squished soundlessly under Mykl's sock-clad feet as they walked the short distance. Mykl reached up to knock, then paused. Light leaked from beneath the door, and a heavy thumping sound came from inside. He dared not look back at Heather. *James, develop some common sense in the next two seconds*, he sent telepathically through the door.

Knocking hard, he yelled loudly, "James, there's a lady out here to take us to see the doctor!"

"Cooomes iiins!" James yelled from inside. The thumping continued. Mykl steeled himself, then opened the door.

A room set at maximum brightness assailed him. Thousands of colored polka dots randomly appeared and disappeared on surfaces everywhere. James, dressed in the same navy blue pajamas and bright new socks as Mykl, was jumping and flopping all around the bed, having the time of his life. Mykl looked up at Heather, shrugged, and lifted his hands in resigned defeat.

"Hellooos!" James said. "This funs, Mykls! You should tries!"

"I see James has figured out how to access the ambiance settings for the room," Heather said. She sounded unbothered by it, though she did squint against the nauseating light show.

"James, get down from there!" Mykl demanded, hands on his hips. "Don't you know how dangerous that is?"

"Aaawww." James awkwardly plopped onto the bed with his butt, and barely missed careening into a wall on the rebound.

James joined them in the hallway, and they continued on only a few steps before passing a darkened room on the left. Peering in, Mykl saw Dawn's book sitting on the desk. "Dawn?" he called into the darkness.

"Those are her quarters, but she's already at the infirmary with the doctor," Heather said.

"Oh." The room's lack of light left him feeling somber, but then again, Dawn had no need of lights or ambiance settings. "James, how did you figure out how to make all those dots?"

"Accidents."

"Why does that not surprise me?"

Mykl ducked a playful swat from James.

Heather laughed. "Simple settings can be accessed by touching two fingers to any wall," she offered. "More complex designs and images can be found in your room computer. A number of live feeds do a spectacular job of creating an open-air illusion. It's an effective remedy if you start to feel stir crazy from living in an enormous cavern."

They continued down the hallway and burst into the full light of the City. Mykl wished he had sunglasses. He raised his hand to block the glare coming from high above. "Is that sunlight?" he asked.

"Not exactly. They try to emulate the relative brightness and path of the sun to keep our bodies in a normal circadian rhythm." Heather pointed to the long strips running from east to west above them. "Physics aren't my specialty, but they use some type of superconductor to gather light from the fusion reactors."

Mykl's mind latched on to the impossible word. He grabbed Heather's arm to stop her. "*Fusion?*"

"Jack will give you a tour later. He's better at explaining things. And I wouldn't want to steal his thunder." She gave him a wink. "Here's our cart. It's just a short jaunt to the end of the block."

James bumped his head on the cart's top as he ducked into the back seat. Mykl hopped in next to Heather, on the verge of a meltdown with curiosity. He pivoted back and forth, wishing his head could turn 360 degrees to take in all the sights. James sat stock-still, moving only his eyes and gripping the cart's hand rail so hard that his fingers were white.

"What's wrong, James?" Mykl asked.

"No doors," he whispered.

"The cart?"

James nodded.

"We're barely moving!" Mykl exclaimed. "You could run faster than this, silly."

But James maintained his death grip on the rail.

Except for a peculiar sheen, and a subtle rounding of the edges, the architecture they passed was much like one would find in any urban area. The buildings cast fuzzy multiple shadows due to the irregular lighting.

"How many people live here?" Mykl asked.

"Several thousand," Heather gave him an indecipherable look, "but it varies."

The combination of the strange look and an inflection in her voice ignited Mykl's internal wariness. He wanted to probe, but he figured he'd have better luck getting answers from Jack.

The cart came to a stop, and Heather said cheerfully, "We're here."

Mykl cringed. He was not looking forward to going to the infirmary. *If this doctor pulls out anything resembling a corkscrew, I'm out of here. Five-inch-thick diamond barriers or not, I am gone.*

The door to the building had no handle, but Heather touched an indentation in the door where a handle would normally be, and the door slid open under its own power. Mykl chuckled. Every futuristic movie and television show he ever watched had self-opening doors. Then again, why not?

The room they entered looked nothing like a doctor's waiting area; it was more like a homey living room. Plush couches and chairs surrounded a low stone table. Fresh flowers, glasses, and a pitcher of water sat atop the table. A trace scent of long-gone cookies made it even *smell* like a home.

"Have a seat, boys. I'll let Dr. Lee know you're here."

Mykl climbed onto one of the oversized armchairs. James flopped in the middle of a couch and began lightly bouncing on the springy cushion. Mykl made a strangled sound in the back of his throat to get his attention and shook a warning finger at him. James tossed back an oft-used "I never get to have any fun" pout.

This homey setting didn't fool Mykl. He knew an arsenal of ice-cold stethoscopes and gleaming silver needles stalked this building, ready to prey on innocent children. Anxiety caused his puncture wound to itch. James, meanwhile, settled into a body-rocking, head-bobbing routine that he often used to battle boredom.

Footsteps clicked ever louder as they approached. A petite woman with Asian features stormed up to them with an aura of confidence and energy. She wore her hair in a straight black ponytail that fell in stark contrast to the white lab coat billowing behind her. Her infectious smile caused Mykl to release the breath he had been holding.

"Good afternoon, gentlemen," she said. "I'm Dr. Lee, but you can call me Cindy. How are we all doing today?"

Before Mykl could respond, James stammered, "J-James goods, how Dawns?"

Dr. Lee's smile became forced as she sat in a chair between them. She clasped her hands prayer-like in front of her. "Dawn is in another facility having more tests done. We're trying to find out why she's having headaches; we'll know more when the results get back in."

Neither boy wished to inquire further about what Dr. Lee chose not to tell.

After allowing them a moment, she asked, "So, who wants to be first?"

Mykl and James pointed at each other so fast she burst into laughter. "Okay, you first then, Mykl. I want to have a look at that leg wound of yours, since you already seem to be able to," she raised her thin eyebrows at him, "run on it."

I knew it! Heather tattled on me. All Jack said he needed to do was keep his room clean, and he had left that a mess as well. He would almost rather get a shot than be in trouble with Jack. *Almost.*

Dr. Lee led him into an examination room that precisely matched his expectations. She touched a corner of the exam bed, and it lowered to an easy height for Mykl to climb on. For all its cold, antiseptic look, the bed radiated a pleasing warmth.

"You're going to have to remove the PJs, Mykl."

Mykl grumbled and complied. Some people couldn't be bargained with, and doctors were the worst.

He was as surprised as Dr. Lee when he exposed his wound. All that remained of it was a small scab that looked close to falling off. Dr. Lee raised the bed and palpated the area around the scab.

"Does this hurt?" she asked.

"Nope."

"Hmmmmm."

"Is that a good hmmm or a bad hmmm?"

"It's always good when a patient isn't in pain, but that was more of a 'This is interesting' hmmm," she said. "And this injury occurred yesterday evening?"

"Yep." Mykl tensed. She was getting that "I'm going to have to give you a shot" look.

"I'd like to get a blood sample from you, Mykl."

Sometimes it was a curse to be able to read people so well.

"I need a single drop from a fingertip," she said, turning to remove a tiny cylindrical device from a recessed cabinet. "This has a microneedle which only penetrates the dermis enough to allow for blood collection. It will be no worse than a mosquito bite—but without the itching afterwards."

He reluctantly extended a middle finger, and she held the end of a collector to it. In the center of the collector was a vial filled with a clear fluid. She pressed a button on the collector, and Mykl detected the barest hint of pressure. A thin crimson ribbon swirled into the fluid.

"All done," she said, setting the sample to the side. "That wasn't so bad now, was it?"

Mykl critically inspected the puncture site by running his thumb over it. No blood, no pain. "Not so bad," he muttered under his breath. He didn't want to give the impression that more puncturing of his skin would be acceptable. Microneedle or otherwise.

After enduring the standard palpations and auscultations, Mykl submitted to a full body scan in an adjoining lab. It didn't take long.

Dr. Lee jotted a few notes as Mykl put his pajamas back on. "That's all for today," she said. "Would you bring James back for me, please?"

"Sure. But fair warning: he doesn't like needles any more than I do," Mykl said.

***

James had switched positions on the couch so he could watch for Mykl's return. Concern painted his face as Mykl approached.

"Dr. Cindy lady nice?" he asked.

"Yeah, for a doctor, she's as nice as they come."

"No shotses?" James wrung his hands with worry.

"No shotses," Mykl repeated. Even James should be able to handle a mosquito bite.

It took some coaxing to get James into the examination room, and once inside, he seemed to shrink in upon himself in half-contained fear. He didn't even look at Dr. Lee.

"Mykl stays?"

"Sure, James. If it will make you feel better."

Dr. Lee patted the exam bed. "Hop on up, James, and take your pajama top off, please?"

How James could get so entangled in so simple a garment as a pajama top in such a short time was one of life's great mysteries. It took both Mykl's and Dr. Lee's help to remove it. But finally, James took his place on the exam bed. Mykl gasped in shock at the ghastly looping scars crisscrossing his friend's back. They had all healed long ago, except for the angry red parallel scratches running diagonally from shoulder to hip.

"James, how did you get all these scars?" Dr. Lee asked sympathetically.

"Accidents," James replied in a barely audible whisper.

Mykl had never seen James with his shirt off before. The notes in James's asylum file had said that a police officer had found him wandering the Las Vegas Strip, but they made no mention of the obvious abuse he had suffered in the past. Mykl felt the greatest pity for him. *At least I knew love from my mother. It's no wonder James sought out the company of me and Dawn. We're likely the only friends he's ever known.*

"And these fresh scratches?" Dr. Lee gently ran a finger along the scabby border of one.

James arched his back away from her touch. "Fences," he said, slumping his shoulders again.

Mykl stared at his socks. "Dr. Lee," he said, "those scratches are about the right spacing if he tore the bottom of the quad fence from the asphalt and squeezed under it. He did it to save me. And in doing so, he saved Dawn too—though he couldn't have known that." It would have taken a great deal of strength and determination, but Mykl had no doubt about what James had done. All in an effort to save his friend from the Angel. His memory of the rest of James's part in the rescue still remained fuzzy.

"Is that what happened, James?" Dr. Lee asked.

James gave a weak nod.

She squeezed his hand. "You did good, James, you did good."

James smiled at her.

"Unfortunately," she added, "you're going to need a tetanus shot like the one Mykl had to get yesterday."

His smile melted into a frown.

Mykl jumped up to grab his friend's arm. "It's okay, James. It's really not that bad."

***

Several crocodile tears and a dozen pokes and prods later, they were allowed to go. Dr. Lee had given them both a clean bill of health and a follow-up appointment to see her again in a week, and Heather took them back to their rooms to get dressed before seeing Jack. Mykl figured if news of their morning antics didn't make it to Jack's desk, then they should have an enjoyable tour of the City. He hoped so: his questions had been growing at an exponential rate.

Besieged by a closet full of new clothes, Mykl experienced a never-before-faced problem: *What do I wear?* Every piece of clothing he touched rated far superior to anything he had ever worn in the Box. Making a decision, he tossed his pajamas on the unmade bed. *If someone thinks I look good in navy blue PJs*, he thought, *then I should do fine with the same color scheme in slacks and shirt.* Another thought struck him as he slipped a foot into a new shoe. *If they have clothes and shoes in my size, then there must be other children here.* But where were they? He hadn't seen any kids since his arrival. He added that to his list of questions for Jack.

"You ready, James?" Mykl called out before he stepped in to collect his friend. James was sitting on the carpet, enthusiastically tying knots in his *long* new shoelaces. Mykl's first instinct was to rush forward and stop him; his second was to cover his eyes. James's blue pants, yellow shirt, and crooked lime green tie created a walking color-combination nightmare.

"Looks goods?" James asked.

"Looks great. I wouldn't change a thing. Now let's go." Mykl pantomimed an ushering motion to get James moving.

"Not finishes," James mumbled. He continued tying knots.

Mykl growled deep in his throat and stared at the moving dots on the ceiling. Those knots were going to be a royal pain to untie later.

"You sounds likes kitteh," James said.

"Done?"

"One mores." James fastidiously looped the last two inches of his laces and pulled with all his might. "Dones!" he said proudly.

Mykl shook his head in frustration as he led James down the hall. He thought he might make a special request to Jack to equip James with laceless shoes.

Dawn's room was still empty. He would just have to fill her in on their tour when they got back. She would enjoy that. He just hoped these people could find a way to fix her headaches.

CHAPTER 30

New voices, low and concerned, spiraled around Dawn's dark world. A vile-tasting film coated her tongue. The monster wielding a sledge hammer behind her eyes tired and began to clench and unclench its fists in the folds of her brain.

"Are you back with us?" a female voice asked.

"Where am I?"

"You were brought to the infirmary here at the City. I'm Dr. Lee. We met earlier. Can you tell me what happened?"

That explained the firmness of the padding under her and the antiseptic overtones in the air.

"Another headache." Dawn furrowed her brows against the pain. "I get them all the time. This was one of the worst though." She ran her tongue around her mouth. "May I have some water please?"

Dawn stiffened as Dr. Lee gently laid a hand on her forehead. "I'm sorry. I can't let you have anything to drink yet. That taste in your mouth is from a sublingual spray. Your blood pressure was exceedingly high for someone your age. The spray was a temporary measure to reduce it."

"Temporary?" Dawn asked. She was certainly not looking forward to more doses of the offensive spray.

"Really, don't worry," Dr. Lee said. "I'm sorry about the taste. We'll get you all the water you need after we finish our tests."

Dawn's first instinct was to ask if the tests were going to hurt, but then she decided they couldn't be worse than what she had already experienced. Breathing through her teeth, she steeled herself and said, "Okay, test away."

Every minute bang and clatter made Dawn twitch involuntarily. Apparently noticing her advanced discomfort, Dr. Lee asked, "On a scale of one to ten—"

"Eleven!" Dawn interrupted. "Sorry."

"Not to worry, dear. We'll start an IV and give you something for the pain." Dr. Lee squeezed her hand, and Dawn forced a smile through gritted teeth.

Within seconds of receiving the painkiller, the tension in Dawn's body dissolved. The pain retreated farther and farther into the dark distance… though the monster still lurked in the shadows.

***

Dr. Lee ran a phalanx of tests. She was an agent of the City because she was honest, skilled, thorough—and she cared. Everything came up negative, until data from Dawn's brain scan arrived. She seethed with anger at the results. She wanted to strangle whoever had diagnosed Dawn in the past. They might as well have been guilty of murder.

***

Dawn drifted like a raft riding swells in a calm ocean. Her gurney gently rolled to and fro, raised and lowered with utmost care, and spun with smooth precision. She knew only that she was alone in a room with a closed door. A swishy-sounding door at that. The medication coursing through had made her loopy, but it had also made her headache tolerable. The pain she felt now, she could live with.

The weird-sounding door swished, and Dawn opened her eyes. Heels stepped inside, paused, and made nimble clicks away from her. There was a soft sliding noise, and then the footsteps returning to her side. Air slowly whispered from the cushion on the stool as Heels sat down.

Dawn lacked the ability to read body language or facial expression, but she excelled at interpreting environmental nuances—and right now, she sensed that something was terribly wrong. Heels had not said a word yet. Her breathing was forced and irregular. Dawn wanted to run in panic.

"Dawn…"

Dawn turned her face to Dr. Lee and waited. Her heart began pounding. The monster was coming.

"I have the results of your tests," Dr. Lee said, her voice just above a whisper. "Your headaches—and your blindness—are not, nor have they ever been, a result of some childhood disease or malnutrition. You have a tumor. You have had it for quite some time. It appears to have started in the occipital region of your brain. It has grown. Like an amoeba, it has sent tendrils through your visual cortex and into the rest of your brain. Its originating location is the cause of your blindness. Its growth is the cause of your headaches."

Dr. Lee took a slow breath. "The tumor is inoperable… and malignant. Our test show that the cancer has spread to your lymph system and organs. The headaches will get worse. Eventually, you will start to lose motor control, and your organs will begin to shut down. At the tumor's current rate of progression, you have about sixty days before you will no longer be able to maintain consciousness."

The monster was in the room. And it was a coward that fed in the dark. Dawn now knew its goal: to convert Dawn into the same insidious creature—a mindless, blind blob—from the inside out. But there was one very important distinction between her and her killer: Dawn was no coward.

"May I have that drink of water now, please?" Dawn asked.

CHAPTER 31

Perched on a ledge near the cavern's entrance was the City information center, where Jack's home and office stood. Its cantilevered foundation extended outward to create a deck with spectacular panoramic views of the community below. None of the City's buildings were more than two stories in height, and their white dome-shaped roofs gave the appearance of squat mushrooms. Evergreen trees, interspersed among the polished domes, softened the alien feel of the landscape. Artificial sunlight glinted off what appeared to be a lake far beyond the City proper.

Mykl stood on a bench to see over the deck railing. He held on to one of James's arms, not for his own support but for James, who was afraid of heights. Heather had dropped them off, and her cart grew smaller as it wound its way down the serpentine road from the ledge.

Twenty-four hours ago, I was writing in my own blood in hopes to save myself from the Asylum Angel, Mykl thought. *Now I'm about to enter the home of a man people call "Jack the Ripper."* What were the next twenty-four hours going to bring?

"James? Mykl? Won't you please come in?" said a pleasant female voice behind them.

"Is this where Jack works?" Mykl asked, hopping off the bench.

"Works, eats, sleeps, lives. This is his home. I am his wife, Delilah." She was a woman of slight build, and she exuded a comfortable confidence and consummate kindness. Mykl couldn't help but stare into eyes so green that they couldn't possibly be real. But when she looked to James, Mykl saw a brief shadow of wariness cloud her gaze. James was contemplating the end of his tie as if he were determining its worthiness to hold more knots. A quick shot from Mykl's elbow to the side of James's thigh brought his friend back to the moment.

They followed Delilah through another self-opening door and into a living space where the walls mimicked the outside view. The interior walls and partitions curved up and in, softening the visual lines. Furnishings with warm earthy tones and hints of primary colors blended with subtle lighting to give a cozy, open-air feel, and the faux transparency of the walls made the room look as large as the cavern outside. Mykl actually backpedaled to reconfirm the outer dimensions of the residence.

Apparently sensing his confusion, Delilah tapped a simple pattern on the inside wall with her fingernails. Instantly the walls transformed to plain white, allowing perception of the building's true dimensions. A simple "ah" from Mykl drew a smile from their hostess and a perplexed head tilt from James.

"I can't wait to experiment with my settings," Mykl said.

"I'm sure you will find something to your liking."

Delilah reset the room ambiance to its previous setting and led them to an arched opening farther inside. Mykl tried to imagine what kind of setting Jack would have for his own personal space. It had to be something spectacular. Perhaps underwater, a moonscape, a space station?

They stepped through the arch, and Delilah indicated an open doorway to their left. "Go on in, gentlemen, I'll bring refreshments in shortly."

Through the doorway was an extremely underwhelming work area. It yawned with plainness. Ordinary white walls with the same rounded sloping at the ceiling and no windows; it felt slightly claustrophobic. Jack sat behind a dark wood desk with two guest chairs in front. Behind him was a short file cabinet with an ancient black telephone sitting atop it.

The only interesting thing in the room was perched on a mantel over a well-worn couch: an exquisitely detailed crystal replica of a clipper ship. Gossamer filaments like spun glass composed the billowing sails. Delicate light glinted off the intricate rigging zigzagging between the masts. Cannon turrets bristled from bow to stern through the transparent hull.

The ship's unique beauty captured James in its spell. He trundled toward it, his arms extended and fingers undulating like suction-cupped tentacles. Mykl, who had been about to sit in one of the chairs in front of Jack, sprinted the short distance to his friend and sprang off the couch to grab his outstretched arm. He pinned his friend with a complex series of facial contortions meant to convey the most dire of messages.

"Boat pretty," James said as Mykl lead him to a seat.

The expression on Jack's face showed that he was not amused. He kept his eye on James until he was seated in the chair next to Mykl. His silence made Mykl squirm. *We're both in deep trouble now; I just know it.* He looked down at his new shoes dangling above the floor so as to avoid Jack's piercing eyes.

After several seconds of awkward silence, Jack spoke. "That ship does have an unusual effect on people," he said. "It was designed as a gift for me from my wife, who developed crystallized carbon technology."

Mykl spared a second glance at the ship and jumped to the obvious meaning. It was made of diamond. If they had the technology to make such a finely detailed work of art, then the applications for diamond were practically limitless. He let his eyes wander about the room and realized that this and every other structure in the City must be constructed of diamond as well.

What would happen if this technology were released to the world?

"I hear you two had an active morning?" Jack said, his expression stern.

This is it. I've heard this kind of question before. It's not really *a question, but a preamble to a scolding. I knew better than to jump on the bed. And James? Well, James is James. Jack doesn't know him as well as I do; I just hope his eccentricities will be taken into account.*

Jack leaned forward to rest his arms on the desk, one hand covering the other as if he were composing himself for a long lecture.

"We all have secrets," Jack began. "I know as well as anyone the importance of keeping one, and I respect your right to keep yours. You won't be punished, or thought any less of, for keeping your own counsel. However, know this: no one in the City got here by denying reality. The truth is simply that—the truth. We deal with it without fear. Otherwise, this facility would not exist."

Jack looked expectantly from James to Mykl.

Mykl weighed his words carefully. He had a free pass out of trouble if he just kept his mouth shut. No such promise had been made about telling the truth. But Jack had given his word that he wouldn't hit him—that he would treat Mykl like a son. Perhaps it was time to fess and begin earning the man's trust.

Mykl sat up straighter in his chair and looked Jack in the eyes. Jack followed suit by sitting up as well, pulling his hands into his lap. A single black casino chip lay on the desk where his hands had been.

Mykl opened his mouth to speak, but James abruptly rose. Without a word, he took determined strides over to the diamond clipper ship and stopped.

Shock pinned Mykl to his chair. This wasn't the James he was familiar with. The posture. That was it. James stood at his full height, shoulders back, proud... like a man.

"This really is quite beautiful," James said in a rich voice as he ran a finger along the ethereal rigging of the ship.

Mykl's mouth hung open as he watched this unfamiliar person undo his crudely made tie and deftly retie it into a proper knot. For fourteen months Mykl had been James's friend, had shared a room with him, had laughed with him, cried with him, and now... Now he didn't know what to think of this—this *stranger*.

He looked back to see Jack's reaction.

Jack was smiling. He picked up the casino chip and tossed it to James. "Welcome to the City, James," he said.

James snipped the chip out of the air between his thumb and forefinger. "Thank you, sir. I see your people found one of my stashes?"

He walked the chip across the back of his fingers like a card sharp.

"Indeed. And I would imagine," Jack said, leaning his chair back and putting his feet on the desk, "that you have quite a story to tell."

James blew a gust of air through his lips. "Nothing that compares to your story. Of that, I am certain. All I did was devise a way to get myself out of begging on the streets."

"You've been *faking*!" Mykl finally overcame his shock and now boiled with righteous rage. He pointed at James's shoes. "You—you tied all those knots on *purpose!*"

James burst into laughter. With no hint of his former clumsiness, he glided across the carpet to kneel and place a hand on Mykl's shoulder. "You're like a little brother, Mykl. I had to find ways to keep that brilliant mind of yours entertained in that abysmal Box." He lowered his head to level his eyes with Mykl's. "Forgive me, my friend?"

"You could have told me." Mykl crossed his arms and looked away, not ready to give in yet.

"Lori was too clever and suspicious. She would have kicked me out if she had caught a whiff of my deception. Either that, or I would have been adopted. So I put on the act, and I buggered up my test results every year. I'm sorry I couldn't be honest with you. I would have left on my own eventually… if it weren't for Dawn. She's very special to me. So are you, Mykl."

"Dawn's going to flip when she finds out," Mykl said.

"Let me tell her? Please?" James asked.

Mykl raised his hands in surrender. "She's all yours. I don't want to be anywhere *near* her when she unleashes her wrath on you." He wrapped his arms around James's neck and squeezed. "Thanks for saving my life yesterday, big brother."

"You're very welcome."

"James, how did you accumulate all of those casino chips?" Jack asked.

"Assisting foreign tourists, mostly." James and Mykl retook their seats. "It helps if you can speak their language."

"And how many languages do you speak?"

"Several. Japanese, all Chinese, French, German, Spanish, and a few others. The library was a wonderful place to learn… and casinos were a perfect place to practice."

"What about those pages of dots you brought with you?"

"Those are my journal," James said with a broad smile.

"*How?*" Mykl asked. "I looked at those stupid dots dozens of times and could never make anything out of them."

"They're private. I had to invent a new language and writing style to safeguard them. The way you plow through puzzles, I didn't think it would be safe if you knew. And some of the pages I left on my desk for you to see were random dots, to throw you off. That and the knots seemed to distract you enough."

"Ha! You're fixing *those* knots yourself!" Mykl said, pointing at James's shoes.

"You *invented* a language?" Jack asked.

"Sure. Kids do it to some extent all the time. I just made mine more complex."

Jack looked contemplative. Mykl stared at James, amazed at how thoroughly he had been duped for over a year.

"How did you beat me on figuring square roots then?" Mykl asked.

"I cheated," James confided with a lopsided smile.

Mykl threw him a pursed-lip scowl.

Delilah entered with a tray full of snacks and drinks. "Hungry, boys?"

"Please. Let me help you with that." James stood to assist.

With a tight-lipped smile at Jack, Delilah relinquished the tray to James. "Looks like *you* are doing dishes tonight," she said to her husband.

"I should know better than to bet against you, dear," Jack said. To his guests, he explained, "Since we both knew of your secret, James, we had a bet as to whether or not you would out yourself after seeing the casino chip. I lost."

"This is going to take some getting used to," James said, setting the tray on the desk. "It's like being dropped into Atlantis. Everyone here is so perceptive. I didn't think I could maintain my ruse much longer anyway, and that chip proved it. The honest thing to do was be myself."

"The mythical Atlantis was destroyed and lost to the world of man," said Jack. "This 'Atlantis' is lying in wait for man to prove that he won't destroy himself first. Then it will arise from the depths of the earth. You have some unique skills that could be of great use to me… if you are willing, James?"

"I can't see how I could possibly refuse—but why would you be inclined to take me in after knowing the *real* me for only a few minutes?"

"Trust does have to be earned. But I would say that your actions, past and present, have more than proven your character to me." Jack began checking points off with his fingers. "You stayed at the asylum to be with Dawn when you could have left and used your intelligence to be very successful in *anything* you chose. You saved the life of your friend from a determined psychopath. *And* when faced with a choice of reality or living a fantasy, you chose the former." Jack lowered his hand. "Your code of values shows that you can be trusted."

Jack shifted his attention back to Mykl. "You were about to say something before James took the floor?"

"Oh, well… I was just going to fess up to jumping on my bed this morning. Until James stole my thunder."

"You were jumping on your bed?" Jack asked.

"Um… yeah," Mykl answered in a small voice. He stared at his knees.

"Well, I'm sure the bed can handle it."

Mykl's head snapped up, his eyes wide in surprise. "I'm not in trouble then?"

"Of course not. I let my own son jump on the bed when he was your age. Just don't get hurt, or Dr. Lee will be lecturing both of us," Jack said with a mischievous grin.

"Speaking of Dr. Lee," James said, "I would like to see how Dawn is doing. They performed some extra tests, and I want to make sure she's okay. Do you mind if I pass on the tour for now?"

"I understand. And I'm sure Mykl will fill you in later," Jack said. "Would you like a ride back?"

"I think I would rather walk and stretch my legs. It will give me a few minutes to prepare a defense for my actions."

"Are you *sure* it's not because you're afraid of riding in a cart?" Mykl teased.

"Ha! I only have one fear now, and that certainly isn't it."

Mykl picked a sandwich off the tray and handed it to James. "Take this—you're going to need your energy. If she reacts anything close to the way she did the last time we tried to play a trick on her, you're as good as dead."

CHAPTER 32

Mykl's thoughts were spinning about in his brain so fast that he had trouble picking one. However, one pesky detail kept nagging at him; it had been doing so ever since he had first met Jack.

"Why me?"

Jack left his chair to come sit in the one James had vacated. "Mykl, the hardest part about running this facility isn't developing technology, or even keeping it secret. It's finding the right kind of people to keep it operating."

"Trouble-prone five-year-olds who like ice cream?" Mykl arched an eyebrow.

Jack laughed. "You might be surprised at how closely that describes them. Acquiring adults who meet our standards has become exceedingly difficult. More so because of the need to change their identities and deal with their ties to society. Adopting bright children out of the asylums and orphanages of the world has proved to be a much better solution."

Jack's answer didn't come close to satisfying Mykl's question, but it was a start. There were many directions one could take to arrive at the complete truth.

"Last night you said this place works on solving world problems, and that you run it. That sounds like a monumental task to undertake in a tiny little office like this." Mykl indicated the space with a sweep of his arm.

Jack tapped a complex pattern on the corner of his desk, and the room darkened. Then its surfaces came alive. The wall to Mykl's left showed an ultra-high resolution map of the world, blazing with pulsing pictograms of light spanning the color spectrum. The wall to his right was checkered with live video feeds. Behind Jack's desk, the wall displayed an immense three-dimensional image of the moon, full, bright, and slightly rotating. Mykl looked over his shoulder. Behind the couch, slightly obscured by the mantel with the ship, was an image of the earth as seen from space. Even the ceiling had changed, now depicting a star field, with colorful glowing icons to mark areas of obvious importance. Some flashed slowly, others danced in a pattern.

"Is that better?" Jack said.

Mykl's eyes darted about. "I think 'frightening' might be a better word to describe it."

He got off his chair and approached the giant Earth. Careful not to touch the wall—he anticipated the images would be interactive—he pointed at one of the icons in orbit about the planet. It looked like a bouquet of angry red balloons, and there were many such icons, not just on this wall, but on all of them, and on the ceiling. "What does this symbol represent?" he asked.

"A nuclear weapon of ninety-nine megatons or greater."

Mykl withdrew his hand and pulled it protectively to his chest. He backed away from the armageddon of color, yet there was no escaping its presence, let alone the realization that thousands of these things orbited miles above in space. "Why?" he asked accusingly.

No longer the smiling, friendly man who had adopted him, Jack now took on the persona of "Jack the Ripper," director of the City. His manner became sharp, precise, and cold, like a blade of truth taking human form.

"I did not put them there, Mykl. Decades-old treaties ban the proliferation of space-based weapons, yet world powers put them there anyway. The offending nations launched them under the guise of communication equipment, weather satellites, and exploratory probes, then gloated over their cleverness. Fortunately, only a handful of City operatives know of this terrible secret. If this ever became public knowledge, the world would be at war within a matter of hours. But I'm afraid it won't take much longer for this secret to be discovered. Regardless of the tools at my disposal, the rapid advancement of detection technology will cause its exposure all too soon.

"My mandate is to provide solutions to issues like this—or to prevent them in the first place. I foresaw this problem when I took on this responsibility, but I lacked the technology or resources to prevent it. The politicians and generals in charge chose to ignore my warnings in favor of increasing their popularity and power bases.

"Yet now, with the technology this facility now possesses, I can render every one of those weapons inert from this very desk. You are now thinking: Why haven't I done that already? The answer is simple: the moment one side realizes they have lost the ability to control those weapons, they will immediately assume that it was the other side that caused it—and we are once again at war. A war that does not have access to these particular weapons, but an ugly, devastating war nonetheless. I don't have the ability to stop *all* attacks with my technology. New York learned that the hard way."

Mykl had been oblivious to how fragile life on this world was until now. His problems in the Box seemed so simple and trivial in comparison. Cockroaches had been replaced with nukes. It appeared that neither pest could be easily eradicated. Shaking his head, he moped back to his chair.

"What about the moon?" he asked. "Why so many there?"

Jack didn't turn to identify the deadly red icons dotting the lunar surface. Mykl guessed he knew the location of every one.

"When it comes to the moon, one corrosive philosophy now dominates every political authority in the world: *If I can't have it, then no one can.* It doesn't apply solely to the moon, either. You almost became a victim of that philosophy with Lori. Her records show that she was recently forbidden from having children."

"That's stupid," Mykl said. Kids acted that way with ratty old toys. For adults to behave the same way was simply moronic. "So, what idiots put the ones way out in space?" He pointed to the tiny glowing balloons above.

"I put those there," Jack said with a hint of amusement.

Mykl raised his hand as if he were in a school classroom. "May I have permission to embarrass myself further by asking more stupid questions?"

Jack chuckled. "Of course."

"Very well then." Mykl lowered his hand. "Why did *you* put nukes in deep space?" The answer to this question should be quite interesting.

"They have been strategically placed from within the orbit of Mars to outside the heliopause as a counter to threats from comets and asteroids. Their fusion rockets are designed to intercept and nudge dangerous targets into a more desirable trajectory. It's one of our most effective operations and has been used at least five times since its inception to prevent devastating impacts. Unfortunately, it's not perfect. The volume of space to monitor is massive, and the odds of something getting through undetected are still relatively high."

"So, how many times have you saved the world?"

"Enough," Jack said wearily.

Mykl scratched the back of his head. He had only asked about one icon and had already discovered two threats capable of destroying the planet. There were hundreds of other mysterious symbols to choose from.

Picking at random, he pointed to a weakly glowing pink flower-shaped icon hovering over South America. "What's this one?"

"That's a biological weapons facility, still under construction," Jack said. He selected a sandwich from the tray.

Mykl rubbed at his eyes with the heels of his hands. "Can we go on that tour now?" he asked, taking a sandwich as well.

CHAPTER 33

A low rumble reverberated throughout the City cavern. James halted his stride to locate the source. He had been walking fast, with purpose, and enjoying the feeling of freedom. Too many years he had been burdened with the need to hide under a lead cloak of deception. With that weight now removed, his spirit soared. It didn't matter that he had no idea what was in store for his future. What mattered was that he now had one.

A city of diamond glistened under the glow of an artificial sun. For all the City's mysteries and secrets, the few people he encountered were generous with waves and easy smiles. He couldn't wait to describe this new world to Dawn. Being her eyes would be so much easier now. *That is, if I can survive her tumultuous temper—or worse, outright rejection—after revealing my deception.*

As if on cue, another angry rumble echoed in the City.

The light dimmed, and the shadows around James softened. Casting his gaze above, he saw a white mist developing all along the ceiling. He turned in a slow circle with his head tilted back. It couldn't be. *Clouds?*

A strobe-like flash around the simulated sun strip punctured the mist, followed by another thunderous rumble. The distinctive smell of moisture permeated the air—then the sky fell.

As if trying to embrace the sky, James bent backward, his arms extended, under a cool rain. Within seconds, his clothes were soaked and stuck to his skin. Had he been at the Box, Mykl would have been tugging on his arm by now to drag him back inside. James laughed at the thought. He loved the rain.

As the water cascaded off the buildings, it made the ingenuity of their designs clear. Elaborate collection troughs redirected water to trees, flower gardens, and lawns. The remaining flow cleansed sidewalks and eventually made its way into a simple gutter system. James marveled at the complexity involved in this one link in the City's ecosystem.

It wasn't long before the rain gave way to a gentle breeze. It made him shiver. But then the misty cloud dispersed, and he felt the warmth from the overhead sun. It left a rainbow circling high above the City.

Combing his fingers through his saturated hair, James resumed his hike to see Dawn. When he'd left Jack's office, his mind had been overflowing with thoughts he wanted to share. But now that he was faced with the imminent conversation, his words evaporated like the clouds above. His confidence eroded with every step. The sandwich in his stomach ran laps around his spine. He had never felt like this before. The old James had no problem at all shuffling up to Dawn and professing his joy at seeing her. The new James… The new James was a mess.

How hard can it be to tell someone that you love them?

James's soaked shoes squished noisily down the quiet hallway. Through her open door, he saw Dawn sitting at the computer desk, hands in her lap. She looked sad, but still so beautiful… so vulnerable. James ached to hold her.

With a shaky hand, he rapped lightly on her door frame.

"Yes?" she said, her voice sounding as if she were much farther away.

James's mouth felt as dry as the last time he chewed several sticks of colored chalk in the Box. "D-Dawn…" he stammered.

"James? Why do you smell like a wet dog?"

"It was raining outside." He didn't stammer.

Dawn started to reply, then her face lost all expression and the silence between them swiftly wound with tension. James wondered if her sensitive ears heard his heart hammering away against his ribs. The thundering flow of his blood echoed in his head, making it even more difficult to think. He dared not breathe, and steeled himself against the verbal lashing about to be unleashed by the woman he loved to the depths of his soul.

But she just clenched one hand into a tight fist and remained silent.

He shifted his weight. His shoes squished in the strained silence. "I... I..."

A smile as bright as the fusion-driven sun lit Dawn's face as she erupted into laughter. "James," she said. "You've finally dropped the act, and *now* you're afraid of me?"

James didn't know what to say. "You—you *knew?*"

"Of course I did. I'm blind, not stupid," she said haughtily. "You slipped in your way of speaking, ever so slightly, too many times over the years for it to be anything but an act. It was subtle, but for someone who lives in a world of sound, it was easy to catch. I even tested you a few times to be sure. Sometimes, when you were escorting me, I would pretend to trip to see if you'd react fast enough to catch me. You always did. I knew the whole 'big clumsy dummy' thing was a show."

The warmth from her radiant smile melted the cold cable of doubt constricting James's chest. He took a tentative step toward her.

"Why didn't you say anything?" he asked.

She stood and unerringly reached out to touch the book lying on her desk. As her delicate fingers caressed its battered border and frayed spine, her smile faded as if she fought some inner demon. "I was afraid."

"Why?" James closed the distance between them and took her hand in his.

She turned her face to his voice. "I didn't know why you were hiding. I was afraid if I called you out on it, you might truly disappear, and I... didn't want to lose you." Her last words came out in the barest whisper.

"You could never lose me. The only reason I pretended to be someone else was to get off the streets and into the Box. I wouldn't have stayed so long, but... but since the first day you arrived, I knew I could never leave without you."

Dawn smiled up at him, and he drew her into an embrace.

"Geeyaaah!" Dawn squirmed away from him. "You're soaking wet!"

Bubbling with laughter, James said, "I told you it was raining."

"We're a half mile underground! How can it rain?"

"Well, I think it—"

Dawn reached up and placed a finger on his lips. "Go change into dry clothes first. Then you can tell me all about it."

"Good idea. I'll be right back."

James took her hand again and gave it a warm squeeze before he left. He had lost the moment to tell her the words locked inside him for so long, but another moment would come. He had all the time in the world now.

***

As James's footsteps retreated, Dawn slumped into her chair. She trembled from the effort it took to appear strong. She knew James loved her. Until today, she would have been elated to have him hold her, free of his pretending. Sadly, this only served to complicate her life. However long it might prove to be.

Dr. Lee had explained her treatment options, but they were very limited. An experimental procedure *might* make a difference. But Jack had to approve the procedure before Dr. Lee would even be permitted to give any details.

Sixty days. That was longer than she would have had in the Box—if Mykl was right that Lori had targeted her as the Ass Angel's next victim. But it wasn't much. And now a man called Jack the Ripper held her fate in his hands. Dawn hated the fact that someone else determined her fate. It rankled every fiber of her being.

But with one choice, one final choice, she could regain control of her own fate. She didn't think of that choice as giving up, but as taking control. And that choice was exclusively hers to make.

For now, however, she wanted to be strong for James. If only for a short time. She owed him that much.

Dawn pulled open the drawer in front of her and picked up the container of pills that Dr. Lee had prescribed. A potent painkiller to keep the monster at bay. There were enough left inside to put the monster to sleep for good. But for now, she took only one. She swallowed it without water, closed the drawer, and bargained with the fiend for a few more moments of happiness.

CHAPTER 34

"Why the rain?" Mykl asked as the last of the drops fell into the palm of his outstretched hand.

"As with light, water is critical to the City ecosystem. We could generate it less dramatically, but rain, with a touch of simulated thunder and lightning, makes for a more visceral feel. It's also the most efficient way to manage dust."

"Interesting. I hope James has the good sense now to not dance around in it like some fool," Mykl said.

They traveled about the City, stopping briefly at points of interest, while Jack narrated its history. The cavern had originally been much smaller but had been expanded along with the needs of the City. With the invention of matter-manipulation technology, the need for heavy machinery to dig, and human labor to build, had become obsolete. Creating tunnels was a simple matter of programming the needed dimensions; within a few days, the job was complete. More advanced applications of the technology configured raw materials for living and work spaces. It turned out that the technology didn't apply exclusively to carbon, but to all elements and compounds—carbon just happened to be cheap and readily available. So why *not* make buildings out of diamond?

With each new technological revelation they passed, a question grew more pronounced in Mykl's mind. He held on to it in hopes that Jack would answer without his asking. It seemed too obvious a question for Jack to neglect bringing it up, but the more Mykl waited, the more he feared the answer. So he skirted his taboo question with others that danced around the issue.

"Do you sell diamonds to pay for all of this?"

"If we tried to fund this operation entirely from our matter technology, world diamond prices would plummet to the value of charcoal briquettes, and people would become very suspicious very fast," Jack said. "In fact, we've never sold anything we produce by our technologies, simply because it's that important to us that we maintain our secrecy. If we began marketing raw materials, we would become an immediate target for scrutiny from any number of businesses and government agencies. No, our funding comes from millions of untraceable investments."

"You're telling me nobody outside the City knows about any of this?" Mykl asked with a sweep of his arm.

"As far as the United States government knows, we are a highly classified consulting agency with unlimited security clearance. The single person outside our agency with limited knowledge of us and authorization to contact me is the president. Within a week of a new president taking office, he or she is briefed on our service and given instructions as to where, when, and why they may contact us. For a long time, presidents had the wisdom to listen and act appropriately to our suggestions. But recently, they have been keeping their own counsel and ignoring our recommendations, leaving the hard decisions for the next person, in order to retain power and voters. This does nothing to deter an impending crisis. When the time comes to act, it may be too late. Blood tends to be the solvent of choice to wipe away inconvenient truths."

They were now approaching the largest structure in the City. It jutted into the center of the lake at the far end of the cavern, its architecture reminiscent of the Sydney Opera House, but more squat and egg-shaped. Chevron patterns on the pearlescent white surface gave the appearance of a reptilian skin stretched tightly over a curved dome.

"This is our Operations Center," Jack said.

Mykl rubbed his thumb up and down on a section of tiny chevrons, It felt rough when rubbed in an opposing direction to the scales. Like everything he had seen in the city, this building demonstrated astounding creativity.

A curious sound came from behind him, like the lid of a cooking pot being lifted and then clattering closed. He turned to find Jack near the rail at the water's edge, holding a clenched fist toward Mykl.

"Hold out your hands," Jack said.

Mykl obliged, and Jack opened his fist to release a cascade of tiny green pellets into Mykl's hands. Dozens escaped Mykl's grasp and rained down about his feet.

"Throw a handful in the water," Jack said with a grin.

Puzzled, Mykl tossed some of his small payload over the rail.

The water below immediately erupted into a boiling frenzy of hungry fish. White bellies, silver sides, and flashes of color slithered to devour the tasty morsels. With a huge grin, Mykl heaved his remaining pellets as far as he could, creating a long plank of feeding fish so thick that he thought he could walk across them. A few bits of the fish food had stuck to his palm, and he flicked them into the water, causing minor eruptions wherever they landed.

"What kind of fish are they?" he asked.

"Rainbow trout. We keep a supply of food for them by the rail here for those that enjoy their feeding spectacle." Jack tapped a miniature Operations Center-shaped box mounted on the rail.

"I can't reach that," Mykl said.

Jack flipped down a built-in step, apparently made so children could help themselves to the fish food. It served as a reminder that Mykl had yet to see a single child since his arrival. Maybe they were all inside?

"Would you like to see inside the Ops Center now?"

"Sure."

The Operations Center lobby offered cushy couches arranged around low tables to create intimate islands for conversation. But there was no one around, and once again, Mykl found that more disturbing than if there had been a hundred people milling about. In this new realm, it appeared that nothing was predictable and no one was quite as they seemed.

A wide high-ceilinged hallway curved beyond Mykl's line of sight. They followed it to a flat-walled dead end.

Jack stood with his hands in his pockets and looked down at Mykl. "What do you think?" he asked.

"I think," Mykl said as he raised a hand, "that you are going to have to do better than that if you want to trick me."

He placed his palm on the wall. It split down the middle, and the two segments slid and disappeared to the sides. One thing Mykl understood clearly now was that any flat surface could be a passageway.

Jack gave Mykl's shoulder a companionable squeeze and said, "It's not my intention to trick you. I think we learn things better by doing rather than showing. And it's much more rewarding."

Ahead, the pearlescent hallway split into two carbon-black openings leading in opposite directions.

"Left or right?" Jack asked.

"I don't think it matters."

"Why?"

"The color. It reminds me of a movie theater entrance designed to trap light and keep it from getting inside. Both entrances most likely lead to the same place. Unless one is a devious trap leading to a machine that grinds up little kids into fish food?"

"I think you were in that asylum much too long," Jack said.

"Agreed. You go first."

Jack laughed. "Incidentally," he said, taking the left opening, "the fish don't eat little kids, but the chickens are quite fond of them."

"Uh-huh. Did you grow up in an asylum too?"

"No. I never grew up," Jack said. He gave Mykl a wink.

CHAPTER 35

An eerie, hushed twilight filled the massive auditorium as Mykl entered. Hundreds of plush reclining seats, on the large size even for an adult, filled the concave floor, facing in seemingly random directions. A blackened ceiling arched high overhead, barely visible in the darkness.

Jack took a seat near the center and beckoned for Mykl to join him.

"How often is this place filled with people?" Mykl asked. He winced at the loudness of his voice. The acoustics were amazing. He was willing to bet he and Jack could carry on a conversation in hushed tones from opposite ends of the room.

"It's been several years since it was last filled to capacity," Jack said.

Another half-answer. Whether Jack was being evasive, or just genuinely careful about divulging details, Mykl had yet to decide.

Mykl crawled into the seat closest to Jack's. His feet didn't even reach the edge of the bottom cushion, and with his arms fully extended to the sides, his fingertips barely made contact with the armrests. His chair was oriented with its back toward Jack's, so he turned around, leaned to the side, and peered at Jack with a "What now?" look.

"My apologies," Jack said. "These seats weren't designed with children in mind. If you lift the inside of the right armrest, you'll find a control pad. Seat adjustments are at the bottom."

Mykl withdrew the thin pad and placed it across his lap. It had an alphanumeric keyboard and a large empty space for drawing patterns, like Mykl had seen Jack do before. Pictograms on the bottom made for intuitive seat adjustments. A light touch rotated him slowly to face Jack. If all the seats had this capacity, then it made perfect sense for them to be spaced so far apart, so they couldn't bump into each other.

Jack ran a finger along the left edge of his control pad, causing the entire pad to glow slightly. Mykl managed to do the same before Jack entered a series of keystrokes that left them in total darkness. The pad in Mykl's lap provided a portable island of light to cling to in an empty black sea. He waited for the show to begin.

Jack's fingers blurred across his glowing pad and then—*Stars!*

It was like staring up into a perfectly clear evening sky. Mykl tilted his seat back and made a full rotation to take in the awesome spectacle. He could gaze at the stars for hours without feeling cold or getting a crick in his neck.

"This is the way the sky above us would look if it were dark outside. A geosynchronous orbiting telescope set to a wide-field view supplies the image feed."

"I like it," Mykl said. "Is the view adjustable from here?" His eyes danced over a long string of numbers and characters low on the horizon.

"All of our satellites can be controlled from any number of locations, including here." Jack began entering a new set of codes.

"Will I be permitted to…" Mykl paused ever so slightly to think of another word besides "play." He was certain that one did not *play* with satellites. "… manipulate any of them?" he finished.

With a hint of a smile and a quick glance at Mykl's not-so-innocent expression, Jack replied, "Once I've finished your orientation here, you will be allowed to… play with them all you wish. Your clearance level won't allow you to cause them any harm."

Mykl's control pad blocked his micro fist pump from Jack's view. He hoped.

Jack changed the star field, then manipulated a tiny circular cursor in the stars and settled it on an extremely faint pinpoint of light. "This is our own sun as viewed from a distance of approximately fifty light years. The unmanned research vessel that deployed the sensor package responsible for this image is still in transit to its destination. With the FTL relay, you could bring up a visual from the vessel, too, but the light would be severely red-shifted. Once it—"

"Wait," Mykl interrupted. Speaking directly at the center of the circular cursor, he said, "You're telling me that you can send commands to a probe that's *fifty* light years away… at faster than the speed of light?" This must be some sort of test. Jack couldn't possibly think he was so stupid to believe such nonsense.

"FTL probably isn't the most accurate statement," Jack amended.

Mykl smirked in the dark.

"Instantaneous would be a more precise term."

Mykl rubbed his eyes with the heels of his hands. "How?"

"There are particles in the nucleus of an atom—so small that they have yet to be discovered by the outside world—that when split, can be utilized for the passing of data almost instantaneously. No matter how far apart the split particles are, what happens to one, happens to the other. Discovering the particle was the easy part. Finding out how to manipulate it… now that was a challenge."

Slowly exhaling, Mykl sensed his mind spinning down into micro-atomic infinity. This sounded more like magic than science. With a deep sucking intake of breath, he brought himself back to reality.

"You have fusion," Mykl said, almost in accusation.

"Yes," Jack confirmed.

"You have FTL communication."

"Yes."

"You can make cities of diamond—out of dirt."

"Yes."

"Why not put all this technology out there for the world to use?"

"Do you know who Prometheus was, Mykl?"

"Um, mythical person who stole fire from the gods and gave it to man?"

"Exactly. Now, what do you think man would do today if he were given all the technology we possess here?"

"I… I don't know." Mykl didn't like the initial dark thoughts that came to him, and he certainly didn't want to share them.

"Take some time to think about Prometheus and what would happen if he were to be put on trial for his actions. Then determine if you would do things differently. Then and now."

"Is this like homework?"

"Your first assignment," Jack said. "You didn't think this was going to be easy, did you?"

"Ha! I didn't know school had started!"

Mykl admired the pseudo-stars. He didn't feel like delving into a philosophical trial for a mythical being yet. There were too many galaxies, stars, and planets to explore. He half expected to wake up from a dream and find himself back in the nightmare of the Box. If not for the very real puncture wound itching like crazy on his leg, he would have pinched himself. *This City could mean the end of science fiction and all its—*

He cut off his own thought to ask, "Are there any aliens down here?"

"Yes," Jack said. He switched off the stars, leaving the two of them in darkness but for the control panels that lit their faces dramatically from below.

Mykl noticed that Jack had answered his question immediately, without pausing to think. No time taken to make up a story or to deceive. Mykl was sure he would have gotten the same type of response had he asked for a drink of water.

"Is there any question I can ask where the answer won't shock me out of my socks?"

"Are you afraid of the truth, Mykl?"

"Is the truth a face-sucking monster?"

Jack laughed. "Would you like to meet him?"

"Who?"

"Our resident alien."

"Love to," Mykl replied. *This is* definitely *the end of science fiction.*

CHAPTER 36

A titanic flowing wave of black diamond leapt from the cavern wall. Frozen at the peak of its curl, it suggested an impending crash of monumental destruction, marking the entrance to the City's Research and Development facility.

"There're hidden fish rendered inside the wave if you know where to look," Jack said as he ushered Mykl inside.

Jack led Mykl down a brightly glowing hallway. Their curving path took them so far that Mykl thought they must certainly be beyond the boundaries of the cavern.

Finally, Jack stopped and poised his hand over a depression in the wall. "Ready?" he asked.

In the half hour it had taken them to get to this moment, Mykl had imagined a menagerie of alien creatures in an infinite variety of shapes, sizes, and colors. Jack had given him no hint or clue as to what to expect, nor had Mykl asked. This was a special moment, not to be spoiled by forewarning.

Mykl swallowed his anxiety and nodded warily at Jack, his eyes never leaving the door.

Swishing efficiently aside, the door revealed a narrow, high-ceilinged laboratory with low workstations bracketing a closed blast door directly opposite them. At Mykl's eye level, tables with wire cages sliced out from the wall between workstations. They all appeared to be empty. Like so much of the City, the room was unoccupied.

"Is he invisible?" Mykl whispered, leaning his head inside with his feet firmly planted outside.

"No, he's just very small. His name is Noah."

At the mention of the name, a small white furry head with tiny ears and beady black eyes popped up to peek through the wires of the closest cage. It wiggled its whiskers at Mykl.

Mykl took tentative steps toward it. The two beings locked eyes and blinked in unison, each no doubt wondering the intention of the other. Mykl furrowed his eyebrows in perplexed confusion. The caged being flicked the fluffy tip of its tail in curiosity. In the last few hours, Mykl had learned of the existence of technologies that could drastically change the future of life on the planet. Now, he stood nose to nose with…

"A mouse?"

Mykl raised his fingers to the tiny beast to let it sniff him. Wispy breaths puffed against his skin. The mouse rose on its hind legs to pat the spot on Mykl's finger where Dr. Lee had taken a blood sample, then in a cedar-scented explosion of wood shavings, it bounded to the far corner of its cage.

Apparently, science fiction was safe—for now.

"It's a very special mouse," Jack replied.

"Did I scare it?" Mykl frowned, but the mouse quickly returned. It reached out between the wires with both paws holding something out to Mykl. A split shell with a greenish seed inside.

"He likes you," Jack said. "He doesn't share his beloved pistachios with just anyone."

Mykl couldn't help but smile as he accepted the offering with thumb and forefinger. "Thank you, Noah."

The mouse raised a paw above its eye, then extended it out to Mykl.

"You pry the shell halves apart and eat the seed," Jack instructed. *He must have guessed that I've never seen a pistachio before*, Mykl thought. Which he appreciated, since he hadn't.

"Yum! These are good," Mykl said. Then he thought about the source of his treat. With a hand covering the side of his mouth, he whispered to Jack, "I'm not going to catch some alien mouse disease, am I?"

"Not to worry. Being an alien isn't contagious, only hereditary—or, in Noah's case, artificially induced."

Mykl blinked. "So it really is a mouse? I mean—an earth mouse? I mean—you know what I mean."

"In your online research at the asylum, did you ever delve into the history of space exploration?"

"Of course. Even when I was still with my... my mom."

"In the mid-1970s we acquired samples of soil, water, and ice from the inner planets, Jupiter, Saturn, and their moons. The most significant findings came from one moon orbiting Jupiter. Europa. Under its icy crust is an ocean teaming with a dormant virus. On the surface, in patches of shade, lives an ice lichen. Nothing intelligent, but—the virus, should it ever find its way into Earth's ecosystem, is capable of killing ninety percent of all multicellular organisms. Including all intelligent life."

Mykl instantly had misgivings about sharing Noah's food.

"The lichens proved to be the most interesting and useful of the specimens. Our researchers postulate that the constant hard radiation from Jupiter forced the lichens to evolve at an accelerated rate. Without constant radiation, dynamic changes could not have happened fast enough for it to adapt and survive in its harsh environment."

Jack removed a clear, puck-shaped item from a nearby workstation and handed it to Mykl. "This is the first sample of another living species in our solar system."

Mykl ran his fingers over the clear material. There wasn't any reason to ask what it was made of—he already knew. The sample inside resembled a heavily weathered rusty green paint chip. He could find something similar in the asylum quad without much effort.

"What makes it so special?" he asked, giving it back to Jack.

"With some genetic tweaking, we infected the lichen with the virus. The adaptive properties of the lichen then allowed for symbiotic interaction with carbon-based life forms." Jack indicated Noah, who waved an empty pistachio shell at him. "Normal lab mice only have a life span of about three years. Noah is sixty years old."

Jack returned the specimen to its place and invited Mykl to follow him. But Mykl paused beside Noah's cage. He felt sorry for the tiny critter. Sixty years in a cage wasn't living—it was a sentence. Fourteen months had been fourteen too many for Mykl in his own asylum prison. Pistachios or not, it seemed wrong.

He waved goodbye to Noah and followed Jack to the blast door.

They entered a space nearly identical to the safety vestibule they came through when Jack first brought them all to the City. Jack performed the opening routine, with Mykl observing every nuance. Finally, with a wait-until-you-see-this smile, Jack pushed open the second blast door and moved aside for Mykl.

Another cavern, even larger than the City's, beckoned. Towering trees near the entrance swayed gently in a warm breeze. The ground sloped down to a manicured park, which then gave way to fields of green crops in rows. Lakes, interconnected by meandering streams, softened the hard lines of the fields. Long shadows stretched away from rectangular sun strips, shining low to Mykl's left.

As Mykl wandered forward, Jack tapped his shoulder and pointed at the wall behind them, where a balcony was mounted. At first glance Mykl thought it was far away, then he realized it was just extremely scaled down. An attached slide spiraled several feet to the ground. He caught a glimpse of a tiny blur of white flying down the last few feet before it scampered off into the trees.

"You didn't think us so heartless as to keep our little friend locked away in a cage all these decades, did you?"

"Never crossed my mind…"

Jack had closed the door behind them, but now it opened again, and Delilah stepped through. She smiled at Mykl, then scowled at Jack.

"You," she said, pointing, "need to remember to carry your phone." She bent down to Mykl. "And you!" she said. "You need to wash up for supper. I bet your hands smell like fish food."

It seemed to Mykl that this woman never lost a bet.

She handed Jack his phone and shared some words that Mykl couldn't make out, but which clearly made Jack concerned.

Jack turned to Mykl. "I'm afraid I have to leave," he said. "I probably won't be back until late tonight. Lahlah will take you back." He mussed Mykl's hair and left in a hurry.

"Lahlah?" Mykl asked, looking up at Delilah, who was straightening his chocolate brown hair with caring fingers.

"Our rascal of a son pinned that one on me when he was young, and it's stuck ever since."

"It's pretty. I like it," Mykl declared to a pair of mesmerizing green eyes.

"Is that so? Well then, I have a proposition for you. How would you like to stay in the house with me and Jack? I'll even let you call me Lahlah."

This wasn't a woman who played fair. How could *anyone* possibly say no to those eyes—and that smile? He felt warm, safe… and loved. All he could manage to say without his voice breaking was, "Okay."

She took his hand to lead him out. "Still have to keep your room clean though, kiddo," she said with a wink.

When they passed by Noah's empty cage, Mykl asked, "With a whole…" Mykl searched for a word, "… world to explore in the other cavern, why would he ever come back to this cage?"

"Because that's where the pistachios are, silly."

CHAPTER 37

"Is he wearing the vest?" asked the agent with the binoculars.
"According to my sensor readings, yes," said the agent with the directional density scanner.
"Well, if he isn't, he's dead. Even with these reduced-velocity rounds," said the agent looking through a high-powered rifle scope.

***

Sebastian stretched after finishing a prerecording of his interview with a local news affiliate known to be sympathetic to whistleblowers. It had not gone as well as he'd anticipated, but in the end, everything worked out fine. They were ignorant as to who they were dealing with. Now, if tonight's viewers deemed his story credible, he could start parlaying his secrets into a meteoric payout.

"Our media people would like to know if you'll be staying in town tonight, Mr. Falstano?" the girl at the news studio's reception desk asked as he passed her.

"I certainly am," he replied. "Got an important dinner date." He paused to put on his sunglasses and admire his reflection in the tinted glass of the lobby windows. Not quite satisfied, he licked a finger to flatten an eyebrow…

***

"Now!"

***

A hole appeared in the dark tint an instant before his reflection fell in a cascade of tempered glass at his feet. Brilliant sunlight and searing pain hit him all at once. The heavy slug impacting his left breast pocket dropped him to his knees. Clutching his chest, he dove to the ground and squirmed through sharp bits of glass to hide behind a couch.

Squealing tires and acrid smoke marked the retreat of his would-be assassins.

Desperately, he ripped open his shirt, thrust a hand under the protective vest, and withdrew it. No blood. If he could have laughed at that moment, he would have. Until his breath returned, primal grunting noises would have to do. Still. *I'm alive!*

And I'm smarter than they are, he thought. Smart enough to be prepared for an attempt on his life. If they had aimed for his head they might have succeeded. If the glass hadn't slowed the bullet it might have had the energy to penetrate his vest. If he didn't always wear his sunglasses he might have been blinded by flying glass.

If, if, if. He had always been lucky. Today, many times over. And now they had given him all the credibility he needed—in the form of a copper-plated slug lodged in the chest plate of his vest.

Damn, that hurt though.

***

"Nice shot."
  "Thanks."

***

With the effortless grace of long practice, Jack drew the polished steel of an ebony-handled straight-edge razor along his neck. The razor had been an early anniversary gift from his wife; probably more of a hint than a gift.

"Rip? *Rip!*" someone yelled from outside.

Jack poked his head out his bathroom, his face half shaven. "Tony? I'm almost done here."

"No time, Rip. The chopper is hovering at the crow's nest. You can finish shaving on the way. We'll keep the ride smooth. Wouldn't want the Ripper cutting his own throat."

CHAPTER 38

James and Dawn were still talking and enjoying supper in her room when Mykl stopped by to pick up his belongings. He told Delilah to wait in the cart since it would only take him a second. His real reason was that it would have taken her a *half* second to notice the mess he'd left.

"Is she going to let you live, James?" Mykl asked.

He barely managed to duck a wadded napkin thrown by Dawn.

"We're continuing to discuss my fate," James joked. "But it's not looking good," he added as Dawn bounced an olive off his forehead.

"Any other comments, minion?" Dawn asked, plucking a cheese cube from her plate and cocking her wrist in Mykl's direction.

"No, no! I'm just passing through to pick up my things. I'll be staying with Jack and Delilah now that you two have each other to entertain."

Dawn frowned. "You're leaving us?"

"I'll only be a few minutes away."

"Well, be sure to visit," Dawn said with a sad pout.

"Between meals, you bet!"

A tiny yellow square whizzed past Mykl's ear as he ducked and ran.

Well, that's a good sign, he thought. She still had her feisty spirit, and James didn't have any new scratches.

He gathered up his pajamas, a spare pair of socks, and Lawrence's jacket to bring with him. The rest could wait. With his arms full, he hooked the pillow on the floor with his foot and flipped it up onto the bed. Shrugging, he thought, *Well, it's a start.*

***

Mykl's new room was no larger than his old one, but it had a homier feel to it, and less generic furnishings. He particularly liked his bed's blanket, which featured detailed sailing ships sewn at random angles. But the current ambiance setting was a dark underwater theme that felt a shade too claustrophobic for comfort, especially after experiencing the wide-open-space illusion in the main room.

Delilah removed all the adult-sized clothes from the drawers and closet, then told Mykl to make himself at home. Judging by the size of the clothes she had taken away, her son was fully grown. It was also apparent from the grooming accoutrements in the bathroom that he still visited every so often. Delilah returned with a brand-new toothbrush and added one more condition to his agreement with Jack.

As Mykl settled in—which mostly consisted of hanging Lawrence's jacket on the back of the chair—he noticed that this room did lack one important thing: a computer. He was about to investigate the desk when Delilah's voice came from the kitchen.

"Dinner's ready. Get it while it's hot!"

Mykl's stomach rumbled in anticipation. This computer issue could wait.

Delilah set their chairs next to each other at a corner of the table for easy conversation. Mykl's chair, while the same height in the back, had a much higher seat. It was an ingenious design of subtle steps and handholds; he could easily get in and out by himself without being lifted into it like a child.

Four steaming bowls sat atop the dining table. The largest overflowed with long, pale, rubbery shoelaces—or at least, that's what they looked like to Mykl. Next to it was a bowl of a cream-colored sauce. The smallest bowl on the table contained a chunky reddish sauce. The contents of the dish closest to him smelled familiar but he had never seen them served in this form before.

"Spaghetti?" he asked.

"And fettuccini," Delilah replied. "Take your pick. Mix and match. Whatever floats your boat."

"Why are the noodles so long?"

"You've never had spaghetti before?"

"We had it in the asylum lots of times, but the noodles were always really short." Mykl indicated a length between his thumb and forefinger.

Delilah gave Mykl a look that he deciphered as pity. She portioned out the long noodles on both their plates and layered on some of the wonderful smelling red sauce; the cream stuff smelled too much like feet, in Mykl's opinion.

"Allow me to show you why spaghetti noodles are supposed to be served long," she said. With one tine of her fork, she selected the end of a noodle and brought it to her lips. Slowly, to Mykl's amazement, she sucked the entire noodle into her mouth. "Now you try."

It didn't look that hard. Mykl scrutinized his noodles for a likely candidate, lifted an end to his lips, and slurped. Too fast. The tail end of the noodle flung to the bottom of his chin and whipped up to pelt him in the nose before disappearing in a wet smack between his lips. He felt slashes of sauce decorating his surprised face.

"And that," Delilah laughed, "is why spaghetti noodles are supposed to be long!"

And that, Mykl realized, *is why the Box kept them short.* Anything that could be used as a source of fun or entertainment was censored, suppressed, or, in this case, shortened.

For the rest of the meal, Delilah showed him all the different ways to wrangle slippery noodles, but none was more fun than the speed-slurp method. Mykl was sure he had sauce in his hair by the time they were done.

After Mykl helped carry his empty plate to the dishwashing "device" (to call it a machine didn't fit, since it had no moving parts), he broached the subject of a computer.

"It's there," she said. "Place your palm flat on the desk and tap your index finger twice. Your access level is already coded."

"Fascinating," Mykl said, arching an eyebrow at her.

She narrowed her eyes at him. "Have you watched any of the early color television science fiction shows?"

"No. Why?"

"You should."

"Indeed?"

She laughed. "You slay me, young man. Yes, indeed!"

Mykl wrung his hands together in excitement. *I have an "access level"!* He didn't know what restrictions they'd placed, but he was sure it meant explicit permission to roam on their computer network. No guessing of passwords, no clandestine midnight missions, and no demons waiting to prey on him from behind. *A computer of my very own.*

"May I go and…" He searched for a suitable word for using a computer in an ultra-secret underground city of diamond.

Smiling, Delilah bent down and, with a finger, lifted his chin to make him look into her twinkling eyes. "You may go *play* with your computer now."

"Thank you, Lahlah." He beamed.

Mykl literally ran to the desk. He climbed up into the chair and adjusted it to its highest setting. It was just right, though he wished something could be done about his dangling feet.

Palm flat. Tap twice. A large home screen flashed to life, level with his eyes, and an androgynous voice spoke in an overly friendly tone.

"Good evening, Mykl."

Oh, hell no!

"Um, voice response off, please?" Mykl requested, though he felt silly for talking to a computer. The text *[Verbal Mute]* glowed briefly, and he exhaled. He wasn't quite ready for a conversing computer yet. Swishy doors were enough for now.

Apart from the generically labeled icons, the screen before Mykl looked like a dark hole he could crawl into. He spared a quick glance to see if Delilah was near before scrambling up on the desk to make sure.

He pushed his hand against the screen. Solid. Any escape through this illusion would have to be made through his own imagination.

By accident, he discovered that sliding his hand along the wall moved the entire screen. If he wanted, he could drag it anywhere he desired. The icons turned out to be touch-activated as well. Lowering himself back into his chair, he got down to business— playing with the computer.

Simple labels such as *Internet*, *Satellites*, *Cameras*, and *Projects* made for easy navigation. He ignored the one labeled *User Introduction*. After all, he had years of experience with computers. They weren't that difficult.

Among the *Satellites* he discovered a subsection for *Planets*. Mykl knew exactly what he was after, and the folder did not disappoint. A page-long list of blue highlighted feeds streamed from Jupiter and its moons. He broke down and peeked into the *User* section to find out what colored highlights meant: blue was for FTL transmissions, green for mixed technologies, and red for external systems only. Good to know. With a few taps on his desk, a real-time image of Jupiter filled the darkness of his screen. If he concentrated hard on one location, he could make out subtle movement. Like watching clouds lazily morph on a sunny day.

"I have something for you, Mykl," Delilah called from behind, startling him. "Oh, got your mind in the stars, have you?"

Mykl simply turned his head and nodded. Guilty as charged. She was concealing something behind her back. He stiffened in alarm. The last time…

Delilah pulled a stunted brown creature with stiff legs and tiny ears from behind her and held it out to him. In the dim light, he couldn't see clearly. Was it dead?

"This belongs to my son, but I don't think he would mind if you had it."

Still in the chair, Mykl pushed himself away from the desk and spun to face her. She stepped to him and, with two hands, placed the creature gently in his lap. He took tentative possession with a loose grip. It certainly wasn't alive. Good thing, too. Its guts were spilling out through a hole in its side. And it was missing an eye. He peered up at her questioningly.

"It's a teddy bear," she said, as if that should explain everything.

"Oh," Mykl said, still not understanding. "What's it for?"

She gave him that look of pity once more. "You've never had a teddy bear before?"

Sadness slowly crept into him from the dark doors of his mind that he preferred to keep closed. His mom had promised him all sorts of odd things—things that he'd never allowed himself to discover the meaning of during his time in the Box. This was one of them.

In tight control of his voice, Mykl replied, "My mom used to say that *I* was her teddy bear." The lifeless blue eye staring up at him threatened to pry those doors open even further. Unbearable pain threatened to flood out if he didn't push them closed fast.

Two warm arms encircled him and squeezed the doors shut. "Of course she did. You'd make a great teddy bear. They're always willing to give unconditional love and protection when you're alone."

"Protection?"

"They keep monsters away."

That explained how it got disemboweled and lost an eye.

"You should give it a name though," she said.

A name. Hmm, what do I call a lovable, lifeless, incomplete hunk of monster repellent?

"What did your son call it... him... her?"

"Stinker."

Mykl felt like he had been punched in the gut. He hugged the bear to him. "Why?"

"Whenever he farted, he would blame the bear."

With his chin resting on top of the bear's head, Mykl spoke as if he were in an empty apartment, alone with his memories. "It's a good name," he said, wondering why his mother had called *him* Stinker.

Delilah ran her fingers once through his hair and scratched his back lightly with her fingernails. "Well, I'll leave you and Stinker to conquer the universe then," she said.

CHAPTER 39

Lori smiled confidently, oblivious to everything but her protective entourage. Law enforcement officials had deemed the city jail too dangerous to detain the Asylum Angel. The media continued to feast on her attempt to kill a five-year-old child, and police feared an angry mob might burn the jail in an effort to carry out vigilante justice. So she had been processed into the only prison for women in the state, for her own safety. The women's prison offered appropriate security and facilities to ensure Lori received the proper protection.

Two large female guards walked her through common areas as if she were on parade. Lori reached back and pulled her hair aside to rub one of the puncture wounds left by a stunner dart. *Bastard.* Another five minutes and that ranger would have shot himself to forget what she had done to that wretched child.

The guards advised that she would be permitted to shower before they moved her to a high-security solitary confinement wing. A shower would be nice. Then she would have sufficient privacy to start devising a strategy for her insanity defense.

The prison was unnaturally silent. Whenever she entered a new section, inmates stopped and stared, their bodies taut, as if they fought to control a desire to pounce. And Lori realized something, something that had been nagging at her from the moment she crossed the threshold

THE PROMETHEUS EFFECT

to general population. All the inmates she encountered had their hair shaved close to the scalp—but hers had been left long and loose. They may as well have tattooed "CHILD KILLER!" on her forehead; the difference made her stand out, as if a spotlight followed her every move, the unblinking eyes of her audience recording every step. The inmates had been forewarned of a visitor; the Asylum Angel had entered the lair of the damned.

All the inmates were women, and all had been sterilized so they would likely never have children again. For this reason, among others, the worst crime one could commit, in their judgment, was taking the life of a child. And walking among them now was the most notorious kind of child predator.

Lori questioned her guards about the security of the shower facilities, but the guards, too, remained silent as they held the door open for her. The large shower area possessed a single, weak light bulb. It struggled to produce a pale glow within the cloud of steam flowing from a nozzle in the center shower station. Hissing, hot mist bellowed forth but never seemed to reach the miniature white tiles below. The smell of sour sweat mingled with the heavy, damp air.

Lori stripped off her prison jumper and took long strides toward the glowing circle in the center. She wanted to hurry.

The brilliant flash of every light turning on at once momentarily blinded her. Then the thundering crash of the door slamming shut echoed through the room. When Lori's eyes readjusted, she found herself surrounded by feral faces.

She screamed for the guards. The door opened immediately, and two guards entered. One set a bottle of bleach on the floor. The second dropped a handful of scrub brushes. They winked at Lori before leaving and closing the door behind them.

Seventeen women circled Lori. One for each child she threatened to kill in the asylum. The shaved bodies of the prison Purity Clan glistened with sweat; they smiled at the opportunity to purify their world. They brandished prison shivs made from spoons, toothbrushes, popsicle sticks, lunch tray shards, even an old pork chop bone. Heat permeated the air, stifling Lori's ability to breathe, yet she shivered as if she were standing naked in the snow.

With a wild growl through teeth like a tattered picket fence, an inmate stepped in to grab Lori's hair. She wrapped it firmly around her wrist and pulled Lori's head back viciously while another woman chopped her fist down on Lori's exposed throat. With a hip thrust and twist of her shoulders, the first woman leveraged Lori off her feet by the hair and slammed her limp body hard, face first, on the slick floor, as if she were no more than a soaked towel. She hit with a sickening wet smack. With her larynx crushed and the wind knocked out of her by the force of the fall, she lay stunned and trembling.

Without uttering a word, the women descended upon her like jackals on injured prey.

Lori felt tiles press into her chest as they pinned her face near the drain, her limbs held in vise-like grasps. The only sounds escaping the shower were Lori's panicked, gurgling attempts to scream, and the soft grunts of her executioners' efforts to make dull shivs penetrate her pale skin. Blood serpentined along moldy grout lines. Eyes wide with terror, Lori watched her life slowly, and painfully, drain away.

CHAPTER 40

"Jessica, my syrup is cold," said a pasty-faced obese woman.

"I'm sorry, ma'am. I'll get you another."

Jessica retrieved the woman's miniature chrome pitcher, sticky with blueberry syrup, and marched back to the kitchen. She had been fortunate to get a job in a run-down twenty-four-hour pancake house. Unfortunately, the only hours offered were for the swing shift. Wearing a nametag and earning minimum wage, serving breakfast when people normally ate dinner, made for a very meager existence. Especially when those wages were garnished to pay off her student loan. The remainder went to her parents to pay the rent they charged her for moving back in with them. Still, it was better than completely giving up and living under a bridge like a troll.

"Here you go, ma'am," Jessica said as she placed another pitcher of syrup on the table, fresh from the warmer.

"Thank you. Could you turn up the volume on the television panel?" the obese woman asked through a mouthful of eggs.

Jessica was aware of the news story about to be aired and had been trying her best to avoid it. They had been pumping the story all day because of the unsuccessful assassination attempt. Her choice would have been to leave the TV off for the remainder of her shift. But she had to abide by the customer's choice.

She dragged a chair to the television and stepped up to adjust the volume.

***

"The government is harboring technology that could fix our energy problems," Sebastian told the interviewing reporter. "Fusion technology."

"And how do you know this?"

"Up until three months ago, I worked as a government agent."

"For which agency?"

"My cover identity was CIA. In actuality, I operated in a special division of the NSA."

"What division would that be? They usually don't intermingle."

"Special technologies." Sebastian smiled and relaxed into his chair. Dealing with reporters usually entailed a mix of chess and poker. He had to think several moves ahead and not pull out his ace in the hole until it was time to checkmate. This reporter seemed oblivious to the fact that he dealt with a pro. Sebastian played the game better than anyone.

"Alien technology?"

"No, of course not."

"Why were you fired?"

"They didn't say."

The reporter consulted his notes before continuing, "Everyone we've interviewed about government conspiracies in the past has turned out to be, if you will forgive the term, a crackpot. What evidence do you have to convince the common person that you are a trustworthy source?"

Sebastian knew if he divulged anything about aliens or alien artifacts, he would indeed be painted as a crackpot, and his credibility would be shot all to hell. He would fare little better if he told the truth. Few people wanted to know the truth these days, fewer still told it, and only a minute fraction lived it. And that truth-worshiping minority was of no use to Sebastian. He needed a much larger audience. One accustomed to living a lie, because it was easier and more comfortable than reality.

"I have NSA credentials and recent pay stubs if you wish to see hard evidence to confirm my previous employment." Sebastian pulled an envelope from his suit jacket and presented it to the reporter. "The badge has a DNA chip in it, though the encryption is likely no longer valid."

"Well, we use a similar security system here at the studio." The reporter smiled into the camera. "We'll take a look at these while we go to commercial break. Stay tuned!"

***

The obese woman most likely never even tasted the pancakes she shoveled away as easily as she breathed. "Jess, dear, may I have another plate of flapjacks please?"

"Sure."

Seeing Sebastian on TV was as close as Jessica ever wanted to be to him again. She was so glad the base guards at Nellis had allowed her to escape in a taxi before he was permitted to leave the bus. She was sure he would have followed if given a chance. But now, watching Sebastian divulge state secrets, she couldn't tear herself away from the train wreck she saw coming. TV reporters loved ruthless questions, and that last smile into the camera radiated pure malice. Sebastian's answers were supplying the rope for his own hanging—she just knew it.

She set another short-stack plate and warm syrup pot on the table.

"Oh, you are a dear. Reading my mind. Where did they ever find you at?"

***

"Welcome back. We're here with Sebastian Falstano, formerly a secret government agent… or was he?" The reporter turned from the camera to Sebastian. "Well, I have good news and bad news." The camera zoomed in on the holoprint ID between the reporter's thumb and index finger. "According to the chip in your ID badge, you are indeed Sebastian Falstano. Unfortunately, you don't even have enough player points on it to earn a free buffet dinner."

Sebastian shook his head. "What are you talking about?"

"Your ID badge is a player card for a local casino," the reporter said. He raised his eyebrows as if this was something Sebastian should already know. "Apparently the card's surface was carefully cleaned and holoprinted to look like authentic NSA credentials. Though, no one really does know what such credentials look like, do they?"

***

The obese lady let out a bark of laughter. Jessica suppressed an impulse to giggle as she lifted another sticky plate from the table.

***

Outwardly, Sebastian exuded calm. Inwardly, he fumed with rage. That card had gained him access to NSA headquarters in Fort Meade, Maryland, prior to his mission to evaluate the artifact. He had kept it in a safe deposit box until last week, and it had never been out of his possession since. Either the reporter was lying to embarrass him, or someone had switched his card out of the box. More likely the latter, but that meant they *planned* to dismiss him. Why?

The reporter pressed on. "The pay stubs you submitted would be even easier to fabricate. Do you really expect our viewers to believe a story about government conspiracies from a man with a fake ID?"

Sebastian unbuttoned his shirt and thrust his chest toward the reporter, exposing a neat circular scar in the center of his sternum. "I was shot and drugged to preserve the secrecy of the technology I witnessed on my last assignment."

"Enough, Mr. Falstano. Are you going to show us scars from your alien abductions next? Concrete proof, sir. If you don't have any, we're done here."

Sebastian maintained his poise. He reached into his shirt and withdraw a large manila envelope. It contained two color prints, which he laid on the table between himself and the reporter. They showed high-resolution satellite images of craters from an old nuclear test site. The same crater was circled in each image, with the differing features labeled.

"If you will compare the images," Sebastian said, "you will notice that a great deal of dirt has been moved to create a crater—and that same dirt has been relocated to add a finger to this mountain range here." He tapped the spot on the print. "Beneath this crater is a massive particle accelerator. Electromagnetic and thermologic jammers camouflage emissions to prevent its detection by foreign spy satellites. The first image can be found on the internet, on almost any nuclear history site. The second image can only be acquired by spy satellites."

The reporter picked up the prints, his eyes scanning rapidly between the two. "Why would the government build such a thing here?"

"What better place to build a secret installation than in an old nuclear crater near an abandoned, yet well-known, secret military base?"

"If memory serves me, that base was abandoned because it was severely contaminated by toxic waste."

"Wouldn't that keep away a curious person in search of concrete truth?" Sebastian tossed back.

The reporter nodded absentmindedly. "Okay. Big question. Why?"

"They developed fusion technology with that accelerator. The applications are limitless. Of course they would want to keep it to themselves."

The reporter dropped the prints back onto the table. "Even with these images, which the government is sure to have another explanation for, you're just a disgruntled ex-employee—if that. One man with a story. Without others to corroborate your evidence…" The reporter shrugged and let his words hang in the air like an invisible rope above his victim.

Sebastian pulled another print from the manila envelope and held it up. "Then ask her," he said.

The camera zoomed in on a photo of a woman.

"She worked in the accelerator facility and was escorted off the base the same day I was. She now works at Sticky's Pancake House. Her name is Jessica Stafford."

Checkmate.

***

"*Oh—my—God,*" the fat lady sang.

Damn that incompetent assassin. Jessica spun away before the plate she dropped hit the floor. Shards of white porcelain tinkled about her heels. She tore off her apron and nametag. With a backhanded flip, she tossed them behind her as she swept into the kitchen to retrieve her purse. One pale fleshy face stared openmouthed at her as she glided back through the restaurant and outside into the darkness.

She had underestimated him. That print of her was recent and actually taken *inside* her restaurant. She had to get away, somewhere, anywhere.

Up ahead, a transit bus was slowing to a stop. She boarded it. Sensors automatically debited the pass in her purse. It didn't matter where the bus was going; she didn't look, she didn't care. As long as it was moving away from the restaurant, that was good enough for her.

The phone in her purse rang. She pulled it out. It was her mother, probably calling to ask if that was her she had seen on television. She ignored the call, switched off the phone, and dropped it back into her purse. She couldn't go home, and she certainly couldn't go back to work. With only ten dollars in her purse and no credit card, her travel options consisted of this bus and her own two legs.

Damn him! He's trying to force me to support his story.

And she could do it, too. She could sell her side of the story and pay off everything. Selling her soul would be so easy. Being true to it had left her broke, jobless, and homeless. And besides, what was an oath besides vibrating vocal cords and scribbles on processed tree pulp? They certainly hadn't treated her fairly, or they would have investigated and known she was innocent. She had never had her integrity put to such a difficult test—

Wait.

Test!

Her hands flew to her face and slowly rose to the top of her head. She grabbed bunches of silky auburn hair in clenched fists.

She suddenly understood. Ever since she had taken that first entry-level civil service exam, she had been discreetly—no, deviously—tested. From the answers already circled on that exam to the classified folder in that polyhedral chamber. Honesty. Integrity. Trust. Words written on every document she signed. Until she proved herself worthy, her oath and signatures were worthless. And that meant… That meant everything she had seen was fake. They wouldn't divulge true secrets until she had proven she could keep meaningless ones.

It was obvious now. It would have been so pitifully easy for them to fabricate everything she had seen. A standard home computer could have run the program mimicking space probe feeds. 3D LCD screens must have been the walls, and the classified folder had to contain a tasty tidbit on some other faux technology. Bastards. *They cuffed me in that seat next to Sebastian on purpose!*

With a new perspective on things, Jessica smoothed back her hair and relaxed.

Her phone buzzed again. That was weird; she was sure she had turned it off. She removed it from her purse and looked at the dark screen. It was definitely turned off.

That's the answer. Sitting right in my palm. If she was right about everything, then she had no doubt they had modified her phone, tracked it, tapped it.

Feeling a tad crazy, she spoke to the powered-down phone. "Your move, Jack."

Melancholy tainted her anticipation. Up until a few minutes ago, faster-than-light technology had existed, and for a brief moment, so did fusion. Someday it still might.

She pushed those thoughts aside. Her immediate need was to avoid Sebastian, the media, and anyone who might recognize her from that broadcast. She couldn't ride on this bus forever; it would eventually reach the end of its scheduled route. She would need to—

The phone vibrated in her hand, sending a chill up her arm that coursed through her body. The screen lit and displayed the text: *E PLURIBUS UNUM*.

Jessica groaned. *Will the tests never cease?*

The E Pluribus Unum, owned and operated by the government, enjoyed the distinction of being the largest casino in Vegas, if not the world, sprawling over two city blocks. The government purchased Caesars Palace and the Bellagio and imploded the buildings in spectacular fashion, then created a new megacasino on the combined property. Even from a mile away, it looked like you could reach out and touch it. In the history of government projects, this had proved the most successful. Not only did it turn a hefty profit every year, but even in the event of a lucky streak by a patron, the government immediately took half their winnings.

Unfortunately, Jessica's bus was heading in the wrong direction. *Well, it's not much farther to the next stop. I can get off and head back on foot. A brisk walk will do me good.*

* * *

At the neon-lit porte-cochère, Jessica slowed her pace. She didn't know where to go, but thought it wise to disappear among the sea of gamblers and tourists inside. Stale cigarette smoke and the drone of thousands of gaming machines filled the air.

A cocktail waitress brushed past her and whispered, "Tower one, elevator five," before yelling out once again, "Cocktails!"

Jessica made her way to the bank of elevators in tower one. A handful of people were already waiting. One kept pushing the call button as if it would speed up the process. She didn't want to be in the same elevator with a button-mashing moron and reverently hoped car number five would be empty.

Strobes began flashing throughout the casino, accompanied by a piercing wail. A calm voice recording began repeating a request to

"Please exit the building." Apparently the fire alarm had been activated.

But no one seemed to care. When the elevators arrived, those inside exited, and those who had been waiting entered. Normally, Jessica would have judged this to be an idiot test, for no intelligent person would get into an elevator during a fire. Fortunately, they had long ago made elevators smarter than the "sheeple" who abused them. During a fire they were designed to return to the lowest uninvolved fire floor, open their doors, and remain open and unmoving until the fire department determined they were safe to use.

It took a few moments of button-mashing for the new occupants to give up and exit the unresponsive transports. Jessica waited until they were clear, then she stepped into car number five.

Every surface inside the elevator mirrored her reflection, except the floor. She tried to make herself presentable. How did one greet Jack the Ripper?

The elevator doors started to close, but before they closed all the way, a man moved swiftly through the slivered opening.

"Hello, Jessica," Sebastian said between breaths as if he had been running. He removed a subcompact pistol from his jacket.

Jessica slowly lowered a hand from her hair.

"Expecting someone else?" Sebastian asked while wiping sweat from his forehead with the back of his hand.

Completely caught off guard, she replied, "That's none of your business."

The elevator rose.

"My business is exactly what this is about. I need you to corroborate my story." He waggled the pistol at her. "You dead works fine with me, but it would be less messy if you cooperated."

Sebastian pushed several buttons on the panel, but they kept going up. "Where are we going?" he asked.

"How should I know?"

"Don't play stupid with me, bitch!" he yelled. "You raced all the way here like you were on a mission. Now what is it?"

They were over fifty levels up now and still climbing. As fast as they were moving, it wouldn't take long to get to roof level. She needed to stall him. "You had me followed?" she asked.

"Of course. You didn't think you could disappear unobserved, did you? I knew who you were before you went to bed that first night home from the base. A hundred dollars goes a long way in bribing a taxi driver, and a thousand will buy a *lot* of pancakes," he smirked.

Now Jessica was mad. She had been nice to that slack-faced cow. To know now that she had been spying on her raised her hackles.

The elevator slowed, and the letter "R" glowed in the destination window.

Sebastian shoved Jessica in front of him as the door opened.

A slender man in a well-tailored gray suit waited in the elevator vestibule. Kneeling at his sides were men with readied automatic weapons. Another stood behind him, scanning the area.

The suited man smiled when he saw Jessica—but then he saw Sebastian, and he clenched his jaw. "I told you to come alone!" He struck Jessica's face with a backhanded blow, sending her sprawling to the back corner of the elevator.

Sebastian raised his pistol.

"Well, well," the suited man said, "if it isn't Sebastian. Shoot him."

"Wait!" Sebastian cried. He immediately dropped his weapon, which was retrieved by one of the armed men.

The suited man made a signal to forestall the execution. "Why should we let you live?" he asked. He pointed at Jessica. "She's selling us fusion technology. What have you got—besides a grudge about having been fired?"

This was news to Sebastian. He had figured Jessica for the goody-goody type, not someone devious enough to toil at a minimum-wage job while marketing state secrets. She had him at a disadvantage. He had to risk upping the ante.

"The location of something even greater," he said.

"Greater than fusion?"

"Yes."

"Bullshit. What is it?"

Sebastian swallowed. "An alien artifact. Recently discovered on the moon. Its technology has been operating for over a billion years with an unknown energy source."

"You expect me to believe that?"

"It's hidden in a cave on Earth now, only accessible by submarine. They drugged me to protect its location, but I found out anyway. According to intelligence reports in a classified file, they're afraid to move it."

"Miss Stafford, can you verify his story?" the man asked.

Blood ran from Jessica's nose and dripped into a shiny warm puddle. She looked up at the man who had struck her—the man who now had the gall to want her to answer his questions. She clenched her jaw in defiance.

"I asked you a question," the man said, stepping toward her menacingly. He went to a knee beside her and pulled the left side of his jacket open. From an inside pocket, he withdrew an ebony-handled straight razor and smoothly thumbed open the blade. In a calm, deliberate motion, he placed its cold edge against the thin skin below her jaw line. She shivered. A simple flick of his wrist would sever her from this life.

"Answer," he demanded. "The truth."

Jessica felt her pulse struggling to beat against the pressure of the razor. He had deceived her, struck her and now he threatened to take her life.

But she was unafraid. For when he had opened his jacket, she had seen, hanging from a silver clip on his inside coat pocket, a military identification badge—with a name she recognized.

She looked up at him. He gave her an imperceptible nod and a wink.

His actions had saved her life. She wanted to hug this man holding a deadly weapon to her throat. Jack the Ripper, indeed.

CHAPTER 41

In a windswept crater, a robotic rover on Mars built a sandcastle at the commands of its new controller. Mykl yawned. This wasn't quite as much fun as he had thought it would be. Nor was the quick tour of solar system camera feeds. The novelty of different-colored dirt wears off fast when you can't actually touch it. He smoothed the castle back into the depression he created and returned the rover to its default settings. Now if a different country's rover happened to come across his work, there would be no incriminating evidence. It was a good thing the City had the only functioning probes on the planet.

"You still up?" Delilah asked from the doorway.

"Too much to explore," Mykl answered.

"Jack is on his way back with another guest if you would like to meet them when they arrive."

"Someone new to the City?" Mykl looked forward to seeing someone else's first reaction to the place.

"Yes, she finally passed her tests to get in."

"Like my tests?"

"Mmm…" Delilah rubbed her hands together and stared at the ceiling while contemplating his question. "Harder, I would say."

"Really? This is someone I have to meet."

THE PROMETHEUS EFFECT

***

Much to Jessica's surprise, Sebastian's weapon was returned to him, and Jack offered him a deal. If Sebastian could bring him the artifact, Jack promised a payout involving more zeros than he had fingers. Sebastian departed happily, his elevator taking the same direction as his fate.

"Please accept my apologies for striking you, Miss Stafford," Jack said. He offered her his handkerchief.

"The way I see it," Jessica said, taking the handkerchief to squelch the blood flowing from her nose, "it's the least painful part of what you've already put me through. But worth it to get rid of that ass."

"Sebastian's predictability makes him one of our greatest assets. Though his mission is still incomplete."

Jessica blinked in astonishment. "He's working for you?"

"He's been volunteering for us for many years now, but he doesn't realize it. He is the best at what he does."

"Did he have to take the same oath that I did?"

"Most certainly."

"But—I'm nothing like him!"

"You wouldn't be standing here if you were."

Jessica had a million questions to ask. But, as a woman, one needed to be asked first. "Why do you go by 'Jack the Ripper'?"

The men standing with Jack appeared at ease with her question, like they had heard the answer many times before. Even in tactical gear bristling with deadly weapons, their faces assumed a look of non-threatening respect. This didn't feel like a group intending to abduct her. It was more like an honor guard here as an escort.

"The original Jack the Ripper tried to improve society by killing what he thought were the undesirable dregs of civilization. My friends call me by that name because I rip from existence the best people the world has to offer—in order to allow them to reach their greatest potential."

"Am I the best the world has to offer?" Jessica asked meekly.

"One of many," he replied. "Would you like to meet others?" Jack motioned to the waiting helicopter beyond the glass vestibule.

"All right, but one more thing…"

Jack raised his eyebrows.

"Why do you carry a straight razor in your pocket?"

***

On the short flight out beyond the city glow and into barren desert darkness, Jack provided answers to Jessica's questions. She still had more as they disembarked at a pine tree-lined mountain ledge. Everyone, she learned, had to pass a test of some sort to become a member of Jack's organization. Her test just happened to be the hardest and most diabolical. Jessica had proven to be one of a very select few with the moral character needed to succeed. Now it was Jack's turn to hold up his end of the bargain.

As the helicopter peeled away, chilling winds from its rotors buffeted treetops and pressed her skirt against her legs. Jack beckoned her to follow him under a rock outcropping. Rough boulders served as solid steps leading upward to a cave suitable for a hermit. Someone had had the wit to mount a doorknob and doorknocker on the back wall.

Jack tapped the doorknocker twice and waited. *This must be another test*, Jessica thought. Then the ground beneath them, a disk of coarse rock, began to descend. Light streamed in in a circle from all sides until glistening clear surfaces of a much larger space surrounded them.

They stepped off onto a textured translucent floor.

"What is the power source for all this?" Jessica asked.

"What would you like it to be?" Jack replied.

She ran her fingers along a wall. It had a soapy crystalline feel instead of slick glass. Turning to face Jack, she said, "I would like it to be *real*."

"Can you survive another ten minutes in an elevator?"

"I'm sure it beats the stairs."

Three parallel tracks ran from floor to ceiling around them. As far as Jessica could determine, they were the only devices holding this transparent cylinder—that Jack called an elevator—in place. Jack urged her to grip a safety railing. Slowly, the illusion of rising walls took hold as they started to descend. Then they became a blur of motion. She was alone and plummeting into the secret lair of a man called Jack the Ripper—and yet she felt safe.

After all, he had been truthful about why he had the razor. The elevator smelled of shaving cream.

Gravity eased its grip, and Jessica estimated they were one third of the way to weightlessness. Minutes passed before she once again sensed the soles of her feet pressing normally against the floor. How far had they dropped? In the final minute of descent, the encompassing rock became dark and an invisible heaviness enveloped her; then motionless silence.

"Welcome to the City, Miss Stafford."

The grand spectacle before her defied the imagination. It couldn't possibly be real. There was nothing on earth like it. If this was another computer-generated illusion, it was far more remarkable than her test in the polyhedral room. She took a step forward with a hand extended, as if to touch it.

"It's real."

The voice came from in front of her instead of behind, and it sounded much, much, younger than Jack's. A small boy in blue pajamas and bright white socks seemed to have materialized out of thin air. He wore a quirk of a smile and stared up at her through inquisitive copper eyes. A tattered teddy bear dangled from his hand, its furry foot hovering an inch off the ground. The kid was adorable, but… odd.

"Where did you come from?" she asked.

"Jessica, this is Mykl… who, at midnight no less, *should* be in bed right now," Jack said.

"Hello," the boy said.

"Hello, Mykl."

***

Mykl took a step back to better see the adults towering over him. The girl was pretty, like his mom, but with a less secretive air about her.

He flung an arm behind him. "Do you like it?"

"Are you sure it's real?" Jessica asked, still not quite certain.

"Can I take her on the tour in the morning, Jack?"

"Sure. Just don't show her any of the secret stuff."

"But…"

Jack winked.

"Funny," Mykl said.

"What's funny?" Jessica asked.

"Come on." Mykl took her by the hand. "We have to kill you now."

"Oh, good," she said. "It's about time. I was already getting way too bored here."

Surprised at having his sarcasm thrown back at him, Mykl looked up at her, and they both burst out laughing. *This one's a keeper.*

Mykl was allowed to tag along with Jack and his new recruit to settle her into a room several doors from his original one. Mykl even performed a brief introduction to the workings of the lights and amenities. They decided on an arctic winter aurora motif for her ambiance setting, then Mykl promised to collect her in the morning for a tour.

Back in his own room, Mykl set his own ambiance to the star field Jack had used in the Operations Center. He didn't find the satellite feed listed in his folders, but it was simply a matter of recalling strings of numbers and characters and entering them as an ambiance preset. With Stinker to protect him, he drifted off to sleep, warm and blissful under a blanket of ships in a sea of stars.

CHAPTER 42

Twelve million miles away, a mindless agent of destruction tumbled silently in the cold vacuum of space at over seventy thousand miles per hour. Camouflaged on its scarred surface was a propulsion system specifically designed for one purpose: to bring the wayward beast home and turn it loose. Like the eyes of a wolf, a stealthy probe kept careful watch on its prey—and the two brothers preceding it.

Mykl awoke with a start to flashing lights all around him. Scarlet red lines slashed brilliantly across his star field as the image rotated and changed perspectives. The visual illusion made his bed feel like a lifeboat being tossed in a stormy sea. More colored trails mirrored the first. He did his best to track the lines and make sense of them. Another perspective change tossed him farther out into space, making him dizzy.

He soon saw that every line terminated at the same fuzzy bluish dot. And as the dot grew larger, Mykl recognized it—for he had played with its replica many times.

Between blinks, the image changed again. Reflexively, Mykl thrust his bear between him and the tumbling asteroid. He pressed himself deeper into his bed as it threatened to crush him.

"Wake up, dumbass," Mykl chastised himself. "It's just a picture."

He jumped down from the bed to find out what was playing havoc with his ambiance setting. The door to Jack's office was open, and the lights within flashed in time with those in his room. He walked to Jack's door and stopped at its threshold.

Jack immediately froze the image with a slap of his palm on the desk. A projected scarlet streak cut Mykl's silhouette in half, from shoulder to hip and through the eyeless socket of the bear at his side.

"What…" Mykl raised his bear to the static image of sharply shadowed rock.

Jack took in a breath and let it out slowly. "I'm sorry, Mykl," he said. "I thought you were asleep."

"I was. All the flashing in my room woke me up."

"In *your* room?"

"I set it to the same star field you showed me in the Operations Center."

"Of course you did," Jack said softly to himself. He crossed an arm over his chest and pinched the bridge of his nose, then moved his hand to cover his mouth and gave Mykl an appraising stare. Finally he lowered his hand to indicate the chair next to him. "Take a seat," he said.

Mykl clambered into the chair with Stinker clutched tightly to his chest. "It's going to hit us, isn't it?" he asked, indicating the asteroid.

"Yes."

"But, I thought you said you were able to prevent that kind of thing from happening."

"I can."

"So…"

"There's a reason."

Mykl leaned back and furrowed his brow. He couldn't think of a single reason why anyone would let an asteroid hit the planet if they could prevent it.

"This asteroid and the two preceding it," Jack said, "are not on a random trajectory. Their courses have been altered to ensure they hit not just the Earth, but the United States. The country controlling them has tried twice in the recent past to do the same thing, but our organization was able to thwart both efforts. However, I can't keep causing 'rocket malfunctions' and 'communication glitches' without them becoming suspicious. Especially when they instituted a triple redundancy of every system, including rockets, on this launch. Were I to put a stop to this, the finger of suspicion could only be directed at the United States. It would be enough to start a war. By allowing this mission to go as planned, it buys us time."

Mykl shook his head. "Buy us time for what?"

"The window for developing alternative energies to replace the world's reliance on fossil fuels closed long ago. Most people believe the published scientific data that claims we still have several hundred years' worth of oil to burn. The truth is, at current consumption rates, we have only twenty. A handful of nations are getting close to discovering this, and they aren't sharing their findings. Instead, they are playing an international game of chess to gain control of the last reserves. It's the main reason the US has relied on foreign oil all these years. The plan all along was to keep its own oil fields in reserve for when the rest of the world ran dry.

"A solid plan, except for one thing: history has shown repeatedly that if one side has what the other desperately needs, desperate measures will be used to acquire it."

Jack gestured to the screens. "China is the country responsible for these three asteroids—although it could just as easily have been any of the other space-exploring countries at odds with the United States. But China does not know the full consequences of their actions. They thought they were clever: they selected asteroids large enough to do precisely enough damage to preselected targets without causing any lasting effects to the planet. What they did not account for, since it is unknown to them, is the Europa virus. It has been found in a dormant state on many asteroids we have surveyed. The release of that virus on Earth would end all human life.

"So: we have neutralized the virus on these three asteroids. Furthermore, I severed China's data feed from the asteroids more than a month ago. Up until the last transmission, everything confirmed an optimal trajectory. But we will allow only one of those asteroids to impact—and at a place of *our* choosing. The other two will bounce harmlessly, albeit quite dramatically, off the atmosphere.

"However, when China fails to achieve their intended goal, they *will* try again—or some other country will do so. Unless we do something to stop them."

Life must be easy for those who go through it oblivious to reality, Mykl thought. As if the threat of nuclear Armageddon wasn't enough, now humans had learned to lob asteroids at each other like snowballs. Lethal virus-laden snowballs at that.

"What are you going to do about it?" Mykl asked.

"You like puzzles. What do *you* think can be done about it?"

"Besides start over?" Mykl replied flippantly.

Jack leaned forward to rest his elbows on the desk. Several seconds of silence passed before he asked softly, "Could you do that, Mykl?"

"Do what?"

"Kill everyone on the planet to settle the world's problems." Jack waited for an answer.

"I—I don't think—"

The thought of a few well-placed meteors erasing major problems in the world popped into his head. No. That was playing with fire. No wonder Prometheus got into so much trouble.

"No. I couldn't. Any solution that involves extinction isn't a solution. It's another problem."

Jack nodded. "Ideas are easy to come by. Finding solutions that don't lead to further problems takes a great deal more thought—and planning."

"Like releasing City technology." Mykl's mind started clacking down the rails into the dark tunnel of that possibility. "If only the United States had it, then other countries would attack preemptively to try and acquire it."

"Or out of fear," Jack added.

"And giving it to the whole world at the same time"—*stealing fire from the gods and giving it to man*—"would mean any country could destroy the world, and they wouldn't need nukes or asteroids. And they could do it…"

"Faster than the speed of light," Jack finished.

Mykl felt a sudden chill. *How do you get people to look past their petty differences of politics, culture, and religion, when* life *is the larger matter at stake?*

Jack blanked all the screens in his office, leaving only the cool glow of an overhead waning crescent moon for light. "Come on," he said. "I'll tuck you back into bed. We're not going to be able to solve all the world's problems tonight."

Before Jack left Mykl's room, he set the ambiance to *Voyager*'s forward camera view. "There you go. It should be smooth sailing for the rest of the night. But if you wake to an alien invasion fleet filling the screen, be sure to come get me. Sweet dreams!"

Stinker's all-seeing eye hid Mykl's smile at Jack's joke. Still, he spared one last glance at the empty stars—just to be sure.

***

Back at his desk, Jack finally had a moment to view his priority messages. Three from Dr. Lee were coded urgent. After reading the first, his expression turned grim. The second had him puzzled and alarmed. And he had to work hard to contain his fury after finishing the third. One of her patients was dying, another was dead, and one was going to *wish* he was dead when Jack saw him again.

No. That kind of anger was irrational and unfair. Fury melted into futility, and finally acceptance, as he reasoned out the ironic inevitability. There was already enough tragedy in the truth, and he was powerless to alter it. And even if he could alter it, no agency could persuade him do so.

However, there were issues in which he did have the authority to make a difference, and no time to waste. He tapped the "acknowledge" link in Dr. Lee's message. While waiting for her reply, he composed a note to the person who, before today, was his most trusted agent.

His desk chimed.

"Cindy? Good, you're still up. Collect Dawn. I'll meet you at the cryo-lab."

CHAPTER 43

Soft sounds spiraled Dawn up from the shadowy well of her fitful slumber. Someone kept calling her name.

"Daherlee? Whatimeisit?" she said groggily.

"It's about four thirty in the morning."

Dawn groaned and scrunched into her pillow.

"Jack approved your procedure. We didn't think we should wait a moment longer than necessary to start. He's waiting for you at the lab to answer your questions."

Dawn's eyes flicked open to a more conscious level of darkness. She started to raise herself from the bed and felt the gentle pressure of a warm hand holding her down.

"Relax," Dr. Lee said. "I don't want you moving around too much. Let us do all the work."

Two pairs of arms cradled her from the warm soft bed, pillow and all, to the cool stiffness of a gurney. Dawn shivered and curled into a fetal position to regain her lost warmth. She hated being cold almost as much as she hated being blind.

**

Once again, Dawn found herself in a foreign place. And it smelled funny, in that it lacked any odor at all. After the door closed behind her, she sensed a pressure in her ears in conjunction with a quick hiss. She suspected the air was sterile but had no idea if its pressurization was to keep something from getting in or from escaping.

Muted, industrious activity commenced behind her. Metallic clinking synced with Dr. Lee's clipped whispering of medical jargon. A smooth warmth filled one of Dawn's hands and squeezed.

"Sorry to have woken you, Dawn," Jack said, completely enveloping her delicate hand with both of his.

"Dr. Lee said time was critical. You've given your consent?"

"It's not my consent that's important right now. It's yours. The choice you make is yours alone. Before you make it, let me fill you in on what this procedure involves…"

Dawn listened intently as Jack recounted the history of the City's amazing medical discovery. Like any medical procedure, it had had its share of failures along with its successes. Unexpected side effects were still being catalogued to this day. The ability to eradicate certain cancers was one such side effect. But it had never been tried on a malignant brain tumor as advanced as hers.

"If curing cancer is a side effect, then what was it originally meant for?" Dawn asked.

"Space travel."

Jack went on to explain the drawbacks and limitations of the human body with regard to travel in the frigid pathways of space. And how, quite by accident, one of their first test subjects thawed the way to make it feasible. While that first test subject was not human, nor a volunteer, all subsequent human subjects *were* volunteers. And only a minute fraction of the thousands of recent volunteers qualified as being *currently alive*.

Dawn's blue eyes stared coldly into the eternal distance beyond her senses. *I must be mad to be considering this. The cure contains elements from my worst nightmares. Who in their right mind… Well, that's it, isn't it? My mind isn't right, and the icy clarity of my thoughts is melting by the minute.*

"So, what you're telling me is," Dawn angled her head toward Jack, "what kills you makes you stronger?"

"That's one way of putting it, I suppose."

"I'm ready to stop living then, if that's what it's going to take to kill this thing inside me."

"Cindy will see to the rest of your needs." Jack brushed a lock of hair from Dawn's face. "Oh, by the way, you will also lose all of your hair… temporarily."

"Dammit. How thoughtful of you to save the worst for last."

Dr. Lee explained the steps of the procedure in detail while her assistants prepped the equipment.

"May I have a pen and paper to write on? I want to try and write messages for James and Mykl before we start."

"I can write for you, if it would make it easier."

"I would rather try it myself so they know it was written by me. I think I still remember how to make the letters. But could you check them when I'm done and let me know if they're right?"

"That I can do."

Dawn knew what she wanted to write; she just had to concentrate on the shapes of the letters. It had been years since her last attempt to write. She practiced the letters in the air with the tip of her pen until she felt satisfied putting them to paper. She was sure the end results were barely legible, but Dr. Lee pronounced them readable enough and placed them in envelopes.

Dawn also requested that two locks of her hair be snipped off, one to be added to each envelope. When that was done, she lay back and waited.

An assistant shaved Dawn's long black hair close to the scalp. Her shorn skin felt tingly and light, though deep inside was the ever-present throbbing menace. Her nightgown was replaced with a protective, hooded skin-suit that provided ports for IVs and a catheter. The IVs were expertly placed; she felt only a tiny pinching sensation. For her comfort, catheterization wouldn't be done until after she was sedated.

"Are you ready, Dawn?"

"I always wanted to be a princess. I never guessed I would end up as Snow White."

"May you live happily ever after," Dr. Lee said as she introduced an alien virus into Dawn's vein.

The cool flow of the IV solution crept up the vein in Dawn's arm from the injection site, then swirled into her heart to be circulated throughout her body. Her heart began to beat more urgently, as if it knew the body's desperate need for this elixir… or perhaps it did so out of abject fear. It would take at least twenty-four hours for the virus to incorporate itself fully into Dawn's cells. Then her life would be suspended.

"I'm going to sedate you now, Dawn. See you soon."

Dr. Lee released the flow of the second IV into Dawn's other arm. Relaxing warmth spread slowly from her navel to her extremities. Her body floated upward to the sky. She wondered if she would ever feel the sun on her face again.

In her last seconds of consciousness, a dazzling flash of light exploded behind her eyes. It was blue—she could swear it was *blue*! Then time… stopped.

"Begin cooling."

***

Wearily, Jack crawled into bed next to his wife.

"Is everything okay?" Delilah asked.

"I've recalled Kyle from assignment. It's time for a family meeting."

"Oh? What's that rascal done now?"

"Patience, my love."

Jack reached out in the dark to caress his wife's cheek. He used the last of his energy to share a soft, lingering goodnight kiss. Then he wrapped his arms around her with a contented sigh.

"Yeah, you still owe me," she said with a smile.

"Mm-hmm," Jack replied as exhaustion finally claimed him.

CHAPTER 44

Stretching like a cat in a sunbeam, Mykl shed the lingering layers of fugue from his mind. Stinker appeared to have fallen victim to a pouncing wild pillow roaming the oversized bed during the night. Its tiny body lay crushed under the pillow's weight, with two fuzzy legs poking out from underneath.

A hint of an unwashed odor reminiscent of the Box tickled Mykl's nose. He determined that the scent was emanating from himself, and he realized he hadn't bathed since right before his abduction interview. A few splashes of water to the face weren't going to cut it today.

The bathroom contained a large circular tub next to a sink-and-mirror setup on one wall, and directly opposite, an opening framed by curving translucent walls. A shallow alcove contained fluffy white towels. Farther in was a domed shower enclosure with a bench seat.

He dropped his pajamas by the alcove and stepped into the shower, which automatically lit up. The controls—assuming that's what the two sets of buttons set in diamond formation were—had no instructions. All four buttons to the left gleamed metallic gold, but the four buttons on the right varied in color: red for the left button, blue for the right, and gold for the top and bottom buttons. *Red and blue. Has to be for hot and cold*, Mykl thought. He touched the blue one, thinking a surprise of cold water was preferable to hot. Nothing happened. He touched the entire diamond array of gold buttons to the left with no effect.

"Well thbbbt."

But when he tapped the top gold button on the right, he was immediately assaulted by jets of cold water from all sides—including above and below.

"CHEEYAAH!" Mykl scampered away from the frosty spray.

Dripping, shivering, and wearing only a scowl, Mykl had an epiphany and tapped the wall next to the alcove twice. A shower control screen appeared. It had a myriad of self-explanatory settings.

Flow Direction. Mykl turned off the floor jets. *That's just weird.*

Force. Medium.

Scent. Why in the world would anyone want scented water?

Temperature. He checked to be sure it wasn't in centigrade, then set it for eighty degrees.

He stepped back into the warm, *unscented* water. Eighty was a bit too low, so he used the red button to bump up the heat to "just right." He raised his arms and twirled in a slow circle, letting the warm jets douse him. *Now this is a shower!*

Soap? He held out his hands to block inconveniently aimed jets from hitting him in the face as he searched for anything that might resemble soap.

Opposite the bench were three plum-sized protrusions. He held his hand under one; nothing happened. He touched it, and a viscous amber liquid squirted to the roughly textured floor. *Oh, the comedy of trial and error*, he thought. This shower obviously wasn't set up for a person of his stature. He tilted his head under the first protrusion, closed his eyes, and tapped it. Soap at last. It even smelled good.

In his exuberance of lathering up, Mykl accidentally drew a hand roughly over his wound. The scab sloughed off, and Mykl looked down expecting to see blood. He was surprised to see only a pink circular scar accentuated by the paleness of his undamaged skin.

Completely healed in less than two days? Dr. Lee would certainly be interested in that bit of news. Which was precisely why Mykl had no intention of letting her know. Curious doctors were the worst kind when it came to poking and prodding their victims. He was healed. That was good enough.

Rinsed, dried, and dressed, Mykl deemed himself ready to keep his appointment with Jessica. He rescued Stinker from his pillow predicament with a bounding leap to the center of the bed and a butt-bouncing dismount to the carpet.

Mykl skipped halfway through the living room before deciding he was getting too old to be carrying a teddy bear around all the time. He tossed it unceremoniously into his room. Two steps later, wracked with guilt, he retrieved Stinker from the floor and propped him up properly on a pillow in the middle of the bed. Giving the bear a pat on the head, he strode away with a smile.

***

Jack's bedroom door was closed, and as he had already implied that Mykl could take Jessica on a tour, Mykl decided he had rock solid permission to leave without announcing he was doing so. Besides, Jack had been up quite late and probably needed his sleep.

A powered cart, smaller than the one he had ridden in on from the tunnel entrance, sat in front of the house. Mykl had no desire to walk all the way to pick up Jessica, and the cart controls looked simple enough. Unfortunately, his feet couldn't reach the accelerator or brake pedals while he sat at the steering wheel. Undeterred by such a trivial setback, Mykl drove off in a standing position.

The first moment of panic came at the bottom of the steep road. The speed of the cart kept increasing as it raced downhill, and he didn't have the weight or leverage to apply the brake. Wrapping his arms under the steering wheel and standing on the brake with both feet while extending his body at last produced the desired effect. He was relieved that there were no more large hills between him and his destination.

He parked the cart outside the residential building where Dawn, James, and Jessica were staying. Inside, James's telltale snores filtered into the hallway. Mykl walked past his room to Dawn's and peeked inside. A twinge of worry poked him in the gut when he saw the dark empty space where Dawn should be. But he told himself that if James slept peacefully, nothing too terribly wrong could have happened to her.

Mykl tapped lightly on Jessica's door. It cracked open, and a shadowed eye peered over Mykl's head and down the hall before looking down. The eye crinkled with a smile and the door opened the rest of the way.

"Ready for your tour?" Mykl asked, rocking onto his toes.

"So you *were* serious last night?" Jessica asked.

Mykl tilted his head to the side and gave a crooked smile. "No."

"No?"

"No, we decided not to kill you."

"Oh, well, in that case, allow me to put on some shoes so you can take me on that tour!"

Mykl left the driving to Jessica while he gave directions and narrated the highlights. Judging by Jessica's oohs and ahs, she was appropriately impressed by the City's scope and beauty. And Mykl continually had to make subtle corrections to her steering vector when she looked away too long from their intended course.

When he directed her to drive to the glossy black precipice at the edge of the City, Jessica's eyes never wandered. She became very quiet. Mykl watched her head slowly tilt back and an expression of awe blossom on her face as they neared the frozen tsunami wave.

Jessica stepped out of the cart, still gazing up at the peak of the massive curl. Finally she turned to Mykl. With a graceful motion of her arm, she indicated the wave while letting her facial expression ask the question.

"Because they can," Mykl answered. "Apparently, the ability to create here is only limited by one's imagination."

"You know," Jessica said, "if it ever rained in here, this would be a great place to stand and not get wet."

"It rains in here all the time," Mykl said matter-of-factly.

"I think you're making up stories now to entertain me."

"Suit yourself," Mykl said with a shrug. "Would you like to be entertained by an alien now?"

Jessica struck a skeptical pose and narrowed one darkly lashed eye at Mykl. "You mean like an *outer space* alien?"

"More like an inner solar system half-alien."

"Half-alien?"

"Partial alien. He's complicated," Mykl said.

"He?"

Mykl moved his hands about, attempting to find the right words. "This'll be a lot easier if I just show you," he said finally, dropping his hands in surrender and walking briskly to the entrance.

He stepped aside for Jessica.

"You first," she said.

Mykl laughed.

"What's so funny?"

"I like you," Mykl said without further comment and led the way to the alien laboratory.

As Jack had done, Mykl paused at the last door for dramatic effect. Jessica wrung her hands, her complexion pale.

"Ready?"

Jessica nodded once.

Mykl opened the door.

Noah was in his cage, peering at them without twitching so much as a whisker. Mykl winked at him, and he could have sworn he received the same gesture in return.

Jessica stepped cautiously into the lab, looking about the area as though some dangerous creature was about to pounce. She turned to Mykl and said, "Well?"

Mykl, his hands in his pockets, gave a side-eyed glance at Noah and tilted his head toward his cage. Noah gave a half-circle wave to Jessica, who leaned forward but didn't move closer.

"It's—a mouse?"

"A very special mouse," Mykl said with pride.

"An alien mouse?"

"Partly."

"Does he shape-shift into a green tentacled blob or something?" Jessica took a tentative step nearer.

Mykl resisted the cheap childish scare tactic of yelling "Boo!" as she brought herself to eye level with the *alien*. He was certain he would lose all rapport with his new friend if he pulled such a trick. And Jessica probably wouldn't be very happy with him either.

"No, as far as I know, he always looks pretty much the way you see him now." Noah twitched his whiskers at Mykl, who wrinkled his nose in return. "And this—" Mykl stretched on his tiptoes to get the diamond-encased lichen, but couldn't reach. "A little help, please? And no 'little' jokes."

"You're a giant among men, my copper-eyed friend," Jessica said. She slid the object closer to him.

Smiling, Mykl held out the alien life form to Jessica. "This is pure alien. It's a lichen from the surface of Europa."

"Europa? As in Jupiter's Europa?"

Mykl nodded.

Jessica tucked a tress of hair behind an ear and examined the flake from all angles. "We've never had a successful mission to retrieve samples from Europa."

"I think you mean: *They* never had success. *We*..." Mykl spread his arms out, "are witness to the City's achievements."

Jessica slowly shook her head. "This is a lot to take in."

A tapping noise drew their attention. Noah held an empty pistachio shell in his paw and was banging it against the lower crossbar of his cage. He was waving his other arm at a nearby jar.

Mykl chuckled. "I think he wants more pistachios. Can you get the jar he's pointing at?"

"He certainly is a smart little guy," Jessica said. "Is that a manifestation of crossbreeding alien DNA?"

"Jack didn't say. He did say that Noah—that's his name by the way—is very old."

"How old?"

"Sixty years."

"Sixty? Six zero?"

"According to Jack, yes."

"That's… whoa, that's not normal. I had biology labs, and these things—"

"Noah."

"Yes, sorry. Noah's kind don't really live beyond three years." She bent to give Noah a pistachio. He took it, turned it over a couple of times, tapped it on the crossbar and handed it back to Jessica.

"What? Oh, I see. The shell isn't cracked. Sorry. Here's a better one." She offered up a fully split-shelled nut to the mouse that was over twice her age.

"I didn't know you spoke mouse?" Mykl said with a wide grin.

"Well, it was obvious. He was letting me know about the shell, and…"

"Maybe he also has telepathic capabilities?"

"You think?" Jessica asked in jest.

Mykl waggled his eyebrows at her.

"You need to teach me how to do that. It's too cute," Jessica said. "So, what else is there to know about besides an ancient alien mouse and a greenish Europan paint chip?"

"Well, we have faster-than-light communication, fusion, and chickens that eat children. Which would you like to see first?"

"Show me the chickens. Those other things sound boring!"

CHAPTER 45

Jessica tossed a large handful of fish food into the lake by the Operations Center with Mykl observing from the top step of the feeder box. She still struggled with a case of the giggles from Mykl's encounter with the chickens.

"Did you really think it was trying to eat you?" she asked.

"It pecked my toe!" Mykl flushed scarlet. He was still embarrassed by the high-pitched squeal that had involuntarily escaped his mouth and the impromptu chicken dance he had performed to escape his attacker. "How do you think you would have reacted if you were my age?"

"I haven't been your age in a very long time. I—" She stopped suddenly. "Mykl?"

"What?"

"How old is Jack?"

Mykl plunged his hand into the fish pellets as he pondered the question. Jack did look older, not old, and certainly not elderly. "I don't know. Maybe fifty?" Mykl dropped pellets into the water one at a time.

"And his codename is Jack the Ripper," Jessica said. She stared out over the lake.

"What of it?"

Popping sounds came from the water's surface as fish eagerly consumed the slow stream of falling pellets.

Jessica leaned sideways against the railing to face Mykl. "When I first arrived for my job at that secret installation…" She paused to chuckle. "Secret. Ha. It may as well have been a public library compared to this place. Anyway. In one of the old airplane hangars, there was an inscription written in the concrete."

Mykl looked up, annoyed that she had apparently decided to make a dramatic pause. He put an index finger to his temple and stared intently into her eyes. "Nope, still can't read minds. You're going to have to tell me what the inscription was."

"A name and a date."

Mykl made a small clockwise circle in the air with his finger.

"Jack the Ripper." She reached out and tweaked Mykl's nose. "2/14/55."

Mykl playfully swatted her hand away. "Jack is *not* over a hundred years old."

"Noah is sixty," she shot back.

"But…" *Symbiotic with carbon-based life*, Jack had said. "Noooo, Jack wouldn't…"

"How long have you known him?"

"Two days."

"Two days? Do you even know his real name?"

"Jack Smith."

"And you believe that. Jack Smi—" She slapped her forehead. "Holy shit! Mykl, I read an article on a study done by a J. Smith when I was working on my thesis. He was delving into the same theories I was: subatomic particles and their energy-producing potential. I think the date on that study was in the mid 1940s."

"That has to be coincidental. There's thousands of J. Smiths in the world," Mykl said, though cracks of doubt began to emerge.

"There are too many coincidences if you ask me," Jessica said.

"Mykl! Jessica!" sang a melodic voice from the shore end of the walkway. Mykl turned to see Delilah waving and beckoning.

"He's not that old," Mykl groused as he tried to keep pace with Jessica.

"Ask him," Jessica said, all but double-dog daring Mykl to do so.

"I will!"

Delilah smiled as they approached. "Sorry to have to cut your tour short, Jessica, but Jack needs Mykl back at the house." She guided Mykl to her cart. "You are welcome to keep exploring if you wish. We may be a while. If you return your cart to any parking space marked with a green circle, it will recharge itself."

"Thank you," Jessica said.

As she watched the two figures in the cart disappear around a corner, she thought to herself: *You don't know Jack.*

CHAPTER 46

Mykl glowed with a happiness he hadn't felt in ages. Spending the morning bantering with Jessica reminded him of spending time with…

No. He couldn't allow himself to open up that door—not now—not yet.

"Did Jack say why he needed me?" he asked Delilah.

"Something about a family meeting. He had one of those cryptic looks that told me he wasn't going to divulge anything more. He does like his little surprises. Our son is on his way here too. He should arrive at any moment. It'll probably be the death of me with both of you getting into trouble."

Jack and Delilah's son? In the current family hierarchy, that would make him Mykl's older brother. Mykl wondered about him. What did he do in this whole City business? What did he look like? Would he want his old room back? *He* would certainly know how old Jack was. Mykl was bursting with curiosity.

Delilah parked the cart in the same spot from which Mykl had commandeered the other one. He felt a tad less guilty about his actions, now that it appeared they were a community resource rather than personal belongings.

"Go on in and make yourself comfortable. I'll see if Jack is ready. He had some priority operational items to discuss with Dr. Lee."

Mykl went inside. He wondered if *he* was a "priority operational item," then convinced himself that he was inflating his perceived value.

Three running steps and a leap placed him in the middle of his bed with Stinker. He grabbed the ratty teddy bear and headed to the living room. Since the house was empty, he took another running leap and dove over the arm of a couch, landing in the middle of the cushions. With Stinker in his lap, he waited.

A cart being driven at a reckless speed skidded to a stop in front of the house, and its door swished open.

"Hello! Hello! Hello!" called a young man in military uniform, stepping in the door.

Mykl stared, openmouthed. He *knew* this man. The uniform made him look different, official, but the smile remained the same.

The man removed his cap and tousled Mykl's hair. "Hello, Mykl," he said, plopping onto the opposite couch and putting his feet up on the crystal-clear table.

"You!" Mykl choked out his words, "*You're* Jack's son?"

The man nodded. His smile was infectious. "I see Stinker has a new friend," he said, pointing to the bear in Mykl's lap. With a mischievous glint in his eyes, he asked, "Did mom tell you how he got his name?"

Mykl laughed. "She did. I didn't believe her—but I do now."

He realized now that he should have guessed who Jack's son was much earlier. All the signs had been there. The comfortable familiarity, the banter—the hug. Subordinates don't hug their bosses, but sons do.

"So, what do I call you?" Mykl said. "Officer Smith… or Kyle?"

"Just Kyle will be fine. Only Mom calls me Officer Smith." He chuckled. "And that's only when she's annoyed with me. She snaps her fingers at you when she's *really* mad," he added dramatically.

"She's too nice to ever get mad."

"Well, it's a good thing your feet can't reach the table," Kyle said, stretching his body out further.

"What do you do that you have to wear a uniform?" Mykl asked.

"My current assignment is as an executive officer on a submarine. I was about to be deployed for a new mission when—"

A rapid snapping of fingers interrupted him. "Officer Smith!" shouted Delilah. "Get your feet off that table!"

"But..."

"I don't care if it's made of diamond, it's the principle of the matter!" Delilah curled her finger. "Now get over here and give your mother a kiss!"

Kyle winked at Mykl before standing to kiss his mother's proffered cheek. He had the tact to look appropriately sheepish under her glare. Mykl, observing from the couch, smiled in confidence that he still hadn't *really* seen Delilah angry. Kyle gave his mother a hug and another loud smooch on the cheek before retaking his place on the couch.

"You may know how to placate your mother, young rascal, but Jack has certainly been in a mood since yesterday. Now which one of you has gotten into trouble?"

The two boys pointed at each other so fast it was as if they had long practice at the maneuver. Delilah rolled her eyes as they both burst out laughing.

***

The laughter rumbled through the house to the balcony where Jack was collecting his thoughts. He couldn't contain or justify the anger he had originally felt for the transgression he now held documented proof of. What he held was simply the truth, and it was time for all parties to face it. Of all the power and technology at his disposal, one force in the universe still conquered all.

With one last deep breath to ready himself, he pulled his gaze from the City and entered his home.

Sustained laughter bubbled from the living room. Kyle caught sight of his father and fell still. Jack now understood the pain he so often detected in his son's eyes.

"What's wrong, Dad?" Kyle began to rise from the couch.

"Don't get up," Jack said, reinforcing his words with an outstretched hand. "You should take a seat too, dear," he said to his wife.

A heavy silence settled over them as Jack and Delilah took seats in armchairs opposite each other. Mykl, eyes sharp and body tense, wrapped thin arms around his bear.

Jack laid a thick leather portfolio on the table. "I'm sorry, but there's no easy way to do this," he said. Reluctantly, he pulled the zipper to access the documents within.

***

The hairs on the back of Mykl's neck tingled at the sound of the zipper's grating teeth. The look on Jack's face as he opened the portfolio made him feel as if the zipper were ripping open his spine and revealing his soul.

"Mykl…"

Never before had Mykl heard his name spoken with such sorrow. Every instinct told him to run, but the cold fist of fear gripped his spine so solidly that he could do no more than tremble inside a numb shell. His dry mouth forbade him to swallow. His body forgot how to breathe.

Jack pulled a rigid sheet from the portfolio. He set it on the table and slid it in front of Mykl. It was a color photograph of a woman's face.

"Do you know this woman?" Jack asked.

Mykl blinked once. The frigid fist released his spine and snapped shut to crush his heart. Stinker tumbled to the floor as he leaned forward and woodenly reached for the photograph with both hands. Unbidden tears stung his eyes and blinded him. He knew in an instant who this person was. He had thought he would never see her face again. He had never seen her hair blond like this, but it didn't matter. It was her.

Her!

A hollow ache deep inside him welled up to close off his throat. He closed his eyes and clutched the photograph to his chest, sobbing in ragged gasps.

The cushion next to him sagged. He felt a warm floral-scented arm wrap around him and a familiar soft body press into his stomach. He pulled Stinker to hide his face and catch his tears, then squeezed it into the embrace with the photograph of his mom.

"Her name is Anya Luchenko," Jack said. "She went missing over a year ago. I am truly sorry about what I said before, Mykl. Dr. Lee has confirmed from your DNA the identity of your mother. She was not a stripper; she was one of our best undercover agents. We have recently discovered that her ability to keep secrets far outweighed her skill at uncovering them. She never told us about you. In fact, she rented a second apartment and led two distinctly different lives in order to keep knowledge of your existence from us and from the dangerous people she dealt with. Even after she went missing, when we searched her assignment-designated apartment, we found no sign that she had a child."

Mykl couldn't bring himself to look up. Still trying to reclaim control of his breathing, he said into the damp head of Stinker, "She… she said… her… her name… was… was Ta—Tanya." So many secrets. *Did I truly know my mother? I know she loved me. That's what matters.*

"Tanya Lush is the assumed name she used as a stripper, as well as on the lease for your apartment. She used an entirely different alias for her official residence. Only her 'Tanya' identification was found with the body. But the police, it seems, found a disposable phone in her locker at the strip club. There were two numbers on the phone, and both were for child care centers. That's how they found you—and we didn't." Jack went back to thumbing through the portfolio.

Mykl concentrated on taking a slow deep breath. He had a question that had to be asked. "Where… Where is she… buried?"

He tried to hold Jack's gaze, but the man's eyes betold more tragedy. It was easier to keep his eyes shut and rest his forehead on Stinker.

Jack answered, "As per policy, and protocol of the county, due to her status and lack of any other documentation… her remains were cremated the day after her autopsy." He pressed his fingers to the table, blanching his fingernails. "Her ashes were disposed of in a landfill outside of town."

Had the tiny bear in Mykl's hands been alive, it would have wailed in pain at the angry fists digging into its hide. Mykl clamped his jaw shut to bar a scream from escaping. He was certain he would never be able to stop if he let it out. White hot anger incinerated the fear inside him, but it had nowhere to go... there was no target to unleash it upon. It burned and burned until he felt as though nothing remained inside of him but cold ashes. He remained motionless, except for the slow tears trickling down his cheeks.

"Did your mother ever tell you anything about your father?" Jack asked.

Mykl felt dead inside now. Nothing remained but a dark vacuum. His small body sagged in resignation to things he had no power to change. Wiping his face with the back of his hand, he looked once more at the photograph of his mother, and without emotion, he answered Jack's question as if he were speaking to her.

"The last thing she said about him was that he was going to be happy to see me." Mykl tuned out the world around him and lost himself in the blue eyes of the woman in the photograph. Nothing else existed.

***

Kyle had barely moved since the moment his father had first placed the photograph on the table. His sole focus had been on the small boy sitting across from him. The boy's face was now blocked by the photograph he held as a shield against his grief.

Jack addressed his son without taking his attention from the portfolio on the table. "Officer Smith."

"Sir?" he answered in a military-conditioned reflex.

"Did you know Agent Luchenko?"

Oh, yes. She was the only woman on earth to Kyle. His Eve. Even though she was forbidden. There were rules, regulations, reasons. But on a chance assignment, her smile and savvy wit had left him defenseless. At the end of the assignment, they parted with an unspoken understanding that they would be together again. The phrase held in check on both their lips had to wait until the proper moment. However, their eyes had held no secrets. There wasn't a day since they were last together that he hadn't thought of her and the words he so desperately wanted to share.

"I do," he said, in the wrong tense to answer Jack's question but in the proper spirit of the feeling inside him.

"You are aware, Officer Smith, that fraternization with other agents is expressly forbidden? Especially so in your case?" Jack spoke with the sternness of command, and the right side of his mouth twitched as though he was suppressing a frown or a smile.

How could Dad know? They had been so careful to avoid any City spying technology. Kyle wracked his brain to think of what he had missed.

Jack handed him three documents. Three DNA profiles. Kyle's eyes went wide in understanding.

In a softer tone, Jack asked, "Did Anya know your full name, son?"

Kyle pursed his lips and nodded. A whirling flood of emotion spun inside his chest, ready to explode.

***

Entirely focused on his mother's picture, Mykl sat completely oblivious to the conversation going on around him—until he slowly became aware that his name was being said over and over. He looked up to see Jack giving him an inquisitive stare.

"Did your mother ever tell you anything about your name?" Jack asked.

Mykl placed the picture of his mother on the cushion next to him. He looked at his hands as he ran them along his legs to his knees. "She said… She said I was named after my dad. She never told me his name." He couldn't make himself look up. He didn't want anyone to see the warm tears that had begun to flow again.

Jack leaned forward. "Mykl, your father's name is spelled M-I-K-Y-L-E. And around here, he is known simply as Kyle."

Mykl looked up, across the table—and into a pair of copper-colored eyes exactly like his own.

CHAPTER 47

Even though he was certain, Mykl wanted to hear the words spoken. "You're... my dad?"

Kyle, his eyes moist, slid around the table and planted himself on the couch next to Mykl. "I am," he said. "I am, I am." He hugged Mykl to his chest while placing a kiss on the top of his head. Mykl endured a pleasant squish as Delilah included both of them in her own embrace.

"How do you know?" Mykl asked, rescuing his mother's photograph from under Kyle.

Kyle—Mykl's father—showed him the three documents that Jack had handed over. "These are the DNA profiles for you, me, and your mother. They prove conclusively that you are my son." Kyle had a mischievous smile. "As far as your name goes, she used to purposely mispronounce mine as 'My Kyle.'"

Mykl nodded slowly. It made sense. He didn't know much about DNA, but he was very good at pattern recognition, and these documents showed similarities. His father's markers were tagged in blue, his mother's in yellow, and the markers they shared in green.

One tag was red— it was on Kyle's record and his own, but not on his mother's. "What's this?" he asked, pointing at the red mark.

Kyle turned to Jack. "Is that what I think it is?"

"It's why those rules about fraternization were put into place. Yes. It is what you think it is." Jack's eyes shifted to Mykl. "Remember what I said about Noah?"

Mykl's eyebrows shot up in surprise. "You mean I'm an—I'm part—I'm like Noah?"

"You're more like your father," Jack said with a hint of humor.

"But... wait. How old are you?" Mykl asked Jack.

A slow smile spread across Jack's face. "I was born in 1926."

"She was right then," Mykl said.

"Who was right?" Delilah asked.

"Jessica put the pieces together after I introduced her to Noah. Something about an inscription in an airplane hangar?"

"She is a clever one," said Jack. "But there is much more to it in your case." He pulled more files from his portfolio. "After years of research and experiments, we needed a human test subject. Though many of our staff expressed a willingness to volunteer, I didn't want to put any of them at risk. So *I* chose to be the first human test subject. My adaptation was satisfactory, but it left me without the ability to have any more children."

"That was *not* satisfactory," Delilah said.

Inclining his head to his wife in acquiescence, Jack said, "The benefits of adaptation include extended lifespan due to the cells' ability to repair telomeres. You see, Mykl, this life form developed on a moon constantly bombarded with hard radiation from Jupiter. That radiation caused a form of forced evolution. The Europa lichen is a master at survival under the harshest of conditions. And after the virus-modified version was combined with human DNA, it developed a *new* set of survivability features. As you may have already noticed from your wound, rapid healing is one of those features."

Mykl scratched at the healed puncture wound through his pants. "So I'm... adapted?"

"Adaptation isn't the appropriate term in your case. Kyle, Delilah, and I had the modified lichen DNA artificially introduced into our systems. After my resulting adaptation, many more genetic modifications were made until we felt ready for more human trials. Kyle was due to deploy on a dangerous assignment before the trials could be completed. He was administered a promising, but untested, version—under the strict guidelines that he not do any 'testing' without City scientists' authorization." Kyle looked suitably cowed as Jack raked him with a glance. "You didn't adapt to the DNA, Mykl. You inherited it from your father. You are, in fact, a mutation… a new species."

Mykl mouthed the word back at Jack. *Species?*

Jack nodded.

"Is that a bad thing?" Mykl managed to choke out.

"Do you *feel* bad?" Jack asked.

Mykl thought for a moment before answering. "Umm, no."

"Well then, so far so good," Jack said. He pulled a translucent sheet from his portfolio and placed it on the table, then tapped a corner of the table with two fingers held together, causing the table to light up with a soft cool glow. "This also explains a lot about you and your unusual talents." The sheet showed a profile cross-section view of what appeared to be a human skull. Jack pressed a corner of the sheet against the table and held it there for a moment. When he removed it, the image remained on the table. With simple taps and finger swipes, the image converted to three dimensions and began to slowly rotate. "This is a scan that Dr. Lee recorded yesterday."

"Is that me?" Mykl asked. "It looks like my head is packed full of stars."

"Synaptic connections, to be precise. One thousand times more dense than a normal human brain. In your instance, alien DNA had the opportunity to affect brain growth. Neurons can only form during fetal development and for a few months after birth. After that, we are stuck with what we have." Jack paused the table display. "What is the earliest memory you have, Mykl?"

"When I was inside my mom, I could feel and hear her sing. I didn't really have a concept of time. Then one day it felt like I was being squeezed like a tube of toothpaste, and I ended up in a tub of warm water. At least, I think it was a tub. I couldn't see all that well. Then I was lifted out of the water and I was cold, couldn't breathe, something was put in my nose, then my mouth, then this whoosh of cold went into me. I was scared. I cried." Mykl picked up the picture of his mother again. "Then I saw her eyes. And I stopped crying. I knew everything was going to be okay." He shrugged.

Jack nodded. "Evidently, the alien DNA wanted you to have all your synapses firing before birth. That, along with their density, is why you are so far ahead of most adults in intelligence. The thing you most lack is simple experience with the world and all its wonders. The power of your mind is going to be truly formidable when you decide what you wish to do with it."

"So, am I… immortal? Am I going to develop a craving for blood? Brains?" Mykl felt quite unsure of what he really was anymore.

"You're not a vampire… or a zombie," Kyle said. Hearing the words made Mykl feel silly for asking.

Nodding toward the image in the table, Mykl asked, "Is this why I've never been sick before?"

Jack nodded. "Among other things. Healing is accelerated, pain thresholds are much greater. As for immortality, I'm afraid not. We don't know how long our lifespans will be extended yet, since none of those who were adapted have died of natural causes yet. But it will happen. And we can be killed by a severe enough injury." Jack leaned in closer to his grandson. "So be careful when jumping on the bed."

"Yes, sir," Mykl said, leaning into his dad for comfort. A father. A real father. *My* father. Mykl smiled. *You were right, Mom; he* was *very happy to see me.*

"When do you have to leave?" Delilah asked Kyle.

"The helicopter is waiting for me up top. They're delaying deployment of the sub under the guise of equipment recalibration, but I'm afraid they can't keep that up much longer." Kyle gave Mykl's shoulder a squeeze. "Want to escort me to my pickup point?"

Mykl set his jaw and assumed a defiant posture. It wasn't fair. He now had a real father and only minutes left to be with him. Every synapse in his super brain told him to scream, "No, you can't go!" But he knew that no matter how much he protested or how many tears he shed, it would have no effect on the eventual outcome. *It's about time I grow up and act my age.*

"As if you could stop me!" he declared, standing up with Stinker held tightly to his side.

***

With Jack and Delilah following behind, Kyle told Mykl about his mom and what she had been working on.

As the digital age grew, cyberspying computers grew so complex in their ability to crack codes that no one's data could be completely secure. Eventually, the only way to make sure another country couldn't pry sensitive secrets out of a crypto vault was to not put them in one in the first place. So a clandestine renaissance took place, where highly trained mind couriers exchanged information person-to-person, with no recording devices save their own memory. Codes were unnecessary as long as they remained discreet. Vegas became a mecca for these spies, and a strip club offered ideal camouflage. The Chinese, in particular, kept a rotation of four diplomats continuously traveling in and out of the country, carrying synaptic secrets under the protection of diplomatic immunity.

Anya took on a long-term assignment to infiltrate the strip club scene and earn the *admiration* of the couriers. Her linguistic training and observational skills made her well suited to pick up bits of conversation between couriers and their invited guests. She was responsible for relaying critical intelligence to the City about China's long-term goals—and their suspicions regarding their failed asteroid missions.

Mykl soaked in the details of his mother's alter ego. It was no wonder she hadn't been able to spend much time with him. She'd held three jobs at once: stripper, spy, and mother. Mykl felt a pang of guilt for having asked her on numerous occasions to stay up and play for just a little bit longer. Her resulting fatigue may have caused her to slip up—and cost her her life. It was unwarranted blame, but he accepted it nonetheless.

"Who killed her?" Mykl asked as they arrived at the lift that would take them to Kyle's pickup point.

Kyle let out a frustrated breath through his nose. "I wish I knew. The last I heard, she was only missing. My dad may know more. I'm sorry."

"Why didn't she have the Europa lichen treatment like you did, if she knew it was going to be so dangerous?"

Kyle smiled tenderly at Mykl. "That one is simple, son. She wanted to have children, so she didn't want to risk the procedure until it was deemed safe for her."

Guilt sliced more pieces off Mykl's heart. Would she have survived the attack if she had been adapted? It didn't matter that he might never have been born. She *might* have been able to survive.

Kyle said his goodbyes to his parents, then he and Mykl rode up the lift together. Father and son stared at each other in silence from opposite sides of the elevator. Both were still in awe at the existence of the other; neither knew what to say next.

Kyle narrowed his eyes at Mykl, making light of their impromptu staring contest. Mykl narrowed his back in fair imitation of his dad.

Kyle farted loudly.

Mykl blinked. "No fair!" he declared, burying his face into Stinker. These teddy bears were useful creatures indeed.

Wind and debris pelted them as the helicopter strafed the treetops to land nearby. Kyle took a knee and placed his hands on Mykl's shoulders. Looking him straight in the eyes, he said, "As much as I wanted to say the words to your mom, I never got another chance. I'm not going to make that mistake again. I love you, son."

Stunned as he was by the words, Mykl was thoroughly incapacitated by the fierce, crushing hug he received from his father. Through tumultuous emotions and a severe lack of breath, he wrapped his arms around Kyle's neck and squeezed in kind.

CHAPTER 48

In the cool darkness of an undersea world, James awoke to bioluminescent creatures performing a slow underwater ballet. This suited him much better than those garish polka dots, and he felt grateful to Mykl for suggesting this particular ambiance setting. A fully inflated pufferfish with tiny fluttering fins sculled into view, reminding James how badly he needed to relieve his bladder.

The instant he touched a wall to increase its illumination, a "message waiting" square appeared under his fingers and began to flash. Another touch to the square brought up a text message asking him to go see Dr. Lee at the infirmary as soon as he was available. She included no other details. Still, it was enough to put his mind working on what she could possibly want. The subject that jumped to the forefront of his thoughts was Dawn.

He took care of business in the bathroom and, out of habit, dressed without any thought of personal grooming. He glanced up to see the now-deflated pufferfish darting aimlessly among other reef inhabitants. *Will wonders ever cease?*

With untied shoelaces snapping at his heels, he dashed down the hall. Dawn's door stood open and her room was lit. Her bed was stripped of linens, and all her drawers were empty. The only hint of her ever having been there was a slight scent of jasmine lingering in the bathroom.

James raced at a dead run to the infirmary, a pace ahead of the panic chasing him. He sprinted along empty streets, past vacant dwellings, and maintained his speed all the way to the infirmary entrance. Dr. Lee met him inside, her hands outstretched in a sign for him to slow down.

"She's fine, James," Dr. Lee said.

James placed his hands on his knees and rocked back against the door frame to catch his breath, his fear somewhat reduced. But "fine" never meant the same thing to women as it did to men. He worked to regain control of his breathing.

"I'm sorry, James. I should have included more details in my message. I didn't mean to frighten you," Dr. Lee said.

"'S'okay," James replied in a quick exhalation.

Dr. Lee took hold of his arm to seat him in a chair. "I'll get you some water."

James nodded and settled heavily onto the cushion. He ran his fingers through disheveled hair, then closed his eyes while he locked his hands behind his head. In the brief span it took Dr. Lee to retrieve the water, James willed himself to control his breathing and mental state.

"Thank you, Doctor," he said, taking the glass she offered.

"By the way," Dr. Lee said, "I like the new James better." She smiled.

After a thirst-quenching gulp, he replied, "My apologies for the deception."

"Jack updated me on your story. Survival often requires unique and drastic measures." Dr. Lee paused. "Which brings us to Dawn."

"You said she was fine."

"She is. As much as we have the ability to make her be at the moment. She informed me that she did not tell you about our findings on her condition?"

Condition. The word "fine" rarely ever pertained to any condition.

"She just said you could dispense medication to keep the pain under control."

He saw from Dr. Lee's facial expression that a lot more needed to be said about this *condition*.

"James…"

There must be some unwritten rule among doctors to use a person's first name and then pause dramatically before giving bad news, James thought.

"Dawn has an inoperable, malignant brain tumor that has metastasized to other organs in her body. When she came here, she only had about two months to live."

"And this is *fine*?" James said.

"But—by her wishes and Jack's permission, we have begun treatment."

"Why was Jack's permission required?"

"This treatment is experimental. The procedure has been extremely successful in treating other types of cancer, but none so advanced as hers. Still, she chose to try it. She didn't want you to watch her spiral down into certain death. She traded sixty more days of blindness and agony for a chance at a real life. A chance to be with you."

James stared at his knees. Dr. Lee had to be making that last part up to make him feel better about the whole ordeal. He had never expressed his real feelings to Dawn, and she had never divulged any romantic notions either. She couldn't, since he had been portraying himself as an idiot. Now he truly felt like one for not having the courage to speak when he had the opportunity.

"She isn't conscious, but you may see her if you wish," Dr. Lee said.

"I would like that."

Dawn was being kept in the next building over. Its interior was sparsely furnished, as if to discourage people from lingering. Very few of Dr. Lee's assistants made their presence known as they traversed two long hallways.

One last turn took them to a short, wide corridor devoid of openings save the one at its end with an illuminated red border. A sign above it read, "Cryo Lab." To James, it was a witch doctor term from the past that involved wealthy people attempting to cheat death. He hoped it meant something else entirely regarding Dawn.

Dr. Lee stopped to explain the entry procedure. "This is a one-way passage into the Cryo Lab. Once we step in, the first door will close and the entry will pressurize slightly. After that, we may proceed into the lab. Questions?"

James shook his head.

Dr. Lee keyed in an entry code. The door slid open, they stepped through, and the door shut behind them. The pressurization was mild—just below the level where James thought he might have to pop his ears—then the interior door opened with a swish.

The next area, labeled "Prep Room," was a large chamber ringed with large interconnecting bubbles. Dawn was in the first bubble; she was the sole patient in the entire area. She lay recumbent with her body angled slightly downward.

James stepped to her side, reached for her hand, and stopped. He looked back at Dr. Lee. "Is it okay if I... touch her?"

"You may. She won't break," Dr. Lee said.

It looked as though Dawn's entire body was encapsulated in a skintight suit with tubing mounted at major arterial junctions. A thick translucent blanket of green hoses crisscrossed her body from shoulders to knees. A clear horseshoe-shaped intubation device barely fogged from her weak exhalations. The suit framed a circle of exposed skin around her face. *She seems so pale*, James thought. *Almost ghostly. No... angelic.* He sensed cold air falling from the blanket covering her. As he took hold of her hand, her chill ran through his fingertips, up to his heart, and down his spine.

"You're going to freeze her," James said. "Aren't you?"

"It's necessary."

"What makes you think this will work?"

"Every person working in this underground city has voluntarily been through the same procedure. Some more than once."

James looked directly into Dr. Lee's eyes. Her face was open and honest.

He turned his attention back to Dawn. She hated being cold. He knew that, and he would do anything in his power to bring warmth back to her world. Until then, he would have to endure the cold loneliness of patiently waiting for the unknown.

Gently, he ran his fingers along the side of her head where there should have been long tresses of silky black hair. Then he bent and, for Dawn's ears only, breathed, "I love you, my princess."

With the words finally spoken, he had one thing left to do. He hoped he would someday soon pay the price for his next action. Tenderly, he laid a kiss on her exposed forehead. The cold lingered on his lips as he marveled at her peaceful beauty.

James reluctantly tore his gaze away and released her hand. "Okay. I'm ready to go now," he said.

After they cycled through the exit airlock, Dr. Lee handed James a small envelope. "She wanted you to have this. She wrote it herself because she wanted you to know that it came from her."

Taking the envelope as carefully as he had taken Dawn's hand, James gave Dr. Lee a quizzical glance. "But she can't write."

"I'll let you be the judge of that," Dr. Lee replied.

The first thing James saw in the envelope was a lock of black hair bundled tightly by strong white thread. It still carried a hint of jasmine. He felt dizzy with the emotion it elicited. The letter had a barely legible column of writing that took concentration to read. As he finished deciphering the last sentence, he brought a hand to his mouth and sat in a chair. She did know him. She truly did.

He squeezed his eyes shut to contain the moisture welling within. "You're evil, Dr. Lee."

"Call me Cindy."

"You could have given me this before I saw her, but it wouldn't have had near the same impact. You did that on purpose."

"Yep. Us girls have to stick together. And, she knows a good man when she sees one. So to speak. I wanted to make sure you knew what you were fighting for. On that note, I believe Jack is waiting for you at the Operations Center. Take a cart. And you might want to run a comb through that crazy hair, too."

"Thank you, Cindy," James said, rising to leave. "I know you'll take good care of her."

THE PROMETHEUS EFFECT

Outside again, under the artificial sun, James took a moment to reread Dawn's letter:

My James

A withheld kiss
A moment lost
So soon we miss
But not forgot
No more hiding
My time is gone
It's always coldest
Before the dawn
Please don't leave
My soul to freeze
I'll need your warmth
To bring me peace

Dawn
PS. You owe me another kiss!

CHAPTER 49

Jessica had spent the last few hours alone in contemplative reflection, dissecting everything she'd learned about the City's technology. They had yet to fully sink in when Jack arrived.

"Still bored?" he asked, surprising her.

"'Overwhelmed into a stunned silence' would be a better way to put it," Jessica said.

"Mykl divulged all of our secrets then?"

"We ran out of time, but I especially like the secret fish food dispenser."

Jack laughed.

Jessica continued, "Actually, I've been sitting here thinking. You have technologies that can remedy almost all the world's problems. Virtually unlimited energy via fusion. Manufacturing of almost anything imaginable with no waste and one hundred percent recyclability. Pollution managed on a scale that actually reverses the damage done to the environment. Farming and food production without fear of weather or pestilence. Transportation. Space travel. Mineral mining of asteroids…"

"Did Mykl tell you anything more about asteroids?" Jack interrupted.

"No, but it's not hard to imagine how easy they would be to mine with your technology. So, add unlimited resources to the list. It baffled me as to why you haven't shared all of this when it's so desperately needed. Then I imagined how one would have to go about releasing this technology." She shifted her position on the bench to face Jack more directly. "You couldn't put it out in individual bits. It's inextricably tied together—all or nothing. And if you made everything public knowledge, it would devastate the world economy." Jack nodded slightly in affirmation. "All utility companies would instantly be obsolete. The same with the professions of building, manufacturing, and transportation. Governments would destabilize. Wars would start all over the world as nations raced to take advantage of the situation. And… They would have all this new technology to make their war machines better and more powerful. So a worldwide release of this technology is out of the question."

She paused before adding, "Not to mention, the fountain of youth?" She waited to see if Jack would deny it.

"Your suppositions are correct. Keep going," Jack said.

"That last thing is enough to start a war all by itself. So, what if it were only America that received the benefit—with the rest of the world starving for energy, food, and resources? Even if America shared its new abundant energy and resources, it wouldn't be enough. Foreign governments that have always been at odds with us won't suddenly change long-standing cultural beliefs and 'adjust to' or subjugate themselves to American domination. They would likely band together and declare war under the theme, 'If we can't have it, then neither can they.'

"Every scenario I can think of leads to someone ending up at war. But I guess these are all problems for you to figure out. You have all the tests and tricks. And now I have been brought here, and for the life of me, I can't figure out why you need me."

"It's very simple," Jack said in a serious tone. "I need you to help me start a war."

Jessica stared at Jack, trying to determine if he was joking.

Behind him, a cart pulled in and parked next to hers. A tall athletic young man ran toward them. His hair was damp and flattened as if he had just showered and had hurried to get here. He gave her a polite nod as Jack turned to address him.

"Good afternoon, James. Glad you could join us. Please, take a seat. This is Jessica. She arrived last night."

Jessica accepted James's offered hand from across the table. "And what do you do here?" she asked.

"Well, I've only been here two days, and up until yesterday, I was the village idiot."

Jessica arched an eyebrow at him.

"I'm much better now," James added.

She raked the younger man with a scrutinizing gaze. "You must be a friend of Mykl's."

James straightened his posture in mock indignation. "Why do you say that?" he asked with a suppressed grin and a twinkle in his eyes.

"Mykl has interesting friends," she replied.

"Oh? How many have you met?"

"Four."

"Four?" Jack and James responded together.

Jessica pointed at Jack. "You, your wife, James, and Noah."

"Noah?" James asked with an inquiring look at Jack.

"Noah is complicated, but in short, he is responsible for making Dawn's treatment possible."

"Oh," James said, his eyes taking on a distant look.

"Which brings us back to the business at hand," Jack said, looking expectantly at Jessica.

"You want me—to start—a war," Jessica said.

James fell still. Jack nodded once.

"With what country?" Jessica asked.

"All of them," Jack said.

Jessica closed her eyes and took in a deep breath. She held it a moment before forcing the air out of her lungs. Flustered and shaken, she said, "I don't understand how a global war is going to solve anything. And I *really* don't understand how *I* could possibly start one."

"You have already aided immensely by preparing the fuse. Now all I need you to do is light it."

Jessica crossed her arms and leaned on the edge of the clear crystal picnic table. No sweetness filled her caramel-colored eyes when, under lowered brows, she said in a demanding tone, "Explain."

Jack made a few rapid taps and finger swipes on the tabletop, turning its surface glossy black. Jessica pulled her arms back in surprise. James sat motionless, his eyes following the choreography of Jack's hands. A large graph with country names and data filled the table.

"This shows real-time and forecasted oil usage for the world. A few major powers recently discovered evidence that suggests there may be less than two hundred years' worth of consumable oil."

"I thought scientists determined that *several* hundred years' worth still existed?" Jessica said.

"That's the number thrown out to prevent a panic—or, more accurately, a lie to buy time. Each country has a plan to deal with the problem. The United States bought foreign oil for almost a century instead of using the reserves on their own soil. When the rest of the world runs dry, they will have the last reserves to themselves. And war will come to the United States."

"But the other technologies…" Jessica started.

"It's too late." Jack updated the graphs. "This is the *actual* amount of oil left. At current consumption rates, it won't last two hundred years; it will last less than *twenty* years. If the outside world knew of this, the war would start today. A very *messy* war."

Jessica shivered and wrapped her arms around her middle.

"At the other extreme, China has opted for a more creative but direct approach to the problem."

Jack's fingers danced across the table. A representation of the inner solar system rotated in the glossy blackness. Multiple colored lines traced from Earth to the asteroid belt.

Jack indicated the lines. "As far as the media and the rest of the world know, these were exploratory space missions launched by China. They were, in actuality, efforts to move asteroids of appropriate size into new orbital paths to impact the Earth at predetermined locations." Jack enlarged the Earth to show the continental United States. Flashing red target symbols marked impact sites, and affected areas painted the continent from coast to coast. "None of these missions succeeded—yet. Because of actions taken by the City." Jack paused to let his words sink in. "If the US government knew of this, we would be at war within hours. If any *one* of these missions had been successful, it would have devastated the US economy, infrastructure, and military—and that's entirely apart from the massive cost in human lives. There would be no stopping China from taking over and dictating a new world order. Unless… the rest of the world went to war against them."

Jack blanked the table, causing humanity's home to disappear. "So, as you already reasoned out, the coming war is inevitable. I can't keep it from happening. But, if I *start* it—my way—I can control it. I can put an end to this, once and for all.

"I know this is asking a lot of you. From what I know, based on our testing and your past, I have decided you can be trusted. Now you have to decide whether you can trust *me*. Our window to make a difference is closing rapidly. You need to make a choice before leaving this table.

"There are basically three options available to you. One: stay here, safely in the comfort of the City. No one will think any less of you for not putting your life at risk. Believe me, you will be in great danger if you leave this place. Two: you can run out and tell the world about me and our secret lair… though you may not enjoy the company of those who claim to believe you.

"I have contingency plans in place, should you choose either of these options. However, those plans will not save the lives of the millions of people who will be killed outright in the next few weeks—nor will they prevent entire cities from being eradicated."

Jessica found it difficult to breathe, let alone speak. She closed her eyes to satisfy an instinctive desire to hide as Jack laid out her choices.

"Three, if you are willing: stay here and help me. Success will trigger events resulting in the deaths of thousands—but will allow uncounted millions to live, and the majority of our planet to remain habitable."

Jessica's stomach surfed waves of nausea. She had gotten herself involved in this whole mess because she wanted a job. No. A *meaningful* job.

Be careful what you ask for, girl. It doesn't get any more meaningful than this.

Jack had kindly tried to convince her that she had freedom of choice. But she knew there *was* no choice. The rails forming the moral track of her conscience allowed only one direction. The question remaining was whether or not her sanity could survive crossing a bridge over a river of blood. Alternatively, she could forever carry the weight of an ocean of bodies within her soul.

"So, I have to start a war. It can't get any worse than that. What do you need me to do?"

"I need you to be the woman that people now think you are."

"Huh?"

"Sebastian left that rooftop thinking you were selling me the secret to fusion technology."

"You set me up!"

"Yes. From the moment you chose not to cheat on that civil service test, you came onto our radar and were carefully screened for this mission. Your own moral code, 'the desire to do the right thing,' is what makes you the person you are. Knowing what the stakes are and how perfectly you have been 'set up' for the job, is there anyone else you would trust to do it?"

She looked into the eyes of the two men watching her before answering, "No, I would not."

"Then I need you to be the woman who sold the secret of fusion." Jack leaned away from her slightly. "And I need you to work with Sebastian."

"*That fu—*" Jessica yelled, biting her lower lip. "He's a piece of shit!"

"Sebastian is a tool," Jack agreed, easing the tension. "And his motivations will be his undoing. But for now, we need him in the picture to do what *he* has been so carefully groomed to do."

Jessica's skin crawled at the thought of spending another moment near Sebastian. To actually *work* with him was unthinkable. If given a choice between starting a war or working with that smarmy sleaze, she would choose war. Now Jack had saddled her with *both!*

"Fine," she said, though she didn't feel fine about it at all.

Jack reached inside his coat pocket and withdrew two envelopes. One he presented to Jessica, the other to James. "In your envelope, Jessica, there are details of what you may and may not discuss with Sebastian, or with any parties he may bring to the bargaining table. In addition, it's almost a guarantee that he will aspire to enlist the aid of China in his quest, but if he proves to be too dimwitted to figure that out, please *encourage* him."

"What happens if Sebastian fails to come through?" Jessica asked.

"China will retain enough military strength to maintain a war effort for decades to come."

Jessica sighed. She handled her envelope with distaste. "Is it going to self-destruct after I read it?" She wondered if the same fate could be arranged for Sebastian.

"No. That would be silly. Memorize the details, then toss it in the trash before you leave."

Jessica frowned in disappointment.

"You will also be provided a casino credit line and a bank account with funds appropriate for the sale you made. Your new residence is the Grand Suite of the E Pluribus Unum, conveniently located one floor below the Chinese diplomatic couriers, who are your number one priority. You are now rich. Act like it. Spend money. Gamble."

"Do I need to keep receipts?"

Jack chuckled. "No, we can absorb any monetary losses. Just keep in mind the bigger picture. This isn't about money; it's about survival."

James touched Jack on the arm to get his attention. "Um, my envelope is addressed to 'Linda,'" he said.

"That's right; its contents are not for you. All you need to know is that I want you to assist Jessica in gathering information—and to watch her back."

"You've obviously invested a great deal of time observing Jessica—so you know you can trust her," James said. "But me? I'm a nobody that got to come here due to Mykl's intellectual prowess and charisma. Why would you want me to participate in this when so many lives are at risk? Aren't there others to choose from? Someone who's better trained?"

"You're right. Normally, you would be subjected to rigorous screening to evaluate what morals motivate you. But I've discovered that a person's free choices are even more predictive of his or her character. And the tests you took—tests you self-imposed—you passed. I ordered a thorough search of your history in our video archives. That search corroborated everything you revealed to us. You told me the complete truth, without knowing I already had proof of your actions. You're not a nobody, James. You are the rare type of individual the world needs right now: an honest man. I've been around a long time. I know when I can trust someone.

"As for other trained agents, there weren't that many to begin with. Maintaining secrets requires a very small talent pool. Everyone else who could do your job has already been placed in more critical positions. We only have a small window of opportunity to make a difference, and you two are our best chance."

"But," said James, "I don't know anything about being a spy, or an agent, or whatever you want to call it."

"How many years did you fool people with your other persona?" Jack asked.

"Well, that was easy. I just played dumb."

Jack raised his eyebrows and gave the young man a wink.

James quickly caught on. "Ah, you want the *old* James back?"

"It will be your best defense; it will allow you to assimilate into your new role without suspicion. You will be returning to the asylum while you are not at work. The letter in that envelope explains everything Linda needs to know to get you back in. As for your job, you will be the room service caterer's third assistant. There are a few long-established agents at the hotel who will be apprised of your mission."

"Which is?"

"Keep your ears open. Once you've been vetted by the people around you, they'll be more apt to speak freely. Especially in other languages," he emphasized. "Use extreme discretion in communicating with Jessica. Your targets are vicious people. Do *not* let your guard down.

"I would like you both to be ready to leave in an hour. Tony will pick you up and convey you to the appropriate portals."

"Portals?" James asked.

"Entrance and exit points."

"Oh. With all the high-end tech around here, I thought you might have meant some kind of instantaneous matter transference device."

Jack wore a curious smile and replied, "One step at a time, James. One step at a time."

"How are we getting back to…" Jessica wanted to say *civilization*, but considering where she was, that would be an insult to the beautiful city around her. "… to the outside world?"

"You will be flown by military helicopter from your portal to a remote landing pad. From there, you will transfer to a luxury civilian helicopter befitting your new lifestyle. It will drop you off on the executive roof landing pad of the E Pluribus Unum. Hotel personnel will meet you there. The rest is on you—though I suggest a trip to the dress boutique, followed by a quick round at the tables to announce your presence to those who may be looking for you."

"Bleh." She scrunched her face in distaste at the thought of having to wear a dress. "I suppose sacrifices have to be made if we're saving the human race."

"I have complete confidence in your abilities," Jack said.

Then he turned to James. "*Your* transportation will be by private vehicle to a bus station in Pioche. Take the bus to Vegas. Walk from the depot to the asylum. You start work in the morning. Don't worry about clothes. The hotel takes care of that." He reached into a coat pocket and presented James with a handful of bright green wire. "Wear this on one of your wrists at all times."

James accepted the offering. "Is this some sort of secret communication device?"

"No, it's a slinky. Wear it as a reminder to keep to your act and as a visual marker to let others know you're *special*. Once they meet you, they will think of you as 'that odd boy with the slinky.' It's cheap camouflage to shield you from deeper scrutiny. People will tend to notice the slinky more than the man wearing it."

As James slipped the slinky over his left wrist, the angular features of his face softened to slackness. "Jack smawt," he drawled with a dull-witted grin.

CHAPTER 50

Assorted images and video clips flickered in and out on the tabletop display beneath Mykl's fingers. Delilah was showing him family memories. While he had definitely inherited his eyes from his father, the rest of his features subtly blended both parents' genes. Delilah even located more images of his mother, which he copied and saved to a file of his own. He was admiring an image of a very young Kyle holding a much less tattered Stinker when Jack returned from his meeting.

"It's time to evacuate," Jack said to Delilah.

She nodded and blanked the table. "How long do you have?" she asked.

"Dr. Lee needs another two hours to finish a few things and secure her facility. Then we leave."

"Wait—where are we going? What about James and Dawn?" Mykl asked in bewilderment.

Jack sat next to Mykl. "We are going someplace safer. James has left with Jessica to assist her with an assignment in Vegas, and Dawn is coming with us."

"There's someplace safer than *here?*" Mykl asked.

"Indeed there is. We would probably be fine staying here, but it's wise not to leave anything to chance."

There was still so much Mykl wanted to do and see here. He had just gotten used to the idea that he had a home, and now he had to leave? It was fitting, in a way: he had finally met his father and *he* had to go away; he had discovered a new James, and now he was gone too. And Jessica. *At least Dawn isn't leaving me.* What he wouldn't give for some stability in his life. No one should have to deal with this much separation anxiety. *Two hours!*

"May I go out and explore for a little bit?" Mykl asked.

Jack fixed him with a penetrating stare. Mykl tried to blank his mind. With all the alien DNA in the room, the potential for telepathy wasn't something to trifle with.

"Be back in one hour and forty-five minutes," Jack said. "You'll need a few minutes when you get back to suit up. Dear, do we still have Kyle's old cart?"

"I think it's in the second level of storage. I'll get it out for him."

His curiosity piqued, Mykl followed Delilah outside. She held him back with a cautionary arm when they reached a large rectangular pad near the side of their dwelling. She entered simple commands into a control panel, and the entire pad began to rise. Three doors became visible as it rose higher. It extended even further, exposing another three, before she halted it.

"How many levels are there?" Mykl asked.

"Four so far. I program in more as we need them."

She opened one of the doors with a tap of her finger. Inside was a scaled-down version of the cart Mykl had appropriated earlier in the morning. Delilah pushed it out and showed him how to adjust the pedals to better fit the length of his legs. The front seat even had safety belts, though the passenger side belt seemed too small even for Mykl. It must have been custom-made for Stinker. As efficient as the setup was, he couldn't help but think it would make for a sickeningly cute picture if he and Stinker were belted in together.

"I'll be right back," Delilah said.

Mykl adjusted himself in his seat and tested the controls. This was going to be a lot more enjoyable than the previous ride.

Delilah returned, and sure enough, she had Stinker with her. She buckled the bear in its seat and said, "There should be enough charge to make a lap around the City if you wish."

"Thank you, Lahlah," he said, and he was off. He wasn't about to stick around for pictures.

The cart's top speed was less than that of the adult version. That was to be expected. In time, he was sure he could reprogram that, if he really wanted. But right now, he just wanted to see the parts of the City he had missed on his brief tour with Jack.

He started a counterclockwise lap of the City's outer ring.

Where in the world is everybody? he thought as he cruised through what looked like a residential area. The architecture of the houses made for plenty of privacy if one so chose, but there were no people to need privacy from—and still no children. Larger buildings that might be restaurants or stores also stood vacant. Had everyone already evacuated? And if so, where to?

The tranquil neighborhood felt eerie and creepy. Mykl stopped to feed the fish—and to make sure they hadn't disappeared too.

With less than thirty minutes left to roam, a thought struck him. In an instant, he ran back to his cart and departed straight for the frozen black tidal wave.

He managed a decent sideways skid to a stop. He unbuckled Stinker and tucked him under an arm for an extra level of protection. One couldn't be too careful when entering an area housing alien life.

He made his way quickly through the security doors. In the lab that held Noah, he found the tiny white mouse standing on top of a pile of empty pistachio shells. Noah stretched up on skinny back legs until he wobbled for balance. When he recognized Mykl, he exploded into a run, sending shells flying everywhere.

Mykl was perplexed by Noah's strange behavior. The cage shook as the mouse raced through piles of wood shavings and bounded off miniature toys that blocked its path. He took a flying leap from the far end of the cage to a swing that hung in the middle. His momentum carried him to the side nearest Mykl. As he leapt off the swing, his feet clasped the slick wires running down the cage. Slowly, extending one spindly arm out toward Mykl, the mouse slid to the bottom crossbar.

"What is *up* with you?" Mykl asked. "Have you been out of pistachios all day?"

The mouse extended its other arm through the wires and made grabbing motions. Not toward Mykl, but toward the creature under his arm. *Stinker?*

Mykl pulled Stinker up to the cage. Noah held on to the wires and began jumping up and down on the crossbar while trying to squish his face through the stiff vertical wires.

"You want the bear?"

Noah ran to the cage door and pointed at the latch. Mykl unlocked it, then held Stinker's face at the opening. Noah leapt from the cage onto the bear's head, then climbed under the right armpit—where it promptly disappeared.

Mykl lifted the bear's arm. Noah's nose and whiskers twitched from beyond a tear in the seam.

"You've done this before," said Mykl.

Noah poked his head the rest of the way out and winked.

"Well, I was coming to say goodbye before we left, but I like your idea better."

Mykl closed the cage and began to leave. A loud, high-pitched squeak stopped him in his tracks. He looked down at Noah, who was waving an arm toward a canister on a nearby table.

"Oh, right," Mykl said. "Pistachios to go."

***

"You're back early," Delilah said.

"I'd seen enough—and I had to pee." Mykl made a beeline to his room, hoping no one could hear the pistachios crunching in his bulging pockets.

Delilah called after him, "Your flight suit is on your bed, along with a travel duffel. I packed some of your clothes but left space for more items if there's anything else you want to bring."

Could she have made this any easier? Mykl carefully laid Stinker on the bed and selected some pairs of socks to stuff nuts into. He looked around; what else was there to bring? Lawrence's jacket still hung from the back of his chair. That needed to go back to the nice man. The ranger probably needed it more than him.

Mykl picked up the dark blue flight suit and put it on. It had long sleeves and a single zipper all the way down the front—and it was *heavy*.

"Why is it so heavy?" Mykl asked, walking out in his socks to model the suit for Delilah.

"Oh, that's a surprise I'm sure you're going to like," she said.

If she was going to play that game, he felt a little better about the surprise in his bear. "Okay." He shrugged and turned to go back to his room, but stopped at the threshold. In his rush to empty his pockets, he had failed to notice a new picture by his door. The wall displayed a candid shot of him and Stinker cruising in the cart. Cute as can be.

A smug chuckle erupted behind him. He grunted in defeat and continued inside to finish packing.

Several minutes later, with Stinker under one arm and the duffel strapped over his shoulder, hanging below his knees, he proclaimed, "Ready when you are." Then he added, "Oh, I still have Lawrence's jacket. Can we get it back to him?"

Delilah smiled. "Just leave it in your room."

"But—"

"We'll make sure he gets it," she assured him.

Jack joined them, suited similarly to Mykl. "I think this thing's shrinking," he said, tugging at the collar.

"Of course it is, dear," Delilah said, patting his belly.

Jack planted a hard kiss on his wife, then they stared into each other's eyes for several seconds. Mykl was certain some sort of telepathy was going on.

Jack reluctantly released her. "Ready to go, Mykl?"

Mykl pointed at Delilah, who wasn't wearing a special suit. "Lahlah?" he asked with a frown.

"I'm needed here to recalibrate the automated systems controlling the City's structural integrity. Once that's done, I'll be right behind you." She kneeled and fully enveloped Mykl in a bone-popping hug. She kissed his forehead, then gave him the same long stare she had shared with Jack. Now he understood. Love doesn't need telepathy.

With a single glance back at his waving grandmother, he took Jack's hand, and they were off.

Jack explained, as they drove past the road to the portal where Mykl had first entered the City, that they would be taking a different route to their plane. The total travel time by underground tram would be a few minutes longer.

They were first to arrive at the portal, which looked like any other vault door Mykl had encountered during his brief stay in the City.

A much larger cart approached. As it got closer, Mykl recognized Dr. Lee and Tony in the front seat. The rear of the cart contained a silver cylinder the size of a large coffin. The cart appeared to be specifically designed to carry the cylinder rather than passengers. Tony executed a 180-degree turn and backed the cart up to the portal ramp. The size and shape of the cylinder put Mykl immediately at unease. Jack had said Dawn was supposed to meet them here, yet she was nowhere to be seen. *Is that...?*

He ran to the cylinder to inspect it. As he touched it, he reflexively withdrew his hand, thinking he had been burned. But it wasn't heat, but freezing cold that had briefly fooled his nerve endings. He looked from his hand to Dr. Lee, silently begging her to not confirm his suspicion.

"Yes, Mykl," she said in answer.

He lowered his eyes, knowing she would now try to explain, justify, and mollify. He listened quietly as she spoke of a tumor, cancer, and mortality probabilities. Mykl was confused as to why she used current tense in her explanation: "was dying," not "has died." Then she used the word "treatment," and relief washed over him. He had foolishly jumped to the conclusion that Dawn was dead. All his nagging questions and contradictory observations crystallized into a diamond-hard epiphany of understanding.

"She's frozen, isn't she?" Mykl said, interrupting. He just needed this one confirmation to make all the pieces fit.

"Not yet. But she will be soon," Dr. Lee answered.

"She's not the only one, either." Mykl turned from Dr. Lee to Jack. "Is she? That's where all the children are… and the adults. Everyone's frozen." He felt a whisker tickle the inside of his fingers holding Stinker. He understood. "This isn't a city; it's an ark."

"And more," said Jack. "And not the only one. It wouldn't be wise to put all our eggs in one basket. Despite the outside world's current efforts, the human race *will* survive. It is my sincere wish that Dawn will survive too. Except for us, everyone still in the City has undergone the freezing process. It is necessary for full adaptation when artificially introducing the alien DNA."

Dr. Lee handed Mykl a small envelope. "Dawn wanted me to give this to you."

Mykl opened it and slid out the handwritten note. A lump formed in his throat, and he couldn't help but smile when he read it.

Shortstuff
Make sure I don't oversleep!
See you soon!

He hugged Dr. Lee. "Thank you," he said, and he stuffed the note into his duffel for safekeeping.

The tram flew smoothly along tracks it never touched. Mykl gazed at his reflection in the window and on the glossy undulating surface of the tunnel's inner surface. An infinity of Mykls stared back at him from the dual reflecting surfaces; he commanded all of them with the slightest movement of his head.

A cold nose pressed against his hand. With as much stealth as he could muster, he retrieved a pistachio from his pocket and stuffed it under the bear's arm. He hoped the muffled crack coming from inside didn't reach anybody else's ears.

CHAPTER 51

A slight shifting of Mykl's weight announced the slowing of the tram. At full stop, the doors slid open on their own. Mykl declined Jack's offer to hold Stinker as he clumsily crawled out with his duffel.

Dr. Lee and Tony manipulated Dawn's cryo-cylinder as if it were weightless. Thin strips with a metallic sheen followed a path under the clear floor. They must have produced electromagnetic levitation like the tram tunnel, but on a smaller scale. Mykl could see, by the ease with which they handled the cylinder, that they had done this many times before. More frozen citizens likely inhabited their destination.

The high ceilinged enclosure they stepped into stored hundreds of dusty, rusting, fifty-five-gallon drums stacked haphazardly. Some oozed sticky goo between ill-fitting lids, partially obscuring yellow radiation emblems. Jack said not to worry: the drums were just props to warn away the curious. As if to prove the point, he procured sunglasses for everyone from one of the drums, stating that they would help when stepping into the brightness outside.

Tony transferred Dawn's cylinder to a large wheeled pushcart while Jack checked the exterior sensors and camera feeds.

As soon as Jack activated the opening mechanism for the massive security doors, a gust of arid wind blew Mykl's hair back.

Beyond the doorway, identical giant mounds of earth zipped in long rows to his left and right, each with a weathered and rusted door, closed and blocked with imposing thick metal beams. *These are fortified bunkers*, Mykl realized. Most of the doors displayed warning symbols with skulls and crossbones. Peeling placards declared the contents of each poisoned Pandora's Box. Behind them, their own placard read, "Nuclear Pathogen."

Jack led them around their bunker to an airplane boneyard of sun-bleached fuselages. One carcass conspicuously stood out among the others: a flat triangle devoid of wings. The tip on the right hand side had been buried by windblown sand. Desert birds made nests in jagged holes throughout the fuselage.

"What is that?" Mykl asked, pointing.

"That is the failed Aurora project," said Jack. "Designed to be the fastest and most stealthy aircraft ever devised by man."

"Why did it fail?"

"They couldn't figure out how to make it fly well enough to be of use. And after billions of dollars invested, and threats of war if they succeeded, they finally gave up. It sits out here in plain view of satellites as proof of their abandoning it in the name of peace. Of course, Russia and China know it's only out here because our military couldn't get it to work."

"Isn't this the kind of thing you were supposed to help with?" Mykl asked.

"I count it as one of our successes."

"A plane that doesn't fly?"

"A war that never happened."

Mykl began to understand better the manner in which Jack answered questions. He never gave a full answer; one had to read between the lines. It was probably an unconscious defense mechanism developed while living in a world of secrets for so long.

Mykl considered. If the failed plane resulted from a program that Jack had successfully sabotaged, that meant...

"Where is the *successful* Aurora project plane?" he asked.

"Right this way."

Jack led them down a path through the junkers.

A nondescript plane waited a wingspan off a poorly maintained runway of weathered asphalt. Yellowish stains streaked from its side rivets to its underbelly. Bald tires displayed a mosaic of cracks around the sidewalls. It even featured a dent in the rear passenger section as if it had been bumped by one the other bones dragged in here to be buried by the elements.

"This thing can fly?" Mykl asked warily.

"It's the fastest plane on the planet right now."

Mykl examined the plane more carefully. The windows were intact and crystal clear. And he noticed a slight shimmer where the outline of the fuselage met the sky. Without taking his eyes off the plane, Mykl asked, "What color will it be when we land?"

"Whatever color it needs to be," Jack replied.

The plane's interior was a clean modern cabin. Mykl had never been in a plane before but thought it odd that handholds should be mounted on every seat and along the full length of the ceiling. Thick padding insulated the walls against the whistling winds outside. He could actually hear his footsteps compressing the dense carpet.

An attendant offered to stow his duffel. He reluctantly relinquished it, figuring it wouldn't be too terribly hard to make an excuse to reacquire it if he needed to. But when she asked if he would like to stow the bear, he gave her a look that let her know not to ask again.

"We don't have your seat configured yet, Mykl, but they have accommodations for you in the cockpit," said the attendant.

Configured? Mykl examined the seats. Each had a multipoint harness with a connecting hub, but they were clearly designed for adult bodies. The hub would rest right over his face. Evidently, non-frozen children were a rarity on this flight. But with luck, perhaps they would at least have ice cream.

In the cockpit, Jack patted a jump seat beside him, behind the pilot. A lap belt served as the seat's lone safety measure.

"Is this enough?" Mykl asked. "The other seats have a lot more belts."

"We aren't going to be setting any speed records today," Jack said.

"Make sure to hang on to Stinker if things get bumpy."

"Where are we going?" Mykl asked. He doubted Jack would tell him anything, but it didn't hurt to try.

"A safe place with a view," Jack said.

Above ground. Possibly a remote mountaintop. Those were the first things that came to Mykl's mind.

"How long is it going to take to get there?" he asked.

"Two days."

Two *days?* Mykl deflated; he was tempted to initiate a toddler meltdown. The fastest plane on the planet, and it was going to take two *days* to get to their destination? If it were up to him, he would vote for setting a new speed record. But it wasn't up to him, and he would have to be patient. Too bad he didn't have any of James's knots to untie.

A pressure on his eardrums coincided with a thump from the outside cabin area. "Doors secure," the attendant reported.

The pilot flipped a few switches, and the plane's front wheel slowly crunched and bumped along the brittle asphalt to the end of the runway. Mykl sensed an ever-increasing rumbling vibration through his seat. Then another problem occurred to him.

"If the satellites can see this area, won't they notice a plane missing? Or flying?"

"We control the satellite feeds. *All* the satellite feeds. And radar, laser, and nonvisible wave frequencies. The only means of detecting us right now is from high-powered optics using visible wavelengths. As it is, we're just a plain old plane," Jack said.

Mykl narrowed his eyes at Jack. "For how long?"

"A few minutes after takeoff. Then we'll start color-morphing to blend in with the sky."

Mykl nodded. That was a much better answer than he'd expected.

The plane made a turn and suddenly thrust forward. Stinker was pressed into Mykl's chest. The roar of the engines, combined with the muffled sound of air shrieking past them, brought a smile to Mykl's face. He watched in amazement as the ground blurred and sped away.

Then the nose of the plane lifted, and blue sky filled the windshield.

One final bump, and they leapt from the earth. Mykl's heart pounded in his chest. *I want to do that again!*

Instead of changing course away from the boneyard as he'd expected, the plane kept flying in a tight spiral, ever upward. He couldn't see anything but a darkening sky and an occasional flash of sunlight through the cockpit windows. How much altitude did they need before they could safely depart to this mystery place?

Up. Up. Up. The sky turned inky black. The pilot killed the engines and flipped other switches. Still they rose. Mykl craned his neck to see out the windows better. Stars began to appear. His weight gradually disappeared. Then it dawned on him: they weren't climbing for safety; they were climbing with a purpose—to reach space.

"Are we going to a space station?" Mykl asked in awe.

"You could call it that," Jack said. "Show him," he said to the pilot.

The plane leveled out, putting them into full weightlessness. Mykl swallowed, glad to not have eaten anything in the last few hours. The pilot slowly rolled the plane and pivoted it so the Earth filled the windshield.

Mykl experienced a sense of déjà vu. *I've seen this view before. Only it was a toy globe. This is real.*

He tore his eyes away from the view. "I still don't understand," he said. "I don't see any space station. Is it color-morphed too?"

"That's beyond even our technology at the moment," Jack said. He nodded to the pilot, and the plane swiveled once again. A much less colorful spectacle reflected light through the windshield. In his surprise, Mykl's mouth formed a circle, like the heavily cratered celestial body framed before them.

"That's no space station!" he exclaimed. "Wait—why are you laughing?"

CHAPTER 52

A deadly-looking black helicopter, bristling with turrets and missile pods, greeted Jessica as she stepped into the sunlight. Two men in full battle gear jumped out and landed lightly on their feet. Feeling unsure, Jessica held her ground as the armed men jogged toward her. When they got close enough, she recognized these men: they were the same ones who had arrested her at the accelerator facility.

Outwardly, she wore a cool blank expression. Inside, her panicked thoughts ran wild. *They're going to recognize me. How do I explain my reappearance?*

"Good afternoon, Miss Stafford," the first man said, shaking her hand while flashing a shy smile. The other one took her still-outstretched hand and greeted her the same.

Jessica stared, only then realizing that they were identical twins. She hadn't made the connection before because of the duress they put her under.

"You two are…"

The first one helped her out by saying, "We're with Jack." The second one added, "Have been for quite some time."

"I'm Robert," the first one said.

"And I'm William. Jack affectionately calls us Billybob."

Jessica blinked in acknowledgement, still too flabbergasted to speak.

These two had terrified her when they first met, and now here they were, babbling on like old friends reunited.

"Normally we make bets between ourselves as to who will pass the test or not," Robert said.

"But in your case, neither of us wanted to bet against you," said William.

"We knew you would make it," said Billybob admiringly.

They had just paid her one of the highest compliments she had ever been given. "Thank you," she said meekly.

"It is now our honor to accompany you on your first mission," said Robert.

"If you will please join us in the helicopter, Miss Stafford?" asked William.

These two men were acting as her protectors. She blamed the dust whipped up by the rotor blades for the moisture in her eyes.

When they were airborne, she asked them how they had come to know Jack. Robert said Jack rescued them ages ago when they were very young. She asked how long ago that was, and William responded by tapping a finger along the side of his nose in the age-old gesture meaning: "Don't ask what you already know." She left it at that.

They circled in for a landing in a spot that had nothing but stunted bushes and drab sand for miles. Robert and William hopped out the moment they touched down.

"This is your next pickup point, Miss Stafford," said Robert as they helped her out.

"Jessica," she said. "Call me Jessica."

They both flashed bright smiles.

When her feet touched the ground, she knew it wasn't desert soil underneath her but rather a high-resolution camouflage pad, hard as concrete. Even this close, its edges blended seamlessly with the natural landscape.

They moved her to the outer boundary of the pad.

"Your ride is ten minutes out," said William. "And I guarantee that no one on that helicopter is an agent. They're private contractors who cater to high-end clientele in need of discreet transportation. We have agents at the hotel, but you are not to seek them out. They will initiate contact with you, if needed, or if things change. The stage is yours."

"Good luck," they both said in unison, and they gave her a sharp salute before reboarding their helicopter.

With an arm outstretched in farewell, she wanted to yell, "Wait," but could think of nothing to justify it except a visceral fear of not wanting to be left alone in the middle of nowhere.

The thumping sound of the rotating blades faded away, and the helicopter became a barely discernable speck. She waited in silence. A silence so profound that she heard nothing but her heartbeat.

She turned in a circle, taking in her surroundings. The scent of sage weighed heavy in the air from rotor-washed bushes nearby. On a rock, a jittery lizard with a black-and-white-striped tail executed pushups in a territorial display. Jessica smiled, seeing that she wasn't alone after all.

She kept a constant scan of the southern horizon, expecting her ride to come from the direction of Las Vegas. Instead, a glint of reflected sunlight appeared in the west. The growing helicopter generated more of a refined humming sound than the aggressive thumping of the military version. Its elegant lines and smooth white finish looked more suited to the shape of a limousine. It landed lightly as far from her as the pad allowed, probably so as not to blast her with rotor wash.

A door on the side slid open, then a short section of steps was lowered and a bolt of red carpet unrolled from the bottom step. Two men and a woman in formal attire approached her at a fast walk. The woman looked like she should be modeling on a catwalk, and her flouncing strides hinted that she might have once done so. The men, a step behind and working to keep pace, carried trays.

The three of them stopped a short distance from Jessica and made respectful bows.

"I hope we haven't kept you waiting, Miss Stafford?" The woman had a foreign accent that Jessica couldn't identify.

The man to her left offered her a warm moist towel from his tray. "To wipe the dust kicked up from our landing, ma'am," he said.

The other man served her a tall glass of cold water. "We also have champagne on board if you would prefer?"

Jessica had never experienced such deferential treatment before. But Jack had advised her to play her role, and it was about time she started.

She dabbed her face with the towel and tossed it back into the man's chest. "Water will be fine," she said, accepting the glass. After a tiny sip, she commanded, "Take me to my hotel," and left them all to follow in her wake to the red carpet. While he hadn't said so in such crude terms, Jack had suggested she act like a haughty bitch. That attitude had never appealed to her in the past, but it was proving entertaining nevertheless.

The interior of the helicopter had been partitioned like a limousine, affording her a peaceful space all to herself, where she was reminded of the sobering reality of her mission. She still harbored anger at being used to start a global war—and she decided to channel those feelings into her role. Had Jack planned that as well? Could he orchestrate and manipulate people so precisely?

She hoped he could. The alternative was a world on fire.

Cool twilight had fallen before their westward arcing flight path brought them to the glittering treasure box of the Las Vegas valley. A straight course would have been appreciably faster, but that would have taken them over restricted airspace, and following interstate freeways would have put them in constant view of Joe Public. This company apparently took its promise of discretion and privacy very seriously.

A minor congregation of hotel security and concierge staff formed a welcome line on the top of the hotel. Jessica was courteously passed off to the hotel's finest and was safely inside the executive elevator before the helicopter took off again. Sharp-dressed hotel representatives advised her that this elevator served only the top two levels, and her encrypted key could override it even in emergency fire control mode. A perk for the wealthy with helicopters, who could afford their own means of rescue or escape. It would not, however, allow her access to the penthouse.

As the elevator began its brief descent, a bespectacled young man with a bean counter aura said, "A hotel account has been set up for you in advance of your arrival, and funds for your credit line were wired to us this morning." He offered Jessica a tablet with her information. "If you will sign on the 'X' and initial for your room, it will activate your keys and debit your first month of tenancy."

Jessica took the pad. One whole *month*. Maybe Jack received a government discount? She read the value of her credit line and had to keep recounting the zeros to be sure she was seeing things correctly. Eight zeros, not counting the decimal places. One hundred million dollars.

She forced herself to breathe normally as she signed. Her breath caught again at the cost of her room. Three million for the month. She initialed quickly and returned the tablet before anyone noticed her hands shaking.

"Thank you, Miss Stafford. Now for your key. Would you like card, ring, pin, or indelible?"

She suffered a long history of losing things and being a bit of a klutz. Trying to remember a pin number in an emergency was akin to flipping a light switch during a power failure. "Indelible, please?" she asked, and cringed inwardly for being so polite. She needed more practice at being a bitch.

She held out her left arm. The bean counter placed a portable indeliprinter on the inside of her wrist and triggered it. The cool spray of indelible electromagnetic ink pattered against her sensitive skin. He removed the device, and she examined the printed area. A perfect color match. Only the slight sheen of drying ink gave it away, and even that rapidly dissipated, leaving no visible trace of the key allowing her access to the casino, her room, and her millions.

She held out her other wrist.

"Both?" he asked.

"Don't make me ask. Just do it!" she said irritably. "I wouldn't want to spill my wine while trying to open a door, now would I?"

He printed her other wrist. "And what wine would you like brought to you, ma'am?"

"The best you've got!" she said, not knowing a thing about wine.

"As you wish. You are in Suite 9902, any of the four doors on your right. The second is the main entry. The suite comprising the other half of your floor is currently unoccupied, should you wish to procure that as well. Please don't hesitate to ask if we may be of further assistance."

She was hastening down the wide, opulent hallway before he'd even finished his spiel. A flick of her right hand over her shoulder was the only acknowledgement she gave him.

She fought the urge to escape into the first door she came across, proceeding to the main entry, which sported intricately carved ten-foot-high double doors of fine walnut. She presented her wrist to the scanner. It clicked from red to green. The door pushed open easily.

Lights came on automatically, flooding a living space larger than she had ever seen. Lacking the energy to explore her temporary home, she flopped face-first into the soft cushions of the closest oversized couch. Limbs carelessly sprawled out, she let out a sigh and closed her eyes to the panoramic city view streaming through floor-to-ceiling windows.

That first test had been easy compared to this. All she had to do before was be herself and do the right thing. Now she had to light a fuse—the consequences of which could extinguish every light in the city, and far beyond.

She buried her face in her arms. *The fuse can wait ten minutes. I need a nap.*

CHAPTER 53

Tom slammed his foot on the brake, and his ambulance shuddered to a staccato stop as the antilock braking mechanism kicked in. A full cup of hot coffee clattered and splattered at his feet.

"That little turd goblin! I swear that's the same kid from the other night!" he complained halfheartedly, then chuckled at the wet mess under his shoes.

"You know," his partner said, "I've noticed that you don't get nearly as bent out of shape as most others do. Why is that?"

"Well. It's kinda like you've said before. Job security."

"There's more to it though, isn't there?" his partner asked, prying for a deeper answer.

Tom tossed a large wad of napkins on the floor mat and began shifting them around with his feet. "Yes. There's more." He drove the ambulance out of the travel lane and popped out the air brake switch. "I used to think we were working against Darwin. We save people from their own stupidity, which enables them to keep breeding."

"You don't think that anymore?"

"Oh, we still save stupid people, always will, but by saving them, they educate others, through their escapades, what *not* to do. Take that drunk driver who killed a kid last week. It would have been so easy to claim I couldn't establish an airway and let the man die in the back of my ambulance. An eye for an eye. He killed a kid, right? No one would care. But—if he lives… If he learns his lesson because of his experience, and influences one other person not to drive drunk—well, that may be one other kid I save by proxy."

"What about the addicts?"

"What about 'em? We've saved more people from overdoses than I care to count. As far as I'm concerned, the addicts are volunteer test subjects for our medicines. The reason we save so many is because our antidotes work so well, thanks to their eagerness to test them. Don't get me wrong: it's not saving the addicts that makes me feel all warm and fuzzy. It's the person who mistakenly took too much medicine or the child who discovered a bottle of pills that the addicts benefit most. Without the addicts as test subjects, I don't think our stuff would work near as well.

"So in the grand scheme of things," Tom said, "I just do the best job I can. I could sit on my ass, do the bare minimum required, and collect my paycheck like a lot of others do. But that's not me. This is my chosen profession. I want to make a difference in the world. And the only way I can see doing that is to do my best. Do the right thing. Even when no one's looking. It helps me sleep better at night. Does that make sense?"

His partner nodded.

"What about you?" Tom asked. "Do you ever choose who lives or dies?"

"Sometimes."

CHAPTER 54

Linda yawned. She yearned to sleep on her beloved couch. But the remembered insinuation that *they* would be looking in on her kept her awake. That, and the security cameras she now knew were being monitored elsewhere.

The outer entry buzzer rang. She looked to the monitor on her desk and was startled to see a giant blurry eyeball filling the screen.

"What the hell…"

The eyeball left the screen and was replaced by an equally giant tongue licking the wide-angle lens. Then the person violating her camera leaned back far enough for her to identify. He waved with a stupid grin on his face.

"Unfrickinbelievable…" she said under her breath. *Please no*, she wished as she buzzed the lock and went to the door.

She opened it, and James fell off the suitcase he stood on.

"Hi Lindas! Misses me?"

"James? Why on earth are you back here?"

James thrust a much crumpled envelope at her. Warily, she took it, saw her name written on it, and opened it. She read with disbelieving eyes as James struggled to get to his feet.

Her hand fell limply in despair. "You're coming back to live *here?*

And you've got a *job*?"

James made a clumsy attempt to stand at attention and executed a sloppy left-handed salute. His slinky half flew off his wrist and hit him in the face.

Linda put a palm to her forehead and closed her eyes. The letter was signed by that Jack guy. She really didn't have a choice in the matter.

"Go in," she said in a tone better suited to the phrase: *Why me?* She looked up in disgust at the saliva-covered camera lens and shuddered.

James stumbled over the threshold and dragged his suitcase through upside-down, its wheels in the air.

"Your old room is still available. Put your things in there," said Linda.

"Okays," he replied.

***

Little had changed in the two days James had been absent from the Box. It smelled like they might have had the couch and carpet cleaned though, and a general look of relief softened the children's faces. With the oppressive cloud of Lori removed from the equation, it was easy to understand why.

Recorded cartoons continued to consume the majority of everyone's attention. With so much of their lives spent in the time machine of television, they had to know by now who the Angel was—and that her tragic accident in prison meant they were safe again.

A few children noticed him and began whispering and pointing. Some looked sad, possibly because they thought his adoption had failed. Others developed a malicious glint in their eyes that told James they were thinking of how to make fun of him for the same reason. With Dawn no longer available as a target, they might choose to direct their torment at him. No matter; he could easily endure it.

Tina disappeared into the quad with a large cup of water. James altered his course to investigate. Peeking out, he saw her dump the entire cup into the dirt at the base of the rose plant where Teeka was buried.

More leaves had sprouted since the last time he'd lain eyes on it. It even had a swollen rosebud with hints of red, ready to bloom. She must have been watering it ever since he left. That, along with the nutrients being supplied by Teeka's decomposing body, stimulated it to thrive.

"Hi Teenas," he drawled.

"James! You're back!" she said excitedly. "Is Mykl back too?"

"Nooo. Mykl gones." He hung his head and put on a pouty sad face.

She rushed to hug him. "It's okay. I missed you too," she said, smiling up at him brightly. "Look at Teeka's rose! Isn't it pretty? I wish Dawn could have it."

James gave a number of exaggerated nods. This little girl's positive energy had always impressed him. Now she had become to him what Jack called a "priority action item."

"Me toos," he said, and he followed her back inside, still dragging his suitcase. "James goes to bed now. Gots works tomorrows."

"Work? Where?"

"The Poorbus Eminems."

Tina's brow wrinkled. Then her eyebrows rose in understanding. "Oh, you mean the E Pluribus Unum, silly."

James nodded. "Poorbus Eminems."

"Well, you better go to bed then. See you tomorrow!"

"Bye, Teenas," he said.

He dragged his suitcase down the hall, letting it paint a black scuffmark the entire way. Except for the linens having been stripped from the beds, his old room remained the same. They hadn't even resecured the bars over his window. That would be convenient if he had to disappear again.

He closed the door and began to unpack. He placed his old asylum clothes back into their original drawers. The slinky he positioned carefully on the desk where he used to write dots. Dawn's letter, containing her lock of hair, he kept on his person. It was much too precious to leave lying about where sticky fingers might find it.

After reading Dawn's letter one more time, he rolled over on the bare mattress and drifted off to sleep.

CHAPTER 55

Sebastian stuffed a hundred-dollar bill into the stripper's stretchy G-string. He knew from classified files that this particular girl was often used as a go-between for the Chinese couriers. Approaching them unannounced or without invitation usually resulted in loss of blood or consciousness, but their favorite stripper would know the right things to say, or do, to get him an audience.

His inside source at the E Pluribus Unum had recounted Jessica's clandestine return and her surprising credit line. Evidently, the man who'd been on the rooftop—the man who'd made a deal with Jessica and had offered Sebastian a princely sum—knew how to invest his money.

Still, that man was only an individual. China represented a population of almost two billion, and they desperately needed fusion technology... or better. If Sebastian could strike a deal with them before Jessica did, or that other guy, then riches beyond his wildest dreams awaited him. True, he didn't have the technical details on fusion to sell, but he *did* know the approximate location of the alien artifact.

Alien. He certainly wasn't going to share that part of the secret with the Chinese—yet. It was only in his panic to save his own skin that he'd blurted it out to the man on the roof. The technology would speak for itself.

If Jessica declined to cooperate, he would eliminate her. Then he'd hope the man who'd made the purchase from her didn't want to resell his newly acquired secret. That would leave Sebastian in position to sell the artifact to the highest bidder.

The stripper thrust a shapely hip at him. She gyrated her best asset to reinforce her demand. He obliged by adding a matching bill to the other side of her single article of clothing.

"They will see you now," she said. "Lucky booth number seven."

Dark carpet, black paint, and scarce lighting maintained the anonymity of clients coming and going from special dances in private booths. Sebastian knocked timidly on number seven.

"Enter," an Asian-accented voice boomed.

Sebastian stumbled into the cramped room. His eyes adjusted enough to discern that two of the four men sitting on the curved couch had handguns trained on him. Weak overhead lighting shadowed their faces beyond recognition.

"Tell me why we shouldn't kill you."

Not again. This was getting ridiculous. Sebastian couldn't tell which one said it. Since the two on the ends held the guns, it was likely one of the two in the middle. The boss. Sebastian had acquired a new vest, but that wouldn't do any good in close quarters if they truly did want to kill him. And he'd had to check his own weapon at the entrance. The fact that these men were allowed to keep theirs confirmed the power they wielded.

"I have information to sell," he said.

"Do not waste our time, Mr. Falstano. Yes, we know who you are. It appears your pretty cohort has already made a sale. Tell us. What did she sell, and what do you have to offer? I warn you. Do not play us the fool."

Sebastian swallowed. Their own intelligence network worked as well as his. Still, he knew things they didn't. "She sold fusion technology. I witnessed the working model before I was released."

"Fired," the man interjected.

Sebastian ignored the comment; he was determined not to be bullied. "From the secret documents I read, the process is only sustainable in the prototype particle accelerator that houses it. I can get the details and formulas from her."

"Why shouldn't we bury you in the desert and purchase the information directly from her?"

"There's an even greater technology being protected at a secret location. She doesn't know where it is or how it works. I alone know its location. The tech is beyond me—you would have to reverse engineer it yourself, but I have complete faith that the great country of China could achieve such a feat. The person who paid Miss Stafford for fusion offered to buy this technology from me if I could bring it to him. I'm offering to sell it to you, exclusively."

The couriers talked rapidly among themselves in Chinese. After some deliberation, the boss stated, "We want both."

"One hundred billion dollars," Sebastian said, prepared to settle for much less if they chose to bargain. He didn't trust the man on the roof to pay the same; if he really had that kind of money, he should be well known—and he wasn't. He didn't even exist as far as Sebastian's efforts revealed.

"Done."

Too quick. Too easy. Either they thought him stupid, or they didn't believe he could produce results. "I would like one million up front, in good faith," he said.

"Very well then. Choose. One crumpled stripper dollar, or you may leave here alive. You may not have both."

Red-faced, Sebastian spun on his heel and left, their laughter chasing him down the darkened hallway.

Later, when he cooled off, he realized the fact he still lived was a good sign. These couriers had a long history of causing people to *disappear*. By allowing him to leave unharmed, they had at least offered him a chance to succeed. He knew he could find the location of the artifact. Now all he needed was to strike a deal with Jessica.

CHAPTER 56

"Why is it that every time you're called away, my boat needs emergency maintenance? Coincidence? I think not. What's your excuse, XO Smith?"

"Family emergency, sir."

"This is a prototype military submarine. They don't expose it to air for family emergencies. Try again, Smith."

"I was called away to be debriefed by my boss."

"That's better. See how much easier it is to be honest? Though it disappoints me to know that *I* am not your boss. So… Smith… what are *our* new orders?"

"We are to make for the southern tip of Madagascar at best possible speed."

"Madagascar? That's on the other side of the planet. It's going to take us a week to get there. What are we supposed to do when we arrive?"

"Wait. Listen. And count."

The commander shook his head in disbelief. "Fine. You're never touching my gun again, by the way. Prepare to dive!"

CHAPTER 57

Stars and the black of space filled Mykl's oval window. Jack had accompanied him back to his seat in the main cabin, where he had shown him the intricacies of his flight suit. The reason for its weight was the highly ferrous materials in its construction. Its design assisted movement on the plane during zero-g flight. Tap-zones on his appendages and torso increased or decreased magnetic attraction. With the right balance of magnetic force, he could almost walk normally. It also worked to lock himself into his seat if he didn't like the floating sensation.

Before Jack left for his own seat to get some rest, he presented Mykl with a small squeeze bottle.

"What's this for?" Mykl asked.

"It's so Noah can drink during the trip. Just fill it with water. He knows how to use it." Jack ruffled Mykl's hair. "He doesn't much care for zero g, so he'll most likely sleep while we're in transit. But he absolutely loves lunar gravity."

Mykl pressed his lips together. "I can't seem to sneak anything past you. I thought you said I was smart?"

"I said you have the *potential* to be. In matters of math and logic, you already are. In matters of life experience, I have over a hundred years on you. Besides, when I went to retrieve Noah for this trip and found his cage empty, I checked the video footage to see where he might be. It looked to me like bringing him along wasn't *entirely* your idea."

Mykl chuckled and patted Stinker, who was buckled into the seat next to him.

"There's a mouse lavatory set up in the bathroom too; you can't miss it. He'll let you know when he needs to use it."

"How many times has Noah *been* on this trip?" Mykl asked.

"A lot. Get some rest. We have at least forty more hours until we touch down."

Jack left, and Mykl returned to the stars beyond his window. Even though they were trillions of miles away, they still looked closer from this perspective. Leaning forward in his seat and pressing his face up against the window, he saw that the plane's wings had folded back to become part of the fuselage. The new non-reflective color of the plane so closely matched the black background that it took the occlusion of stars to discern the wing's edge.

Mykl yawned and leaned his seat back. Next stop—the moon.

CHAPTER 58

The moment Jessica's mind released its grip on consciousness, elegant chimes sounded throughout her suite. A low growl of frustration escaped from deep in her throat.

The video panel showed a sharply dressed waiter standing outside her door, cradling a bottle of wine. She rubbed her tired eyes. She didn't even *like* wine. It was an excuse she had made up on the spot because she'd thought it would enhance her persona.

"Your wine, madam," the waiter offered, despite her sleepy scowl. "Would you like me to open it for you?"

"No. Set it on the bar," she said waspishly. Being interrupted within seconds of entering a blissful nap canceled any need to feign grumpiness.

He set the wine down and held out a thin pad for her. She hesitated a moment and then understood: of course, a tip. It wasn't his fault. He was just doing his job, and doing it well. She added one hundred dollars to the staggering wine cost, then, as an afterthought, added another zero before tossing the pad back. To the man's credit, he didn't even check the amount. A professional through and through. He bowed to take his leave.

"Wait," she said. "Can the chimes be disabled temporarily?"

"Of course." He walked her through the suite personalization menus next to the video panel. This side of the world had a long way to go to catch up to the technology of her previous room.

This time, she proffered him a genuine thank you. Some people were best not to antagonize.

Standing in the middle of an expanse of polished marble tiles, she pursed her lips. There was no going back to sleep now. And it dawned on her, she had absolutely nothing to wear, apart from what already covered her body. Time to spend some money.

Her wrist key called the elevator. Inside, only four options illuminated for her selection: Roof, Shop, Casino, and Valet. Which reminded her: Jack had told her to buy a car. Add that to the to-do list.

She selected "Shop" to begin her spending spree.

Much to her delight, the elevator opened into a secluded private foyer with canapés and fresh flowers. She stuffed two of the savory morsels into her mouth and nicked a third when a woman entered the foyer from behind a stained-glass door.

"May I help you, Miss Stafford?" she asked, bowing slightly, her hands clasped at her waist.

Jessica, her mouth stuffed, found it impossible to speak. She mimed a drink to the woman. A chilled bottle of sparkling water was opened, poured, and offered to her before she finished swallowing.

"I need clothes," she said after clearing her palate. "Dresses, shoes, undergarments. You name it." She modeled her current attire. "This is all I have at the moment. I was… um… caught unprepared for my… vacation."

The woman crossed her arms and scrutinized Jessica, tapping a perfectly manicured nail to her lips. "Let's take some measurements and get started," she said, producing a cloth tape as if by magic from a tiny pocket at her waist.

Jessica stood with her arms apart as the woman quickly took note of her dimensions without having to write them down.

"You choose. I make fit," the woman said, holding the stained-glass door open.

Jessica stepped through into a fitting room area which opened into a luxury dress shop. The woman followed as Jessica meandered through the store, saying, "This one, this one, that one, two of these, some of those…"

The woman never wrote anything down the entire time.

"I'll need shoes to match the dresses. Use your best judgment," Jessica said. Shoe and wine shopping were definitely not in her repertoire. She'd tried to wear high heels once for a high school dance, with embarrassingly disastrous consequences. "Make sure there are a few pairs of flats as well," she added. "And have everything sent to my suite!"

"It will be done." The woman disappeared into a work area and snapped orders to unseen employees.

Jessica took that as her excuse to make an exit and get on with her list.

The escalator to the casino level glittered with signs and flashing arrows. Gamble, Jack had said. If this were actually *her* money, she sure as hell wouldn't piss it away gambling; this city thrived on losers. She paused at the bottom of the escalator, unsure how to proceed.

A suited man with a hotel nametag approached her. "May I help you, Miss Stafford?"

Jack had said he wanted her to be seen. And it appeared that everyone involved with the hotel already knew her. They must have circulated her picture among the staff so she could be singled out for preferential treatment.

"I…" She rubbed her hands together. "I would like to gamble."

"Please allow me to show you to the private cashier."

He led her past the main cashier cage where long lines of people with plastic cups waited to exchange colorful tokens. At one point, the casinos had gotten rid of tokens altogether, opting instead to do business with purely electronic transfers. But they had soon realized that, psychologically, people felt better about using the tokens in the game of surrendering money. Plain electronic debiting of their coin left them feeling coldly swindled.

She opted for a tray of ten-thousand-dollar cheques. The private cashier informed her that the table maximums had been removed for any game she wished to play, and that the tables were sufficiently funded so as not to inconvenience her on a big win. She felt it unnecessary to thank them for such generosity. It was more likely that *she* would be the one funding the tables.

The high roller area sported plush chairs and subdued lighting. It served nicely if one desired to lose money in comfort, but it wouldn't serve her purpose at all: she wanted to follow Jack's plan to be visible. So she roamed out to the main casino.

Cradling a one-million-dollar tray of cheques, she pondered where to start. Her previous gambling experience had been limited to spare change donated to grocery store slot machines. This was altogether different.

Table games ringed the floor. She decided to see how far her stacks would last around the loop before she lost it all.

The elaborate spectator sport of dice-dancing appeared to be going on at the table nearest her. She knew nothing about craps, but from a discreet distance away, she observed and absorbed the lingo. It seemed to be only as hard as one chose to make it. When a man sulked away empty-handed, she sidled into his spot. The rail still held his warmth. The men nearest her surreptitiously glanced at her tray of cheques with envy.

"New shooter!" a dealer called out. The man to her left picked up the dice. He ground them together in his palms and sent them spinning across the table.

"Six! The point is six!" the dealer said in a booming baritone.

With the grace of a klutzy physicist, Jessica selected an entire stack of cheques between thumb and forefinger and dropped them on the green felt with a resounding *thunk*.

"Hard eight," she said.

Everyone at the table instantly became statues. Conversations and dealer chatter stopped. All eyes marveled at the beautiful stack of glittering violet cheques. Then they all stared at her. No one moved.

"Please?" she asked when it appeared they needed assurance from her to resume operations.

The box man regained his composure first. "Of course, Miss

Stafford," he said. His eyes appeared to hold a measure of sadness for her, as if he were certain of the fate of her money. A low murmuring spread among the other players. Some tugged on the shirts of gamblers at nearby tables to get their attention. Within seconds, a large crowd of attentive patrons had formed concentric rings around the table, all wanting to witness this once-in-a-lifetime roll of the dice.

The stick man slid the dice to the shooter. He tentatively picked up the dice and cradled them in his palm. Then he crushed them into his fist, pounded his fist twice on the padded rail, and said to the dealer, "I don't want to be responsible for this." Staring at the two-hundred-thousand-dollar stack in the middle of the table, he opened his hand and held out the dice to Jessica.

It was a breach of casino protocol as well as poor table etiquette. The dealers all looked to the box man in charge of the table. "Any objections?" he asked, scanning the bettors' faces.

None objected.

"The dice are yours, Miss Stafford," he said.

Tension quieted the crowd.

"Coward," she spat contemptuously as she snatched the dice. In the same movement, she redirected her hand to nonchalantly toss the dice against the rubber pyramids across the table. The crowd of bodies pressed in to see the result. Two tiny red squares ricocheted off each other and then spun to a stop.

A raucous roar erupted and reverberated throughout the casino. All heads turned to see what had happened to cause such an outburst. Two dice lay motionless on the green felt, their faces staring up into the lights and security domes. Painted indentations graced all four corners of the top facets.

Hard eight. Winner.

Jessica had thought it was going to be a challenge to get people to notice her. Now she held the attention of the entire casino. Men wanted to pat her on the back in congratulations, or touch her for luck. Her cold demeanor kept them at bay. She'd almost tripled her gambling stake on one roll of the dice. The box man pulled her stack into his racks and slid two one-million-dollar plaques toward her. Her payout for nine-to-one odds.

"Congratulations, Miss Stafford," he said.

She took possession of the two plaques and slid them under her cheque tray. Feeling quite generous from her big win, she took an entire stack of the ten-thousand-dollar cheques and set them in the center of the table. She ran an index finger up its length and toppled them toward the box man. After making brief eye contact with the table crew, she said, "Gentlemen," and turned to leave.

The crowd parted for her in awed respect.

"Wait!" the previous shooter called out. "Would you... would you roll my six for me? ... Please?"

She smirked, took the dice, and sent them flying once more.

"Hard six! Winner!"

Everyone within earshot now knew her name.

By the end of her two-hour gambling run, she had become a legend. She had lost wagers, of course, but the outrageous bets she won made them forgettable. And by the time she'd tasted all of the table games, she cradled ten million dollars more than she'd started with.

Security stopped her entourage of followers at the high-roller entrance, and she was glad to be free of her hounding shadow. They leached her energy to create the charged atmosphere around them. She felt drained.

A lone gambler, an older Asian man, sat at a baccarat table with his back to her. Curiosity about a game she hadn't yet played drew her closer. He was playing at five thousand dollars a hand, and using a score sheet to record the results of his bets. Judging by the look of the sheet and the horde of empty cocktail glasses, he had been grinding for hours. And judging by the size of his meager stack of cheques, he wasn't doing very well.

Jessica started to ask how the game was played, but it appeared the casino did all the dealing and drawing. A no-skill game; just bet and wait. Feeling a shade guilty for shaving the casino's profits with money that, in actuality, didn't even belong to her, she placed a million-dollar plaque in the betting circle.

The man looked up from his recording sheet and scowled at her. She gave him a "deal with it" sneer and smiled sweetly to the dealer.

A king and a nine snapped into her betting circle. An ace and six to her table partner. The dealer revealed his own pair of threes, then drew a card from the shoe. A two of hearts.

"Player wins," the dealer said to Jessica. He withdrew a plaque to match hers from beneath a covered stash and slid it next to her bet.

"Player loses," the dealer directed at the Asian man, and swiftly removed the last of his remaining stack.

"Well, that was easy," Jessica said. One stack of ten-thousand-dollar cheques remained in her tray. She placed the tray on the table and slid it to the dealer. "Yours," she said.

The dealer respectfully bowed his head in acceptance.

Picking up her two million-dollar plaques, she said, "Mine," smiled, and sauntered away, ignoring the furious glare of the Asian man. She didn't know she had badly insulted the boss of the Chinese couriers. Nor the danger of such an action.

"Would you like this deposited to your main bank account, Miss Stafford?" the woman at the cashier window asked her.

She remembered now that Jack had mentioned something about a bank account. The number of zeros in her credit line had effectively wiped out any thought of there being *more* money available to her.

Jessica pushed her plaques under the bars of the window. "Yes, please," she said. The cashier counted out eleven million dollars in plaques and made an entry into her computer. She then passed a receipt across the polished granite counter.

"Is there anything else I can do for you, Miss Stafford?"

"No," Jessica said, taking the receipt. She read it. Her mouth went dry. She read it again. "No," she repeated as she walked away.

Her account held three *billion* dollars. Plus the pittance she had just deposited.

Jessica suddenly felt very vulnerable. This kind of money made people a target. She now understood why the super-rich became recluses and lived in the tops of hotels. She wanted nothing more than to disappear into her suite now. Everyone wished for money. But at what point did it become a curse?

Jessica inhaled deeply to soothe her anxiety. *Only one more thing to accomplish tonight. The rest can wait.*

She approached the nearest security guard. "I need a few bodyguards for a while. Can you arrange that?"

The security guard relayed her request into his collar radio. "They will be right here," he said.

Three large men in loosely fitted suits soon arrived. Their jackets hung open. From the front, one could easily see an arsenal of holstered firearms. No one in their right mind would mess with even *one* of these men, let alone three. Jessica's tension eased slightly.

"Gentlemen," she said, "I need to purchase a car at the dealership across the street."

The men made tiny nods and head movements at each other as if they were telepathic. Then one said, "Follow me."

She followed. The other two tucked in close behind her. They moved through the casino like a spear, penetrating the mass of bodies between her and the exit. Rarely did her point man need to touch anyone to get them to make way. Whether it was his facial expression or the visible butts of his weapons, people eagerly stepped aside.

At the shady car dealership, her guards established a no-nonsense screen of muscle to shield her from shenanigans. Classier places existed nearby, with much larger selections, but Jack had insisted she make her purchase here. The dealership divided its lot into two halves. One side rented ego cars to that certain class of men who lacked the income to purchase one and the self-confidence to do without. The other side catered to the type of clientele who never negotiated prices or even asked what they were. If they wanted something, they bought it. All of those cars prowled behind polished glass in a glittering showroom, unsullied by grubby hands unable to afford them.

Jessica wouldn't have been at all surprised if a salesperson came out wearing an outfit split down the center: one side in a suit, the other in a

T-shirt and dirty jeans. Instead, the man who greeted them wore baggy velour sweats and oversized sunglasses, even though it was dark out.

"Whatcha want?" he asked. "I'm the owner."

"I want to buy a car," Jessica replied.

"Do ya now? What about your friends?"

"They're selling cookies."

He pulled down his glasses to peer at the bruisers behind her. "Yep. Seen 'em before. Show me the money. I show you the cars."

Jessica immediately tagged him as a douchebag. He seemed as if he couldn't care less about selling her a vehicle. But Jack must have had his reasons for picking this place. One might be that they accepted casino credit in lieu of cash. That was normally illegal, but when money is concerned, deals can always be made.

The man held out a portable scanner, and she presented her wrist with a wry smile.

"Will that cover it?" she asked haughtily.

"You got a license?"

"No." While she knew how to drive, she had never actually owned a car before—the outrageous fuel costs made them too expensive. Hence she'd had no need for a license.

"That'll be extra."

"Fine."

He swished an open hand at his showroom. "Pick your poison."

Every car sported sleek precision lines only possible in handmade automotive art. Luxury models appeared to lean back in relaxation against an invisible wind. Sport versions hugged low to the ground like a predator, ready to pounce, and able to catch anything that moved. She didn't know a lot about cars, but Jack had said she wouldn't have to. *Buy the best one on the lot*, he'd said. *You'll know it when you see it*. It would have been a lot easier if he had told her exactly which car to buy, but he'd said she would look more natural to those observing if she found it on her own.

"May I make a suggestion?" the owner asked.

"Make it quick. I'm in a hurry."

Gesturing with his whole arm like a striking cobra, he pointed at a car precariously perched on a sculpted pedestal and said, "That one."

It radiated color like fresh lava pouring out an angry volcano, and it looked equally as hot to touch. Jessica wondered why the snow-themed pedestal beneath it didn't melt. The owner depressed a switch on a nearby desk, and the pedestal slowly retracted into the ground, fulfilling the illusion of melting snow. If any car could intimidate Jessica, this one achieved it in one big goose-pimply shiver.

Jessica dared to run a finger along the polished paint. She was disappointed that it didn't make a sizzling sound. "Why this one?" she asked.

"Because you can afford it."

Jessica leveled an irritated stare at the man.

He held up his hands defensively. "You're the first person to visit that can afford it since it came in on consignment. The owner's a crazy old man who's asking way too much for it, but he pays the rent on the floor space on time, so…" He shrugged.

"What's so special about it?" Jessica began a more critical evaluation of the beast.

"Hell if I know. It's satellite-locked and requires an encrypted download to unlock the doors. *I* haven't even sat inside the damned thing," he said petulantly.

"So you don't even know if it runs?"

"It looks pretty." He flashed her a *That should be good enough for you* smile, then quickly switched tactics. "You're probably not going to be allowed to purchase it anyway. The wannabe buyer's details and credit information have to be approved by the owner first. Not sure how he would feel about a woman without a license driving his baby."

Righteous anger simmered within Jessica. She wanted to whack him upside the head with one of those million-dollar cheques she'd cashed in. Lucky for him, "crazy old man" was a decent description of Jack. Which meant this was the car she needed to buy.

"Send him my details. I want to see inside."

He mocked a submissive bow with the words, "By your command."

Then he smirked and disappeared into his office. Jessica suppressed an extreme urge to kick the car and walk off the lot.

The salesperson wore an entirely new expression when he returned—an expression that said he had just completed a sale. He confidently approached the car, opened the driver-side door, which scissored upward, and gestured for her to look inside. "Have a seat? See for yourself. Get a whiff of that new car smell."

The narrow driver's seat was deeply contoured and fitted with racing style safety belts. Jessica squirmed into it. *Damn, this feels good!* Its soft curves and indentations matched her body. It was almost as if the seat was made for her. And then she realized: it *was* made for her. Specifically for her.

As if she needed brick-over-the-head confirmation, a line of text only she could see flashed on the digital steering display: "Buy it! —J."

She wrapped her fingers around the steering wheel and gave the owner a side-eyed glance.

"Push the green button on the dash to start it," the man said.

"Inside?"

"The exhaust is connected to a ventilation system. It's safe."

She did as instructed and started the engine. It didn't have the roar and rumble that ego cars needed. This one purred contentedly, satisfied that it had no match in this jungle or any other.

The owner removed his sunglasses and leaned in further. "You know, with the commission on this, I can retire and move to Australia."

"What does this red button do?" Jessica asked, reaching for it.

"Whoa! Never touch the red button!"

Jessica jerked her hand back.

"Just kidding," he said. "That's the kill switch to stop the motor. Sorry." He looked less than apologetic.

She mashed the red button and searched for the door release. He assisted her out and back to her feet.

"So…you like it?" he asked, sounding supremely confident that this was a done deal.

She wasn't ready to put him into retirement just yet. "I don't know." She tsked. "Does it come in black?"

CHAPTER 59

An angry air horn and sirens in the distance had woken James at false dawn. He scrounged for food and snuck out of the Box before anyone else woke.

Now he wandered about inside the main entrance to the E Pluribus Unum. Not many people filled the casino at this hour, but cocktail waitresses unceasingly ran drinks to the early risers and yet-to-call-it-a-nighters. It had been years since James had hustled the casino sidewalks for tokens, and even back then, he had never taken the opportunity to explore the inside much. He found himself at a loss in the maze of shops, slots, restaurants, and gaming tables. *Where is this caterer's kitchen?*

A cocktail waitress called out to him. "You. Hey, you. Slinkyboy."

James pointed at himself.

"Yeah, you." She sashayed up to him with a tray full of empty glasses balanced on one hand, scowling like a lifelong cocktail waitress whose timeworn beauty relegated her to the lower-tipping morning shift. Her harsh voice suggested years of smoking, but her eyes remained savvy. "You lost?" she asked.

"James look for caterman."

"Caterman?"

"James supposed to work for caterman." He fidgeted with his slinky and glanced at her nametag. *Rose.*

"You work *here?*" Rose asked.

James made exaggerated nods.

"Say… you're some kinda special. Aren'tcha?"

"James not special James stupid," he said rapidly.

"I bet you are," she said slowly, giving him a once-over. "So you're going to work for the caterman. Well, friend, I can help you out. They're probably going to send you out on errands and food delivery. Let me fill you in on a little secret."

James hunched down and leaned in closer.

"They have this test they won't tell you about. When you deliver food to people and they give you money, you're supposed to bring it to me. That's the test. Don't tell anyone I told you and you won't get into trouble. Remember, it's a secret. You bring me the money and you won't lose your job. Got it?"

James nodded gravely. "How long James bring nice lady moneys?"

"At least a year. Sometimes longer. They really like to test you here."

"Okays."

"See that giant slot machine *way* off in the distance?" She pointed toward the west side of the casino.

James nodded.

"When you get there, take a left. That's the side you got your slinky on. Keep walking down that hallway and it will take you to the caterman."

"Thank yous," James said. Inside, he seethed.

"Welcome, hon." She turned and shouted, "Cocktails!"

How could a person be so devoid of common decency as to take advantage of someone with James's apparent deficiencies? And he had little choice in the matter. If he didn't surrender his tips to this evil woman, he risked blowing his cover.

He followed the waitress's directions to double doors with eye-level windows. A brass placard above them read, "Caterer's Kitchen." Just as James pushed on the swinging door to his left, something hit the other side hard enough to push him backward. A cacophony of porcelain carnage erupted from the other side, followed by a five-second lesson in the art of cursing.

James pulled the door this time instead of pushing.

A spindly young man, barely older than himself, lay sprawled on the polished tile, surrounded by broken dishes and the scattered remains of salad greens, steak, and lobster. Some type of cream soup had spilled all over his white apron.

"Hi," James said.

The young man continued cursing. He retrieved his empty tray and began filling it with the larger shards. "This is America," he said, not looking up. "We drive on the *right* side of the road." He glared up at James. "Not the left!"

James carefully kept his face blank.

"Who are you anyway?"

"Me James. Me work here," James said proudly.

"*No.* Boss!"

"What's all this ruckus?" someone yelled from deeper in the kitchen. A stocky man in a food-stained apron appeared before them. He wiped his hands, adding more blotches to the apron. "What happened?"

The young man pointed at James, "New guy."

The man noticed James for the first time. "Oh, no. Please tell me you're not stupid?"

"But James *is* stupid."

"Dammit!" He massaged his temples with the thumb and middle finger of his right hand. "Why do they keep sending me these fart-brained morons?"

"James work hards."

"Let's start with working *not* stupid! Now go see the laundry guys back the way you came and get fitted for a work uniform."

***

When James returned, he wore a long-sleeved white shirt and black slacks. The pants rode a few inches too high, but that bolstered his camouflage—along with his slinky.

"What's that spring thing on your arm?" the head caterer asked.

James protectively cradled his slinkied arm to his chest.

The man extended his arms. "Easy now," he said. "Don't be throwin' no fit on me. You can keep it. Just don't let it get in the way of your work. Got it?"

"Yes, sirs," said James.

"Don't be 'sir'n' me either. Call me Al." He held out his hand for James to shake. "We're hittin' a hard reset and startin' over, James. You're a workin' man now. Act like it."

James grasped Al's hand as if it were a ball of cotton candy he feared to crush.

"Not like that," Al said. "Like this." He squeezed solid and firm.

James squeezed back minutely harder than before.

"We'll work on it," Al said.

"Timmy!" Al shouted. The same young man as before appeared, still sullen and soaked with soup. "James, you stick with Timmy here a while. Timmy, show him the ropes. I gotta get back to work."

Timmy mouthed a few hushed curses and tugged at James's shoulder. He grabbed a wooden handle from around the corner and thrust it at James. "See them tiny ropes at the bottom of this stick? That's called a mop. This here's a bucket. Let me show you how to use it."

CHAPTER 60

The master bedroom in Jessica's suite flaunted comfortable opulence. She regretted not having found it sooner. After her exploits last night, she had returned so wiped out that she had curled up on the same couch as before and immediately fell asleep.

Before she drove away from that car dealership, she had instructed the owner to give each of her bodyguards whatever vehicle on the lot they desired and to put it on her bill. A receipt slipped under her door while she slept showed that they had negotiated for much less. One wanted nothing more than new tires for his personal vehicle; another asked for his transmission to be serviced. The last one respectfully declined any type of reimbursement whatsoever, and a smiley face was drawn by his name. Her entry camera playback showed that he was the one who brought the receipt back.

Jessica called security and asked to speak to the man. She thanked him and asked if he cared to help her again.

"Of course," he replied.

She tasked him with finding Sebastian and sending him to her suite. After she hung up, she immediately redialed and, as much as it pained her to do so, added the word "unharmed" to her request. She then ordered a room service breakfast.

Every room in her suite included so many features that an entire day spent exploring would still not allow her to experience half of them. First, she needed a shower… or a bath. The oversized tub had space to accommodate four people. But the thought of that many people occupying it simultaneously in this venue made her opt for the shower instead.

Squeezing out her damp hair as she stepped out of the gold-accented black marble shower, she went to explore the walk-in closet. It was larger than her parents' trailer; her new clothing and dresses took up only a tiny fraction of the available space. The lady from the shop must have delivered everything while she was out last night. While Jessica didn't care much for dresses, she couldn't help but rub the luxurious fabric of a gorgeous red model between her fingers. *I must try this on!*

She slipped the red dress over her head and tugged it over her soft curves. With a respectful amount of apprehensiveness, she pulled on the matching heels as well, then inspected her reflection in a full-length mirror. Jessica had never thought of herself as pretty, but now, freshly showered, shaved, and lotioned up, and in the most gorgeous dress she had ever seen, she was almost ready to reconsider.

She managed to accomplish several poses in the mirror without falling—though she did wobble a little. Turning around, she evaluated how the dress made her butt look. Not bad.

The visitor announcement chimes rang throughout the suite. She checked the bathroom security monitor. Two men waited at the main entry. The sight of one of them ignited an anger that flushed her cheeks to match the color of her dress. Bottled violence supplied all the balance she needed to storm across the slick tiles and thick carpet to meet them in her heels.

CHAPTER 61

A half cup of cold, bitter coffee was all Sebastian had to show for his efforts to confront Jessica. Concealed by a ball cap and sunglasses, he stared past the rim of his cup and evaluated his options. Sending a message directly to her suite would never work; she would surely turn him down, or worse, ignore him. He had to catch her alone and *force* her to listen.

He'd spent all last night stalking her, but that crowd following her everywhere she went had made it impossible to make a move. And then she acquired those three meatheads, who followed her around like guard dogs. She probably treated them that way, too. *Well, I'm no one's lapdog,* Sebastian thought. *I will find her and show her how things are done.*

He adjusted his sunglasses and pulled his ball cap lower. It wouldn't do for her to notice him before he noticed her. Surprise was a valuable tool. And when that didn't work, violence achieved the same end.

A hand clamped down on Sebastian's shoulder from behind, like the bite of an angry pit bull. Suddenly no longer able to control that arm, he dropped his coffee cup to the table. The man applied more pressure to the nerve plexus; he definitely commanded Sebastian's undivided attention.

"Sebastian Falstano. Miss Stafford would like to see you," the man said.

Sebastian didn't have to think too hard to realize who this man was. It took a big man to exert that kind of pressure.

"Okay," was all he could manage through the pain.

The man released him and pulled Sebastian's chair away from the table with him in it. "This way."

The man ushered him onto the escalators that Sebastian had been staking out. They exited in a shopping area, marched through a men's clothing store, and then proceeded through an opening at the back. They stopped at an elevator foyer that Sebastian never knew existed.

The man used a ring key to call the elevator, then pushed Sebastian inside. "When it stops, take a right. It's the third door on your left."

"You're not coming up?" Sebastian asked, rubbing his shoulder.

"Miss Stafford can take care of herself."

Sebastian nodded. This was going to be easy. *What a gift!*

"Excuses pleases?" A large young man with a lime green slinky on his wrist crowded into the elevator, pushing a food cart. He mashed the already lit button for the ninety-ninth floor until the door closed. Then he farted loudly. "Woof. James stinky!"

Sebastian stuffed his nose under his shirt. He was rewarded with an odor that was only marginally better, since he hadn't showered in two days. Fortunately, the elevator traveled fast. The idiot with the slinky hummed off-tune the whole way up while polishing the handle of his cart. Whenever he glanced up to make eye contact with Sebastian, he bashfully looked away.

Sebastian knew he could easily intimidate Jessica. She lacked the internal fortitude that he possessed for dealing with pressure situations. *All I have to do is step in and take control. She doesn't have a chance. If she tries to act tough, a good slap will put her back in place.*

"Are you taking that to Miss Stafford?" Sebastian asked.

"Not tellin'. Can't makes me," the young man said, shaking his head vigorously.

Sebastian pulled out his wallet. "How about if I give you a dollar?"

"James not dumbs."

"You're pretty smart, huh?"

"James stupid."

"How about *two* dollars?"

"Okays!" James agreed.

Sebastian handed over the bills.

"Yeses," James said.

"Yeses? Yeses what?"

"Yeses."

"Yes, you're taking that to Miss Stafford?"

James gave Sebastian a blank look.

The elevator stopped on the ninety-ninth floor. "How about I follow you?" Sebastian said.

"Okays."

James pounded on the main suite door with his fists. "Miss Jessica! Miss Jessica! James has you foods!"

Sebastian rolled his eyes, reached over, and pushed the visitor announcement button.

A cross between a growl and a grunt burst from behind the doors as both flew open in a synchronized whoosh. Jessica fumed in the entryway, her arms and legs extended from the effort to yank them open. Sebastian barely recognized the strikingly beautiful woman posed aggressively before him, wearing a sexy red dress, her hair still damp and wild from a shower. She curtly motioned the slinkied idiot inside, then stepped back to block Sebastian from entering, injecting him with a venomous stare. She stood so close he detected an enticing fresh scent wafting from her body.

He reached out to touch her.

She slapped him—*hard*. His cap and sunglasses went flying. Stars filled his vision.

"Listen—" he began.

She slapped him again, harder. He fell to his knees. The room spun uncontrollably. She gracefully lifted her leg, placed the heel of a dazzling shoe under his collarbone, and kicked him backward. His head rebounded off a solid column. He reeled from the impact.

"*You* listen!" she said.

He blinked his eyes to try and get them to focus. *There's something I'm supposed to be doing. A plan.* The details eluded him.

"What?" he asked, not knowing why.

Jessica cocked her arm back to deliver another blow. He cowered behind a decorative plant.

"*Never* try to touch me again."

He nodded and lowered a hand to his waistband.

Her voice sounded chilling as she said, "Touch that gun and I will holster it in your ass."

He lifted his hands in submission.

"Now," she said. "I want you to get me an audience with those Chinese diplomats upstairs."

"They're couriers."

"Whatever!" she spat back at him. "Just get me an appointment and don't be there when I show up. They don't seem to want to talk to me for some reason."

"You're a woman. Of course they don't want to talk to you." He looked up to see her lording over him, hands on hips, nostrils flaring. A posture that made her look even more enticing.

"What about the artifact?" she asked. "Have you found it?"

Sebastian looked to James, who had stopped with his cart just behind her, looking unsure what to do.

Jessica followed his glance. "What? You're worried about *him*? He can barely tie his own..." She looked at James's feet. "What, in the name of little green slinkies, did you do to your shoes, kid?"

"James like knots."

"Right." She whirled back to Sebastian. "He likes knots. I don't think we need to worry about *him* overhearing anything. Now speak!"

Sebastian swallowed. He tasted blood in his mouth. "What do *you* know about the artifact?" he asked, trying to regain his dignity.

Her body seemed to relax. She plucked a ripe strawberry from a plate on the food cart and took a bite. She chewed deliberately while staring directly at him. It unsettled him further. Right when he thought she wouldn't answer, she said, "I don't know any of the names, but they showed it to a few highly trained experts without revealing its location. All but you are still 'on the reservation,' so to speak. Probably locked away in some dark hole now that you're on the loose.

"The physicists involved with its original evaluation are spinning in their smocks to shoot another proton at it. One expert confirmed that there may be an alien language contained in it. I know that they're afraid to move it. The information I read, and heard in meetings, was that it was being stored someplace safe in case it turned out to be dangerous. With the potential energy it possesses, I can assume it's not within a thousand miles of a US coastline. That's what I know. Now. Where is it?"

This was great news to Sebastian. He had been afraid they might move it before he acquired enough resources to act. Without realizing it, Jessica had confirmed not only the artifact's location but its validity as well. He had wondered why they had chosen a location halfway across the globe to secure it. Now he knew. Information empowered him.

"I won't tell you."

A half-eaten strawberry hit him in the face.

"You don't have enough fruit to make me talk!" He wiped his face and retrieved his cap. The now lens-less glasses were a total loss. Leaning back, he assumed a more relaxed posture. "One billion dollars, and I will tell you where it is." He flashed his most insolent smile.

"Counteroffer," she said without a trace of humor. "One *million* dollars. To the man who sent you to me… to have you *erased*!"

Sebastian's smile vanished. He knew that man would gladly kill him for far less. A thousand dollars would be sufficient motivation. One million was overkill. Still, dead was dead, and she had cash to spare. It was time to utilize his most dependable skills.

"Greenland," he lied.

"I don't believe you."

"You'll have to kill me then," he bluffed.

She took a bite of another strawberry. "Perhaps later. I'm hungry now. Go get me that meeting with the Chinese. Don't show up at my door again. Call the suite and leave a message. Go. Now!"

Sebastian leaned against the wall to get his feet under him, still a little unsteady.

She pushed him into the hallway and yelled, "Fetch!" Then she slammed the doors with gusto.

At least no one else had seen him in such disgrace, he thought as he careened down the hallway to the elevator. That idiot with the slinky certainly didn't count. And even though he had completely failed to ally himself with Jessica and her fusion technology, he knew he could leverage his new information about the artifact into an earth-shattering payout for himself. *And* he didn't need to rely on anybody else's help to do it.

***

Jessica covered her mouth and looked back to see James doing the same. Stifled laughter escaped through their fingers.

"That felt so good!" Jessica said in a hushed voice.

"You were amazing!" James said. "Remind me never to piss you off!"

Jessica took a step and stumbled. James caught her. "That's enough of these," she said, pulling off her heels and tossing them aside. She padded across thick carpet in bare feet to retrieve something from the bar. She tossed it to James. "Your tip," she said.

James examined the token. "This is a thousand dollars! All I did was deliver food."

"And support me with backup muscle if I needed it. With you present, I felt a bit more emboldened."

"I think if I hadn't been here, you might have killed him," James said.

"Jack said we still need him. I had to be nice."

"Uh-huh. Nice. Right." James pocketed the token.

"Did you really tie those knots yourself?"

"Yep."

"That's messed up."

"Everybody has a superpower."

"Well, you better go rescue Sebastian, Knotboy. He should be at the elevator by now, and he can't leave without a key."

"Can I have a strawberry?" James asked.

"Don't make me hurt you," Jessica said.

James quickly snatched one off her plate and popped it into his mouth with an impish smile.

CHAPTER 62

Sebastian searched around the elevator for a call button. Nothing. Only a key code reader, and he had no key. He was stuck.

A familiar off-key humming approached from down the hall.

"Did she give you a tip?" asked Sebastian.

The idiot pulled a bill out of his pocket and brandished it. "One dollars!" he said excitedly.

"One dollar, huh? How about I give you *five* dollars and you use your key to take me one floor up?"

The kid mouthed the word "five" in awe and held up four fingers. Sebastian nodded and pulled out his wallet.

"James not supposed tos. James gets in troubles."

"I promise. I won't tell *anyone*."

"Promises?"

"Promise and hope to die," replied Sebastian.

"Okays then." James placed his slinkied wrist to the reader, and the elevator opened immediately. He did the same inside and pressed the button for the one hundredth floor a dozen times. "Moneys," he said, holding his hand out.

Sebastian forked over the five.

The kid farted again when the elevator closed. Almost as if he was doing it on purpose. Maybe he was; one never could tell with tards.

Sebastian held his breath until the doors opened again, and bolted out as soon as he fit through the opening.

"Bye, bye!" said the big kid with the slinky. The elevator doors closed.

As Sebastian let out his breath to take in a lungful of fresher air, a strong hand grabbed him from behind with enough force to bounce him off a wall. His eyes crossed as he registered the gun pointing at his face.

The man holding it asked in thickly accented English, "What are you doing on this floor?" Another man to Sebastian's right also aimed a weapon at him.

"I'm here to see Fan Kong," he said. "I have business with him."

The first man barked an order in Chinese to the second man, who nodded and disappeared down the hall. "Do not move," the first man commanded Sebastian, pressing the barrel of his gun sharply into Sebastian's sternal notch while he patted him down. Upon finding the handgun in Sebastian's waistband, he released the magazine and ejected the round in the chamber one-handed before tossing the gun aside. He must have been expertly trained to execute such a task so easily, Sebastian thought.

"Turn around," the man said.

Sebastian did so and received a thorough search down to his ankles.

The other man returned. "Fan will see him."

"I am Gang," the first man said, his gun pressed to Sebastian's spine. "If you bring a weapon here again, you will need a surgeon to remove it from you."

Sebastian nodded his understanding. Jessica and this man had a lot in common.

"That way. He is waiting," Gang said, smacking the cap off Sebastian's head and giving him a none-too-gentle shove in the right direction.

The hallway ran much shorter on this level; the presidential suite probably encompassed the entire top floor. Sebastian expected to step into a palatial display of the most rare and expensive comforts available to man, but instead, he found himself in the half circle of an anteroom with an imposing desk in the back center. Fan Kong sat behind it in the one available chair. The desk looked sturdy enough to stop a bullet.

Sebastian took in the configuration again. The desk took up the only defensible position; no doubt it *could* stop a bullet.

He also suspected that Fan's cohorts were hidden in strategic firing positions. Should he try something, or should Fan give them a signal, only the subsequent bullet holes would reveal their locations.

Sebastian sighed. He had really wanted to see the inside of the suite.

Fan gave an impatient tilt to his head. Sebastian immediately performed an appropriate bow, as was custom for those who did not want to be killed or severely beaten.

"Fan Kong, I have your information," he said.

Fan's face divulged nothing. He sat like a mannequin with unmoving eyes. "You have nothing," he said.

Sebastian concentrated on his breathing.

"You come with nothing on your person. Not even a phone. Do you expect me to believe that you have memorized all the details needed to make fusion possible?"

Sebastian relaxed. So *that's* what he meant. This he could work with. He had stopped carrying his phone for fear of it being tapped or tracked. They would believe that.

"One doesn't need technical toys to carry vital information. Nor is it wise to do so. As you well know." Sebastian bowed again briefly to Fan. "As for fusion, the girl has proven to be selfish and wishes to talk to you in person. She is naïve in thinking that she can bargain with you better than I. You will find her to be an easy victim."

"I wonder. Who is the greater victim here? Since we now have no need of you." Fan reached under his desk.

"Wait." Sebastian extending a calming hand. "She confirmed the location of the other energy source, and there is no reason to believe it has been moved. The US government stored it far away from their own soil because they feel it is dangerous. It is close enough to your own borders that you could easily claim it for yourself."

Fan retracted his arm.

"The location is safely stored in my head," Sebastian continued. "If you wish to know it, you must pay."

"One step at a time, my traitorous friend," said Fan. Sebastian bristled at being called a traitor. He was no patriot by any means, but he liked to think of himself as more of a *trader* than a traitor. "We will meet with this Jessica first. Then, if we need you, we will let you know." Sebastian withered under the predatory smile Fan directed at him. "Tell her to meet us here," Fan planted a finger in the middle of his desk, "at six this evening. Alone."

Fan backhanded a wave at him. "You may go."

Sebastian bowed and hurried back to the elevator. While he thought the meeting had gone well, he couldn't escape fast enough.

Gang held the elevator open. With the same unnerving smile Fan had used, Gang returned Sebastian's unloaded gun and empty magazine. The threat and the dare were obvious. *Try bringing it back again.*

* * *

With Sebastian on his way back down the elevator, the wall behind Fan split in the center and swung open. Traditional red and gold furnishings spanned the main room. Fan's subordinate couriers held their weapons at rest.

"Split up," Fan said. "Search her suite when she leaves. Place listening devices and mount the tracker on her car in valet. Whether she wishes to deal or not, we will get that technology."

CHAPTER 63

Everyone in the passenger section of the plane dozed, read, or otherwise kept themselves occupied. Jack received a nerve tingle notification from his phone. Only critical messages triggered the tingle setting.

He checked the short line of text. Eight hours until Jessica's first meeting. Time to make a phone call.

He drifted silently along the aisle so as not to disturb anyone, and entered a compact office cubicle at the back of the plane. He tapped the magnetic setting of his suit to keep him secured in the chair and dialed the number of his party. They answered on the second ring.

"Hello?"

"Mr. President, this is Jack."

"Jack? Jack who?"

"Jack the Ripper."

Silence.

"You said you would never call me unless it was absolutely necessary."

"Your life is in danger," said Jack.

"I'm the president. My life is always in danger."

"This is a danger your Secret Service cannot protect you from."

The president chuckled. "Aren't you part of my *secret* service?"

"No. To you, I am an advisor."

"I called you for advice about my re-election campaign. You rejected me."

"It's not my job to elect presidents, only to advise them when absolutely necessary."

"*I* am the president. You work for *me*. What gives you the right to pick and choose what advice to give?"

"The wisdom of your predecessors and the survival of the human race."

"Wait. Are we talking nuclear?"

"Mr. President, listen carefully. You need to get to Bunker 17."

"Never heard of it."

"Then someone has done their job well."

"What's wrong with my new state-of-the-art bunker they recently finished in the Rocky Mountains?"

"Everyone in the world knows where it is."

"Fine. Where is this 17 at?"

"After we conclude this conversation, dial the number 17, one seven, on the hardline. When a person answers, say the word 'Execute.' Your people will know what must be done. Do not take your mobile phone with you. It's being tracked."

"You didn't think *that* bit of information was important enough to tell me about sooner?" the president asked indignantly.

"You may take your wife with you, if you wish," Jack added. "Do not take your mistress. She cannot be trusted."

After a brief silence: "This isn't over," the president said, threateningly.

"No, Mr. President, it's just beginning."

Jack disconnected the call.

CHAPTER 64

Only halfway through his shift, James had already tallied over two thousand dollars in tips, including the thousand-dollar token from Jessica. He had thought his slow-witted ruse might cost him tips, but it did the opposite. People took pity on him and tipped more. As much as he wanted to withhold some from that wretched waitress, he didn't dare risk it. She could be working in concert with someone else to actually test whether he surrendered everything.

Begrudgingly, he trudged to the waitress's work station and dumped a double handful of crumpled cash, coins, and tokens. She lifted painted-on eyebrows in surprised delight, as if she hadn't really expected him to follow up on his promise.

"James do good?" he asked.

"I was expecting more," she said. "You aren't holding out on me, are you?" Her face hardened, and her eyes tunneled into him.

James gulped and turned out his empty front pockets. "James gives everythings. James gets mores. Okays?"

"You do that, hon. Remember: I'm watching you."

With his outturned pockets flopping as he went, James hobble-hopped like a gimpy duck all the way back to the caterer's kitchen. He didn't want to spend another moment more than he had to with that despicable woman.

THE PROMETHEUS EFFECT

***

The hour of Jessica's meeting was fast approaching. Sebastian's message had told her to come alone. Even though she had specifically told him she didn't want him there, the manner in which he had said to come alone left her uneasy.

She had already made plans to circumvent that demand anyway. Hopefully it wouldn't arouse suspicion. Now, if she could just make a decision on a dress.

Red was out of the question. They interpreted that as lucky, and frankly, she looked too damned good in that dress. She wanted them focused on business, not her. She finally chose black. It matched her mood. And no heels this time. Though, the stiletto pair matching the dress would make formidable weapons.

An elaborate clock of rotating crystals displayed five minutes to six. It was almost time to strike the match and light the fuse. As she left the suite, she repressed thoughts of the horrible word hanging in the air. *War.*

She made a fist and presented her wrist to the elevator code reader. She didn't want the sight of her trembling fingers to remind her of how nervous she felt. Sebastian's message had stated that the elevator security man would grant her access to their floor. With barely enough time to take in and exhale a deep breath, she rose one level.

A burly Asian man greeted her. "I must search you for weapons," he said. His thoughts were plain by the leer on his face.

Situations like this seemed to bring out the best in her. Instantly, her resolve hardened into cold steel. "If I needed a weapon, I would have taken it from Sebastian when I beat his sorry ass into submission," she said.

The man laughed. "So that is why his face was so red." He bowed to her in respect, then withdrew a slender black rod fastened to his belt. "Please permit *me* to save face and use the wand?"

Jessica acquiesced. After scanning her, he allowed her access to the hallway. "Fan is ready for you," he said.

When she stopped at the entrance to the courier's suite, she wondered if such a thing as chromatic shock existed. If it did, she was experiencing it. *It's a good thing I didn't wear the red dress. If I stopped moving in here, I would become invisible.*

"Welcome, Miss Stafford. I am Fan Kong. Won't you please come in?"

***

"James! Get your slinkied ass in here!" Al yelled into the kitchen.

James bumped into Timmy as he lumbered to answer Al's summons. "Sorrys," he said.

Timmy muttered something under his breath.

"Boss, Al, sirs? James do bad agains?"

"Stop with the 'sir' already. And no, you didn't do bad. You done very good in fact. The bitch queen on ninety-nine requested you again. She wants you to deliver a bottle of champagne to the red dragons on one hundred."

"She nice lady," said James.

"Not from what I hear. But I guess she likes you. Good tipper, too. Hope she's treatin' you right?"

James nodded. "She nice lady."

"Right. Well, she wants her champagne delivered right after six o'clock. That's in about ten minutes. I already put the bottle on ice and in your cart so you can't accidentally drop it. And *whatever* you do, *don't* let them talk you into opening the bottle yourself. You might kill someone."

Timmy chuckled as he left the kitchen with a tray of hors d'oeuvres.

Al waited for the doors to stop swinging and leaned in closer to James. "Come here," he said, and retreated into his disheveled office.

James followed, fiddling nervously with his slinky. Al thrust a conical paper cup filled with murky liquid at him. "Drink this," he said.

With two outstretched hands, James cradled the cup, sensing a peculiar change in his boss's behavior. He liked Al, but he didn't yet trust him enough to drink an unknown liquid handed to him out of the blue. He had made up his mind to spill it when Al cupped his chin gently and made James look at him.

Al's eyes pleaded for him to listen, and when he spoke, it was entirely without his usual dialect. "James, whatever happens, act appropriately. Any slip-up now could cost you your life. Jessica's as well."

So. Al was an agent. James nodded to him, then downed the contents of the cup in one gulp. It tasted bitter and orangey. Without looking back, he left with his cart to the executive elevator.

A warm flush began spreading throughout his body. He suspected the liquid was some kind of strong painkiller. He wasn't looking forward to finding out why Al had given it to him.

During his trip to deliver Jessica's lunch, she had shared her plan for a champagne delivery shortly after the designated hour. She thought a witness, any witness, might deter mischief by the couriers. James had agreed. It seemed a sound idea.

Now he watched the elevator's floor indicator. At approximately five minutes to six, it went from ninety-nine to one hundred. That was his cue. He called for the elevator; Jessica would be alone with them only briefly while he traveled up.

Before coming down to his level, the elevator paused again at ninety-nine, then rose back to one hundred. He hoped she hadn't changed her mind.

At thirty floors up, his thoughts started growing fur. *Pretending* to be slow-witted and clumsy wouldn't be necessary; it would come naturally. Perhaps that's why Al had made him drink that concoction? To force him to stay in character? He hoped that was all.

The elevator opened, and James found himself staring at the deadly black circle of a gun barrel. He quickly held up both arms.

"What's your business here?" the large man demanded.

"James brings shampans!"

"We didn't order any."

"Nice lady asks James to bring shampans?"

"She did?"

James nodded and pointed at the bottle in his cart while keeping his hands raised.

The man motioned with his gun. "Out," he said. "Face the wall and keep your hands where I can see them."

James placed his nose against textured wallpaper and held both his hands out to the left side of his body, below his shoulders.

"Not like that, idiot." The man roughly placed James's hands high above his head. "Keep them there!" He thoroughly frisked James and searched his cart. In Chinese, he announced down the hall that an idiot food server was coming. James didn't mind being referred to as an idiot, but the way the man added "new guy" at the end of his announcement put James on edge.

Down the hall, he found Jessica lounging at the far side of an expansive main room, admiring a view she didn't have from her own suite. She turned at the commotion.

"You ordered this?" Fan Kong asked of her.

"Yes. In hope we would have something to celebrate with, should we come to a deal."

"You were instructed to come alone. Were you not?" Fan spat in anger.

"The kid has half a brain. We may as well be alone," she said.

"You *know* him?" Fan asked. The other courier took a position behind James.

"He's been delivering my meals. What of it?"

Fan made a gesture to his man near James. With lightning speed, he planted a fist deep into James's stomach. James buckled to the ground, unable to speak or breathe.

"What are you doing?" Jessica screamed. "He's only a dumb kid!"

"We shall see," said Fan.

James covered his face as the man continued to pummel his back and kick at his legs. *Thank you, Al*, he thought; the painkiller dulled the worst of the strikes. He just hoped Jessica could keep herself together, for both their sakes. She didn't have the same magic of modern chemistry to help her cope. Guilt and blame were painted on her face.

"Search him," said Fan as James wiped his bloodied nose.

Hands dove into his pockets and ripped his shoes away. He panicked when they tore off his shirt. Dawn's letter, with her lock of hair, was buttoned securely in the pocket. James tried to reach for the shirt, but had his hand slapped away. He wasn't faking his anguish when they discovered the letter. Jessica looked to be on the verge of tears.

"What is it?" asked Fan.

"I can't read it. It looks like it was written by someone more stupid than him."

"Let me see," demanded Fan.

James made short sobbing noises as he tried to regain his breath.

"Your girlfriend, perhaps?" Fan asked, studying the letter.

James nodded vigorously.

Fan marched to the balcony and slid open the glass doors. Stepping through, he locked eyes with James—and slowly crumpled his most treasured possession. Then he dropped it over the edge.

James wailed in grief. "Noooo, James's friend give that!" He lowered his blotchy face to the carpet and coughed against the blood running down the back of his throat. "James's friend," he said again mournfully, and closed his eyes. The act was fake, but the tears that wet his face were entirely real.

"Fan?" the man who assaulted James asked. "Look at these scars."

James knew what the man was referring to. The thick looping scars crisscrossing his back.

Fan walked over. "Ah, allow me to demonstrate," he said. He unplugged a heavy marble lamp and ripped the cord from it. He doubled over the cord and began whipping James.

James flinched and cried out under each blow. But the painkiller was doing its job, and his screams were an act. But his pain at the loss of Dawn's letter was real. They could inflict no pain greater than that. *Let him swing*, James thought. *Do your worst. My dad hit harder than that.*

"There. See?" Fan said to his subordinate. James supposed he would soon have new scars to match his old ones.

"How did you know?" the other man asked.

"I have three children of my own," Fan said proudly. He stuffed a dollar bill into James's hand. "Now leave the cart and go. Next time we give better tip."

CHAPTER 65

Breathe, Jessica told herself. Now was not the moment to show concern. She knew it was all her fault, but now was not the time to battle guilt, either. She wanted to run after James to apologize, to make sure he was all right.

Get ahold of yourself, Jessica. You still have a job to do. James is safe, and he gave you a golden opportunity to secure your credibility. Use it!

"If you think making a special needs kid cry is going to impress me, you are sadly mistaken. I thought men of your stature were above such pettiness," she said.

Fan forced a toothy smile. "You enjoyed embarrassing me at the baccarat table. I saw that you had a liking for the boy. Consider us now even. Do not become indebted to me again. I exact swift payment."

Petty, insecure twit, Jessica thought. *He did this because he needed to save face.* How many wars had been fought for the same reason? Fulfilling the requirements of Jack's mission were going to be easy with pathetic men like these in charge. Today, the carrot, tomorrow, the *stick*!

"Business then," Jessica said. "By now, you already know that I sold technical specifications to create stable fusion to a private buyer for three billion dollars."

Fan interrupted. "And one hundred million in casino credit. We know. My government is also prepared to offer the same—if you can prove it works."

"That's a very capitalistic offer, and I'm sure your government would like that deal. However, I prefer a more communistic approach. From each according to their ability to pay, to each according to their need for power. That *is* the essence of your government's political philosophy, is it not?"

Fan stood dangerously still. Jessica detected his tension winding ever tighter. He would be a terrible poker player.

Feeling more confident, she began to wander about the room. "Since you represent, by proxy, the government with the largest population in the world, it's only fair that I ask one hundred billion dollars for my information. The technology works. I've seen it. I can replicate it."

"Such greed from someone who extols communism."

"A girl's got to make a living."

"Sebastian offered to sell us his secret for far less. I hear his is the greater energy source in this deal?" Fan countered.

Jessica tossed her hand to the side as if swatting away an offending fly. "I have no doubt he could take you to the artifact's location. But it's unproven technology. Potentially dangerous. Who knows how long it will take you to reverse engineer it?"

"Artifact?" Fan asked, his interest obviously piqued.

"He didn't tell you?" Jessica gave a smug chuckle. "The coward. He's probably afraid you won't believe him. It's not of this earth, gentlemen. *Alien* technology. Unknown energy source. My fusion is tried, tested, reliable, and safe."

"You are sure of this?" asked Fan.

"Fusion? Of course," said Jessica.

"No. The artifact is alien?"

"Absolutely. The files I read stated they don't even know what it's made of yet. And they're afraid to store it anywhere near the continental United States. I don't blame them. Who would want to be near something that could potentially blow up the planet?"

Fan looked thoughtful. This pleased Jessica. *This one's all yours, Sebastian. May you choke on it!*

"I can see you need a while to think," she said. "How about we meet again in twenty-four hours?"

Jessica bowed and took a step to leave. When Fan's courier grabbed her arm, she slapped him across the face before he could react. "It's now 125 billion," she snapped. "Keep your dog on a leash!"

Red-faced, the courier reached into his jacket. Jessica quickly stepped into his personal space. She had him at a height disadvantage by several inches. "How much is *your* honor worth, *little* man?" she growled.

"Enough!" Fan said. "Please accept my apologies," he bowed slightly, "for my associate's indiscretion. I assure you, he will be dealt with appropriately. Six o'clock tomorrow evening then?"

Jessica nodded curtly and left unhindered to the elevator. She hoped she had given enough carrot. She had definitely given more stick than she'd planned.

CHAPTER 66

Blood gushed from James's nose as he rode down the elevator. He tried to stanch the flow with his shredded shirt. Red streamers soaked and stained the fabric.

James checked his back in the elevator mirrors. He'd definitely been subjected to much worse in the past. And he felt comfortably numb to the worst of his injuries.

A security camera monitored the elevator, so he still couldn't afford to let his guard down. He kept an ongoing babble about blood and mean men while impatiently rocking back and forth.

Shirtless and shoeless, he stumbled into the kitchen with a blood-soaked bundle of cloth clutched over his heart. Blood from both nostrils dribbled over his lips, down his chin and neck, and smeared across his chest.

"James bleeding!" he announced to the kitchen with teary eyes.

Timmy's face paled, and he swooned on rubbery knees. "Boss!" he yelled. "Aw, James, those bastards really did a number on you." He helped James to a chair. "*Boss!*"

Al scurried from his office. "Jeez, Timmy, I'm right—" He stopped. "Timmy, get the med kit. James, come to my office. We'll get you fixed up, okay?"

"Why dey so bean to Jabes?" he asked as Al tilted his head back to wipe blood off his face. The flow began to pool in his swollen nasal cavity and trickle down his throat.

"Try not to swallow too much, James. You'll get sick. Spit in this trash can," Al said.

"Oday."

Timmy observed with concern over Al's shoulder. "You should tell someone, boss. This time they've gone too far!"

"It won't do any good, Timmy. The hotel is not about to do anything to upset its best customer. It's the dragon's initiation thing for new people. You went through it yourself."

Timmy's face soured at the injustice of it all. "They only punched me in the stomach. They didn't bloody me up and near whip me to death!"

James breathed heavily through his mouth and spit out dark gelatinous clots every so often.

"Timmy, hand me the antiseptic spray and a couple of the rolled gauze bandages," Al directed. "James, your twelve hours are over today. You go home and rest. We'll see you bright and early in the morning. And don't worry about the uniform. They'll give you a fresh one tomorrow. Get another pair of shoes before you leave, too. If they give you any trouble, tell them to talk to me."

"You're making him come back tomorrow?" Timmy asked, aghast.

"He's a probationary employee, Timmy. If he doesn't show up, he'll lose his job."

"'S'not right," Timmy muttered, and walked away.

James felt a pang of guilt for having made a new friend under false pretenses.

Al finished dressing James's wounds without another word between them. The only communication that took place was a reassuring pat to James's shoulder from Al, and a discreet wink from James. *Mission accomplished. All in a day's work.*

Back in his old asylum clothes, James limped his way out of the casino. His pockets held a miniature tin of tablets that Al had given him for pain, and a crumpled, bloody, one-dollar bill. He looked forward to getting rid of the bill.

To James's surprise, the cocktail waitress still waited at her station. She should have been gone by now. It would be in her nature, James thought, to wait around for him to leave so she could collect his tips. After what he'd been through, he wasn't in the mood to play stupid. But his knowledge of the bigger picture kept him focused. That, and his slinky.

Still, although he had to keep up appearances on the outside, in his mind he was free to think and speak without filters. And when the waitress eyed him expectantly, he thought: *That's right, bitch. I have your bloody tip!*

James dropped the bill, still sticky with blood, by her hands on the workstation. The red matched her nails. "James has bad day," he said. "James sorrys." *Not!* He hung his head lest he crack a smile.

Disgusted, she picked up the bill with a cocktail napkin and deposited it in the trash. As greedy as she was, he was surprised she threw it away. "Unacceptable," she said. "After such a promising start, this is how you finish the day?" She shook her head at him, showing not an ounce of concern for his fresh bruises. "You're going to have to do better than that if you want to keep your job."

"James tries harders," he said.

"You damn well better." She plucked a flimsy plastic bag from a box next to a row of drink condiments. "You like cherries?" she asked.

James nodded.

She placed two long-stemmed cherries into the bag and dropped them into a brown paper sack she pulled from a lower shelf. She folded the top of the sack over and handed it to him. "Here's two cherries for the work you did today. Do good, and you get more cherries."

"Okays. James like cherries!" James thought the blood boiling inside him might erupt through his pores.

"Now don't open that until you get home. I *mean* it," she warned.

"Yeses," James said fearfully. She certainly enjoyed being a *mean* "it." He wouldn't put it past her to follow him to the Box to make sure he did as he was told.

As he turned to leave, she yelled at his back, "Remember, tomorrow dawns a new day!"

Her words hit him like a pitchfork skewering his soul. That vile, nasty witch had cast an evil curse upon him with that reminder of his loss. He brooded all the way back to the Box.

***

Linda let him in. "James, what happened to your face?"

"Bad days. James tired." He kept trudging to his dorm.

Tina bolted from the couch and gave him a hug. "James! Come see! Come see! Come see!" She tugged at his hand to take him to the quad.

"What see?" he asked.

She pointed at Teeka's rose. The bud had opened during his absence, and in the waning light, he detected a vibrant red emerging. A beautiful flower patiently waiting to bloom.

James hunched to examine it. "Pretty," he said.

Tina touched his face lightly. "Oooooh," she cooed. "What happened?"

"James trip. Fall downs." He shrugged. She didn't need to know anything more than that. As he had once protected Mykl, he would now protect her. Her spirit deserved a chance to bloom as well. He had a plan.

Tina adopted an attitude far too serious for her size. She pointed at him sharply. "You need to be more careful! You should go to bed right now!" She stared up at him with hands on her hips.

If it weren't for the sting seeping through the fading dose of painkiller, he would have laughed at her preposterous posturing. "Yes, Teenas," he said. "James go sleepytimes." She had drawn a smile out of him that he was hard pressed to suppress.

As soon as James had closed the door to his room, he gulped down two of Al's tablets. He sat on his bunk and stared at the paper sack in his lap, torn by competing desires: on the one hand, he wanted to throw it away; on the other hand, he actually liked cherries. The cherries won.

He opened the sack and reached for the bag inside. But he felt something else in the sack. An envelope. The small kind used for distributing tips. Could she be returning a share of his earnings? Unlikely—and if she was, he was certain it wasn't very much.

He opened the envelope, and a thunderbolt of guilt hit him squarely in the chest.

The envelope contained a crumpled letter and a lock of hair.

He held it to his heart. Tears stung his eyes. He lay back on the bunk and instantly regretted doing so. Rolling to his side, he reread Dawn's letter. Her lock of hair still smelled of jasmine.

He secured them both back into the envelope. It was obvious now that he didn't hold a monopoly on deception. Only one possibility explained this miracle: the cocktail waitress was an agent. If Jack's people were able to build an underground city of diamond, then they certainly possessed the technology to track objects thrown from a balcony one hundred stories high. And she had retrieved this particular object.

Her position probably allowed her to track the goings-on of the entire casino, like Al did with the hotel. Her name fit her so well. She came off as thorny and painful to be near, but James knew now that in reality, she must contain a beauty she rarely showed.

Even in pain, James steeled his resolve to do his part to help bring about a world where such beauty need never be hidden. He hadn't been able to bring himself to use her name before. Now he would never forget it. Ever.

CHAPTER 67

Somewhere west of DC. That was all the president could be sure of regarding his location. A pair of military men in battle fatigues had shepherded him and a couple of trusted Secret Service agents to a rarely used northwest tunnel leading away from the West Wing. They had emerged unseen from a Civil War soldier's tomb at Oak Hill Cemetery. A sporty private helicopter had met them not one hundred feet away and taken them to a light prop plane on an abandoned airstrip overgrown with weeds. After several hours, that plane had bounced to a landing on a bumpy meadow, where two men in combat fatigues—twins, oddly enough—emerged from vehicles camouflaged to match the natural surroundings. It took another three hours of travel on bumpy, monotonous, neck-jarring roads before the president was finally able to stretch his legs on solid ground, and a half-hour hike through dense trees to a hunting cabin.

Now the president rubbed his neck as he surveyed the layers of dirt and decomposing leaves gradually composting the building from the ground up. But to his surprise, they didn't enter the cabin. Instead, they led him around the back to a detached root cellar dug into a hill. A pair of moles scurried away when the door was opened.

The cellar's stale air smelled of wet, rotting leaves. There was no hint of human presence. One of the men in uniform held a featureless black device the size of his fist up to an empty shelf on the back wall. Whirring and grinding noises issued from some hidden mechanical device on the other side, then both military men planted their feet and shoved hard to get the wall to swing back.

Fresh air blew against the president's face. A cascading sequence of lights illuminated a long square corridor leading straight into the hill. They followed it, passing through numerous blast doors along the way. The president was informed that they would all be secured before the military men left.

The president wondered why Jack thought an unassuming hill would yield more protection than an entire mountain. Then they came to an open-cage mining elevator, and things quickly started to make sense. The elevator dropped for several minutes through the earth's strata before they exited—only to walk to another elevator cage several hundred feet away. They zigzagged deeper into the earth this way for another hour.

Before the military men left, they told the president he would be contacted in approximately twenty-four hours. The closing of the final blast door left him and his two protectors in complete silence, and his imagination conjured up a suffocating feeling of compression from the incredible mass of surrounding rock. They had to be more than a mile underground.

The president's Secret Service men secured the facility. They soon confirmed that there were no threats, and that there was enough food and water to last years.

The president ventured off to investigate his new home away from home, and he found it woefully lacking. The place resembled a time capsule. A museum of outdated technology, containing relics from well before his era. How was he supposed to run a country when the only phone to be found was a nonfunctioning antique? A black Western Electric 302 on a pedestal covered by a dusty glass dome.

CHAPTER 68

The lights of Las Vegas began igniting as twilight descended upon the city. Jessica contemplated the scientific achievements involved in transitioning from natural to man-made light while standing behind the thick glass of her suite windows. The war she was tasked to start threatened everything in her span of vision. She wondered if she would act when the moment came.

If not me, then who?

This was her endgame. The most dangerous part of her mission. She had already lit the fuse. She hoped the end result wouldn't blow up in her face.

When she'd returned to her suite after the meeting, she'd discovered signs that someone had rifled through her belongings. The old trick of wetting a strand of hair and placing it in strategic locations had served her well. Someone had entered her balcony and bedroom, and it certainly wasn't housekeeping. They'd even inspected her underwear drawer. Of all the places to discover an intrusion, that was the one she'd most dreaded. *Perverts!* Fortunately, she'd preemptively stashed a few pairs in the room safe. It made her skin crawl to think about touching the ones in the drawer now.

She found it decidedly abnormal to try to go about her normal routine when she knew they were listening in on her. When James returned in the morning, loudly announcing the arrival of her breakfast, she met him with a finger to her lips. She tapped her ear and gestured toward the room. He nodded his understanding, pointed a thumb at his chest, and gave her the "okay" sign with a winning smile. She felt much better knowing that he had come to no serious harm.

That relief waned as the day wore on. She had made it clear in her original hiring interview that she didn't want to work on the development of new weapons. Now, instead, she was about to *unleash* a weapon. She didn't know which was worse; the end result would be the same however she looked at it.

Time's up.

Jessica closed her eyes to the twinkling city and tried to set it in her memory. She hoped the lights would still be there tomorrow.

CHAPTER 69

"We should kill her."

Fan Kong had listened to such grumblings from his underlings all day. They lacked the finesse and wisdom needed for the bigger picture. Yes, they *should* kill her. But not until she furnished them with needed information. Fan knew his government would pay her full asking price, *if* she could prove everything she promised. Fusion would lift a great burden from a Chinese empire starving for energy. They would no longer need to bow to imperialist demands. It was unconscionable that America should possess such technology and China should not. It also disrupted the global balance of power.

Every effort had been made to locate the person with whom she had made her first deal, but the man had simply vanished. No record of him even existed. It didn't make sense. A person worth billions had to exist *somewhere*. And naturally, this made Fan's government suspicious. This man couldn't be working on his own behalf; he had to be a front for another country. Russia, most likely, though Russia denied it. They would deny the sun rising on their own country if it served their interests.

Still, the fact remained that she had sold *something* to *someone*. One does not pay that kind of money for *nothing*. And Fan would find out her something. If she did not tread carefully, she would be the one who paid.

"She's here. And she insults you again."

Jessica strode in wearing a white dress. *The color for funerals. How prophetic, Miss Stafford.*

He bowed slightly to her. "Welcome back, Miss Stafford. I trust you slept well?"

She exhibited beauty without question, though dark thoughts seemed to cloud her expression. She also seemed irritable and in no mood for pleasantries. Perhaps she thought her position in this transaction weak and could be motivated to cut her demands? Fan planned to make this difficult for her.

"I slept quite all right," said Jessica dismissively. "Does your government accept my offer?" She held up a matte black cigar-sized cylinder. "Or shall I find a buyer for this elsewhere?"

Fan's lieutenant took a step toward her.

"Ah, ah." She waved the cylinder gently. "The information in this is protected by a self-destructing incendiary charge. If it drops, or if someone tries to open it improperly... poof."

Fan uttered an order in Chinese for his man to step back. "Information," he said to Miss Stafford, "does not fulfill your burden of proof."

The girl eyed his man warily. "I would like to continue this conversation on the balcony. Alone," she said. She looked distressed. Good. He did not need the presence of his men to foster that feeling in her.

"Very well," Fan said. "After you?"

Jessica strode to the breezy platform, nervously tapping the cylinder on her palm. Fan followed closely at her side. She walked to the far edge and leaned against a polished gold rail. It would be so easy, Fan thought, to push her over and be done with this fawn. Of all those he and his men had disposed of, none had met the fate of a one-hundred-story drop. *She shall be the first*, he decided.

"Proof," Fan spat.

"Proof," Jessica pointed in a northwesterly direction, "is at the accelerator base. They currently have the only functioning model in the world. I have"—she lightly tapped the cylinder on the rail; Fan cringed—"the formulas and equipment specifications to build one."

Does she realize how badly she weakens her position?

"Without concrete proof, I am afraid that my government cannot meet your asking price, Miss Stafford. You waste my time."

She fidgeted fearfully. *She will know fear*, Fan promised himself. The minutes she had left to enjoy her newfound wealth diminished by the second. If she only knew how many billions his government *had been* willing to pay for the contents of that cylinder. The cylinder she had so foolishly brought with her…

"I have a counteroffer then," she said, as Fan knew she would. "Since I cannot provide you with a working model in a reasonable amount of time, I will reduce my asking price to fifty billion. Half the original amount. I think that is fair."

"No, Miss Stafford, it is not," Fan replied. He enjoyed her discomfort. He noticed her hands trembling. She would take anything he offered now. Or perhaps give anything he demanded when faced with a deadly alternative. "I am authorized to offer you one billion. No more."

Her pupils dilated in fear. Fan had learned much in reading people across a poker table—though he had never possessed the luck required to win. She would fold, if not kneel before him and beg for more. He wished her dress showed more cleavage.

Her face suddenly hardened. This puzzled Fan. She made a fist around the cylinder, and her pupils constricted like coiling snakes. Her irises reflected the dominant red colors bleeding through his massive suite windows. She took a sharp intake of breath as if she were about to breathe flames.

"And this is *my* final offer," she fired back. "With one hundred billion, I could have made myself comfortable somewhere no matter what you did with this technology. Now I have to ensure you don't botch up the planet by making weapons from it. Before I was fired from my job, I stumbled across a very interesting report about your government and its weapons programs."

Fan forced himself to swallow. *What is she getting at? What could she possibly know about our weapons programs?*

"If you want this technology," she said, brandishing the cylinder at him, "you're going to have to pay me twenty-five billion dollars, *American*—or I'll let the rest of the world know about your kinetic and nuclear space-based weapons platforms."

"No!" The word escaped Fan's mouth involuntarily. He said it in response to her knowledge of the weapons, not the money she demanded. He didn't mean to say it at all. She had surprised him.

In his position, he had to know something of his country's greatest secrets; it was necessary if he was to be effective in culling truth from fiction in his dealings. So he knew that China's space-based weapons were the darkest and most closely guarded of these secrets. They were China's only assurance of first-strike capability. And if *she* knew, then her government did as well. This was disastrous. If she revealed it to the world...

"Then we are through here," said Jessica.

With a simple flick of her wrist, she flipped the cylinder in a high arc out from the rail.

Fan instinctively reached for it. A useless gesture. He had no chance of catching it. She had embarrassed him again by making him act like a dog, snapping at a tossed treat. He watched the cylinder fall until he could no longer see it. When he turned back, Jessica had already marched past his men. She paused to peer back at him with a curious smile. Fan clenched his jaw. She had better learn how to fly before the end of day.

"And don't think about threatening me," she said. "I have numerous countdown notifiers in operation to release your secret, with proof, should you prevent me from pausing them in any way." Jessica strolled out as if she hadn't a care in the world, head held high and shoulders back.

"You're letting her go?" Fan's lieutenant asked.

"For now," said Fan. "I have to contact our government immediately. Take Gang, find Sebastian, then take him to the airport. I am sure we will be leaving soon. The rest of you: make sure the girl does not leave this hotel!"

CHAPTER 70

A half bottle of whiskey and a fully loaded pistol rested on the table. Sebastian knew the bottle held enough courage for him to use the gun. It was funny, he thought, how everyone wanted to shoot him, and yet he would be the one who finally pulled the trigger to finish the job.

He'd often wondered what thoughts a man might battle with before sending a bullet to chase them away. Pain? Despair? Hopelessness? Well, two out of three worked.

The whiskey did a fair job on the pain, at least.

He'd used the last of his money on the hotel room and booze. It wasn't even a *nice* room. Not like Jessica's. He wanted to be rich and powerful like her. The bitch didn't even know how to *use* her money and power. If *he* had it, he would *be* somebody. But now, he drank to being a failure. A fraud. A *parasite*! Alcohol mercilessly revealed the truth to him; it was the cheapest truth serum money could buy.

Still, it had its purpose. With a finger on the trigger, he upended the bottle and attempted to swill the amber liquid as fast as he could. If he did this quickly and stopped being so analytical, it would be over quicker.

When his door blasted off its hinges, he saw two men, no, three— maybe it *was* two—rush toward him. Before he could react, they secured his gun and frog-marched him out to the hallway.

THE PROMETHEUS EFFECT

Ah, they do *need me*, Sebastian thought.

CHAPTER 71

Deeply shadowed lunar craters drifted serenely below Mykl's window as their plane executed a wide loop to approach the mythical "dark side" of the moon. In reality, it received as much light as any other side of the moon, but since observers on Earth couldn't see it, they assumed it was dark. In the current position of its rotational cycle, shadows spilled miles long at every crater. The craft's wing coloration fluctuated to match the surface like lazy waves rolling on an ocean.

The plane's momentum and elevation dropped as they approached their destination: Hippocrates Crater. By now, Noah rarely made appearances outside of Stinker, but Mykl held the bear up in case his friend wished to witness another moon landing. Long whiskers protruding from beneath the bear's arm lightly brushed the diamond-clear window.

The plane came to a hovering stop. Midway up the crater face, mere feet from the rounded nose, a section of rock split in two. A sharp clunk jolted them as something latched on, and they were slowly pulled inside. The rock closed behind them as they passed, leaving them in total darkness.

Bright lights suddenly flashed on all around the plane. Mykl flinched and squinted against the harsh illumination. A squeak from Stinker told him that he wasn't the only one startled. They were floating in a gigantic hangar. Mykl counted seven similar planes docked to their right.

Jack emerged from the cockpit. "Welcome to the moon, Mykl."

Mykl pointed to the other planes. "How many people are here?"

Another solid *kachunk* resounded from the front exit hatch.

"Most of our Operations staff have been relocated here temporarily," Jack said. "That's why the City has been so empty, in case you were wondering. There are one hundred and seventeen people working here at present."

"And how many total?"

"We have thousands in cold sleep chambers in the deeper levels of the base." Jack seemed to be more forthright now; maybe because Mykl finally knew what questions to ask.

"How long has this been here?"

A hissing sound emanated above the front exit hatch.

"Five years after the last publicly known manned landing, this facility became operational."

Outside the window, suited figures on tethers began inspecting and securing the plane. Mykl poked his thumb in their direction. "There's no atmosphere out there?"

Jack leaned down to see what Mykl was pointing at. "The lunar hangar is quite large; it would be impractical to maintain an atmosphere in it. Also, in the unlikely event of a leak, people on Earth would suddenly be wondering why the moon was off-gassing oxygen. Can't have that, now can we?"

The hissing stopped, and the hatch swung inward.

"Clear the settings on your jumpsuit once we're past the main airlock," Jack said. "You won't need magnetic assistance beyond that." He retrieved Mykl's duffel from an overhead bin.

Mykl thought for a moment. "You control gravity here," he said.

"That's right. If we didn't, prolonged exposure to the weak lunar pull would play havoc on our bodies. You can adjust it to moon-actual in your quarters. It aids sleeping, and, as I'm sure you'll find out, it's Noah's favorite part about being here."

"Aren't there satellites and other devices that can detect gravitational anomalies?" Mykl asked as he secured Stinker under his arm. "I mean, how do people on Earth not know we're here?"

Jack put a hand on Mykl's shoulder. He took slow steps with him into the enclosed walkway that had been extended out to the plane. "If we didn't control the chips on all of their sensors, they would. But we can, and we do. The only anomalies they see on the moon are the ones we want them to see."

"You *want* them to see anomalies?" Mykl asked.

"There are always anomalies. To not have any would be suspicious in itself."

Mykl stumbled over a raised seam in the walkway. He felt like he was falling in slow motion. Jack caught him by the shoulder strap of his jumpsuit and planted him firmly back on the ground.

"It takes considerably more concentration to walk in lunar gravity until you become accustomed to it," he said. "Oh, and I wouldn't advise jumping on the bed." He leaned down to whisper to him so Dr. Lee wouldn't hear. "Unless you have the gravity on full Earth norm," he added with a wink.

They reached the main airlock. As Mykl's leg passed over the threshold, it felt suddenly heavy, and as though he was being pulled through the opening. Noah gave a muffled squeak. After two days of weightlessness, full gravity felt oddly strenuous.

Mykl followed Jack through a portal like those installed at the City. A tram exactly like the ones on Earth waited for them.

"Are we there yet?" Mykl asked.

Jack laughed. "The main base rings a craterlet inside a larger crater named Byrd."

"Like the explorer?"

Jack gave Mykl a scrutinizing look. "You really *have* spent some significant time exploring the nets to know such trivia."

Mykl shrugged.

"Yes, the explorer," Jack said. "There are some adherents who believe that during his explorations, he found the Earth to be hollow. They also think he encountered someone not of this world who warned him that man should pursue peace over the horrors of war."

"Did he?" Mykl asked. "Meet someone not of this world?"

"Then? No, most likely not," Jack replied. "If the same thing happened today…? There would probably be a great deal of truth to it."

"Hmmm. So this tram goes *through* the moon to the other side?"

"In almost a straight line. When we arrive, you'll be able to see the Earth, though the lunar-camouflaged view window distorts the image slightly. You can bring up a clearer image with ambiance controls."

Numerous people came and went once they reached the Earth side of the moon. It was by far the most people Mykl had seen since his arrival at the City. Nods of greeting made it clear that everyone knew Jack, but they all moved with the speed of purpose, and none stopped to chitchat. They all appeared to be working on something, and the tension of that something was as palpable as an immovable deadline.

Stepping out of foot traffic, Jack knelt next to Mykl and directed his attention to the wall beside them. Jack drew a circle on its surface with an index finger, and a directory appeared with glowing letters.

"After you bring up the directory, just navigate through the list until you find what you're looking for. Then draw another circle on the place you want to go. An H&G trail will illuminate to direct you," Jack explained.

"What's an 'H&G' trail?"

"Hansel and Gretel."

"Bread crumbs. Right."

"And little Noah doesn't get fat from eating them," Jack said. "Double-tap the screen to clear the directory, and draw an X on the trail when you no longer need it." Jack demonstrated by asking for a trail line to Mykl's room—which was actually named "Mykl's room" in the directory. The base had obviously been notified of his arrival. *There had better be ice cream then.*

An aqua-colored thin line appeared in the floor, starting from the wall where Jack had been tapping. They followed it around corners and through more pressure doors until they arrived at a door marked with a flashing circle of the same color. Mykl stepped inside.

To his surprise, it was set up exactly like the one he used at the City, right down to sailing ships on the blanket. He almost tossed Stinker on the bed out of habit before remembering that the bear now carried a passenger.

"Well, I have work to get to," Jack said, "so I'll leave you two to settle in. Gravity controls are accessed via the ambiance settings. Noah prefers moon-actual," he added, quirking a smile and closing the door.

Mykl set Stinker on the bed. Noah crawled out immediately and started making energetic jumps on the blanket. After a few jumps, he stopped, stared at Mykl, and pointed to the nearest wall. Mykl understood: the mouse wanted him to adjust the gravity. So he pulled up the settings and lowered the gravity as far as it would go. Moon actual. His arms drifted from his sides, and his guts felt like they were redistributing.

Noah responded by making spectacular—for a mouse—leaps from one end of the bed to the other.

"Is *this* why you like the moon?" Mykl asked.

Noah responded by doing flips and twists in the air. With careful use of his tail, he could control his tiny body to land *mostly* feet first.

"Well, at least someone gets to enjoy jumping on the bed."

Light streamed through a squat window recessed into the wall—a thick pane of glass, only a few inches high. *Glass? Who am I kidding?* It was most likely diamond. The window sat too low for an adult to conveniently look through, but still too high for him. No matter: he just reached up to the ledge and pulled himself up to peer out.

A brightly lit, starkly shadowed lunar landscape filled the lower half of his thin panorama. Shades of gray upon gray made up the Byrd Crater. Above that, in the dark abyss of space, hung the Earth, in a living, vibrant blue.

The scene struck Mykl as fantasy. Here he was, a new species of human, on the moon, staring at the Earth, with a half alien mouse at his side. Only five days ago he'd lived on the Earth, gazing at the stars, wondering if anyone was out there. *What adventure will my next week of life bring?*

Noah leapt from the bed to Mykl's shoulder, then hopped into the recess to observe with him. But even in one-sixth gravity, Mykl's arms were already starting to tire, so he lowered himself back to the floor. Noah stayed to watch, alone with his tiny mouse thoughts.

The opposite side of the room held a large, blank, unadorned wall, with no furnishings against it. Mykl knew precisely what to do with it. He adjusted his chair and activated the computer.

"Good evening, Mykl," the computer voice said.

"No, no, no. Voice commands off! Still creepy."

He located the folder with satellite feeds. He wanted a real-time image of the Earth. But the perspectives he found weren't quite right. He finally found image feeds from cameras located on the moon, and from one of these, he zoomed in to get the perfect angle. A vibrant blue planet filled his wall from floor to ceiling.

Noah had finally tired of Earth-gazing and was now playing Supermouse by flying from perch to perch across the room. No wonder he went ballistic at seeing Mykl enter the lab with Stinker. From the looks of it, he was having the time of his life. Even when one of his landings missed, he just tumbled lightly to the floor.

Mykl watched as the half-alien mouse suddenly stopped his leaping and zipped under the bed. A moment later he shot back into view and leapt onto the desktop with his rear end swinging around wildly and his back legs kicking in the air, scrabbling for traction. He was holding something in his front paws, and he set it on the desk. It looked like a round blue disk.

Mykl leaned closer to examine it. "You've found a blue button," he said, confused.

Noah darted to the end of the desk and gripped his hind feet on the edge. He sprang out and upward to the bed. With a late flip, he landed near Stinker, clawed his way up the bear's head, and tapped the missing eye.

"You found Stinker's eye!" Mykl exclaimed. "That means…"

Of course *that's what it means,* he said to himself. *That means my dad lived up here when he was a kid. Like I am now.* That explained the unusual window height; it was probably set for his father's height on his last visit, a few years older than Mykl was now.

Mykl rolled the button around in his fingers. He decided he would have Delilah sew it back on, so Stinker would have two good eyes the next time he battled a monster.

A horrifying thought came to his mind. Mykl quickly looked under the bed—and felt ridiculously relieved to find nothing there.

Mykl returned his attention to the computer. Jack had given him limited access to his administrative files, so that Mykl could peruse the problems within and try to think of viable solutions. But right now, Mykl just wanted to check on his friend James. Folders had been added for both James and Jessica, and he browsed their contents, which included early recordings of them on assignment.

Then he discovered a very recently added video clip that shocked him. It showed James pulled roughly from an elevator and held at gunpoint. Then the video cut and started up again from a different feed. This one was in a room decorated by someone infatuated with the color red. Jessica was already there, and James entered, pushing a silver cart. A short man seemed angry. As the first sucker punch landed, Mykl's hands flew to cover his face. He wanted to intervene, but he knew this had already happened, and nothing in his power could change that. His heart broke as James wailed for the man not to throw away Dawn's letter. He flinched harder than James did as each wet smack of the lamp cord left a new mark.

Finally, mercifully, the clip ended.

Mykl trembled in his chair. He felt sympathetic pain and a tight tingling of his own back.

Full of trepidation, Mykl opened the written report attached to the video file. It read: "Wounds not serious. First aid applied. Medication given for pain. Agent performance exceptional. Al."

Mykl breathed a sigh of relief. Why, why, why would Jack put James, or Jessica for that matter, in such a dangerous situation? Were they agents now? Like his mother had been? He didn't want them to suffer her fate.

THE PROMETHEUS EFFECT

A light flashed from Mykl's Earth-wall. He whirled to see several more flashes appear in sequence, and then nothing. Mykl replayed the feed from the first flash. They didn't originate on the planet, but in space above it. This struck Mykl as very wrong. He had to tell Jack.

Stinker watched him run out of the room with his one good eye.

CHAPTER 72

Stains of cherry juice covered the front of James's crisp white uniform shirt. He pulled two more fresh cherries from a clear plastic container and popped them into his mouth, then once again wiped his sticky fingers on his shirt.

James brought his tips to Rose on a more regular basis now. She pretended to be just as ornery as ever, and he played along just as stupidly. Since the other cocktail waitresses tended to avoid her, she was much easier to catch alone than Al was in his busy kitchen.

Today, when he arrived for work, James had slipped Rose a message. In it, he both thanked her and made a request. He needed a sedative for a six-year-old child, approximately twenty kilograms. All he offered for a reason was: "She deserves better than the asylum."

And Rose had come through. Just now, when he had stopped by her station to drop off his tips, she had given him another paper bag of cherries—in which she'd stashed a fingernail-sized dermapatch with the sedative he requested. She'd whispered to him that the medication absorbed painlessly through open skin, and that within minutes, the subject would fall asleep and stay that way for several hours, or until the patch was removed.

James was immensely grateful, even though if things went perfectly, he wouldn't have to use it.

Things never went perfectly for James.

When he reentered the bustling kitchen, Timmy beckoned for him to come over. "You doin' okay, James?"

James barged right into Timmy's personal space and bent down nose to nose with him. He said, "James okays! How Timmys?"

"Whoa!" Timmy exclaimed, taking a step back, "Two squares! Two squares!" he said, pointing to the twelve-inch-square tiles on the kitchen floor. "This is my space, that's your space."

"James like Timmys."

"I like you too, buddy. Two squares. Okay?"

James gave him a wild thumbs up, almost losing his slinky in the process.

"James," Al called out, "a word with you, please?"

James trudged to his boss.

"Can you stay for a few hours of overtime?"

Timmy's head shot up at the word "overtime."

"I can't pay you though."

Timmy quickly made himself scarce and disappeared. Everyone else in the kitchen was too busy toiling away at tasks to notice anything.

Al waved James into his office and dropped the charade. "James, there's something going on with the dragons. We have video and audio in their suite, but they've always suspected that, so they routinely pass notes. And today, they've been doing it all day. Now everyone is gone except for Fan. I need to you go up there and see if you can find out anything."

James arched an eyebrow in a wordless question.

"You've been vetted now," Al replied. "There shouldn't be any more trouble like yesterday."

James nodded his acceptance.

"Oh, one last thing," Al said. "If things go bad, don't come back here. You and Jessica need to get back to her car and get out of town. *Fast.* Use your best judgment."

And *that*, James thought, was why he'd requested the sedative. "If," in these cases, often turned to "when."

As James left the office in search of an empty cart, Al yelled loud enough to his back for the kitchen staff to hear, "And don't forget the silverware! They leave it sitting around all over the place!"

***

When the elevator opened up on the one hundredth floor, James already had his arms up in anticipation of facing another gun. But no one confronted him. In fact, the hallway was deserted. Pushing his cart forward, he heard Fan speaking tersely in Chinese inside the main room. The entry lay wide open, and he warily pushed the cart through, as if he knew there was a hungry tiger inside waiting to pounce.

Fan was speaking into a bulky phone that was attached to a briefcase with a twisted cord. From the briefcase, another line ran to a portable reflector dish on the dark balcony, aimed up at the stars. He stopped in the middle of a sentence and raked James with a death-to-you glare.

"James gets dishes, please?" he asked meekly, fidgeting with his slinky.

James knew by the look in Fan's eyes that his life hung on the edge of a cliff. A few tense seconds spiraled into infinity before Fan snapped, "Be quick," and went back to his conversation.

The handset volume allowed James to make out most of the other side of the conversation, but James found it difficult to manage all three of his priorities simultaneously: playing stupid, interpreting the conversation, and searching for dirty dishes. But he found the dishes everywhere, including in potted plants throughout the main room, and that allowed James to get progressively closer to Fan.

The top of his cart teetered with dishes by the time he made it to the open balcony sliders. He was running out of places to search for dishes, and if he didn't leave soon he would risk suspicion. But the conversation flowed too rich with unguarded words for him to leave now.

Speaking rapidly in Chinese, Fan said into the handset, "This line may not be secure."

"*Doesn't matter. Nothing they can do to stop it. Our plane has arrived and is preparing for EMP."*

"Excellent. We have Sebastian in our possession and the girl has not left her suite. What do you want me to do?"

"You only have a few minutes until launch. Bring the traitor... Kill the girl."

<click>

James knew he had involuntarily flinched upon hearing Jessica's fate. Had Fan noticed? He didn't know, and he couldn't afford to make eye contact now. He knew the fire in his own eyes would give him away. His adrenal system dumped a cascade of biochemicals into his bloodstream.

Time slowed down.

Pretending to search the base of a densely leafed plant, James surreptitiously observed Fan's reflection on the polished steel handle of his cart. It severely distorted the image, but he could tell that Fan was reaching for something on the table next to him. James kept his back turned and tried to hum, but his dry throat produced a croaky cough instead.

Fan lifted the object off the table and stalked with carefully placed footsteps to stand behind him.

James forced himself to relax. He would be faster without tension in his body. He slowly drew breath as Fan raised something over his head.

At the moment of Fan's commitment to an executioner's blow, James pivoted on his knee like an uncoiling spring. He caught Fan's descending wrist in his left hand and squeezed it with adrenaline-fueled strength. The thin bones of Fan's forearm snapped audibly. Dark and unbelieving eyes gazed into a merciless titanium gray stare.

Before Fan could utter a sound, before the marble lamp fixture even fell from his hand, James grabbed Fan by the throat and lifted his feet from the floor. Like a wet blanket being tossed over a clothesline, James drove Fan's spine down onto the hardwood crest of a high-backed chair. Made to last for generations, the beautiful chair never moved, and the top of Fan's thoracic spine proved to be no match for the quality workmanship of his ancestors. Bones shattered, paralyzing him from the chest down. His bladder and bowels released their contents. His legs quivered beyond his control.

Though his would-be assassin now trembled helplessly, anger and the demand for justice still raged through James. It had been a long time since he had last contemplated taking a man's life. Then, he had chosen to run and live on the streets instead. Now, he would have to run again. Every moment that passed put him and Jessica in more danger.

"Who... are... you?" Fan managed to whisper.

James ignored the question. There wasn't enough time to get acquainted now. He grabbed Fan by the front of his shirt and carried him out to the balcony. If Fan's men found him, he would tell them it was James who had injured him, and it would be all but impossible to escape the hotel. Only one reasonable choice remained if he and Jessica were to make it out of this alive.

James swung Fan over the railing like a rag doll.

His legs dangling limply, Fan gripped the rail with his one working hand. Fear distorted his face. "No," he pleaded weakly.

Bright flashes in the distance silhouetted the northern mountain ranges. One came from the direction of the City—and Dawn. Electric blue crackling sparks danced at lightning speed along the power lines gridding Las Vegas, and then all the lights in the city went out in a muted hush. The high-pitched squeals of tires—followed by concussive impacts—echoed from far below. Then the screams.

"Why?" James demanded, pulling Fan hard against the rail.

"P-power," Fan answered.

"Your country would destroy the world for power?" James asked.

"Not destroy. Enlighten. Under a new world order."

The hotel shook and shuddered, causing James to tighten his grip further, lest he drop Fan. A distant rumbling boom echoed off mountains ringing the deathly dark valley.

"That wasn't just an EMP, was it?" James demanded. "*Was it?*"

"*That*... was your destiny!" Fan said, grabbing James by the collar with a challenging look in his eyes.

James placed his forehead against Fan's. In Chinese, he said, "You

are without honor. A disgrace to your ancestors."
Then he released his grip.

CHAPTER 73

Fan's fingers slipped from James's shirt and caught the end of his slinky. James held on to the other end and watched the coils straighten until it was yanked from his grasp. *Damn*, he thought. He had started to develop a sentimental attachment for the thing.

James grabbed the satellite phone, along with its components, and threw them off the balcony. Followed by his cart. With a little luck, Fan's men wouldn't find out what had happened until he and Jessica were long gone.

Taking the elevator was out of the question. James felt sorry for all the people in the city who must be trapped in them. James knew that emergency stairwells existed at the end of each hotel wing, and an exterior maintenance ladder ran the entire height of the building. But the emergency lighting in the hotel had also failed. He'd have to navigate his way through a pitch black room and down a hallway to the closest stairs.

James felt more sympathetic for Dawn after he barked his shins on chairs and low tables. Once he made it to the hallway, his pace quickened. He jogged while keeping one hand in contact with the wall. At the end, he pushed the panic bar on the stairwell door and entered a spiraling trap. He sensed a constant vibration on the handrail and heard a thrum of noise rising from below. There must be thousands of people trying to get out of this dead building. If a fire started now... No—*when* the fire started. The only reliable source of light was open flame: lighters and matches. And the building's fire protection system would need electricity to operate. This hotel was destined to burn.

James skidded down a dark flight of stairs to Jessica's floor.

Another problem: a key card was required to exit the stairwell on this floor, and even if he had one, the locks operated electronically. He searched near both sides of the door until he located the fire extinguisher case. Using his elbow, he broke the center glass panel and removed the extinguisher. It wasn't an axe, but perhaps it would serve for knocking the locking mechanism off. It took several blows, but at last the lock plate swung free. James fished out the broken pieces and worked the bolt open with his finger.

Running along the hall, he stopped at the first door he came to and tried to kick it in. The frame splintered with the first kick and the door crashed open with the second. James ran inside and stopped immediately. It would not be good to get trapped in a maze. He yelled, "Jessica!"

A faint reply filtered back to him.

Damn, this suite is huge.

"Keep coming to my voice!"

He didn't dare move any farther inside. He knew how to get out from where he stood. He heard Jessica's voice getting closer.

"Keep coming!" he called back.

"What happened?" she asked when she finally reached him.

James grabbed her by the arm. "EMP. Come with me."

He led her back up the stairs and out onto the roof. A helicopter would be really nice about now, he thought.

From the roof of the E Pluribus Unum, he could see the huge fires already burning all around the city. And not a siren was to be heard. Another fireball erupted in the low mountains to the south, and James watched as a plane, now electronically dead, fell from the sky.

"This way," James said, pulling Jessica along. "We need to get to your car."

"Look around us. There isn't a car in the city still working!"

James stopped to face her. "If there's *one* car in the entire city that might work, which one do you think it would be?"

She nodded. "You've got a point. But the roads are going to have dead cars everywhere. They'll be impassable."

"Hey, I was instructed to get you to your car," James said, "so that's where we're going. If you think of a better idea before we get there, I'm all ears."

It felt treacherous running along a dark rooftop well over one thousand feet above the ground. When they reached the edge, James started climbing over the side.

"What are you *doing*?" Jessica half-asked, half-yelled.

"There's a caged ladder right here. It leads all the way down to the roof of the parking garage. We can take the stairs once we reach the garage."

Jessica peered over the edge. James could tell by her shaking hands that she was not comfortable with the extreme height. But she took a deep breath, and he knew she'd manage.

"I'll go first," James said. "If you slip, I *will* catch you. I promise." He extended a hand to assist her.

"Where's your slinky?" Jessica asked.

"It, um, fell off Fan's balcony," James said. Probably not what she wanted to hear right now.

"Where is Fan now? Is he coming after us?" she asked.

"I'm pretty sure he's still holding on to the slinky," James answered with a trace of irony.

With one foot on the top rung of the ladder, Jessica stopped and spun sharply to James. "You killed him?"

James leaned back from the rung to see her better. "*He* was ordered to kill *you*. And he *tried* to kill me. I've been instructed to protect you… and to use my best judgment. Fan Kong has been judged. Let's leave this place before they find him."

Jessica nodded and advanced over the edge.

They descended for ten full minutes before she spoke again. "Thank you," she said.

It wasn't the kind of "thank you" one received for giving a gift, James thought. It was the kind offered in forgiveness for making a life-altering decision. He had killed a man for her. That had to be as hard on her as it was on him. Her words made him feel less like a monster and more like he had done the right thing. They were healing words. To say "You're welcome" would diminish them, so he didn't.

"You okay?" he asked. "Do you need to rest?"

"I'm good. Let's keep going."

By the time they reached the top of the parking garage, the buildup of lactic acid burned in their thighs. When they reached the garage stairs, they both had to use the handrails to take weight off their noodle-like legs.

At every level of the garage, hundreds of people holding cigarette lighters for illumination milled about their cars. Someone had succeeded in hotwiring a headlight directly to a car battery. Lost souls in the dark migrated to the light like moths to a flame.

When they reached valet level, James said, "We need to get your key."

"It doesn't have a key. It's all biometric," she said.

"Then how did the valet drive it?"

"It has a valet setting and a GPS leash to keep them honest."

James pondered this. "Then how were they supposed to retrieve it for you?"

Jessica shrugged. "I assumed the car would know. It's City technology after all."

"Well, some of that tech would be useful right now to help us locate the car in the dark."

"I asked them to keep it close. Let's check the first level by the entrance and hope they found my tip persuasive enough."

They found the car parked sideways across two parking spaces, facing the exit. "I think your tip worked," James said. "How do we get in?"

Jessica placed her left palm on the driver-side door. It automatically unlocked and began scissoring upward. Diffuse light filled the interior.

She ducked in and slid into her seat while touching the passenger-side open icon flashing on the dash. "Quick, get in!"

James hopped in the other side and closed the door.

"Okay. Now what?" Jessica asked.

"Now," said a male voice that came from the dashboard, *"it's time for you two to come home. You're going to—"*

James interrupted. "We need to go to the asylum first."

"That's not in the plan, son. And certainly not advisable, given the state the city is in right now."

"I'll go by myself if I have to. There's a little girl that I am *not* leaving behind."

James waited through a long pause. He had just moved to open his door and get out when the voice spoke again. *"Sit tight. We're taking you to your friend. Better buckle up. It's going to be bumpy."*

They both harnessed themselves in. Jessica asked, "Where am I driving?" She placed her hands on the wheel.

"I'm driving. You two just hang on."

The car's engine fired up with a low growling purr.

"I know you, don't I?" Jessica said.

"We'll meet soon."

The car rolled forward into the darkness. They were being driven without headlights, but an enhanced night vision view appeared in their windshield. James figured the driver had his own screen for navigation, and this view was just for James and Jessica's comfort.

Instead of driving out the main valet exit, the car turned deeper into the garage and veered straight for the security fence enclosing the first level—and accelerated.

"Hang on."

The car punched through the fence—and the ground dropped out from under them. James's stomach leapt to his throat. Reflexively, he pushed himself deeper into his seat. From the look on Jessica's face, she felt the same sensation.

They hit the ground with a jarring impact and began to slide sideways down a steep slope.

"We're in the flood channel!" James said.

"*Less traffic.*"

The car picked up speed on the flat bottom of the channel.

"What about the trolls?" James asked.

"*I prefer to call them 'extreme urban outdoorsmen.' And they will be fine. Our routes are clear.*"

James appreciated the man's thinking. This was a genius method of traversing a city whose surface streets were choked with dead vehicles. And one of these channels went right past the asylum's quad.

They negotiated the channels without encountering any obstacles. As they approached the asylum, the car suddenly veered up onto the left slope then quickly swung back to the right and raced up the slope on the other side. It ripped through the fence beside the asylum and landed squarely in the quad.

"*We'll have that fixed,*" the voice said. "*James, tell Linda that as long as she stays to help the remaining children, she will receive all the support she needs.*" The car's headlights came on and lit up the quad.

"Right." James pulled himself out of the car. He ran to the quad door and pushed. Locked. Of course—without power, the residents inside were all trapped by the electronic locks. James checked the window to ensure there was no one standing behind the door, then he kicked it open. *Add that to the City's list of things to fix.*

Candles flickered throughout the dayroom. A small body removed itself from those clustered around a weak circle of candlelight. It walked cautiously toward him.

"James? Is that you?" Tina asked.

He knelt before her. "That's right, Tina. Come on. We have to leave now."

Tina's body stiffened. James instantly realized she had never known him as anyone other than the old James. She must be terrified right now. *Way to go, stupid.*

"What happened to you?" Tina asked with a mixture of fear and curiosity.

"Before now, I was always pretending to be… the way I was. It was just so they wouldn't kick me out. This is the real me. There's no need to be afraid."

"Oh… Well, that makes sense. And I'm not afraid. I'm happy for you."

"Why is that, little Tina?" James asked.

"Because you're not super stupid anymore. Only a little stupid." She pointed at the knots in his shoelaces.

Linda appeared from the darkness. "James?"

James returned to his feet. "Linda, I don't have a lot of time," he said. "There's been a catastrophic failure of the electrical grid. Jack asked me to inform you that if you stay with these children and keep them safe, you will receive all the support you need." He knew the voice from the car wasn't Jack's, but all that mattered was that Linda be persuaded to do the right thing for these children, and he knew the name "Jack" would have the desired effect on her. "I'll be taking Tina with me. She has a new family waiting for her."

Tina latched on to his leg and hugged it tightly.

By the look on Linda's face, she seemed to be struggling more with James's transformation than with the power failure. "What happened to you?" she asked.

"Let's just say, Jack found a cure for stupid."

He knelt again in front of Tina. "Wait here for a second, Tina. I need to get something from my room."

He sprinted to the boys' dorms in three giant leaps. He didn't need light for assistance. After so many years of living here, he knew the layout well enough to find his way in the dark as well as Dawn did. In his room, he lifted an edge of the top bunk off its support. Inside the gap where the support fit, he dug out Dawn's letter. With that in hand, he returned to Tina.

"Ready?" he asked, placing a hand on the back of her arm and surreptitiously pressing the dermapatch onto her skin. They walked through the quad toward the headlights.

"Wait!" Tina said as they reached the car. She ran back and stopped at the planter. "What about Teeka's rose?"

James followed her to the planter box. He looked from her to the plant standing tall in the harsh light. He'd almost forgotten about that part of the plan. "We're taking it with us," he said. He pulled low on the stem, uprooting the entire plant.

Tina frowned in concern.

"We'll replant it when we get home," he reassured her.

"Home?" she asked.

"With Mykl," he added.

"I don't think he likes me," she said, getting in the car to sit on James's lap.

"Oh, I think he does." James tucked the rose plant behind his seat, then turned to Jessica. "Jessica, this is Tina. Tina, this is Jessica. She's really nice."

Tina leaned into James for big brotherly protection before smiling bashfully and saying, "Hi." She yawned widely.

"She's adorable," Jessica said.

"Hang on to her tight, James. It's going to get bumpy again."

The headlights went off and the night vision view reappeared. With a sharp turn, the car hurtled back into the flood channel and took off. It squealed around turns and exceeded a hundred miles per hour on the long straightaways. Tina was terrified at first, but the sedative acted quickly, and soon she was asleep in James's arms.

When they neared the city boundary, the car slowed and the voice spoke again. *"Okay, here comes the tricky part. You should be aware that you are being tracked by Chinese agents."*

Jessica said irritably, "How in the hell are they able to track this car?"

"Normally, we wouldn't allow that, but in this case, we are."

"Are you using us as some sort of *bait*?" Jessica asked. "We have a child in the car!"

"No, not bait. Think of it as a magic trick. They have to see you die. Otherwise they will keep searching. Your existence complicates our efforts."

"You're not really going to kill us though?" Jessica asked.

"Of course not. We have a fireworks show planned. The Chinese will be most satisfied. Trust me, we have to let them catch up to you."

"Wait—their vehicles still work?"

"Of course; they were prepared for the EMP. They posted vehicles at all exit points to the city in case you tried to leave. But your vehicle is better."

Their car emerged from a tunnel, exited off a service ramp, and blasted through a locked gate. They cruised at a moderate speed to an interstate connector and stopped.

A pair of headlights approached rapidly from the southwest. The night vision shut off, and the car's headlights and taillights engaged. *He wants to make sure the Chinese see us*, James thought. Then with a screech of tires, the car took off again, entering the interstate heading northeast out of town.

James twisted to look back at the dark city vista. The former treasure box of glittering lights had ignited into a seething cauldron of smoke and fire. The twisting flames blazing atop the E Pluribus Unum made it the brightest spot in the city. Jessica didn't turn around, but her moist eyes kept returning to the rearview mirror.

James could tell that this car's mysterious driver was making sure they didn't lose their tail. The Chinese agents were allowed to stay close—but not too close.

Playing the role of prey, they exited the interstate at the last possible moment. The surprised Chinese driver behind them lost ground in the dirt from turning too late, but he caught back up quickly.

"Be on your toes. It's showtime. Here's the plan…"

CHAPTER 74

"I don't understand why her vehicle functions when the EMP disabled all the others," said the passenger in the pursuing vehicle.

The driver replied, "She paid a fortune for that car. It is possible that the electronics are shielded same as ours. It most certainly has projectile protection as well. But don't worry—she can't possibly travel much further with the hole we drilled in her fuel cell. And when she stops, we'll have her. Just remember, we want her alive. We take her head only if she proves too resistant to cooperation."

"Look! Ahead of her. Three cargo trucks. Why are they still functioning?"

"They must be government auto-drive trucks taking supplies to the base they deny existing."

"Well, they'll have to slow down for the curve, which means so will she. Should we force her off the road?"

"Didn't I just tell you we want her alive? We're not trying any dangerous maneuvers—*What is she doing?*"

The sleek, ground-hugging work of art ahead of them accelerated into the oncoming traffic lane to pass the trucks. There would be no actual oncoming traffic with all the vehicles disabled, but this was a blind curve, and there could be any number of stopped cars around that corner. A desperate move.

THE PROMETHEUS EFFECT

As the car passed the convoy, it clipped the front wheel of the rear truck. Not only did the car fishtail dramatically, but the truck's tire failed in spectacular fashion, and the truck began to jackknife. It tipped to its side, taking the elongated trailer with it.

The Chinese pursuers narrowly avoided a collision as their car screeched to a halt behind the skidding, overturned truck.

"We can't lose her! Go around! Go around!" said the passenger.

"I know! Which way?" asked the driver. He couldn't see beyond the thick dust cloud.

"My side! There is room!"

The driver backed up and maneuvered around, off the road. His tires threw rooster tails of gritty desert sand until they regained the asphalt. But when they cleared the dust cloud, their prey was nowhere to be seen.

"She's gotten away!"

"There's nowhere for her to go. Once we clear these curves, we'll see her lights again—There! She's stopped!"

The deafening roar of two fighter jets startled the Chinese agents. The panicked driver jammed his foot on the brake. The jets screamed, flying ridiculously low, and headed straight for the stopped car a half mile ahead. Afterburners suddenly kicked in as they thundered upward at blazing speed, never breaking formation.

Before either agent could comment on the spectacle, two successive detonations occurred at the red car's location. Two growing fireballs became one. The Chinese agents ducked into their arms too late to protect them from the incendiary flash. Supersonic shockwaves lifted their car off the ground amid a swarm of shattered glass. Bits of debris steadily rained from the sky.

They stumbled from their windowless car.

Blinking to clear the searing afterimage, the passenger asked, "Why?"

"Perhaps the last truck in the convoy carried the ice cream?" the driver replied. They both laughed. "Don't mess with fat Americans' ice cream!" More laughter. Both men were in a state of shock, and it had made them punchy.

The driver regained his composure first. "More likely, they found her out. The United States government doesn't care for traitors any more than we do."

"Should we check for a body?"

The driver pointed to the deep flaming crater where the car had been. "What's there to check? The body's been vaporized. Even the car's been vaporized. No, our job is done. Let's move on to the safe house and send in our report."

Off in the distance, the fading marker lights of the remaining two government trucks continued north for an on-time delivery.

**

"Wow, that was loud… and impressive," said Jessica as she watched the distant fireball from an opening in the cargo truck's rear panel. James peered over her shoulder, cradling the sleeping Tina.

After the truck crashed, their car had accelerated at full speed to the first truck in the line. Its back door had clattered to the asphalt as a modified ramp, and they'd decelerated to let forward momentum carry them into the truck. It was a maneuver Jessica had seen frequently in movies, but to experience it felt truly exhilarating. The Billybob twins had been perched on an elevated shelf in the truck's cargo area, out of the way, and they dropped down to help her and James get out of the car. Since James had his hands full with Tina, Jessica retrieved the plant he seemed so infatuated with.

As soon as they had all exited the car, the twins pushed it back down the ramp. It slowed to a stop, and as soon as they had reached a safe distance and the pursuing car was in sight—*Boom!*

"How does it feel to be dead?" a voice asked from behind Jessica. She had thought the voice sounded familiar when it had spoken through the dash; now she was sure of it.

She whirled to face the man. He certainly resembled the man who had fired her so unjustly, but the lack of a uniform and the addition of a smile—she hadn't thought him capable of one—made her uncertain.

"Colonel?" she asked.

"Not a colonel anymore, after tonight. I'm dead like you. Along with the EMP, they annihilated the accelerator base with a spaced-launched kinetic weapon."

Jessica swallowed against her sudden cold nausea.

"According to the uploaded logs, I died at ground zero along with a few others. The rest had long been evacuated. A few rats certainly perished. Rest your mind, no humans were actually harmed at the base. My name is Cutter, by the way. But you can call me Chip."

Again the smile, and he held out his hand. Jessica took it.

"Well done, Miss Stafford. Well done. Please forgive me for any grief I may have caused you in the past. That test is not an easy one. From either side."

"An oath without actions to back it up is an empty oath."

"Well said, Miss Stafford."

"Please, call me Jessica… Chip," she said, returning his smile.

"And you," Cutter said, turning to James. "That was quite a performance the last couple of days." His tone turned serious. "Whatever you may be feeling now, know this: you did what had to be done. If you hadn't, the two of you might not be alive. And in all honesty, you may have saved that man from the horrors of burning to death. I've been in your shoes. If you need to talk…"

James nodded his understanding. "What about Tina here?" he asked, adjusting the sleeping girl in his arms.

Cutter brushed the hair from her face in a fatherly manner. "We'll find a place for her. I promise you that."

"Where are we going now?" Jessica asked.

"Back to the City. Our job is done. Jack has it from here."

CHAPTER 75

The world around Sebastian spun uncontrollably and had been doing so since Fan's men took him. Faces were nothing more than blurs.

He vomited. He felt better.

Two men on either side of him jogged clumsily, supporting his weight under each arm. Sebastian's legs moved solely from his feet hitting the ground. If he lifted his legs, their task would be easier, but making things easy on people wasn't in his repertoire.

It looked like they were in a private airport terminal. But why was it so dark? People scurried all around with flashlights.

They burst through an emergency exit. No alarm sounded.

A jet with its turbines revving waited on the runway. An acrid smell of burning plastics registered in Sebastian's sodden brain.

As the men ran, he continued to let his feet drag, ruining his shoes. So what. He would be rich soon.

The men muscled him up the rolling stairs to the plane. Here at last, the lights were on.

Two voices spoke in a language he registered as Chinese. One of them belonged to Gang, the muscle from the hotel. The other was a man in uniform. Sebastian listened and watched, hoping to catch some phrase or body language he could interpret, but understood nothing.

THE PROMETHEUS EFFECT

The man in uniform finally turned to him. "I am China's Deputy Minister of State Security," he said in slightly accented English. The Chinese writing on his nametag resembled a stick figure samurai standing next to a guillotine.

Sebastian's surroundings started to spin again. The whiskey had begun to reach its peak effect. He vaguely realized that the alcohol would continue to evoke its truth serum effect. His inhibitions and ability to filter thoughts were becoming more compromised by the second.

"My name is Ji Bo," the man said. "You will address me as Deputy Minister."

Sebastian nodded. He felt queasy again and didn't trust opening his mouth.

The plane accelerated along the tarmac. Gang and Ji took seats facing him and secured themselves. Splotches of flickering orange briefly flew past Sebastian's window, as if the world outside moved and he sat motionless. The engine roar grew, and the nose of the plane lifted sharply. Sebastian closed his eyes and tried to concentrate on a single thought to stop the extraneous motion in his mind. It didn't work.

"Mr. Falstano," Ji began. "You are now our guest."

Gang's severe expression contradicted Ji's words.

"This plane carries no parachutes," Ji continued. "You may remain as our guest, or leave as our entertainment." He paused to allow his words to sink in.

Finally, Sebastian thought. *Someone who doesn't want to shoot me.* He didn't want to die, but if it was to happen, he wanted his death to be spectacular. Something the world would remember for generations. Being thrown from a plane would be spectacular. But wait... did Ji ask a question? He tried to get a grasp on his oily short-term memory. His thoughts kept slipping away like slimy fish.

Ji slapped him. "You will now tell me the location of the artifact," he demanded.

Sebastian's mental filters had completely dissolved in the alcohol. Ji's mere mention of the location immediately brought it to his mind, and it tumbled to the tip of his tongue with nary a hint of resistance. His head lolled forward as if the word rolling out of his mouth carried weight. "Seychelles," he said. Then he passed out.

***

Ji regarded Sebastian with a combination of interest and revulsion. *Did he say "seashells"?* No. It was more like Seychelles. That would make more sense. He would give this information to the chief minister so that his forces could act on it.

And if it proved to be false, Sebastian would face a firing squad.

CHAPTER 76

Numerous old-style tube televisions formed a vast mosaic of news feeds. The president darted from screen to screen, these flickering windows into the world, reading the tickers at the bottom of each square. The United States had been attacked, but by whom? No one had come forward to claim responsibility. Only sporadic, and sometimes staticky, details came through, though that didn't stop the media "experts" from putting forth any number of speculations and theories.

One of the televisions flashed an "update" banner. A drone feed showed a smoking crater where the White House had once been.

The president swore and threw a television remote in exasperation. It shattered against a concrete pillar.

"Bastards!" he yelled, damning both the attackers and those who had placed him in this bunker with no means of modern communication. "One Goddamned phone," he growled through clenched teeth. "How stupid do you have to be to design a bunker without a decent *phone*?"

His Secret Service men stood mutely as far away from their boss as protocol allowed. They had already offered up their own phones, but unfortunately, the bunker's depth and thick barriers made them useless—and their batteries had since been depleted in the struggle to acquire a signal.

"The country probably thinks I'm dead. Or worse, a coward. It's an election year!"

The president stomped around in frustration, searching for something else to hold on to—and eventually throw. His shoes crunched over the remnants of the ancient black phone's protective glass dome. He had kicked it to pieces in a previous tantrum. The damned phone wasn't even *connected* to anything! No wires. No cords. No batteries. It was a Goddamned *paperweight*. Who the hell knew what it was for? A seashell produced more sound than that phone. He glared at it.

It rang.

The bell rang sweet and clear, startling the Secret Service men. The final strike of the bell hung in the air, dying slowly, then the ring sequence started again.

"You've got to be kidding me," the president said. Despite his words, hope surged into him. He kept the inward flow of that feeling in check. It was easy to allow hope in; it required more effort to rid oneself of disappointment.

He picked up the receiver and said, more confidently than he felt, "This is the president speaking."

"Mr. President, this is Jack."

The president set his anger aside. He was essentially a prisoner in this bunker until Jack allowed him to leave. Threatening one's jailer never worked out well for the prisoner. But once he escaped this backwards cave of a home…

"I'm listening," the president said.

Jack got straight to the point. "China has initiated a preemptive strike with space-based kinetic and nuclear weapons."

"That's an act of war! *And* a violation of the Outer Space Treaty."

"The United States also has weapons of mass destruction in orbit," Jack said.

The president remained guiltily silent. Jack's knowledge of deep secrets disturbed him.

"Washington, DC, Cheyenne Mountain, Rocky Mountain, a prototype particle accelerator, and numerous military bases have been attacked by both EMP and kinetic weapons. Two nuclear-tipped kinetic weapons also detonated in the Ghawar and Khurais oil fields of Saudi Arabia. The Riyadh military base has been completely destroyed. Washington and Las Vegas are without power, burning, and in the midst of rioting. The good news is, loss of life is minimal thus far—though that will change when our own people in Washington and Vegas take advantage of the power outages."

"We need to launch a counterstrike *immediately!*" the president shouted.

"Mr. President, the affected military bases had long been closed or were previously evacuated out of caution. And those oil fields ran dry and were taken over by extremists years ago. China is using force to send you a message."

"They tried to *kill* me."

"No, Mr. President, they did not. They could track your phone. You had it taken to your house outside the city. Your wife and children are fine."

The president clenched his jaw. How could Jack possibly know these things? There must be a mole in his inner circle.

Jack continued. "And while they didn't know where you were, they certainly knew where you were *not*. They knew you were not present at any of the selected targets. Those targets were chosen not to hurt you, but to demonstrate the effectiveness and accuracy of their weapons—and force you to negotiate."

"Negotiate for what?"

"Fusion."

Silence.

"We don't have fusion," the president finally said.

"China thinks you do."

"Is this all because of that crackpot on the news a while back? China can't honestly believe that!"

"When countries harboring a mutual distrust for one another place weapons in space, against long-established treaties, anything is possible. Sometimes people's belief in things overrides reality. The fact is, China believes you possess the technology to control fusion. And if they can't have it, neither can you. That's why they destroyed the particle accelerator."

The president thought for a moment before asking quietly, "Did we have a working fusion generator there?"

"No. They were merely working on fusion experiments. China was manipulated into believing otherwise."

"Who is responsible for instigating this?" the president dared ask. He would accuse Jack, but what did the man have to gain by starting a war? Jack wasn't motivated by power, or fame, or money. No, this couldn't be Jack's doing. *Else why would he have warned me and placed me in this bunker?*

"The woman responsible for inciting China to act on this misinformation has been iced. She will no longer be a problem."

Iced, the president thought. *Jack uses the euphemism so calmly.* This man truly personified Jack the Ripper. "So this was all a mistake? A misunderstanding?"

"The weapons in space are also a mistake. They were put there with a full understanding of the consequences of using them. When China realizes there is no fusion to bargain for, they will have no choice but to gamble with the rest of their arsenal. There are not enough fossil fuels left to supply the world at the present rate of consumption. The last reserves of any significance are along America's coastlines. As past governments have predicted, the United States will soon possess the last available fuel on earth. But Mr. President… the missiles aimed at your country have all the fuel they need."

"So we're left with no choice but to go to war. An all-out liquidation of our own arsenal will at least put us on even ground when the dust settles." The president no longer harbored any ill will toward the mountain fortress enveloping him.

"Mr. President, a scorched-earth policy threatens the extinction of the human race."

"They started it!"

"Did they? In the many years I have held my position, a number of presidents have come and gone. All but one held reelection as their top priority. The atmosphere of distrust among nations has grown with every passing year. No, Mr. President, they did not 'start' it. Nor did anyone in the last one hundred thousand years.

"It started with a nomadic group of hominids encountering a new tribe and deciding that their tribe had a greater need than the other. It started with Prometheus stealing fire from the gods and giving it to men who had not yet earned it. Through the use of fire, he hoped men would acquire new knowledge and attain a greater level of productivity. But the corrupt underlying philosophy of 'If we can't have it, neither can they' remained. We have now reached the endgame of Prometheus's misdeed. The products of that knowledge are now poised to exterminate all life. Will you be the one who brings that philosophy to its inevitable conclusion?"

"Don't preach to me. Tell me what to do!"

"Be the president who is remembered as having had the wisdom *not* to destroy the planet. Call the Chinese president. Use your diplomatic prowess. Explain the misunderstanding. Most importantly, stall for time. Ask for a week to investigate the matter and tend to your frightened nation. Control of time allows for more rational actions, Mr. President. A lot can happen in a week. They should be eager to comply. And in the end, you will most certainly be reelected."

Finally, Jack was talking some sense. A week was an easy commodity to bargain for in the political world. It wasn't a complete solution to the problem, but it was a start. "What am I supposed to do after the week passes? Sit around and do nothing? What's to prevent this from happening again?"

"I like that you're starting to think about the future, Mr. President. There may be hope yet. You buy that week, and I will come up with a solution to the rest of the puzzle. Agreed?"

Do I have a choice? "Agreed," the president said grudgingly.

"Good. The exits leading out of the bunker are now unlocked. There is a vehicle waiting to take you back to work. Good luck."

The line went silent.

"Jack? ... Jack! ... Dammit."

The president replaced the handset on its base. Then he picked up the entire phone and examined it from all angles to see if he had missed something. It was the same as before, unconnected to anything. Another one of Jack's mysteries.

Of all the tasks waiting for him, the one he least looked forward to was seeing his wife. *Should have left the phone at the White House,* he thought.

CHAPTER 77

"Action message coming in, Commander," the person monitoring the sub's communications center said.

The submarine commander took the printout and read the short message. Kyle waited stoically two paces behind him. "Attack on US soil. Space-based kinetic weapons. Heavy damage to targets. White House destroyed. Minimal loss of life. President not harmed. Stay on mission."

The commander looked to Kyle for some sort of reaction and saw none.

"Stay on mission?" the commander asked. "An act of war has been committed, and we are to 'stay on mission'? That doesn't make any sense at all! Unless the agency that put us on this mission *knew* this was going to happen."

Kyle remained respectfully silent.

The commander presented the message to Kyle. "You have permission to speak," he said.

Kyle took the message but didn't read it. He didn't have to. Everything was going according to plan. Except the suspicions of the commander. He had to give the commander credit: the man was sharp. "You seem to be implying something, sir?" he asked.

"*Implying*? Let me make this crystal clear. I am accusing you of having knowledge of this mission that was not shared with the commander of this vessel. I will not be treated like a puppet. It compromises the safety of my crew when vital information is withheld."

"Sir—"

The commander flashed a palm at Kyle to forestall his response. "If you don't have something relevant to tell me, then don't talk until you do." He lowered his hand.

Kyle stood at attention. "Sir," he said gently, "as long as this submarine is in the water, you are her commander. My job is to follow orders within the chain of command."

At face value, he hadn't said anything of merit—certainly not enough to let him off the hook—but if one jumped to the obvious key phrase, "chain of command"… So that was it, the commander thought. Someone higher up in the chain thought it necessary to keep him in the dark. Who *was* this Kyle kid anyway? The commander thought he knew, but a gulf of mistrust had been developing within him since the spook incident.

Wait a minute…

"XO Smith."

"Sir."

"After we picked up that spook and someone took over our navigation remotely, how long was it before we dropped him off?"

"Approximately seven days, sir."

"And from the moment you returned to the boat until we reach our destination, how many days will have passed?"

Is that a hint of a smile on my XO?

"About seven days… sir," Kyle replied.

"Seems to be one hell of a coincidence. I don't believe in coincidences, mister. I want to know what's going on."

"Sir, if you feel that you can no longer trust me, I will step down and let one of the other officers take my place. Have me sedated in the infirmary if you feel it's necessary for the protection of the crew and this boat. I will not, however, violate my orders." Kyle stood like a man awaiting final judgement.

The commander fixed him with a stare. His XO had withheld information—was still withholding information. Of that he was certain. He was also the most capable XO he had ever served with, and would make a fine commander someday. He'd noted that bit of praise in the XO's last evaluation. The commander tried to imagine himself in the XO's shoes. Would he cave in to his superior's demands in the face of higher orders? His answer surprised him: *When submarines fly!* He would tell his commander to *shove it*. That's why he wasn't an admiral by now. His honesty and integrity had left him with no stomach for political niceties. And Kyle must hold a great deal of respect for him to make the offer of stepping down. His concern for the safety of everyone involved seemed genuine. He wasn't playing fair. The kid was really putting him to the test.

"That won't be necessary, XO Smith. Return to your post," the commander said.

CHAPTER 78

In a lavish bunker complex under the mountains west of Chengdu, China, four men lounged in stately chairs surrounding an ornate desk. The president of the United States had requested an audience; they had agreed, and had instructed him to call back in six hours. This gave the men opportunity to gather for the occasion. No translator would be needed, for they had all spent semesters receiving education in American colleges. It is money well spent when your enemy teaches your spies and future leaders.

The phone on their desk rang at one minute past noon. It was well past midnight on the other end of the line—a planned inconvenience.

"Good morning, Mr. President. How nice of you to call," said China's paramount leader, keeping the phone on speaker for all to hear.

"President Feng, thank you for taking my call. It appears that we are both victims of a gross misunderstanding."

"Our intelligence reports state otherwise, Mr. President," Feng said. "One does not deploy one billion dollars' worth of aircraft and ten million in ordnance to fix a misunderstanding. However, it is very much the type of thing one would do to protect a secret. Wouldn't you agree?"

"We don't have fusion, Feng."

"Of course you don't. We took that ability away from you by bombing the only place you *did* have it, *Harold*." If the US president wanted to do away with traditional niceties, so be it.

"I don't know what to tell you, other than you have been deceived. If it were reasonable for us to do so, don't you think we would have launched a counterstrike by now? There is no need to escalate aggression over a *mistake*! I'm sure your spy satellites can confirm that we are not preparing to retaliate."

Feng made a gesture to the military general at his side; the man nodded in confirmation. "Such action would be foolhardy indeed," Feng said, "considering we have the ability to target and destroy any American city of our choosing within fifteen minutes. Including the office you now sit in."

"Dammit, Feng. I'm here in good faith to show we have nothing to hide. If you launch another weapon, anywhere, we all lose."

Feng spoke slowly. "Is that a threat… Mr. President? Your country is no longer the superpower of years past. I suggest you select your words carefully."

"President Feng, and anyone else who is listening in, give me a week to sort this out. Allow reason and cooler heads a chance to prevail. Will you agree to that much? For the sake of both our countries… and everyone else who stands to lose if we fail?"

Feng made a toothy smile. The president was all but groveling at his feet. This was even better than he had hoped for. One week. Plenty for China's needs. And for the United States to experience China's *true* weapon.

"You may have your week, Mr. President. Use it wisely."

Feng killed the connection before the president could respond.

"Their navy is in full recall to protect their coastlines," the general informed him, "except for one carrier group en route to the Seychelles area—to retrieve the artifact, we assume. The carrier and her support vessels are some of the oldest and most obsolete in their fleet. They will be no trouble. Half our fleet and the majority of our submarines are already in the area. The US forces will be vastly outnumbered."

"Excellent," Feng said. Turning to his Director of National Space Administration, he asked, "And what of the stones we have thrown toward the American side of the pond?"

"According to the last telemetry data, all are on optimal trajectories. We are unable to verify the asteroids' locations visibly, but infrared scans confirm telemetry. If the American navy remains on the coastlines, they will be destroyed along with major coastal cities. The mission is guaranteed to succeed this time, President Feng."

Feng drummed his fingers on the desk. "Keep the kinetics armed. We may still have some cleaning up to do after the impacts."

***

Two men in the white uniforms of the Chinese navy guarded Sebastian as he huddled over a safety rail of China's flagship aircraft carrier. The fresh air was supposed to help with the seasickness, but staring down at the relentless waves exacerbated it instead. His hangover added its own vile twist. High winds ripped streamers of bile sideways from his mouth with each retch.

He closed his eyes and attempted a breathing exercise. He retched again and felt something tear in his abdomen. *How could a ship this big have so much motion?* When his bladder threatened to burst, he tried peeing through the rails and off the ship. Howling wind blew urine back in his face.

The men behind him wore expressions of revolted amusement. Why were they even there? They stood too far away to prevent him from jumping. Not that he would try; he had too much to lose now. Even if he did jump, he doubted they would mount a rescue. That attitude would have to change. It was a good thing he had passed out before revealing everything he knew.

When their flight from Las Vegas landed, he and the deputy minister had immediately boarded a waiting military transport jet. When they landed on the carrier, Sebastian had run straight from the jet to his present location. He had yet to see the inside of the carrier.

He retched again. A groan escaped from his lips as he let his face fall against cold steel.

Someone grabbed the back of his head, and he sensed pressure being applied to the side of his neck. When the pressure released, it felt like a rough bandage remained.

"For seasick," said a uniformed man in passable English. He spoke with the air of a doctor. "Your presence is expected inside when it takes effect." The doctor turned smartly on his heel and marched to the island control tower.

After ten minutes, Sebastian's body began to relax, though his mind remained fuzzy. A fair trade. He wiped his mouth on his sleeve and signaled his readiness to go inside.

His guards led him to the tower, but barred him from entering. One guard stepped inside and came back with a wet towel and a change of clothes. "Strip," he ordered. "You stink."

Sebastian was more than happy to oblige. They tossed his reeking clothes over the side of the ship. The new ones felt coarse and rough on his skin, and they were orange, like prison garb. But they were clean.

"You may enter now," the guard said.

Inside, a tiny man with a face of stone stood next to the deputy minister. Judging by all of his medals, pips, and tassels, he had to be an admiral of the Chinese navy. On second glance, Sebastian recognized the man's face from news stories. This man enjoyed taunting US warships. The media had labeled him a dangerous warmonger. Sebastian had no desire to test this man's patience, but his goals required him to do so. If he gave away everything now, he would be fish bait.

The admiral spoke to Sebastian in Chinese. The deputy minister translated. "We will be in the Seychelles area in two days. Our satellites and reconnaissance flights show nothing out of the ordinary. You will now tell us, please, exactly where the artifact is being kept."

No, I won't, Sebastian thought. "I don't know *exactly* where it is," he said, which was true. "Do you have an aerial map of the area?"

The admiral led them to a digital navigation table. A glossy touch screen comprised the entire tabletop. It sat awkwardly lower than customary for one obvious reason: the admiral's small stature. No self-respecting admiral wanted to command while sitting in a booster chair.

The admiral pulled up a static satellite image. Sebastian knew they possessed technology to show real-time feeds, but he supposed they were reluctant to show it. Their sonar and reconnaissance data had determined the placement of numerous ships and submarines, all of which were marked with icons. A Chinese armada converged on the Seychelles, closely followed by unwelcome guests. A good portion of the Russian fleet shadowed them. A spattering of North Korean ships was attempting a blockade of the Russians.

Sebastian couldn't contain his curiosity. "What's going on here?" he asked, pointing at the North Koreans.

The deputy minister responded, "It's nice to have trained flies. They are not your concern." He tapped the table lightly. "Where is the artifact?"

"Can you center the image over the Seychelles?"

The admiral did so. Evidently he understood English but chose not to speak it.

Chinese submarines surrounded the area. That would be very fortuitous, when the moment was right.

Sebastian whirled his finger in the air over a spot on the plot. "My best guess is that it is being kept in one of the islands in this group here." A lie. "The entrance is only accessible by submarine. A smaller attack submarine at that. I doubt one of your Dynasty class boomers would fit." Enough truth to keep him needed—and alive—for two more days. Once he kept his end of the deal, he was sure the sight of the artifact would quash any negativity they felt toward him. *I must see the look on their faces when they witness it for themselves.*

The admiral paced once around the navigation table, contemplatively rubbing his chin. As though remembering Sebastian still remained in his presence, he turned to the guard, pointed at Sebastian, and spoke his first word of English.

"Brig."

CHAPTER 79

The moon's Operations Center shared similarities with the one planetside, but whereas the City's ops center offered relaxing chairs for long brainstorming and planning sessions, the moon's had been designed for quick and efficient implementation of action plans and dealing with emergency situations. In a fraction of the space used in the City building, technicians manned wrap-around work stations and deeply recessed alcoves along the walls. The flow of information flashed holographically around the room in synchronized patterns.

Mykl slipped in unnoticed and took a seat in the protective shadow of a work station. He had a perfect view of Jack, manipulating video feeds on a chest-high virtual screen circling him. The computer system redisplayed and magnified everything he accessed on a larger curved surface to keep everyone updated.

Mykl observed from his hiding spot for two hours. He should have brought Stinker to keep him company—and to keep him calm. The images he saw educated him on the abominations of war. His thumping heart wanted him to run. Only Jack's seemingly unfazed affect kept his own emotions anchored.

He had mixed feelings when Tina was rescued. She was a nice enough girl but… she was a *girl*.

The conversation with the president showed a side of Jack that Mykl hadn't seen before. He learned much from it.

When the operation finally wound down and the lights were turned up, a man with a clear view of Mykl outed him. The man made no accusations, just a simple nod toward him while making eye contact with Jack.

Jack wore a should-have-known expression on his face. "How much?" he asked.

Mykl crawled out from under the work station. His butt ached from sitting on the hard floor. Stinker would have made an excellent cushion. "I came here right after I saw the flashes in space on my wall screen," he said.

"Of course you did," Jack said.

"Ladies and gentlemen, thank you," he said to all present. "We can go back to normal staffing for now. If something unexpected comes up, we know where to find you."

That drew a few chuckles. All but three people left the room. They gave Mykl smiles, nods, and hellos as they filed past. None seemed put off by his spying.

Jack hooked an empty chair with his foot and sent it rolling toward Mykl. "Questions?"

This wasn't to be a "bad boy" lecture then. Good. Mykl climbed into the adult-height chair and scooted his butt to the back. The soles of his shoes pointed at Jack. "You could have stopped those missiles, or whatever they were, from launching. Couldn't you?" he asked.

"They were EMP and nuclear-tipped kinetic weapons. Who do you think China would suspect if all those weapons failed to launch?"

"Us. No, not *us,* but the US," Mykl replied.

"And when they feared that their space-based weapons had been discovered, they would attempt to launch a preemptive strike with missiles even more powerful. And when they found those to be nonresponsive?"

"More blame," said Mykl.

"And more fear. It doesn't take computers to run a war. They only make them more efficient. I've been preventing this type of incident from happening for decades. It's time for the madness to end, and it had to start somewhere. Nations of the world that aren't already at war are mobilizing resources to join in. America is currently being viewed as a victim, and the world is waiting for their response before taking sides."

"And you still want me to think of a solution for all of this?"

"If you can. It's not easy when the pieces to the puzzle keep changing, is it?"

Mykl didn't need to respond to that. Jack had been at this almost a century, yet his best solution to the current state of the puzzle involved allowing bombs to fall on American soil. What did he expect Mykl to come up with to prevent the next bomb from falling out of the sky? Magic and fantasy saved the world just fine in books, but this required something real. Something extraordinary. It would take substantially more thought—and computer resources.

"I need full, unrestricted access to all files and camera feeds," Mykl said. "And I need the most up-to-date and real-time information available. Future plans would be beneficial too."

"There are some secrets that I cannot allow you to see… yet. All other restrictions to your access will be removed before you return to your computer."

The world once again revolved at Mykl's fingertips. What wonders would reveal themselves now?

"I'm going to check on Dawn first. Then I'll get started," Mykl said.

"She's on sublevel six," Jack said as Mykl got up to leave.

"Oh—and the restroom?" Mykl asked.

Jack pointed to his right.

***

Six levels deep inside the moon base, the elevator opened onto a large area with the stillness of a cemetery. And it was *cold*. Long hallways radiated from a central hub, connecting concentric rings of compartments like the spokes of a wheel.

Mykl zipped his jumpsuit to the top. Dr. Lee noticed him and waved him over.

"What can I do for you, Mykl?" she asked.

"Dawn?"

Dr. Lee set down a stylus and asked Mykl to follow her. Dawn resided one room over. That made Mykl feel better. She hadn't been stored away in some random out-of-the-way location.

Dr. Lee slid open a side view panel so he could better see inside Dawn's cylinder. Mykl tentatively touched the view window. It made a tiny fog spot at his fingertip, which rapidly went away as he withdrew it. He held his breath in order to better detect any movement from inside, but he observed no signs of life. A fine layer of rime dusted Dawn's eyelashes.

"By definition," Dr. Lee said from behind him, "she is clinically dead. Biologically, her life is suspended in time. At 173 degrees Kelvin, she is in a dreamless sleep. Her cancer is no longer killing her."

Mykl tuned out after hearing the words "clinically dead." "She can be awakened again, right?" A silly question. He knew that. But sometimes one needed to hear the answers to silly questions again and again before they could be believed.

"The process is complete. We could start the reanimation procedure right now, but James wants to be present when we do. She expressed the same desire."

"So she'll stay like this?" Mykl asked.

"For as long as needed."

"What's the longest someone's been kept like this before reanimation?"

"About fifty years. That was before I started here. Jack rescued a little boy in the late stages of a neuromuscular disease from a terminal care center. The boy had been bed-ridden for most of his life and knew very little of the outside world. He knew only that he was trapped in a body that had failed him. When our knowledge on nerve regeneration was sufficiently advanced, we woke him. We watched in amazement as his damaged myelin sheaths began to heal. Without this treatment, he would certainly have died."

"And he's still okay now?" Mykl asked.

"Of course. Except for being skinny and hating all vegetables. James has met him. His name is Timmy."

Mykl had seen Timmy in the hotel kitchen when he was searching the video feeds in James's folders.

"When we deemed Timmy fully recovered, he was adopted by one of our agents who works on an ambulance in Las Vegas. Considering that Timmy was thrust ahead fifty years in a time machine, he's adapted beautifully. But he has no knowledge of the City or his father's affiliation with it."

"How long is Dawn's 'time machine' set for?"

"That's not preset in advance," Dr. Lee answered. "It could be a day, a year, or a hundred years. Until the situation on the planet is resolved, it's not safe, or fair, to wake everyone."

"Thank you, Dr. Lee. I'm going to go back to my room now." Mykl gently rubbed Dawn's cylinder. Whether for luck or goodbye, he couldn't say. All he knew was the gesture made him feel less cold inside.

On returning to his room, Mykl discovered a long section of toilet paper unrolled to the base of the windowed wall, its end shredded. Noah was asleep in the window slit, nestled on a fluffy white cloud of his own making.

Mykl tore a few extra squares off the end of the roll and laid them over the sleeping mouse like miniature blankets. He remembered all too well what had happened to the last creature he had given protection from the cold. Too many mean people existed in the world. Acts of kindness went a long way.

With Noah snoozing before a panorama of moon and Earth, Mykl decided to begin in earnest on Jack's problem. His personal folder contained new files—a good sign. The contents of Jack's "Operations" folder had exploded as well. If he had reserved secrets, it couldn't be many.

A new folder labeled "Children" immediately caught Mykl's attention. Inside were alphabetized subfolders for all the world's countries. There was also a folder containing video feeds, which Mykl began scrolling through. A rolling time stamp showed them to be live images.

The scenes he witnessed made Lori seem like an angel. Thousands upon thousands of children were starving to death from too little food, while the men guarding them obviously ate too much. Boys not much older than himself carried rifles too big for their undeveloped muscles. Mass graves piled high with tiny bodies grew as expressionless men threw in more without looking back.

How? Why? The stupidity of it all made Mykl sick. *Don't these people know they're literally throwing away their future?*

Then he came to the girls…

He closed the files immediately. That was enough. He couldn't watch anymore.

Jack couldn't save them all; there were too many. And Mykl knew for certain that any one of those children, given the chance, would gladly live in the conditions of the Box. Even with Lori running it.

Mykl rubbed his cheeks. He didn't realize he had been clenching his jaw for so long. Any solution he came up with would definitely take into account the children of the world.

Intelligence gathering reported massive troop deployments on every continent. Navies had stepped up patrols and established lines of defense at major ports. All except China and Russia, who appeared to be playing a game of cat and mouse in the Indian Ocean, heading toward East Africa. Mykl couldn't find any reports to explain the strange convergence of so many vessels. That was undoubtedly one of Jack's secrets he didn't care to share.

Mykl set his wall globe spinning and made the computer plot in red every city currently targeted by nukes. His room turned eerie from the haunting glow. He then computed the affected areas after detonation and overlaid those in pink. The color completely saturated every landmass. The only unaffected areas were deep in the oceans. He adjusted to show one week after an all-out nuclear event. Now even the oceans filled in with the deadly color. He saw no need to run the mortality rates. This could never be allowed as a solution.

With two keystrokes, Mykl brought back the normal globe. *If it were only that easy*, he thought. He brought up a saved picture of his mother. She had lost her life working on the front lines of this battle; Mykl felt like he was letting her down. Before he knew it, he was scrolling through every picture of her. It was far better for his psyche than the graphic scenes he'd discovered in the other folders.

He wanted to see more pictures, so he entered a search for her cover name. A police evidence file sat at the top of the list.

Don't open it, he told himself. *Nothing good can come of this.*

He removed his hands from the keyboard and placed them in his lap. No one had ever told Mykl *how* his mother died. Only that she had been killed.

He hopped off his chair. It wouldn't make any difference to know the details.

He drifted to his bed and took Stinker in his arms. *It won't change anything. It won't bring her back.*

He stared at the computer screen, a debate rampaging in his brain.

He finally retook his seat, with Stinker in his lap. Uncounted reasons swam in his head telling him why he shouldn't open that file. But his need trumped them all. *I have to know the truth.*

Firmly holding Stinker to his chest, he opened the file. It contained all the official documentation on the incident. Police reports, coroner and witness statements. The presence of an attached security video clip caused Mykl the most fear. *Can't stop now.*

He played the clip—and immediately froze the blurry image. His mother was walking toward what appeared to be a back entrance. *At this moment in time, she still lived.* He could leave it at that. Shut off the computer and walk away with that memory… and be forever haunted with not knowing.

He allowed the playback to resume.

Two masked men rushed in from opposite sides of the frame. One drew a long knife hard against her throat while the other pulled her to the ground. The buckles on her boots glinted in the harsh lighting as she thrashed and kicked at her assailants. They were too strong. Again and again and again, they raised knives high in the air. After each plunge, the blades came back up a darker shade of red, until the kicking stopped. The men ran in opposite directions.

Mykl watched the pool of blood grow. He leaned forward in his chair to analyze the scene. Muddled emotions sloshed in his mind. Absentmindedly, he rubbed one of Stinker's ears between two fingers. He truly experienced sorrow for this woman who had been so brutally killed. But—this was not his mother. She had worn boots with laces that evening. Not buckles.

The first thought in Mykl's mind was to run and tell someone. *She could still be alive!* Then he realized no one was more suited, or motivated, to find out what happened than him.

There *have* to be more camera angles, he thought. City technology had the capability to tap into any security system. He located the address of the strip club from the police report. It took him only seconds to access the club's video archive. While the club itself didn't store records for very long, the City boasted virtually unlimited capacity for data storage. What others deleted, the City archived.

Recalling the date of the incident was an easy matter. One does not readily forget their own birthday. He found dozens of security cameras within a one-block radius. The club's camera on the employee entrance confirmed her showing up to work with lace-up boots. Mykl fast-forwarded the playback of an interior camera a few minutes before the woman's attack. He caught someone briefly conversing with his mother. They pointed, as if describing something behind the club. His mother rushed outside. The same camera that recorded the murder confirmed her leaving. But it wasn't her who came back.

Odd.

He needed another camera angle. An industrial building directly behind the club granted a high, wide-angle view. Mykl entered a timecode thirty minutes before the attack and fast-forwarded. A truck driving through the club's rear parking lot stopped, then suddenly backed into his mother's car. Then drove away. No wonder his mother rushed out. As she surveyed the damage, a dark van, with its side door open, blazed into the lot and screeched to a stop behind her. Three men jumped out and muscled her inside. The camera showed no other people who could have witnessed the event.

As the van's side door slammed shut, the passenger door opened, and a woman got out. She looked identical to his mother, and she was dressed the same—except for the buckles on her boots. She spent a moment adjusting her hair after the van drove off. So, she was part of it. But surely she didn't know what her assignment was. Her grisly death was about to be used to cover up an abduction.

Still alive, Mykl made himself believe. *But where?*

Enough cameras existed along the van's route for him to track it to one of the city's smaller airports. Men removed his mother's limp body from the van and carried her into a private jet. *She's drugged*, Mykl thought. The alternative was unthinkable.

The jet's registration number indicated that it was of Chinese ownership with diplomatic status. Its flight plan showed its final destination as Cabo San Lucas. From there, Mykl had to dig into the City's archive data on aircraft tracking. If the plane had a computer chip, all movement was logged, regardless of whether or not it filed a flight plan. He found airport security footage that confirmed each landing and refueling of his mother's plane as it made hop after hop to the tip of South America. But it wasn't until an airport serving Punta Arenas that he finally reconfirmed his mother's presence. Her body still limp, she was taken from the plane, and new faces loaded her into another van.

Mykl wiped his moist hands on Stinker's fur. *If they're going through this much trouble to move her, they aren't going to kill her.* Rationalization gave him courage to keep going.

The van proceeded to the docks, where his mother was loaded onto a large vessel registered as a Chinese research ship. Not only were the ship's onboard cameras turned off, which normally wasn't a problem for City technology, they were also completely shrouded. So—the people behind this were so suspicious, they didn't trust the surveillance cameras on their own ship. Mykl instead had to use satellite imagery from the City tracking database. For three days, the ship cruised along

Antarctica's coastline. Then it anchored in an iceberg-clogged bay. He could only enlarge the image so far before it began losing critical detail. He detected a helicopter leaving the ship, but could not positively identify his mother being transferred aboard.

Deep in the Antarctic wasteland, the helicopter landed next to a track-wheeled snow vehicle. Mykl strained his eyes to make out details in the pixels of those who left the helicopter. Three people. He could be sure of very little, but he was certain that one was smaller than the other two. That had to be her.

He brought up another screen to show the same image in infrared. The ice and snow turned black; anything with warmth glowed brightly. The glow of the ice vehicle floated along a curving path as he sped up the playback. It finally came to a stop at a base station made of square buildings. Mykl pulled up the informational report for the base coordinates: Kunlun Station, one of the coldest places on Earth. The perfect place to interrogate a spy without fear of them escaping.

Mykl zoomed in on the base, now tracking both normal and infrared side by side. No one would leave without him seeing. He gradually increased the speed of the playback.

One day… two… three… Only a single person at a time ever left the buildings.

Four days… five…

Finally, on the seventh day, a person came out and entered a tractor to take it beyond the base perimeter. Mykl ignored it. Soon after, three people emerged from a central building.

Mykl clicked the playback to normal speed. The person in the middle glowed brighter than the other two. It dawned on Mykl that the other two must be wearing climate gear to protect them from the cold. They walked in the direction the tractor had gone.

No!

Mykl backed up the recording to the point where the tractor left the base. This time he followed it. Just past the base perimeter, it stopped and made a deep pit in the snow pack. Cold fear flowed into Mykl's soul. There was no question what—or whom—that pit was for.

The three glowing dots approached the edge of the pit. Mykl zoomed in as far as he could. The person in the center no longer glowed as brightly as before; the cold was taking its toll. For several minutes, the dots barely moved. Then an infrared flash scattered incandescent bits of the center person toward the pit. Tiny heat signatures disappeared quickly as the warm blood droplets froze. Then the person fell into the pit, unmoving.

With the execution complete, the tractor pushed broken ice and snow to cover the body, and the warm glow of Mykl's mother disappeared.

In desperation, he ran the satellite feed all the way to present. Nothing changed. He rested his forehead on the desk and cried.

CHAPTER 80

Lawrence's shift had so far consisted of an uneventful morning and afternoon, so what happened in the early evening balanced everything out. In the twistiest part of North Shore Road, at the far border of his patrol area, he came across fresh skid marks intertwining through a blind curve. The right-angle start to them meant a significant impact had occurred.

Heavily damaged vehicles had ended up on opposite sides of the road. The first was a classic muscle car—or had been. Its mutilated corpse now lay belly up to the dimming sky, and its driver was sprawled halfway out a shattered window, cold and stiff. The accident must have happened after the end of Lawrence's rounds yesterday. The driver had apparently lived long enough to enjoy one last beer, judging by the half-empty can still clutched in his hand. Numerous others littered the scene and the interior of his ruined ride. At least he was the only one in the vehicle.

Lawrence notified his dispatcher to send a coroner. Nothing worth saving remained on this side of the road.

He hustled over to the other side, hoping, but not betting, he would find a brighter outcome.

Scorched desert painted a sooty halo around the charred husk of the second vehicle. Lawrence knew no life existed in the burned car, but he executed a thorough search of the area in the dim hope that someone might have been ejected from the vehicle. He found nothing.

Reluctantly, he then inspected the burned car. He needed the VIN number and an occupant count. The tally-box for total fatalities on his accident form reported the number as "two" when he was done: one in each vehicle. The VIN came back with no registered owner, and there was little to identify the victim. Jane/John Doe temporarily filled the ID section of his report. He thought the victim might be female, but he couldn't be certain. Fire does horrible things to human flesh.

***

After helping the shorthanded coroner load his vehicle and signing the tow man's book, Lawrence returned to his truck. Time to call it a day. Reheat some dinner. Rinse. Repeat.

A clicking sound came from underneath his right boot as he stepped from the desert back onto the road. He reached down and pried off a shiny object stuck to his sole.

"Damn thing. Why won't it stay put?" He wiped sooty dirt off his nametag and went to refasten it to his old jacket. But then he blinked in confusion. He was already wearing a nametag.

He shrugged. "Must have been an extra that fell out of my pocket. Heaven knows I've bought enough of them in my career." He pocketed the extra nametag and started home.

***

Five hours later, warm light from a sputtering old kerosene lantern cast flickering shadows in the stillness of Lawrence's trailer. The lantern's constant noise sounded to Lawrence like an exhaled breath, which made him think of it as a living entity, glowing brightly, providing warmth and security. It masked the sound of his finite heartbeat and the deadly silence encroaching from outside. Almost out of fuel, it hissed and coughed. None remained to refill it. A half-melted emergency candle sat at the ready. After that burned away, the only light would be from stars and the glowing orange smoke plumes beyond the nearest mountain.

Lawrence had been a soldier and a survivor. He would survive this too. Every electronic device in his domain now lay dead and useless. Even the battery-powered ones. He'd had to walk the last five miles home after the flash scuttled his truck. A military-grade EMP was the only reasonable explanation. If so, it would take years for the government to remedy that—and that was if something worse didn't happen first.

Nothing remained for him here. He decided the moment had come to move on. Retire. Start living. Maybe go someplace with a creek or a pond full of trout. He missed fishing.

For more times than he cared to count, Lawrence re-read the name on the business card he had held for the last two hours: Jack Grey. Too cliché, he thought. The name had to be fake. There was nothing fake about the helicopter or the men he showed up with, though.

The business card's edges were worn and dirty from hours of handling. He flipped it over again, hoping a contact number might magically reveal itself this time as opposed to all the other times he'd checked. Still blank. Only the man's name had ever been on the card. *Why give a card without contact information?*

Not for the first time, he held the card up to the lantern to examine it for a watermark he might have missed. Nothing. And as he watched, the lantern gave one last spitting gasp and died. His heartbeat returned to fill the silence.

No need to light the candle yet; it was too valuable. He could manage in the darkness of his trailer easily enough. The sun would rise again in the morning, and he would start his journey. Pacific Northwest sounded good. They still had water and trees. He put the business card in a zippered pocket of his tattered old coat. *I wonder how that boy is doing.*

Strong gusting winds suddenly rocked Lawrence's trailer. Sand and tiny pebbles pelted his windows. He extended his arms to brace himself against the walls of the narrow interior walkway.

"What was *that*?" he asked the darkness.

He opened his door and stepped out. Thanks to the stars, there was more light out here than there was in the trailer. *Not much in the way of clouds. What caused the wind?*

Footsteps crunched toward him in the gravelly soil.

His hand shifted to his sidearm. "Who's there?"

A brilliant beam of light split open the darkness. He shielded his eyes. The light lowered and refocused to form an oval shape at his feet.

"Good evening, ranger," said a woman's voice.

Lawrence moved his hand to the side to see her better. Her short skirt revealed a magnificent pair of fishnet stocking-clad legs.

"Looks like you could use some company," she said.

She stopped a few steps away and assumed a saucy posture with hands on her shapely hips. She wore the uniform of a cocktail waitress. Lawrence wrinkled his forehead in befuddlement.

"How did you get here?" he asked, hoping she planned to stay longer.

She raised one hand and twirled a finger in the air. Lights flashed on behind her. The outline of a helicopter, black as a desert beetle, sat on the road a hundred feet away.

Lawrence touched his pocket with the business card.

"That's right," she said, gesturing toward the helicopter. "It's the same one. You've been fiddling with that card enough over the last few days that we thought you might be ready to join us."

"How would you know about that?" Lawrence asked.

"Biometric sensors in the paper. If you weren't interested in Jack's offer, you would have thrown the card away. We've found that those who *are* interested hang on to the card. Literally."

"I'm finding that hard to believe."

"Less believable than a cocktail waitress showing up in a stealth helicopter to recruit you after an EMP attack?"

She made a *very* strong point. Perhaps his skepticism needed a kick in the ass.

"How's the boy?" he asked.

"Oh, he's fine," she said. "Over-the-moon happy, you might say, now that he's been reunited with his real father. But we're here for you,

Mr. Hansen. What do you say? Would you like to join us?"

"But... you don't even know me."

"Mr. Hansen, your life is as transparent to us as a perfect diamond—and equally as flawless. Well, except for that incident when you were nineteen. Boys will be boys," she said with a knowing grin.

Lawrence flushed. He found it difficult to look her in the eyes now. "But, I don't know *you*."

"Momma told you not to ride with strangers?" She sashayed to him with an arm extended. "I'm Rose."

Lawrence tentatively took her hand. She squeezed his encouragingly and smiled. He gestured back toward his trailer and made his decision. "I have other firearms and ammunition inside. I can't leave them for some child to discover."

"We have technology to take care of that," she said. Without moving her eyes from his, she reached into a utility pocket in her skirt and pulled out a single strike-anywhere match.

Lawrence understood, and took it. "There won't be a body for them to find in the rubble?"

"After tonight, there are going to be a lot of missing bodies. And much bigger issues for them to deal with."

Light from the helicopter shined through the trailer windows, giving Lawrence enough visibility to commit his first-ever felony: arson. He justified it in his mind that it was for the greater good. With a snap of his wrist, he lit the match and tossed it onto the mattress.

Trailers were notorious for burning hot and fast. His was no exception. When the flames started licking the ceiling, he exited to rejoin Rose.

"Is there any place to fish where we're going?" he asked.

"Sure enough. I'll even teach you how," she said with a wink.

CHAPTER 81

Tears once again dampened Stinker's fur. Mykl tried to convince himself that he couldn't have done anything to change the outcome. This had all happened over a year ago. If only he could go back in time, he might be able to make a difference. Phenomenal technology surrounded him. Faster-than-light communication. Gravity control. Matter manipulation. Prolonged life. *Why not a time machine?*

But Mykl knew, even if they did have one, the dangers would be too great to risk altering the life of one person. Hibernation—like with Dawn—was the only "time machine" they could safely use.

Something niggled at his mind. Like Dawn...

Like Dawn!

Mykl tugged at his hair. Jack had asked him about his earliest memories. He thought back to those now. The water in the tub: did it have a color? Yes. It had a pinkish tinge. Blood. Did any of his own blood mix with his mother's inside the womb? If so, could she have been exposed to the alien DNA, and possibly adapted? Maybe the gunshot didn't kill her. And if she had hung on, even for a little while... There was no better location for a person to freeze solid than the coldest place on the planet. Could she have won the race between hypothermia and exsanguination? Could she be in hibernation, like Dawn?

In the lowered gravity, Mykl reached his door in one bound, his feet never touching the floor. He had to find Jack.

CHAPTER 82

"We have not found the entrance to this cavern you speak of," the deputy minister said, shoving Sebastian into the carrier's command tower. "If it is not located soon, you will be thrown overboard and allowed to search for it on your own."

"It's there," Sebastian said with more confidence than he possessed. "Perhaps try tightening the search area to these three islands?" He tapped a new area on the navigation table. Now that the Seychelles were visible on the horizon, he felt comfortable divulging his best estimate.

"You don't really know, do you?" the deputy minister said.

Sebastian schooled his face.

"This is fantasy. You know nothing." The deputy minister called to the guard.

"Wait," Sebastian said. "Please?" He strode to the navigation plot and, via hand gestures, asked the admiral for permission to access it. The admiral acquiesced. His expression read: *Sign your own death warrant.*

Sebastian zoomed out to show China's coastline from the Sea of Japan to the South China Sea. He selected the mark-up function and began drawing in different colors, scribbling lines all along the coast and out to sea. Some zigzagged, others looped back on themselves. He had run out of colors by the time he reached the bottom of the map.

The admiral's eyes narrowed and his fists clenched.

"What is this mess?" the deputy minister asked.

"Those are your secret submarine patrol routes as of my last day of employment. The organization kept them in the same classified folder holding the details on the artifact."

The admiral quickly erased the mark-up and nodded to the deputy minister. All of the submarines normally patrolling these routes would now be searching the Seychelles for the cavern entrance, but Sebastian could tell by the look on the admiral's face that the patrol routes were correct nonetheless. The admiral said something in Chinese and left the tower. Probably needed to contact his superiors.

"We will keep searching," said the deputy minister. "What other of our secrets do you wish to share before you return to the brig?"

Sebastian quickly learned the fleeting power of information after one ran out of things to say.

CHAPTER 83

"Action message coming in, sir. Juliet Romeo priority."

"Send it to my quarters," the commander said. He faced his XO. "We'll decode it there."

His XO appeared puzzled. That was a first.

In addition to the commander's personal safe, two redundant code safes occupied his quarters—one each for him and his XO. The letters and symbols of the action message glowed on a panel between the two safes. It looked to be an extremely short message, but one never knew for sure until it was decoded. The two men inserted their keys and, per protocol, covered their dials as they spun their safe combinations. The commander finished decoding first. Two words.

"Initiate Blackbird," the commander read.

"I concur," replied XO Smith.

XO Smith remained coolly composed under the piercing stare of his commander. Stressing each word, the commander asked, "What is Blackbird?" His patience with his XO was running thin.

"The details are in your personal safe, sir," XO Smith said.

"And how do *you* know what's in my safe?"

"There is a false wall in the back. Entering your combination in reverse order will release the locks and allow you to access the rest of your orders."

"Sometimes I wonder who really is in command of this boat," the commander muttered.

He turned to his safe, dialed the reverse combination as instructed, and pulled open the heavy gray door. The contents were just the same as he had left them. A heavy-caliber revolver sat atop his own personal and confidential documents. He reached in and pushed against the back of the safe. It swung outward, revealing an envelope sealed in a clear waterproof bag.

The safe remained open behind him as he tore through the waterproofing plastic to access the contents inside. The front of the envelope bore one word in bold block letters: **BLACKBIRD**.

"You already know what this says, don't you, XO Smith?"

"Yes, sir."

"Always a step ahead of me," the commander said as he broke the seal on the envelope. "When is there going to be honesty and trust between us?"

He read the short message three times before he believed it. No signature claimed responsibility for the orders; only a code. The same code his orders had required him to memorize before he'd taken this assignment. His superiors had told him the code would validate and/or override any orders he may receive in the future. He held his future in his hands, and it appeared to be the end of his career.

The orders instructed him to turn over command to his XO, Mikyle Smith.

"Right now, sir," Kyle said. Respectfully, he added, "With your permission?"

The commander turned back to his safe and paused. He slid the message back in its envelope and placed it on top of the revolver before closing the safe. *I am truly a puppet now. Will my crew be able to see the strings?*

"Let's make this official, XO Smith. Come with me." He led the way to the control room.

If this was to be his final act as commander of this ship, he would at least do it by the book. He would let no dark mark of insubordination sully his record.

He switched his communication mic to ship-wide transmission. "Attention all hands, attention all hands. As of this moment, XO Mikyle Smith is in command of this vessel. I repeat, XO Mikyle Smith is now in command of this vessel."

He passed the mic to Smith. "She's yours now," he said. "I'll be in my quarters."

Kyle accepted the mic. "Sir, you need to stay here for this," he said. Before the commander could retort, Kyle said into the mic, "All hands, this is XO Smith. Ready the ship for flight. Repeat. Ready the ship for flight."

The men nearby all bent to their new task without question or hesitation. None reflected the surprise the commander knew was showing on his own face. They knew what they were doing as if they had done it a hundred times before. His XO wasn't the only one with secrets.

"*All* of them?" the commander asked.

"All of them," Kyle confirmed with a single nod.

"Then… what am I?" the commander asked, no longer sure of anything.

"*You* are the man who has been deemed fit to command this vessel once I train you how to fly it. Then she will truly be yours. I'm sorry for all the deception, but I assure you, all these men hold you in the highest regard."

"Fly?"

"Yes."

The commander scratched at the graying stubble on his scalp. The phrase *When submarines fly* danced in his memory. "Well, I suppose I'll believe it when I see it," he said.

"These orders came in ahead of schedule. I need to check in and find out why," Kyle said.

"We're at six hundred feet. We need to get to periscope depth," the commander offered.

Kyle punched in the radio frequency for a rarely used test setting. He spoke into the mic. "Blackbird initiated. Awaiting orders."

An unfamiliar voice came through the control room speakers so clearly that the person talking could have been standing right next to him. "Copy, Blackbird. Proceed to the Chinese research base at Kunlun Station in Antarctica. Maintain stealth at best possible speed. We may have found Anya. Coordinates and details are being relayed to your control station."

So. This submarine also had topside verbal communication capability while at depth, and without the assistance of a comm buoy. Amazing.

"Who's Anya?" the commander asked.

"The mother of my son."

"I didn't know you had a son."

"I didn't either until last week."

"So you really were away for a family meeting?"

"That's the absolute truth, sir."

The sonar man swiveled from his console. "We are configured for flight mode. Course has been laid in for optimal speed to target while avoiding visual detection. Shall I take her up, sir?"

"Do it," Kyle said. "Commander, would you please join me at the control station?"

The men took the two empty seats at the station. "I suggest you strap in tight, sir," Kyle said, securing himself in the seat's five-point harness. The commander followed suit. Forward velocity pressed them back into their seats as the submarine's up-angle increased.

Kyle gestured at his console to get the commander's attention, and as he entered keystrokes, he explained to the commander what he was doing.

The dark gray surfaces around them turned transparent, and an unimpeded 360-degree panorama materialized. Murky water rushed at their faces. The commander reflexively leaned away from the distressing view. It was one thing to be aware of crushing water enshrouding a submarine; it was quite different to actually see it. Usually, that foretold a burial at sea.

Gradually, the water changed from a dark green to a lighter blue. The commander could now detect the rippling barrier where waves met surface air. On each side, dark undulating shapes near the hull became distinctly wing-like. *Where did those come from?*

Without breaking speed, they crossed through the foamy surface. The commander braced himself for a post-breach impact that never came. Instead, they continued to rise. He looked over at Kyle with a genuine smile blossoming on his face.

"She really can fly?" the commander asked.

"Best speed," Kyle said into his headset.

They surged back into their seats again as the faceted black-winged wedge gained altitude and speed.

"How?" the commander asked, burning with curiosity.

"The missile tubes house gravity generators. This vessel has no weapons other than electronic countermeasures. If someone did happen to fire a missile or torpedo at us, it could be redirected back at the aggressor with the push of a button. The outer skin can morph into any shape or color. You could stand on it as it parked on a mountainside and not detect it. All the propulsion noises you are familiar with have been simulated. The prop is merely for show. Control screens also simulated radar and transducer signals. The vessel actually uses a far superior system which can detect objects with perfect clarity, at unlimited range, and completely undetectable. Technically, it's a submersible plane. It's meant to be a peace-keeping apparatus when the time comes."

"When will that be?"

"Soon," Kyle said. "You are the person we would like to entrust with that mission."

Commander of a submersible plane? The XO had to be out of his mind. Still, how could he possibly refuse? "Let's rescue this Anya first. You can tell me about the mission on the way."

***

Kyle read the notes on his console. "This may end up being a body recovery, Commander." He could practically feel Mykl's hope radiating from Jack's message. She had very little chance to survive this. He filled the commander in on as much as he could.

A stark white coastline had come into view far below. Active camouflage changed the Blackbird's outer skin to arctic white as they descended to the snowpack.

"Luck appears to be on our side, Commander. The base is deserted."

"So we pick her up and leave," the commander said.

"Not quite that easy. She's buried under several feet of ice and snow."

"I don't understand."

"We're going to have to dig her out. Her service has earned her the right to proper handling of her remains." Kyle chose not to mention the possibility that she might be revived. The possibility was still quite slim. Besides, a flying submarine was enough surprise to spring on the man for one day.

After landing next to the furnished coordinates, Kyle sent a squad of men to check the vacant base for digging tools. They returned with enough picks and shovels for them to work in shifts.

"This is going to take hours," the commander said, shivering in the cold as he dug.

"So be it," Kyle said. "She's coming with us." He flung his pick angrily into the frozen ground.

***

It didn't take hours. It took an entire day. The men could only work short intervals in the extreme cold. They kept up a continuous rotation between digging and warming themselves. No one complained. The commander developed a new respect for his crew.

They finally reached the woman's body in an air pocket created by a large slab of ice. She had been shot in the chest; red-tinged frost marked areas of frozen blood. To the commander's surprise, she wore what looked like a stripper outfit. Her arms were tucked in close to her body, with her hands covering her face.

The XO called for blankets and a body bag.

With great reverence, the commander helped Kyle roll the frozen body into a blanket, which they then slid into a thick, zippered bag. The icy tears on his XO's face told him all he needed to know: she may have died in the service to her country, but she meant something much more to him.

Six men, with Kyle and the commander leading, carried the woman's body past saluting men and up a ramp into the flying ship. They made a space for her in the coldest part of the walk-in freezer.

The commander placed a hand on Kyle's back. "I'm sorry, son," he said.

"Let's take her home," Kyle replied.

When they were both back at the ship's control station, a fireball began streaking through the upper atmosphere.

"I've never seen one that big before," the commander said.

"It's time to go. We don't want to be here when the other one impacts."

CHAPTER 84

The submarine's infirmary had been a five-star accommodation compared to the Chinese aircraft carrier's brig. All Sebastian had for amenities were a woven grass mat and an open bucket for bodily waste. The brig certainly incented him to keep out of its confines.

A clanging of the cross bolt on his cell announced the arrival of a visitor.

The deputy minister spoke from behind two guards framing the door opening. "We have found the entrance to your cavern. An underwater drone confirms no mines or traps, and the air inside is breathable. You will now accompany us to the artifact."

Sebastian breathed a sigh of relief. As long as the artifact remained inside, he would be back on top in the realm of power brokers.

"Were there signs of anyone inside?" he asked.

"We detected artificial lighting. That is all."

Sebastian nodded and fell in step between the guards.

They moved down through the decks until they arrived at an opening in the side of the ship. A temporary gangway had been put in place, its bottom edge scraping the top of one of their smaller attack submarines, bobbing on the waves. Sebastian smiled inside at seeing the admiral already on deck. It took a lot to get an admiral to leave his ship. They believed him now.

Sebastian enjoyed much better accommodations for this trip: they permitted him to stand in the control room, as long as he kept out of the way. A strike force of elite Chinese commandos rode the outer deck of the submarine with special breathing gear. Their orders were to neutralize any threat as the submarine surfaced, and then secure the immediate area. Sebastian's anticipation bubbled wildly.

Much to his dismay, his traveling companions chose not to speak any more English once they submerged. He would have liked to have known their thoughts.

Soon, scrabbling noises filtering through the hull from the upper deck told Sebastian that they had surfaced again. They must be inside now.

The muzzle of an automatic rifle directed him to the deck hatch. He hoped this would be the last time anybody pointed a weapon at him. Once they saw the artifact, they would show him the respect he deserved.

The deputy minister and admiral ordered him to precede them out the hatch. Their faces were more wary than respectful. Sebastian understood; if anyone was going to get shot at, they wanted it to be him.

Dank air hit him as he crawled through the hatch. Commandos ringed the upper platform. Without waiting for the others to emerge, Sebastian climbed the ladder to get a glimpse of the outer vault. To his surprise and dismay, the door stood open. Not by much, but it was definitely open. If the artifact had been removed, he would never leave this place alive.

The admiral and deputy minister came to his side.

"Lead the way, Mr. Falstano," the deputy minister said, his words heavy with skepticism. Perhaps he too saw the open door as a bad omen.

It could be a trap as well, thought Sebastian. He carefully judged where he stepped, and he tried not to cringe when turning on the same light switches he remembered the woman using. They walked past the hydraulic lifts holding the concrete block ceiling in place. Relief flooded him at the realization that he wouldn't have to endure the acoustical trauma of their lifting noise. However, he was unsettled to not know how the ceiling remained in the up position—and whether it would stay that way.

Sebastian's heart leapt at seeing the circular hatch to the artifact chamber. It was closed! *Please let it be unlocked.* With his entourage of armed guards and Chinese leadership, he turned the wheel… and pulled.

The door opened to the most beautiful sight he could have wished for. On a short pedestal in the dark interior, a swatch of thin white cloth lay draped over a glowing sphere. He located the flashlight and ducked through the opening. How he longed to get another look at this marvel from another world.

"Stop where you are, Mr. Falstano," said the deputy minister. "Step away from the artifact."

Sebastian stepped aside with the graciousness of a dinner host, indicating for his guests to see for themselves. *Let them see and be humbled.* He pointed the flashlight beam at the ceiling to light the area. Being smaller in stature, the admiral and deputy minister had no need to duck as they entered.

With great caution, the deputy minister lifted two corners of the cloth. He dropped it to the ground behind him. Both men hunched over to gaze into the translucent, glowing sphere. Their expressions turned rapturous.

In rapid-fire Chinese, the two men argued. Then, boldly, the admiral lifted the sphere off the pedestal to examine it more closely. Sebastian held his breath. He had not seen anyone physically touch it yet, and he had no idea how it might affect the artifact—or the person holding it. The admiral lifted it close to his face while slowly rotating it in his hands.

Suddenly, he stopped and clenched his jaw. Without saying a word, he held the artifact out to the deputy minister, indicating a spot on its surface. The deputy minister examined the spot. His eyes went wide, and he turned away in disgust and strode right to the door.

What just happened? What did he see?

With a savage grin, the admiral threw the artifact at Sebastian's feet.

It hit the rough floor with a crunch. Sebastian reflexively grabbed it to keep it from hitting the wall and getting damaged further. The admiral gave a backhanded wave, joined the deputy minister, and the two men left the chamber. To Sebastian's horror, they closed the hatch and spun the wheel, locking him inside.

As soon as the wheel came to a stop, the ground jolted sharply. A thundering impact came from the other side of the hatch, so powerful that it threw him off his feet. This could mean only be one thing: the deputy minister and admiral had been crushed by the falling ceiling.

In a panic, Sebastian lunged toward the hatch and tried turning the wheel. It didn't budge. The circular walls of his tomb threatened to crush his sanity.

Fear welled up in Sebastian's mind. Why had the two men reacted so? Desperately, he began examining the sphere's surface with the flashlight. And he saw it. He understood.

On the bottom, where the sphere had contacted the pedestal, was a tiny inscription: *Made in China*.

Sebastian screamed.

He tried to make sense of the series of events that had led him here. Clearly, it had all been an elaborate ruse—but to what end? To kill the admiral and deputy minister? No. Couldn't be. They were expendable pawns in the Chinese power matrix. To kill… *me?* Sebastian felt a speck of self-importance. But no. As much as the thought pleased his fragile ego, it was impossibly farfetched.

When did this start? When did they lead me down this path? He had no answers. They hadn't even given him the dignity of understanding. He seethed. He wanted to kill whoever had done this to him. He wished upon them the most horrible death imaginable.

The light of the flashlight flickered and dimmed. He tapped it and edged closer to the glowing sphere for comfort.

Before the flashlight died completely, a soft click came from the pedestal. Concentric rings of bright light circled the low domed ceiling, surrounding a pinpoint of light just above the pedestal. Then a door in the side of the pedestal swung open to reveal a hollow interior. Sebastian hurried over. Behind the door he found a bottle of water, some peanut butter crackers, and a handwritten letter.

Sebastian grabbed the letter and read.

Mr. Falstano,

Thank you.

Only someone of your expert talents could have made this mission a success. Your actions may well have saved humanity and the planet it inhabits.

Sebastian blinked. Did one of the light rings just go out? He couldn't be certain. Munching on a cracker, he continued to read.

Your contributions to society will be remembered for generations. Children of the future will learn of, and be influenced by, your life choices. You are to be commended for volunteering for this mission. All suicide missions require a willing volunteer.

Sebastian spluttered cracker crumbs everywhere. *Suicide mission? When the hell did I volunteer for that?*

He took a swig of water. A muffled boom reverberated through his manmade cave. The commandos were attempting to blast their way in. He knew it would take weeks—and he would die of dehydration long before that.

He took another drink. No sense rationing it.

If you're looking for someone to blame for your current accommodations, look no further than yourself. You were not coerced or ordered in any way. You were merely presented opportunities. At any time, you could have chosen differently. Any shred of honor or decency would have disqualified you from this mission and sent you down another track. Your own choices brought you to our attention—and eventually to this place, this tomb.

Cheating on your college entry exams started you on this path. Your eagerness to covet an unearned and unlearned education kept you on it. Murdering an innocent student to protect your lies paved the way. Do not say that you are now surprised at the consequences of your actions. Stupid, you are not. Ignorance and lies have brought you to face judgment before the blade of truth.

You sought information to gain power over people. Here is the intelligence update most pertinent to you now: China has altered the trajectory of three asteroids so that they will hit this planet. Two will miss. The third will strike the island where you are now trapped. When the last point of light above you goes out, you will have sixty seconds before the asteroid impacts at seventy thousand miles per hour. No more opportunities remain available to you. Your choices have sealed your fate.

Truly
—Jack

Another ring went out, followed by the muted sound of a distant explosion. Death approached Sebastian on two fronts. At least no one would shoot him this time. Then again, an asteroid was just another projectile, far larger and traveling faster than any bullet.

Jack was right. He had brought this on himself. He had wished to kill the person who had done this to him. Some wishes come true.

***

Sebastian closed his eyes and concentrated on the glowing afterimage of a pinpoint of light that had just gone out. He curled into a fetal position and made wish after wish in hopes that one would come true.

Unfortunately, the truth cannot be wished away.

CHAPTER 85

Back in the solitude of his room, Mykl watched the recovery of his mother's body through the weirdly shaped submarine's external cameras. He wanted to watch until they delivered her back to the City, but the appearance of three asteroids burning their way through the atmosphere heralded a whole new set of problems.

The first two asteroids broke into several spectacular fireballs as they flew deeper into the atmosphere. The pieces skipped into the cold oblivion of space without ever touching the planet.

The largest asteroid was over three kilometers wide and its projected impact area was unthinkable. He bounded over to his globe-filled wall and pulled up the live image from a City satellite.

A black shape began blocking stars at the top of his visual feed. It didn't look to be traveling all that fast as it tumbled toward the Earth. Its leading edge began to glow. Jack had said he couldn't keep China from succeeding indefinitely without them becoming suspicious and resorting to more direct measures, and it looked like Jack was now allowing China to have their way.

The glow intensified and transformed to a white-hot dot as the asteroid entered the lower atmosphere. From the comfort of his vantage point on the moon, the impact was almost anticlimactic.

Then the post-impact fireball began to grow.

Mykl zoomed in. The radiant fireball had already engulfed numerous nearby ships. When it finally began to dissipate, a twenty-mile-wide swath of glowing sea floor, seven miles deep, bled molten rock like a fresh wound. Another twenty miles beyond that, the surface of the ocean boiled. Tsunami waves raced outward as if attempting to escape the cataclysmic event that bore them. How many people had Jack allowed to die? A hundred thousand? A million? More?

Then Mykl remembered that these asteroids had been altered from their original courses and impact areas. How many people had been spared in comparison? It couldn't have been an easy choice to make.

And if Jack hadn't neutralized the virus on that asteroid, the Earth would now be experiencing an extinction-level event like the dinosaurs. Come to think of it, that virus was very likely the culprit that had caused their extinction as well. China had gambled with ending the human race, if not all life on the planet. What were a few million lives compared to that?

Mykl brought up a feed from a non-City satellite. Random static filled his screen. He tried others. All dead. Every last non-City satellite had ceased to function. Communications, navigation, weather, research, military…

Wait. Militaries without satellites were virtually blind. The lack of access to satellite data would cripple everyone's ability to launch strikes against their foes.

Mykl checked the Chinese orbital weapon platforms. They, too, drifted dead in space. It was too coincidental. Mykl was suddenly certain that Jack used the asteroids as an excuse to kill every satellite and launching station in orbit. Sending up replacements would take weeks if not longer. Good thing they abandoned the space station long ago.

Updates began flowing into the open Operations file. China had lost seventy-five percent of its naval fleet from the impact, including ninety percent of its submarines. Russia lost less, but their position as a superpower was severely weakened. North Korea had only minutes before the tsunami decimated every significant warship in its fleet. More unlikely coincidences? No. Jack had somehow influenced those fleets to be in the impact area. Those fleets would take years, if not decades, to rebuild.

Leaning back in his chair, Mykl understood that the world rotated as a safer place—for now. A major asteroid impact had just occurred, and countries would want to sit tight and evaluate potential post-impact issues. Without satellites, that would be a daunting task. China and Russia dared not instigate anything militarily with their weakened navies, and their intercontinental ballistic missile targeting would be down without satellites.

Sure, people would be without their up-to-the-minute news and entertainment—but they were safer now than they had been in decades.

Mykl knew it couldn't last. Eventually they would replace the damaged satellites. Probably the space weapons as well. And if the world discovered China's involvement in directing the asteroid, severe repercussions would follow. Or others might attempt to tame asteroids for their own nefarious purposes. No, this wasn't a final solution to the problem.

Is that why Jack put this on me? This series of incidents had bought him time—that was all.

The possibility existed—Mykl had entertained the thought before—that an impactful event such as this could bring everyone together in unity. Perhaps the world would now dismiss their petty differences for the good of all. But such possibilities functioned like wishes: they hardly ever worked out the way you wanted. A true solution needed to be predictable. And that required complete control over the problem.

Noah leapt onto Mykl's desk from his perch at the window. His head poked through a square of toilet paper, fluttering behind him like a cape. He surveyed Mykl's desk as if he was searching for something. Apparently not finding it, he launched himself to the bed. Mykl wondered if he had any mouse friends or children of his own. Being the pioneer for the modified virus studies, he, too, probably lacked the ability to have children, like Jack—

An explosion of thoughts hit Mykl all at once. What if? How fast? How long? How many?

THE PROMETHEUS EFFECT

He had a solution. Now it was a matter of logistics. The virus just needed to be modified further, and he required a distribution method.

Mykl frowned at the tedious task of searching through massive City databases. As much as he hated to do it, he activated the computer voice recognition system.

"Computer voice activation *on*," he said, hoping the system would be that user-friendly.

"Good evening, Mykl," said a disembodied voice.

Mykl cringed, while Noah cocked his head and scanned for the visitor.

"Computer, how many modifications to the Europa virus are there?"

"You may call me Vale."

"Vale?" Mykl said, not at all happy that this had suddenly turned into a conversation.

"Voice Activation Language Emulator."

"Very well… Vale. Answer the previous question… please?"

"That information is restricted."

Mykl stared in disbelief. Restricted? *I'm supposed to have* unrestricted *access, except for a few things Jack wants to keep secret. So—this was one of Jack's secrets.*

"Vale, what types of drones does the City have at their disposal?"

Vale rattled off an impressive list, but none fit the need Mykl had in mind. And when he inquired about such a drone, Vale once again pleaded "restricted access."

Anger, mixed with betrayal, grew inside him.

"Vale, can you track all City technology that utilizes gravity manipulation?"

"Yes, Mykl."

"Display the location of such devices on my wall map."

The asteroid impact site remained centered in his satellite's field of view. A large plume of steam and smoke had now climbed high into the atmosphere, obscuring the boiling crater. Wind currents pulled the plume in an easterly direction.

Mykl placed his hands far apart on the wall and quickly brought them together. The image zoomed out rapidly. Floating dots blanketed every population center on the planet, as he'd expected.

"Vale, same request, but show me the distribution two weeks ago," Mykl ordered.

Only a tiny fraction of the lights remained.

"Back to current time," he demanded.

He selected a dot and zoomed in on it. The City satellite at his command transmitted impeccable resolution. He zoomed closer and closer until the drone loomed larger than life. Color-morphing made it almost undetectable. Mykl identified it as a fat disk with protrusions along its perimeter.

"Vale, what is this drone's function?" Mykl asked, knowing exactly the response Vale would give him.

"That information is restricted," Vale answered.

"Computer! Voice interaction *off!*"

Out of habit, Mykl grabbed Stinker in his rush out of the room.

***

Mykl slid to a stop at the Operations Center. The people monitoring post-impact effects noticed him this time. So did Jack. The man's lean body sagged in a chair, and his face seemed to have aged decades since the last time Mykl saw him.

"I need to speak with you… alone," Mykl said in a fair imitation of Jack's command voice.

Eyebrows raised behind every work station. Jack politely gestured to his private office connected to the main room. Mykl remained standing as Jack closed the door and sat. He looked at Mykl expectantly.

"I found a solution to your problem," Mykl said. "But you already knew it."

Sadness haunted Jack's eyes as he nodded confirmation.

Mykl pressed on, ready for a fight. "You used me."

"Mykl…"

"What?" he demanded, not happy about having his prepared spiel interrupted.

"Delilah's dead."

Stinker fell to the floor.

Jack shared his pain, and his love, in a communicative stare.

"Lahlah?" Mykl whispered softly.

Jack closed his eyes in silent affirmation.

Mykl dropped to his knees and buried his face in Stinker's fuzzy belly. "HuNyOOOOOOOO!" he wailed into the bear.

Jack moved to sit by his grandson. He pulled Mykl and Stinker into his lap. Stinker heroically attempted to absorb their grief, but there was only so much one teddy bear could do. They would need each other for the rest.

After Mykl's sobs subsided, he leaned back to look into Jack's eyes. "How?" he asked.

Jack paused. "She was on her way to return Lawrence's jacket… when a drunk driver hit her head-on at high speed. She didn't feel anything. The impact was too great."

A few of the bear's stiches popped under the tension of Mykl's grip. His jaw muscles quivered as he stared into the realm of things that cannot be undone. His irrational thoughts weren't ready to be let go.

"You could have implemented the solution fifty years ago," he said. "None of this would have happened! My mom, Lahlah, the asteroids, none of it!"

"*You* might not exist now if I had done that."

"*I DON'T CARE!*" Mykl threw Stinker across the room.

Jack spoke calmly, though his face reflected Mykl's grief. "The number of innocent people has always been far larger than the number of those who would do evil. I had to give them a chance. Generation after generation came and went, until we finally reached the tipping point to self-destruction. It's not their fault. Humanity's foundation was broken from the start. Scattered. They developed strengths that, in cooperation, would take them to the stars. But they held on to their petty differences to the detriment of the species.

"I gave them those fifty years to create a new foundation. They failed. It can't be forced upon them, or simply handed over. Another fifty years won't make any difference. If I hadn't neutralized the virus on those asteroids, all intelligent life would be extinguished in a year, in the most horrible apocalyptic conditions imaginable. My solution saves them from that, as well as from a destruction of their own making… And it allows for a new start."

Mykl had been rubbing at his eyes the entire time Jack spoke. He was surprised at how quickly he could recover his composure, but then again, he had always possessed that ability. Perhaps it was a manifestation of his alien DNA. A new survival trait: the ability to not dwell on the past.

"You can't save everyone," Mykl said.

"No. I can't," Jack said. "Nor can I make everyone happy. No one can."

"Why did you ask me to come up with a solution when you already had one?"

"It took decades to develop mine," Jack said. "You discovered it in what, five days? Not a day goes by that I don't feel like some kind of monster. You came to this of your own reasoning. When a five-year-old boy—a brilliant, innocent boy at that—reaches the same conclusion, it takes some weight off my old heart."

Mykl didn't feel all that innocent. *Solution.* Such a nice, unthreatening word for what Jack planned to do. It had a more appropriate and accurate name. "When are you going to implement this…?" Mykl couldn't bring himself to say the word.

"Now," Jack said.

"How?"

Jack carried Mykl with him as he went to sit at his desk. Then he entered the most complex series of taps and swipes Mykl had witnessed so far. A slowly flashing red circle, the size of an apple, appeared on the desk. "All I have to do is place my palm on that circle, and the sequence will initiate."

Mykl's anger softened. This mortal man had carried the weight of the world on his shoulders for too long. Would Jack's adaptation also protect his human conscience after committing speciocide?

Mykl lunged forward and slapped his hand on the circle before Jack could react. He then fell into Jack's lap and pressed his head into the older man's chest. Jack's heart still beat strongly.

With Jack squeezing him tight, Mykl said, "You're not a monster."

They remained in each other's arms until their tears dried, not saying a word. Each was lost in his own thoughts… as the race of humans on the planet began to die.

CHAPTER 86

Three Weeks Post-Impact

"Did he have anything to say?" President Feng asked of his military's highest-ranking officer, then coughed. This cold had latched on a week ago, and he couldn't shake it. Everyone around him seemed to have it too.

"The space administration director maintained his innocence up until the rifles fired at his execution," the general answered.

"And his family?"

"Nothing. They have been relocated to a labor camp."

"What of the reactions to the asteroids? Has anyone placed the blame on us?"

"No one. If anything, the other governments pity us for our losses."

Pity, Feng thought, and he coughed in disgust. He had defanged his country by his own actions. The catastrophic EMP created by the asteroids passing through atmosphere had ruined everything in orbit. With luck, they might be able to launch a simple communications satellite in the coming week. Their military would likely require decades to rebuild.

But one thing was for certain: *someone* knew of China's role in bringing the asteroids to Earth. For the impact to have occurred at the *precise* location where their fleet had been directed... that was no coincidence.

THE PROMETHEUS EFFECT

Feng coughed and pounded a fist on his desk in anger.

***

"What happens now?" Mykl asked.

They had said teary goodbyes to his mom and Delilah at their memorial service the day before. He now sat with his father in Dr. Lee's homey office.

"Now it's our turn to go into hibernation," Kyle said.

"Is it going to hurt? Will there be needles involved?"

"I think Dr. Lee can put you to sleep before she uses any needles. After that, you won't dream or feel a thing until you wake again."

"And that will be…?" Mykl asked.

His father knelt next to him. "When the world is ready for us, Mykl."

CHAPTER 87

Three Months Post-Impact

In the CEO's office of a major manufacturer of pregnancy tests, a heated discussion takes place.

"Have you gotten my messages? We've been bombarded by numerous complaints from all over the country," the CEO says.

The flustered quality control manager replies, "There's *nothing* wrong with our product! I've personally run tests on thousands of random samples. New *and* old. The detection rate is greater than 99%."

"Then why are none of our customers seeing positive readings on their tests? Answer me that! Are *all* the women in the world suddenly unable to get pregnant? This is ridiculous. Recheck, recalibrate and do whatever is necessary to resolve this problem. Or I will find someone who can…"

***

In a fertility clinic, a lab technician attempted for the ninth time to artificially fertilize another egg. Everything goes smoothly. Rubbing the fatigue from her eyes, she places her work in the incubator. But when she returns to work the next day, the microscope reveals zero cell division among all attempts. These failures have been going on for at least a week…

THE PROMETHEUS EFFECT

***

The president doodles leisurely at his desk in the Oval Office. He won reelection in a landslide. Now his science advisor is prattling on about a disturbing drop in conception rates across the nation. He has four more years to enjoy his presidency. A few less babies being born doesn't concern him in the slightest...

***

Six Months Post-Impact

Panic has spread across the world. No new documented cases of conception have occurred since two weeks after the asteroid strike. Microbiologists traced the culprit to a heretofore-unknown virus, likely introduced into the atmosphere by the asteroids themselves. Initial infection is believed to be related to the post-impact common cold pandemic. No one died from the infection, but it left the entire population of the planet sterile. No one was immune.

Scientists working on a vaccine or treatment are baffled by the virus's gene structure and resiliency. It affects not only humans but also the greater apes. Hopes for success are slim. Still they try.

Religious zealots worldwide have finally found their calling. Their signs stating the world is coming to an end no longer receive looks of ridicule and disbelief. The messages are now viewed as fact and certainty...

***

Ten Months Post-Impact

The last baby is born. Her mother names her Hope. World population numbers dominate nightly newscasts as a countdown to extinction. Even countries with terrible histories of exploiting children now treat them as national treasures.

Orphanages throughout the world empty like the shelves of a looted store. The curator of the Las Vegas Foundling Asylum sees her last charge adopted by a worthy family.

Scientists develop a promising vaccine. With no suitable animals to use, and in desperation, they risk testing it on the last born child.

Hope dies…

***

Five Years Post-Impact

Elementary schools close their doors due to declining need. Manufacturing of children's products comes to a halt. Many companies go out of business. World population has dropped by ten percent. Previously adversarial nations now work together to find a solution to prevent extinction. The world is at peace…

***

Twenty Years Post-Impact

The sound of children laughing exists only on recordings. Playgrounds and schools have been repurposed. World population has dropped by thirty percent. Inhabitants of the planet find that food, water, and energy are plentiful. The last members of the global workforce begin taking jobs. Resignation sets in that there will be no miracle, no cure, and no more children…

***

Fifty Years Post-Impact

No schools of any kind remain. People have accepted that they already

THE PROMETHEUS EFFECT

know all that is needed to take them to the end. The workforce ages, and production drops. Yet all live in comfort. The remaining population naturally begins to migrate to better climates for convenience and social needs. Individuals from enemy nations become friends. It's better than being alone. Abandoned cities become weed-ridden wildlife sanctuaries…

***

Ninety Years Post-Impact

A group of old men gather solemnly at a sheltered table by the sea. A massive pod of whales blows misty plumes into the air as if in salute to the ceremony. The men have just consigned one of their own to an ocean teeming with life. Their brittle bodies no longer have the strength to dig graves. Their softening minds no longer have the will. As far as they know, they are the last living people in the world.

One of the men attempts to break the somber mood. He claims he saw a submarine fly out of the water and disappear beyond the horizon. The other men look at each other in heavy-hearted silence. Hallucinations are a sign of advanced dementia. They know their friend will not be with them much longer.

Against the backdrop of a red rising sun, they return to lonely homes to tend to their gardens…

CHAPTER 88

Ninety-Seven Years Post-Impact

Earth's last survivor of the impact generation has been trapped for three hundred days. A fall injured his knee, and he no longer possesses the ability to navigate the steep steps leading out of his beautiful cove by the sea. A freshwater stream has met all his needs for thirst, but without the ability to reach his garden, he has thought, for three hundred days now, that he would soon starve. However, every morning when he awakes, fresh food awaits. He saw the flying submarine years ago, and he wonders if his mind decided to follow.

A deep fatigue in his bones and a shallow flutter in his chest tell him that the setting sun measures his remaining moments. Sadness envelops him. He feels certain that he is the last. He ponders the possibility that he has already died and lives now in the afterlife. If that is the case, besides the loneliness, it isn't so bad. And perhaps this next death will reunite him with his friends.

With one last look at the sunset, he lies in the sand and closes his eyes. The ocean breeze caresses his deeply lined face. Sea birds call to the sky. He releases his physical body from further need.

I am ready to go…

A small warmth fills his palm. Not furry, like a creature, but smooth, like soft skin. He opens his eyes again. A small boy kneels beside him, with chocolate brown hair and copper-colored eyes.

The boy holds his hand and speaks to him. He can't understand the language, but he knows in his failing heart that the words are kind.

The sun is setting too fast… or does his heart beat too slowly? No matter. He smiles at the boy and closes his eyes for the last time. Happiness graces his last thoughts.

I'm not the last, after all. Where one child lives, there are bound to be more…

CHAPTER 89

"That was very nice of you, Mykl," his father said after he recounted his visit to say goodbye to the last man.

Mykl and his dad were enjoying a picnic in a cool breeze on a sun-warmed beach. The large city behind them changed hourly as matter-manipulation bots recycled it. Lawrence and Rose frolicked with Tina in the surf. Her shrieks of laughter mingled with the sounds of hundreds of other children playing in the sand.

Mykl shrugged and stared at the teddy bear in his lap. Stinker was a proper bear with two good eyes now—though Mykl had asked Dr. Lee to leave the tear under his arm, in case Noah ever had need of it again. Noah, however, seemed quite happy to entertain the children from the comfort of his new outdoor habitat.

"I didn't think he should die alone," Mykl said. "The least I could do was let him know that everything was going to be okay."

When sensors determined that only one man remained on the planet, the reanimation plans were initiated by the few City agents who had remained awake and unseen over the long years. Mykl and his father were among the first to be awakened. That was some six months ago. Today, they celebrated Mykl's sixth birthday, though one hundred and three years had passed since his birth.

An old thought came to his mind.

"Dad?" he asked.

"Yes, Stinker?"

Mykl struggled to speak through the grin breaking across his face. "I was wondering: what do you think Mom was going to give me for a present on that night she disappeared?"

His father looked at him with that special sort of smile fathers use when they know a deep secret. He leaned over and whispered, "You're holding it."

Mykl's mouth popped open in surprise.

His father laughed. "Happy birthday, Mykl." He kissed his son's forehead. "She planned on taking you to the City after she finished her mission that night. She thought it was time for you to meet the rest of your family. My old teddy bear would be a perfect present."

"You made that up!" Mykl said.

"Did I?"

Mykl dropped his head into Stinker as he thought it over. His dad was probably right.

He sat up and surveyed the area. Sweeping an arm out to the children and the city beyond, he asked, "What do we do now? Everyone's awake."

"We start over," his father said. "This is a new world without borders. Everyone is free to be whatever they want to be. A new planetary constitution has been ratified that spells out individual rights, including the rights of the planet itself. Because, without the planet, there is no *us*."

"Can I be a surfer when I grow up?" Mykl asked, admiring the waves crashing in.

"We'll talk about it," his father said in a tone that certainly meant "no."

"Then can I have a sword?"

His father stifled a laugh by coughing into his hand. "Why don't you go play with Tina? She's been trying to get your attention for a while now. I think she likes you."

Mykl blushed. He really wanted a sword. But, as much as he tried to hide it, he liked Tina too.

CHAPTER 90

One last task to complete, Jack thought as he and Jessica entered the deserted and sunless City. With its purpose fulfilled, there was no longer a need for anyone to hide. But it would continue to operate on minimum maintenance power, remaining available in case a new crisis should arise. Without the fusion-driven sun overhead, the City streets would lie suspended in perpetual twilight.

They decided to walk rather than drive to the Operations Center. It gave them both time to think. They passed by the fish feeder, which was now empty; while the lake remained, all the fish had been transplanted to lakes and streams. Only insects and single-cell pond creatures would remain as the city's caretakers.

Inside the Operations Center, Jack showed Jessica how to access a locked enclosure known only to a select few individuals. It housed an elevator shaft that went even deeper into the earth. Quietly, in pitch black, they slipped downward, their eyes adjusting to the darkness. The elevator and the five stronger-than-steel cables lowering it radiated no energy. More efficient ways to move the elevator certainly existed, but technological devices and power were kept to a minimum down here.

When the elevator stopped, Jack pulled open the doors manually and led Jessica out. Directly across from them, a vault door emitted a weak blue light through its view window. Jack noted that the glow was neither dimmer nor brighter than it had been the last time he visited—almost one hundred years ago. He found the observation discomforting.

THE PROMETHEUS EFFECT

He signaled for Jessica to be cautious with her voice and movements, and they crept forward to peer inside.

Hard vacuum filled the vault's interior. Securely perched on a pile of moon rocks, to mimic the environment in which it was found, sat a glowing sphere. Mysterious symbols clouded its translucent interior, and scars and scrapes marred its diamond-hard surface—a result of its long voyage. It appeared unchanged. Jack breathed a sigh of relief.

Jessica's eyes grew wider, and she held her breath. Her face was dramatically side-lit by the glow.

"The artifact?" she asked in an awed whisper. "It's *real*?"

Jack nodded. Turning back to the sphere, he closed his eyes in acceptance of its unchanged presence. He could have observed it using passive sensors embedded in the vault lining, but he'd had to see it with his own eyes. He'd had to be sure. The sphere posed too many unknowns. City technology couldn't penetrate it—yet. It was not of this Earth, and until proven otherwise, it was dangerous… and a problem for another day.

When they returned to the top, Jessica blew out her breath as if trying to expel her disbelief. "Does Mykl know about this?" she asked.

"He does not, and I would like to keep it that way, for now," Jack answered. "His curiosity and love of puzzles would cause him to obsess over it. He's done enough for the time being. Let him experience childhood for a change. He's earned it. He needs it.

"Once the human race has reestablished itself here, it can begin venturing to other planets. Diversifying the species among many worlds is the true key to survival. But someone, or some*thing*, is already out there…"

CHAPTER 91

A frigid river swept her along with merciless force. Chunks of shadowy ice spun in the current's dark eddies. The cold made her arms and legs sluggish in responding to her mind's commands, but one hand clung for life to a smoldering log. It should have burned her, but instead it felt warm and safe. Almost as if, were she to let go, it would maintain its hold on her.

As long as she had strength of will, she would never let go.

Something clawed its way up her body, attempting to pull her under and away from the log. She coughed and gagged as foul water threatened to drown her. *No*, she wanted to cry out, but the icy cold rendered her mute.

Panic chipped away at her sanity. Determined not to give up, she kept fighting the current and the creature whose claws raked up her back. When it reached her head, it opened its maw and sank serrated fangs into her skull. Her back arched in a futile effort to throw the creature off. She dug her fingernails into the log. If she could only scream… If she only knew it was a dream…

***

"Sedate her," Dr. Lee said as her patient arched off the bed, writhing in pain.

"What's wrong?" James asked, fear and concern draining the blood from his face.

"The tumor is dying. But as it decays, it's producing waste products that her system must eradicate. That process is causing her a great deal of discomfort." Dr. Lee studied a monitor. It showed Dawn's brain activity returning to an unconscious and dreamless state. "She started to show normal brain activity as she approached consciousness. That's a good sign, James. For now, we'll keep her sedated and comfortable. The rest is up to her."

"She's a fighter," James said, still holding her hand tightly. Beads of blood oozed where her nails had dug into him. "She won't give up… ever."

CHAPTER 92

One Year After the Great Awakening

On a soft, grass-covered dune by the ocean, with her bare toes extended toward the waves, she sat with her eyes closed, feeling the warmth of the setting sun on her face. A light breeze blew strands of her silky black hair across her long, dark lashes, tickling her nose. She puffed the offending filaments away in frustration and tucked them behind her ear again.

Crunching footsteps plodded through the sand toward her from the left, as they had every evening since she had discovered this secluded dune. She smiled… and opened her eyes.

The footsteps came to a stop beside her. She felt no need to ask who was there. She knew. He would always be there. A perfect red rose lay in her lap as proof. It numbered one of eleven he had given to her earlier that day. An odd number from an unusual man.

"I have something for you," the young man said as he kneeled beside her.

Determined not to rise to his bait, she lifted the beautiful rose with two fingers and said, "But I have everything I want."

"But not everything you *need*," he said gently.

She tilted her head down toward him, letting her hair tumble over her bare shoulder. She lifted a hand to his cheek. Such a handsome face. An electric thrill ran through her. And those eyes—those titanium gray eyes. She could spend eternity gazing into them. Right now they held a mixture of mischief and love. She took a moment to catch her breath.

"Are you so sure?" she asked, smiling coyly and fluttering her eyelashes. Two could play at this game.

He twisted from his kneeling position to retrieve a large white box from behind him. A preserved rose lay on top of the lid, and several holes ran along the sides. He placed the box between them. Curious, she set her rose to the side and knelt before the box as well.

"It's Teeka's rose," he said.

She stroked the petals with two fingers as if petting a sleeping kitten. Her eyes peered up at him, moist and questioning. Holding her gaze with his own, he tilted his head to the box. A tear tumbled down his cheek as he lifted the lid.

Her hands immediately went to her mouth to stifle a sob. A tiny white kitten with a black smirk of a mustache lay curled in a soft, sleeping ball, next to a grimy old shoelace.

Dawn's tears fell unchecked on the fur of the innocent wonder before her. Her subdued sobs awakened it from its peaceful slumber. It stretched and yawned mightily. Then a pair of kitten blue eyes gazed serenely into her own and slowly blinked, forging a trusting bond that healed past pain. She stroked its tear-dampened fur with a trembling hand.

"They were able to take genetic material from the root of the rose to give her a second chance at life. She's identical to Teeka in every way," James said.

Unable to speak, Dawn mouthed the words, "Thank you."

The kitten rediscovered the shoelace and began playing.

"I have… one more thing," James said. He pulled from his shirt pocket a roughly carved driftwood box, and presented it to her.

With a tear-streaked face, she looked questioningly from the box to him.

"Diamonds are a dime a dozen these days," he said, "so I made something special. I hope you like it."

Using her thumbs, Dawn popped open the little box. It held a ring, crafted from a section of new shoelace. James had unraveled the individual threads and retied them to form a delicately petaled rose where a stone would normally sit. Dawn admired its complex beauty.

"I love you, Dawn... Will you marry me?" James asked, his voice husky with emotion.

"You're crazy," Dawn half-laughed, half-sobbed.

"I'm not crazy," James said. "I'm stupid." He smiled.

"Whatever!" Dawn slipped on the ring. "Yes... Kiss me."

And James kissed her. Until the sun fell from the sky and the stars danced in celebration. And every morning they woke next to each other for the rest of their lives... which was a very... very... long time.

end

ACKNOWLEDGEMENTS

Before a book can be written, there has to be a spark of inspiration to light the candle of one's imagination. I give credit for that inspiring spark to Terry and Jeri. Your accomplishments and words of reason (along with your friendship) made me understand that if I had a story to tell, I need only have the discipline to write it, and the courage to share it.

Many profound thank yous go to Stephen, Tom, and Rebecca. When my writing candle began to flicker, you took it and used it to light a fire under my ass.

To my seafaring beta readers, Elizabeth, Kathy, and Kristy, who, after reading about the death of billions, demanded the Grim Reaper take a few more. Cheers, my friends. I hope you are satisfied!

Scott, Stephanie C., and Crystal, thank you for taking time out of your busy days to show me where my pen strokes fell short.

As a first-time author, I can't thank my editors, David Gatewood and Crystal Watanabe, enough. I learned more from your feedback than any book could ever teach me. My next project will be better because of it. I promise.

Susan, the beauty of your art is a reflection of yourself. I hope the words on the pages do your cover justice.

This book was a learning experience for me. I had doubts that I could even write. No more. Now I have a desire to do better. Thank you ALL for igniting that fire inside me.

Made in the USA
San Bernardino, CA
28 January 2018